SUMMER SESSION

A Selection of Recent Titles by Merry Jones

THE NANNY MURDERS
THE RIVER KILLINGS
THE DEADLY NEIGHBORS
THE BORROWED AND BLUE MURDERS

SUMMER SESSION

Merry Jones

This first world edition published 2011
in Great Britain and in the USA by
SEVERN HOUSE PUBLISHERS LTD of
9–15 High Street, Sutton, Surrey, England, SM1 1DF.

British Library Cataloguing in Publication Data

Jones, Merry Bloch.
  Summer session.
  1. Women veterans–Fiction. 2. Iraq War, 2003- –
  Veterans–United States–Fiction. 3. Post-traumatic
  stress disorder–Fiction. 4. Cornell University–
  Employees–Fiction. 5. Falls (Accidents)–Fiction.
  6. Brain damage–Patients–Rehabilitation–Fiction.
  7. Suicide–Fiction. 8. Suspense fiction.
  I. Title
  813.6-dc22

ISBN-13: 978-0-7278-8044-4 (cased)

All Severn House titles are printed on acid-free paper.

Severn House Publishers support The Forest Stewardship Council [FSC],
the leading international forest certification organisation. All our titles that
are printed on Greenpeace-approved FSC-certified paper carry the FSC logo.

MIX
Paper from
responsible sources
FSC
www.fsc.org   FSC® C018575

Typeset by Palimpsest Book Production Ltd.,
Falkirk, Stirlingshire, Scotland.
Printed and bound in Great Britain by
MPG Books Ltd., Bodmin, Cornwall.

To Robin, Baille and Neely

Acknowledgements

I am indebted to many people for their help with this book, including:

my agent, Rebecca Strauss at McIntosh & Otis, for her relentless enthusiasm and energy;

my editors, Amanda Stewart and Rachel Simpson Hutchens at Severn House, for their incredible insights and vision;

Dr Ron Kotler for his generosity in sharing his knowledge of sleep disorders, treatment and research;

Dr Susan Solovy Mulder for her contributions regarding Post Traumatic Stress Disorder and related treatments;

Dr Michael Zasloff for his patient answers to questions and guidance to articles on the brain, frontal lobe injuries, learning processes and aphasia;

members of The Philadelphia Liars Club – Jonathan Maberry, Gregory Frost, Jonathan McGoran, Leslie E. Banks, Kelly Simmons, Marie Lamba, Dennis Tafoya, Solomon Jones, Keith Strunk, Edward Pettit, Don Lafferty for their never-ending supply of supportiveness and good cheer;

Lanie Zera, Janet Martin, Nancy Delman, Sue Francke and Jane Braun for their soft shoulders and continued encouragement;

HealMyPTSD website founder, Michele Rosenthal for providing a much needed and accessible resource to people coping with the condition;

two generous female Iraqi war vets, who wished to remain anonymous, for details of their experiences there;

Baille and Neely for the constant inspiration and amazement they generate;

Robin for being my first reader, discusser, re-reader, re-discusser, etc.; a giant among men, my love and best friend.

Late April

Falling, Hank Jennings had three distinct, almost simultaneous thoughts. The first was to deny that he was actually falling. He couldn't be, not after his years of scaling the steepest mountains and exploring the darkest caverns in the world. It would be a cruel joke for him to die in broad daylight, falling off his own roof.

His second thought – this as he gained momentum and spread himself flat, scraping the skin off his fingertips while trying to dig his nails into the shingles – was of Harper, how hard his death would be on her.

His final thought, just before his head slammed the chimney, was about his own stupidity. Obviously, the roof had been the wrong place to have an argument.

June

Graham Reynolds puzzled at the large black eyeball staring at him from the pillow beside his head. What he saw made no sense. He closed his eyes, not yet fully awake, but when he opened them again, the thing was still there. Dark, steady and unblinking.

He squinted, focusing, gradually convinced that it wasn't an eye. Of course it wasn't. It was the barrel of a gun. Oh right, the gun. He'd bought it a few days ago in Manchester. He shut his eyes again, irritated by the light pouring through the window and his own sticky sweat.

Gently, he raised a hand to cover his forehead and rolled on to his back, the damp sheet sticking to his skin. He tried to remember. Had he shot anyone last night? A bunch of drunk frat boys had been making a racket across the street. He remembered staring out the window, ready to fire at the next one who made a sound, but, oddly, he wasn't sure if he'd actually pulled the trigger. If he had, though, there would have been cops, right? Sirens. And, like on television, a barrier of yellow tape? So probably no one got shot.

But now his room was stifling hot. And an angry bubble was swelling in his belly, even before he was out of bed. He turned his pulsing head, saw clumps of dirty clothes. Empty bottles. Scattered books. An upside-down sneaker, his work boots. His computer. Graham sat up, cursed the pain in his head and glanced at the clock. The numbers nine–one–nine didn't register. He picked up a vial of pills, turned it upside down. Empty. He picked up another. Empty. Damn. He'd have to dig into the stash, which no doubt would piss everyone off because each bottle he opened was one less in the pot. But what the hell. Speaking of the stash, he had to go get it, package it up. That guy from the city was coming. Where the hell had he put the padlock combination? Shit. He had no idea. Well, no biggie. He was pretty sure he knew the number by heart. Twenty-two, seven, two. Something like that.

Repeating numbers to himself, Graham stood unsteadily, went to the john, splashed some cold water on his face. When he came out, he noticed the clock again. Nine thirty. Wait. Was it Tuesday? Shit. He had class. A quiz in half an hour. Class? Was he seriously supposed to sit through class? With that insufferable twit Larry and his girlfriend – why couldn't he ever remember her name? Monica? Whatever. She wore pink. All pink, all the time. Pink tops, pink skirts, pink shoes – no doubt pink panties, too. If she sat near him today, he might have to rip her pink little head off. His hands tightened, aching. Maybe he'd kill the TA, instead. Wait until she handed out the quiz, and then: Bang. No more TA, no more quiz.

Fuck it. Maybe he wouldn't even go to class. He sat on the bed, not thinking.

'Hey – Graham.' Larry banged on his door.

'What?' Graham looked at the gun. Thought about popping Larry.

'You ready to go?'

Graham picked up the gun and aimed at the door, pretending. Bam. Bam.

'Graham?'

Graham pictured Larry's ear against the door, waiting for a response. Go ahead, he told himself. Respond. Shoot the little shit.

'Graham?' The doorknob jiggled.

'Don't come in, Larry. Don't even think of it.'

'Well, then answer—'

'I'm answering: Go away.'

Graham pictured clotting blood spatter in the hallway, clumps of brain matter. He hesitated, his finger on the trigger, considering which would be harder to take. Larry? Or the mess that Larry would make? His head pulsed blinding light. His finger tingled, aching to pull the trigger.

'Well, if you're coming, hurry the fuck up. I'm out.' Graham heard footsteps, the creak of the floorboards. The little turd was walking away, had no idea how close he'd come.

Graham let the gun drop on to the mattress, pressed his fingers against the hammering behind his forehead. Then, sweating, he pulled on some clothes, bright colors to counter the stark white-ness pounding his head.

Nine fifty-one. For support, Graham stepped into his work boots. Then he drew a deep breath, grabbed his book bag and headed out the door.

*   *   *

Harper Jennings parked her Ninja in the lot behind Willard Straight Hall, stowed her helmet, grabbed her iced chai and big black leather sack and began climbing the hill to campus, sweating off the jasmine scent of her three-minute morning shower. As she walked, her left leg ached from her hip to her ankle.

The pain was chronic, had been with her for more than five years, sometimes intensely, others quietly, but it was always there. Considering its cause, though, she couldn't complain. She was, after all, still able to feel it, unlike others in her patrol. The dead couldn't feel anything anymore. No, by comparison, a little, even a lot of pain wasn't so bad. In a way, it was her duty to carry it with her, a reminder of those who hadn't come home.

But it wasn't just a reminder. It was also a warning. The explosion that killed nine soldiers and thirteen civilians and forever damaged her leg had lasted maybe two seconds. An eye blink. A breath. Proving that life could change or end that quickly. Like Hank's fall. The time it had taken her husband to drop from their roof to the cement ledge below had been – what? Four seconds? Three? No time at all. Catastrophes gave no warning and took no time; she had to be prepared for the unexpected. Her leg with its ragged nerves was, in its way, a constant personal red alert.

Still, on the third Tuesday morning in June, as Harper ascended the steepest part of the hill to campus, she wasn't thinking about danger or possible catastrophes but about the positives in her life. Starting with her iced chai. Lord, what a luxury. Cold, spicy, sweet. In Iraq, there had been days when she'd have eagerly sold a body part for just one sip.

Or for the shade of an old oak tree. And now, here she was, surrounded by them. Not just oaks, either. Pines, elms, maples – dozens of species of trees and shrubs thrived all across Cornell's campus and the surrounding hills. The land was alive, fertile. Not like the barren deserts of war.

Harper paused, letting her left leg rest. A couple of wrens flew overhead, flitting on to a tree branch, chirping. A squirrel darted under a bush. A car accelerated. All around her was peace. Finally. Yet another reason to be thankful. At least for now, the war was leaving her alone. Weeks had passed since her last flashback. Even with Hank's injuries, she'd remained grounded in the moment, able to deal with crisis after crisis without being overwhelmed or interrupted by the past.

Starting up the hill again, Harper thought about Hank. More than anything else, she was thankful for his survival. God, she missed him. But when she'd visited that morning, Hank had actually shown progress. She'd asked about his breakfast, and he'd declared, 'Oat. Meal.' His eyes had twinkled, teasing the way they used to.

Lord. How had it happened? How had Hank Jennings, a man who'd scaled the world's highest mountains and worked atop oil rigs in the turbulent North Sea – how had he been so clumsy as to fall off his own roof? The accident had left him unconscious for days, critical for weeks, and now his brain was damaged, maybe permanently. Mercifully, he seemed oblivious to that possibility. Another thing, Harper supposed, to be thankful for.

The last few yards to the top of the hill were toughest. The physical therapist had advised that walking would be good; she'd figured that climbing would be even better. Wincing, she drew a deep breath and dug her purple Keens into the slope, pushing her weight up toward the top. Counting out the steps. One and two and three and four. Inhale. One and two and three – and there.

Harper paused, gazing back over the panorama. Her reward for her daily uphill trek was to view the lush idyllic hills surrounding Lake Cayuga, the town of Ithaca nestling its shore.

Ten minutes until class. Harper sat on a bench, watching people pass, attempting to cool off by sipping her chai. Lord, the weather was sizzling. Only June, and before ten o'clock in the morning, eighty-five humid degrees. This wasn't the dry, dusty heat of Iraq where the air was loaded with fine, grimy, clinging sand. No, here the air was thick and wet. Soupy. Like oatmeal.

Time to go. Harper stood and made her way past Olin Library and across the Arts Quad to White Hall, the traditional nineteenth-century stone building in which her class met. Maybe, Harper hoped, its thick walls and high ceilings would insulate it, offering cool relief. But as she entered the building, close heat enveloped her. By noon, when her recitation ended, the place would be a steam bath.

Climbing the four flights of steps, Harper remembered that hot air rose; the higher she went, the hotter it got. Brutal. At least the classroom had a fan. She'd distribute the quizzes and plop in front of it. And stay there. Yet another thing to be thankful for.

'Morning, Loot.'
  'Hey, Loot.'
  Early in the summer, talking about how she'd come to study Archeology, she'd mentioned her military service. Someone had asked her rank, and since then no one had uttered her name.
  'Morning.' Harper smiled and dropped into her seat, holding her lukewarm chai to her forehead, concentrating on the weak swirl of warm air from the fan.
  'We're melting, Loot. Puddles of protoplasm.'
  Grumbling about the heat continued as Harper dabbed her neck with a limp tissue and scanned the room, taking attendance.
  Pamela, her hair sun-bleached almost white, was talking to Jeremy about going out on her Hobie Cat.
  Preppies Dustin and Jason, in summer school to amass credits for double majors, were as usual razzing Monique. 'So, what can we infer from your obsession with pink? Do you fear other colors?'
  Jason smirked. 'Like yellow – what's wrong with yellow?'
  Monique scoffed. 'Deal with it. Pink's my comfort zone.' Her sundress, book bag, flip-flops, lips, nails, bracelets – her entire ensemble was, as always, pink. Harper didn't comment. She understood comfort zones of color; hers were neutral, tans and grays, nothing that would draw attention. Camouflage tones.
  As usual, Anna sat at the back of the room, alone, separated by rows of empty chairs. Anna's thick black hair had frizzed with the humidity; her face was hidden behind a book. She didn't look up when Harper called her name.
  Terence, by contrast, flashed a smile and a thumbs-up. A tight end for Big Red football, he was retaking the course so his C average wouldn't cut him from the team.
  Behind him was redhead Gwen, a transfer student making up credits. Straight A pre-Law students Dustin and Jason sat together, still cramming for the quiz. Kevin and his long amber dreadlocks sprawled beside the window, mellow as always. English major Cathy sat posture perfect, blonde hair pulled into a tight bun, muscles taut as if about to begin a sprint. Larry from Brooklyn and Esoso from Nigeria reclined like mirror

images, legs extended, and Shaundra, a drama major, sat by the door, munching a bear's claw. Finally, Graham anchored the middle of the room, his tangled curls emerging above the other heads like a rose on a too-long stem.

Harper scanned her group, wondering how this course in Archeology would affect them. None was majoring in the field; each was taking the class to fill an electives requirement. Still, when she'd been their age – just seven or eight years earlier – she'd had no idea what interested her; she'd been in ROTC with no clue that she'd pursue a PhD, let alone in Archeology. Maybe this introductory course would inspire someone to continue. She pictured it: huge Terence lumbering around fragile relics on a dig. Or Shaundra, emoting like Lady Macbeth while carbon dating—

'Loot?' Esoso had his hand up. 'Take pity on us. It's too hot for a quiz.'

Jeremy agreed. 'It's like the core of a molten volcano—'

'No, more like Hades itself,' Shaundra feigned anguish, swaying for effect.

'This isn't hot,' Harper smiled. 'Try lugging eighty pounds of gear in a hundred and ten degrees. You guys are soft.' She put check marks beside the names of the absent students – Kelsey and Greg – and took the quizzes out of her big leather sack. 'Try not to melt on your answer sheets.'

As Harper distributed the papers, Graham Reynolds' skinny arm went up.

'Loot, can I open that?' He pointed to the window closest to her desk. It was raised only halfway. Of course he could open it. Not that it would help.

Graham stood, and Harper blinked at his selection of wardrobe: fiery orange madras shorts, heavy construction boots and a red sleeveless T-shirt labeled 'LIFEGUARD'. Were his clothes some kind of anti-fashion, anti-conformity statement? Or just a random compilation of garments? Who would have put those pieces together? And, good God, why? Harper shook her head, amused. Cornell was a far cry from the military with its inspections of spit-shined shoes and pressed uniforms. Maybe Graham was just a free spirit. Or maybe he was color-blind.

Slowly, Graham moved past his classmates to the front of the room, stepping around desks and over book bags. Thin and some inches over six-feet tall, he was delicate featured, almost pretty, yet he tackled the window with surprising aggression, shoving too hard, forcing the pane up only an inch or so before jamming it and engaging it in battle, attacking with his full body.

Harper didn't watch him. She settled into her chair by the fan, waving her grade book to stir the heavy air. Noticing, not for the first time, that Anna appeared to have dozed off. What was with that girl?

Dustin raised his hand, asking if they could go outside since, seriously, no one could take a quiz effectively in this heat. Larry, Monique and Shaundra chimed in with a chorus of 'Please, Loot'. Maybe Graham heard, maybe not; he'd finally unjammed the window and raised it as high as it could go.

Harper was thinking that it was a good idea, going outside. She wasn't paying attention to Graham. So she didn't notice him lifting one leg, then the other over the sill, didn't look his way until she saw her students' gaping mouths and disbelieving eyes and followed their gazes just in time to see Graham purposefully lower himself over the ledge. His tangled curls dropped out of sight until all that was visible were his fingertips on the window frame.

Instantly, Harper was out of her chair, bolting to the window, leaning out and grabbing his wrists. She reacted reflexively, with precision and dexterity, calling for assistance. Graham hung there, gazing up at her with hazy green eyes. For a few endless seconds, Harper strained to hold on, tightening her grip, tugging at his thin, slippery arms, but she couldn't get leverage to pull him up, didn't have the body mass. Larry, Terence and Esoso joined her at the window, crowding her, reaching out, yanking at Graham's forearms.

'Graham,' Harper ordered, 'grab hold of my hand.'

But Graham didn't even try. Without a word, his eyes still fixed on Harper's, he let go of the windowsill and pushed off of the wall with his legs. His wrists slipped from her hands and, silently, he dropped four stories to the ground.

For a moment, nobody moved. Everyone was silent. Stunned. Then chaos erupted. Shrill screams. People running in circles, yelping, making frantic calls on cell phones. Shaundra stared at the window, strangling her bear claw; Gwen bent over, holding her belly, yipping, her voice drowned out by Monique's.

The room around Harper became fuzzy; she smelled gunfire, heard explosions. Oh God, she thought. Not now. She couldn't allow a flashback now. Grabbing a pencil from a nearby desk, she dug its point into her palm, using pain to ground herself in the moment. She concentrated on the present, on panicked cries, on the commotion of chairs scraping the old wooden floor. Her students needed her. She pulled away from the open window and, as trained, left the dead in order to protect the living.

'Listen up, everyone. Hey!'

No one listened. They continued shouting, moving in a dance of confusion.

'OK, then,' she muttered. Drawing a breath, Harper let out a shrill, ear-bending whistle.

Instantly, the room was silent. Fourteen pairs of eyes turned to her, lost and childlike. Reflexively, Harper shouted orders. 'Get your belongings. We're moving out.' Scanning the room, she saw that, amazingly, despite the havoc, Anna still slept in her seat.

'Anna!' Harper called to her. 'Somebody – Jeremy – wake her up.'

Jeremy looked at Anna, muttered, 'Jesus Christ,' and rolled his eyes in annoyance as he jostled her shoulder. She didn't wake up. Didn't react at all.

'Come on, Anna.' Jeremy shook his head, impatient. Finally, he leaned over and bellowed into her ear. 'WAKE UP!'

Anna didn't budge. Didn't move.

OK. Never mind. Harper would come back for her.

The class stood at the door, staring at Anna, asking what was wrong with that girl? Wasn't she strange? Tsks of disapproval among the panic.

Harper kept them moving. She called out names: Jeremy. Cathy, Shaundra. Gwen, Kevin, Larry. Pam. One at a time, touching each on the arm, she guided her students to the staircase; from there, she ushered them down the four flights to the door.

'Everyone stays here.' She put Jason in charge. 'Nobody moves. Nobody goes near Graham or even glances at him until I get back.' She hurried to the side of the building where a mere glance told her that Graham was beyond help. Then, ignoring the pain in her leg, she climbed the steps again to the classroom to get her remaining student.

Anna looked around in confusion. 'Loot? Where is everyone?'

'Outside.' Gently, Harper took her arm. 'Come with me.'
Anna resisted, pulled away. 'I heard shouting.'
'There's been an accident. I'll explain—'
'Why was everyone shouting?' Anna refused to move. 'What happened?'

Harper was getting annoyed; Anna was taking too much time and attention, shouldn't have been sleeping in class to begin with. 'Graham fell. Now let's move.' She started for the door.

Anna followed, asking questions. 'He fell? Where? How? Is he OK?'

Harper didn't answer; she ushered Anna down the stairs to the spot where her classmates huddled, flustered and shaken. Anna remained apart, tagging along as the group moved silently on to the landscaped quadrangle. When they came to the mangled body in orange madras shorts and a red tank top, the silence shattered with a scream.

'Whoa—' Kevin reached to catch her, but too late. Anna had already collapsed, out cold.

Students blinked at her and looked away, disapproving. Shaking their heads.

Harper hurried to her, feeling at fault. Granted, Anna was different. Always by herself. Often asleep in class. Even so, Harper shouldn't have been so abrupt, should have better prepared her for seeing Graham's body. Now the girl had fainted. Harper knelt, checked her pulse. Lying on the grass, Anna resembled an overstuffed doll, her torso cushiony and pillow-like. She seemed unhurt, but her skin felt clammy, and she remained disturbingly still, eyes closed, not responding to her name or Harper's touch.

'She'll be all right,' Harper assured herself as much as the others. Then, although several students had already done so, she used Jeremy's cell to call the police. Bystanders gathered, gawking and asking questions, but the class clustered around Graham, listening for sirens, protecting their freshly dead class-mate, unsure what else to do.

Harper watched over them, struggling to process what had happened. One moment, Graham had been taking a quiz; the next, he'd jumped to his death. Poof. No warning. Unless she'd missed something. She replayed the morning. The students in their seats, the suffocating heat. The weak buzzing fan. She'd given out the quizzes, and Graham had asked to open the window. Had there been any desperation in his voice? Any anger? Or sadness? She tried, but recalled nothing of note. Harper could still see Graham's unwavering eyes, feel his slick skin slipping from her grip. She also heard distant explosions, a low rumble of gunfire. No, she insisted. Not now.

'OK, everybody. Listen up.' She refocused, looking each student in the eyes, one at a time. 'I don't know what the hell happened to Graham. Why he did this. But we're going to be OK. All of us. The police are on the way. For now, stay together. And stay strong.'

Nods. Tear-filled eyes. Hugs. Sniffles and whimpers. Students stood arm in arm or sat leaning against each other, except for Anna, who lay beside them on the grass. Despite the heat, Harper shivered as she paced in circles around them, guarding her pack, touching Gwen's shoulder or patting Cathy's head. Her students depended on her, so she remained in control, fending off the flash of explosives, the flames nipping at her belly, the bullets whizzing past her ears. She pressed the pencil point into her palm, hoping that pain would hold her in the moment. Or that Graham's broken body would magically mend itself and stand, revealing a tasteless practical joke. Or an acrobatics trick. Or some reason, however misguided, for his death.

Finally, an endless few minutes after Graham crashed on to the quad, lights flashed and sirens blared. Campus cops, Ithaca police, firemen and an ambulance arrived, closely followed by local news, the dean, a cadre of university officials and even more curious onlookers.

'Attention, everyone.' Detective Charlene Rivers' voice blared into a megaphone, even though it was hardly necessary; people could easily hear her without amplification. Fortyish, broad-shouldered and dark-skinned, she'd assessed the scene quickly and taken over. 'Paramedics are here to check you out and see if anyone needs attention. Meantime –' her voice jolted to a stop, interrupted by a blare of feedback – 'nobody go anywhere; we need to talk to each of you, individually. Who's first?' She eyed the group, waiting for a volunteer.

Jason raised his hand; officers escorted him to a nearby bench.

Harper wandered after them, intending to eavesdrop. It wouldn't be easy to hear their conversation, not with machine guns firing in her head, but she was determined to find out why Graham had killed himself. What her students knew. Inconspicuously, she sat on the grass not far from the bench, listening.

'Loot – our instructor – she tried to stop him. But there was no time – nobody could do anything.' Jason's voice was flat, emotionless. 'He just climbed out, hung on for a few seconds and let go.'

Dustin was next. 'Threaten? You mean to kill himself? Never. Well, not that I know of.'

Gwen called Graham a comedian. 'I met him freshman year. He had a droll sense of humor. Real wry. When I saw him going out the window, I thought it was a joke.'

Pam sniffled. 'He seemed a tad eccentric. But not destructive or dangerous. Just in his own world.'

Terence shrugged. 'I didn't know the dude. No disrespect intended; it's just we never, you know, actually hung out.'

Monique fumed. 'Sorry, but I'm furious at Graham – selfish bastard. Did he think about anybody but himself? His family? His friends? Was his life so unbearable that he had to do this?'

Larry, Graham's room-mate, chewed his thumbnail. 'He gave no sign. No warning. Well, this morning, he was pretty grouchy, but – truthfully? Graham was grouchy every morning. Nothing seemed different.'

Anna awoke and gave her statement in a whisper too low for Harper to hear.

Jeremy threw up behind a tree.

Finally, Harper went back to the group, having listened to parts of fourteen statements and learned exactly nothing.

Dean Van Arsdale addressed the group, his smooth baritone bellowing through the borrowed megaphone. '. . . And remember, free counseling is available for any and all who need or want it. Make sure you fill out the forms being distributed by my assistant, Marge, and take a brochure about the university's mental health services and ways to access help.' He urged students to seek support, reminding them that they'd been through a terrible ordeal. A trauma. Explaining that the effects of a trauma could be unexpected and lasting. Harper listened, blinking away sniper fire.

When the dean finally finished, Detective Rivers took the megaphone again. 'If you think of anything relevant to Graham Reynolds' suicide, get in touch. Meantime, everyone is excused.'

'Wait. Ma'am?' Harper didn't want to overstep authority, but it was, after all, her recitation. 'I'd like to say something.'

The detective offered the megaphone, but Harper didn't take it. Instead, she let out another attention-getting whistle. These were her students, her responsibility. Fourteen faces – not counting those of the dean, the onlookers, the cops or the press – turned her way.

'Next recitation is a memorial.' She spoke quietly. 'Dedicated to Graham. Write something about him. Or to him. We'll share them as a group. Before we go, anybody have something they want to say?'

Eyes diverted; heads shook.

'RIP, man,' Terence finally offered.

A few voices mumbled, 'Amen.'

Nobody added anything.

'OK, then. Stay strong. See you in class.'

With that, most of the students and bystanders wandered off. Gwen and Shaundra stopped to give Harper hugs. Larry lingered a few feet from Harper.

'Larry?' Monique hefted her pink book bag. 'You coming?'

He didn't answer, didn't even look at her. Finally, she stomped off alone.

Larry didn't say anything. Didn't leave.

'You OK, Larry?'

He shrugged, watched the grass. 'Sure.'

Clearly, he wanted to talk. Harper watched him, saw tension, small twitchy movements of his head and neck. 'This must be hard for you, losing a room-mate.'

Larry shook his head. 'Truth is I hardly knew the guy.'

Harper was confused. 'But I thought you lived with—'

'I only met him a few weeks ago. At work. Graham needed a place; I had an extra room. So he moved in.'

An edgy silence. Larry twitched, cleared his throat, shifted his weight. Getting up the nerve to say something?

Dean Van Arsdale was talking with the police. 'Mrs Jennings.' He gestured to her. 'Would you join us, please?'

She nodded, but didn't move. 'Larry, if you need—'

'No, Loot. It's cool. Thanks.' He backed away. 'I'll catch you later.'

Harper watched him as he took off after a pink form crossing the quad.

The police asked Harper the same questions they'd asked the students. Had she known Graham Reynolds well? Had she noticed any changes in his behavior? Any signs of depression? Any personal crisis?

She answered, No. No. No. And no. She felt useless, frustrated. And surprised that no one was blaming her for Graham's death, even though she'd been in charge. In fact, as he left, the dean squeezed her hand and offered his sympathy and support.

Detective Rivers offered her a ride home, but Harper had her Ninja parked on campus. Besides, the gunfire in her head was escalating rapidly; she couldn't fend it off much longer, so she thanked the detective and told her she wanted to linger a while. Finally, when the police, the media and university officials had gone, she sank under an oak tree, leaning against the sturdy safety of its trunk.

There was not even the hint of a breeze. No matter where Harper looked, she saw Graham's red tank top disappearing out the window, his curls dropping beyond the sill. Again and again, his skinny wrists slipped from her grasp.

No, she repeated, shaking her head, trying to reject the emotional triggers. Think of something else. Repeat your wedding vows; picture the sparkle in Hank's eyes. Or try to find a squirrel to feed. Or count the trees on the quad. But it was too late. She smelled gunpowder, saw explosions. Her mind had already begun its spin, would have to cycle through, so she sat stiffly, arms crossed, waiting for her flashback to pass.

Harper pressed her back against the wall of a blown-out building and clutched her rifle. No, wait – it wasn't her rifle; it was Graham's wrists, and she clung to them, felt them slide out of her hands, saw his eyes watching hers as he fell. But no, it wasn't Graham who was falling. It was her husband, Hank. She was home in the yard, planting tulips. She smelled damp soil, glanced up at the roof where Hank was fixing shingles.

Hank didn't make a sound. Not a grunt, not a curse. He simply fell.

Watching him for the thousandth time, Harper still couldn't take a breath. Couldn't move or stop her brain. Shutting her eyes, she waited for Hank to hit the chimney, then the ledge; she anticipated the thud of impact.

But there was no thud. Just a bang, a flash of white-hot wind.

Men were shouting, guns popping. Dust and smoke, an acrid, burning smell. Weapon raised, Harper dashed to take cover but stumbled, glanced down to see what she'd stepped on. The boy. He had no face. It was entirely gone, blown away. His head, a ball of red.

Or was that the red of the tulips? Back in the garden, digging, she paused to look up at the roof. Again, Hank slid, limbs akimbo, his head smacking the chimney, his body tumbling over the gutters and falling through the air.

Hot air. Dusty air. Someone was approaching through the haze: a woman. Sameh. Harper knew her name, saw her every morning as she passed the checkpoint on her way to the market. Sameh, in traditional black garb, with shining eyes. Often, she had children with her – two young boys. But not this time.

Marvin was jabbering about an old movie. 'The guy's a genius, but when the schoolteacher chick's around, he trips, falls, bumps into things—'

Sameh came toward them, crossing the road. Harper nodded a greeting. Sameh nodded back, eyes smiling. Marvin talked. '. . . He's a complete buffoon . . .'

Was there a burst of light? A bang? Harper saw, heard nothing. She was vaguely aware that she'd left the ground. She was flying . . .

Downward, from the classroom window. Whooshing through hot air, four stories to the ground of the Arts Quad.

No, not to the Arts Quad. To her garden. Harper raced across the flowerbed, stomping on her new plantings. 'Hank!' His name erupted from her belly, a soul-wrenching howl. Hank's eyes were partly open, but he didn't respond to his wife's frantic calls or her desperate rattling of his body. She needed to get help.

But Harper couldn't move. She smelled smoke and burning flesh, tasted metal. Blood? She was on her back, her arm on her belly; her hands felt sticky clumps – oh God, were they her guts? She closed her fingers around something, lifted it. Saw a red fleshy glob. Oh God, oh God . . .

'Oh God—' The voice came from above, from the roof. Trent's voice. Trent Manning, Hank's colleague, close friend. He'd been up there, helping Hank with the repairs. 'Christ – Harper. I'm coming down. Don't move him.'

Move him? Harper couldn't move him. Lord, she couldn't

even move herself, lying there holding a glob, trying to call out but making no sound. What the hell had happened? Where was Marvin? Sameh? The others – Cooper? Phyllis? Mike? Were they OK? Why couldn't she move her legs? And the blood on her belly – she must have been shot. Must be dying. But she didn't feel pain – wasn't that interesting? Death didn't hurt, wasn't as bad as she'd imagined. She lay still, watching the empty sky, aware of flickering light. Waiting to be dead.

But she didn't die. She was on her feet again, running for help. Breathless, pushing through enemy fire, seeing bodies drop around her. Stepping on the kid with no face. Holding her body low to the ground, dashing past overturned trucks and wounded comrades, up on to the deck and into the kitchen where she grabbed her cell phone. Every action took too long, and her thoughts were jumbled, interrupted by surges of gunfire and cries of pain. And by Graham turning into Hank and falling, landing with a muted thud and an understated rustle of dogwoods.

Which, absurdly, she noted needed trimming. Their old house needed so much work. The upstairs bathroom was gutted; the kitchen only half redone. Shingles were coming up on the roof . . . and – damn, there went Hank again, falling. Or was it Graham? Marvin chattered; Sameh stepped through the dust, about to cross the street.

But Harper was beside Hank again. Time stopped. Gunfire hiccuped intermittently; white light flashed with deadly explosive pops. Harper knelt beside Hank, stroking his face, promising him, the others and herself that everything would be all right. Hank was tough. Hank would survive. Unlike Graham – or Marvin, Phyllis, Cooper, Sameh and the boy without a face – Hank would be fine.

But Hank wasn't fine. His head had slammed first the chimney and then a concrete ledge, and his brain had ricocheted against his skull. There was damage to the frontal lobe, particularly on one side. For weeks, doctors repeatedly operated to relieve swelling and pressure inside his skull and waited to see how much permanent harm had been done, not sure he'd recover. Harper had prayed, had made deals with God, promising never to curse again, to give to charities, to install solar panels on the house and minimize her carbon footprint, even to make peace with her father – anything if Hank would get well. A month

and a half later, though, Hank was still in the clinic of the
Cayuga Neurological Center, still not fine.

Neither was Harper, for that matter. Hunkering down with
her weapon raised, she watched for potential suicide bombers
and told the suspicious-looking Iraqi boy to halt, but he didn't;
he kept approaching. She called out again, warning him. 'Stop
right there.'

He didn't. Two more steps and she'd have to follow protocol,
firing at him. Dropping him to the dust.

'. . . you OK?'

A voice drifted through the smoke and dust.

'Miss? Are you all right?'

Harper peered out from the alley where she'd sought cover,
her gun aimed and ready. Through the clearing smoke, a skinny
guy with glasses peered back at her. He wasn't in uniform. He
wasn't even in Iraq.

'Miss? Can I help you out of there?' He frowned, not an
angry frown, though. A worried frown. And he stepped closer,
offering his hand. Why wasn't he afraid? Didn't he believe
she'd shoot?

'Step back,' Harper breathed, aiming at him. But when she
glanced down, she saw that she wasn't holding her firearm. Her
gun, in fact, was a twig. A short, fat, pathetic twig.

The guy stepped back but took out his cell phone. 'Do you
need assistance? Should I call somebody?' He eyed her warily.

Oh God. Harper closed her eyes, opened them again. The
streets of Iraq were gone. The war, her yard where Hank had
hit his head, all of it had retreated, fading back into her head.
She looked around at the building behind her, the bushes, the
skinny guy with glasses who gaped at her. Another man joined
him, older, bearded. Wonderful, she was drawing a crowd. She
should put out a hat, sing a little tune, get contributions. The
two stood watching her, talking. Harper heard them mumbling,
'. . . needs help . . . maybe campus police . . .'

Campus police? Oh God, not again. 'No, no – I'm fine.' She
swallowed, looked around, getting her bearings. She was outside
Olin Library, across the quad from White Hall. How the hell
had she gotten there? Lord, had she really gone running for
cover? Time had passed, but how much? A few minutes? An
hour? She didn't know.

She stood tall, hoping to convince the men that she was all

right. Dropping her twig, she slapped dirt off her hands, brushed off her khaki capris and stepped out of the shrubbery.

'I'm OK – really.' She attempted a composed, authoritative voice. 'Just fine.'

The men didn't move. They stared, assessing her.

'Seriously. Everything's cool.' She straightened her back, met their eyes. Her tone might have been too emphatic, skin too flushed, eyes too wild. But she walked away with deliberate dignity, as if she weren't smudged with soil and sweat, as if she didn't still want to dive for cover in the shadows.

Harper felt the pair watching until she turned at the library and hurried out of their line of sight. Then, looking back, making sure they weren't following, she stopped, bent over and clutched her stomach. It was over; she was OK. The gunfire, the explosions hadn't been real. They'd been just another damned flashback.

She stepped off the path and touched the library wall, scraping her fingers along the rough concrete, making sure. Leaning against it, she pressed her hands against her eyes, pushing away memories. It was almost comical, the repetition. The absurd replays of people blowing up and falling down. If only she could add a little music – piano, like in Charlie Chaplin movies – she'd have some real entertainment. Could sell tickets. If not for the stomach-knotting, heart-flipping fear. If not for the horrific realities behind them, the flashbacks would be hilarious.

But she wasn't laughing. Not even snickering. She was mad at herself for having another flashback, for losing control. Her shrink insisted that the flashbacks weren't her fault; they were mental scars from the war. From what happened there. Even so, she'd thought she'd gotten better. That the images, the smells of fear and death would leave her alone.

Until a few years ago, the only dead person Harper had ever seen had been Grandma Emma, who died at eighty-eight, crocheting an afghan in her living room. In her coffin, Grandma Emma's face had been brightly rouged, her eyelids dusted with startling blue shadow, her silvery hair elegantly coiffed. She had been dressed in a rosy Jones New York suit fit for the symphony.

But then came Iraq. Harper had seen the dead without styled hair or cosmetics. Often without limbs or faces. There, she'd learned not just what death looked like but what it smelled like. What it *tasted* like.

This knowledge, like a parasite, had moved into her mind and made a home there, ready to rear up at the slightest trigger, dominating her thoughts, overcoming reality. In the war, Harper had sustained physical injuries, but they'd been neither as permanent nor as painful as her invisible, mental ones.

The diagnosis was PTSD. Post Traumatic Stress Disorder. Harper had learned all about its causes and symptoms; the condition was epidemic among veterans of Iraq and Afghanistan, as common as a cold. Like many other vets, Harper saw a therapist and had pills that were supposed to but didn't really help. The fact was that there was no cure for her condition, so she tried to tough it out and control it on her own. And, even after Hank's fall, she'd managed to reduce the frequency and intensity of the flashbacks.

Until today. Until Graham Reynolds' death. On her watch.

Sweat dripped down her back, beaded on her forehead. Harper tried to get her bearings. The sun had risen high overhead; a cluster of students picnicked under a nearby tree, others sat on a bench eating pizza. So it was lunchtime. Between noon and one. Harper stretched her sore leg and looked around, missing something. Her big leather bag. Damn. Where was it? Back in those bushes? Or had she dropped it while running for cover? Without its weight on her shoulder, she felt naked. Defenseless, as if she'd lost her gear. Her mind rattled off the list: Rifle, 175 rounds of ammunition, gas mask, canteens, chemical suit, boots, medical kit, helmet, bulletproof vest, compass, knife, baby wipes. Stop, she told herself. Stop. She wasn't separated from her gear – she didn't have gear any more, wasn't in a combat zone, wasn't in actual danger. She was looking for a sack, not a survival kit. Still, all her stuff – phone, keys, papers, books, money, driver's license and credit cards – everything was in that bag. Lord. Where was it?

And then she remembered. Her students had taken their things out of the classroom with them, but in the confusion she must have left her bag in the building, upstairs. That had to be it. Smearing sweat from her forehead, Harper started back across the Arts Quad to climb the stairs of White Hall yet another time.

The room was just as they'd left it; apparently, no other class had been held there yet. The lights were still on. And the fan. The chairs were jumbled, shoved randomly out of order. Harper

moved one, putting it back in place, but stopped. The arrange-
ment of chairs and neatness of the room didn't matter. She
needed to stay on task, get her bag and go before her mind
began replaying what had happened, taunting her with what she
might have done to prevent it.

Quickly, Harper found her leather sack, stuffed her papers
into it, jammed the grade book on top and started for the door.
Glancing back, though, she noticed a single green book bag in
the middle of the room.

Graham's?

It had to be. And, on his desk, his unfinished quiz.

Maybe Graham had written something on it – maybe a note
that would explain what he'd done. Harper made her way
through the scattered chairs and picked up his quiz. A piece of
paper slipped out from under it, drifting to the floor. She scooped
it up. But, no, it wasn't a suicide letter. Just a bunch of numbers.
Was it a cheat sheet? No, not unless the answers were coded.
There were no letters, no A, B, C or D for multiple choices.
Maybe a phone number. Or a student ID, or a computer password. Well, it didn't matter. She stared at the digits –
16719220702 – wondering if they were the last things Graham
had written. But that didn't matter, either.

Harper stuffed the numbers and Graham's quiz into her bulky
leather sack and picked up Graham's book bag. Wait. Maybe
he'd left a note in it? She set it down, unzipped it, pulled it
open.

Inside, she found no note. Just Graham's textbook, his phone,
a half-eaten bag of Doritos, a Mountain Dew, a vial of prescription pills. And, at the bottom, lying beside three tens and six
crisp one hundred dollar bills, a shiny black nine-millimeter
handgun.

Harper sat down, staring. A gun? Why did Graham have a gun?
And, if he'd wanted to commit suicide, why hadn't he just shot
himself? Why did he bother to jump out the window?

It made no sense. Graham seemed too oblivious and gawky
to be involved in anything as dark as a gun. She wondered what
the pills were for. And the money – it was a lot for a college
kid to carry around.

The heat was suffocating, made it difficult to think. And Harper
reminded herself it wasn't her responsibility to investigate

Graham. The bag and its contents would go to the authorities. She'd call that detective – what was her name? Waters? Harper checked the detective's card. Rivers. Charlene Rivers.

Harper pulled out her cell, made the call, arranged to meet the detective at three. She had almost two hours. Hoping to fill them, she made another call.

'Hey. I was wondering – taking a chance you have an opening today. To see me.' Harper hated to sound needy even to Leslie, her therapist, so she kept the message brief. 'Something happened—' She stopped herself, avoiding a whine. 'Anyhow, let me know?'

Harper hefted her bulky bag on to one shoulder, Graham's gun-laden book bag on to the other, and made her way around the jumbled desks to the door where she stopped, unable to leave yet. Steeling herself, tightening her fists, she turned and made herself look.

It was just a window. Wide open. No fingers grabbed at the sill. No curls dropped from sight. Harper waited, but there was no flashback; all she saw was the empty stillness of framed glass and painted wood.

Letting out a breath, she turned off the fan and the lights and left. Halfway down the steps, her phone beeped a text message from Leslie. 'CU 4 p.m.'

Harper stood outside White Hall with nowhere to go. Almost two hours until she was to meet Detective Rivers, three until her appointment with Leslie. She felt like calling a friend, but, in truth, not many were around. Even before Iraq, she hadn't had a huge social circle, preferring small intimate groups to crowds. But since her return, she'd kept even more to herself, uncomfortable with most people unless she had to perform a designated role – like instructor. Maybe it was her damaged leg, but probably it was deeper. The war, what she'd seen and done, had changed her. Harper felt different from 'civilians'. Well, except for Hank.

Hank wasn't like other people; he'd been in Iraq – a consultant. He understood. But apart from Hank, Harper had spent the last three years primarily in her own company, except for a few close friends. But most of them were gone for the summer. Janet and Dan were in Italy, Ruth in Maine. Ethan and Cathy on a dig in Belize, and Vicki and Trent – supposedly her closest friends – had been scarce since Hank's fall. Before the accident, Trent had wandered into their home as easily as his own, and Vicki had come over daily for morning coffee. But not lately. Harper hadn't talked to them in days. Possibly weeks.

So, lugging Graham's book bag and her own leather sack, Harper wandered the quad, alone. Ignoring the ache in her leg, she followed the path to her favorite spot, the Suspension Bridge, and crossed it halfway, stopping to gaze down into the gorge, at the greenery bursting from its steep rock walls. And the rushing stream at the bottom, slowly, patiently carving its way through rock.

Harper loved this view; it was the opposite of the desert but had the same effect. The stream gave perspective, demonstrated how small and fleeting life was, how time and nature went on despite human concerns, oblivious to suicides or injuries or even wars. After a while, calmer, she turned and backtracked, crossing campus the other way, towards College Town. From there, she kept moving, wandering along Dryden Road down to Eddy Street and up again. She walked for miles, ignoring the burn of her leg muscles, passing head shops, coffee houses, pizza parlors and bars, noticing none of them. Harper focused only on her body's motion. One foot after another, sweating, lugging heavy bags, Harper walked until she was light-headed and thirsty. Only then did she realize that, although she'd gone in a roundabout way, all along she'd been heading back toward Hoy Road, to the only place she really wanted to be – the Neurological Center. And Hank.

Now that she had a clear destination, she picked up her pace. She was going to see Hank. Her Hank. She pictured their first meeting in Iraq, at a reception for civilian contractors and consultants. She'd been on duty, but Hank hadn't cared; he'd offered her a Martini and tried to pick her up. He'd been swarthy and strong, his dark eyes twinkling when he looked at her, as if seeing her amused him. She'd refused the drink and walked away, thinking him cocky and full of himself. She'd thought nothing of it until she'd run into him again at a briefing. When a colleague introduced them, Hank had grinned, feigned a wince and covered his crotch.

'I've already met the lieutenant. It took her maybe ten seconds to bust my balls.'

Everyone had laughed. Sexism, overt and unashamed.

Harper hadn't blinked. 'Ten seconds? That long?' she feigned surprise. 'I must have been having a slow day.'

Hank had laughed. And hung around. Harper quickly found out that he wasn't just another horny guy with a handsome face. Hank was gutsy and quick, smarter than almost anyone she'd ever met. At thirty-six, he was not only consulting for the army in Iraq; he was also up for tenure as a professor of Geology at Cornell. Hank had changed her view of the world. And herself. With him, she had dropped her guard, had discovered how to love and trust. With Hank, she'd found the confidence to pursue her PhD in Archeology and begin a career. And, with Hank, she hoped to have a child, raise a family. That's why they'd bought the house. That's why they'd been rehabbing it. Again, Harper saw Hank climb the ladder to the roof where Trent was examining shingles.

No. Harper slammed the door on that image, refusing to revisit Hank's fall. Not just his, but Graham's, too. She would think only of this moment. Of Hank. As she walked, her steps seemed to pound out his name: Hank, Hank, Hank, Hank. She walked in rhythm with his name, up the driveway to the massive, ultra-modern Neurological Center, and when the automatic doors whooshed open and the cold of the air conditioners assaulted her, she could still hear it repeating, strong and simple, like a mantra in her head.

Harper stopped for a drink at the water cooler, but, in the suddenly chilled air, her thirst seemed to have died. She signed in and greeted Laurie, the perky receptionist at the front desk, and, wearing her visitor's pass, took the elevator to the third floor where she found that Hank wasn't in his room. The nurse at the desk wasn't Lulu, who worked in the morning, or Sybil, who worked evenings. This one was new; her name tag said Marcy. Marcy seemed reluctant to speak to Harper, eyed her oddly.

'Mr Jennings is off the floor for a procedure,' was all she would say, nothing about what kind of procedure or when he'd be back.

Having nowhere else to go, Harper set her bags on the floor of Hank's room and sat in the reclining chair, waiting, trying not to think. She turned on the television, but the talk shows and commercials annoyed her, so she turned it off and watched the blank pale-green walls, the doors of the built-in pine closet,

the view into the white-tiled bathroom. The place was impersonal. Cold. Depressing. Institutional. Well, it *was* an institution,
and Hank wasn't there for the decor. And his stay was only
temporary.

Chilly, Harper got out of the chair and on to his bed, pulling
up the blanket, trying to recall his bear-like warmth. How long
had it been since they'd slept in the same bed? A few minutes?
A century?

Aching, she pressed her face into his pillow, searching for
his scent, but the pillow smelled sterile, like bleach. There was
nothing of Hank in this room, not his wit or his passion, not
even his smell.

Harper got out of bed, unable to stay still. She fidgeted with
the flowers her mother had sent, removing dead blossoms,
pinching off wilting petals. She watered the potted plant from
Hank's cousins, removed the withered grapes from Trent and
Vicki's ageing fruit basket. She avoided the Godiva chocolates
from Dr Hayden, Hank's department chair, and tacked the cards
from various colleagues and friends neatly on to the bulletin
board. Maybe the room looked cozier now. She sat again, looked
around. No, the room was still impersonal, still institutional,
just dotted with Hallmark cards. Harper gazed out the window.
The sky had darkened; thick clouds had blown in. Maybe there
would be a thunderstorm. Maybe the heat would break.

Meantime, she hadn't eaten lunch. And the chocolates looked
awfully good. Rich and dark, filled with nougat or caramel or
raspberry cream. Maybe she'd have just one. Or two. They were
small.

Six chocolates later, she heard voices – an orderly telling the
nurse that he was bringing 307 back to his room. 307? That
was Hank's room; Hank was back.

Harper's fingers were sticky with melted chocolate. She ran
to the bathroom to rinse them, glanced in the mirror. And gasped.
Her cheeks were streaked with sweat and mud; her hair mangled
and matted. She recalled Marcy, the nurse, backing away from
her. Of course she had; Harper would back away from this face,
too.

Leaning over the sink, she splashed away soil and sweat
marks, smoothed the clumps out of her short blonde hair. Even
then, the woman in the mirror looked haggard, disheveled. But
the orderly was wheeling Hank's chair into the room; there was

no time for major repairs. Harper straightened to her full five foot three-and-a-quarter inches, took a cleansing breath, slapped her cheeks to redden them, and opened the bathroom door, a little giddy, a lot needy. Hank was back. Her Hank. And his big bear-like presence would steady her.

The orderly saw her and smiled. 'Looks like you have company,' he told Hank.

Hank looked around, wide-eyed. He hadn't been expecting anyone. His face was pale and too hollow, but when he saw her, his eyes brightened, laughing. Did she look that funny? He forced himself up and out of the chair, using mostly his good arm and leg, and he stood, off balance but independent, grinning at her.

Harper wanted to run to him but knew better; he was still wobbly. She might knock him over. So she moved slowly, planting a gentle kiss on his mouth.

'I had some free time, so I thought I'd surprise you.' Maybe he's better now, she thought. Maybe this last procedure improved his brain function. Maybe he'll talk.

But Hank stood, silently watching her. So she kept talking. 'It's so hot outside, Hank. Lucky you have air conditioning. White Hall was—' She stopped mid-sentence, recalling how her class there had ended. She blinked, changing the subject.

'The nurse said you were out having a procedure. So I straightened up a little.' Stop chattering, she told herself. Stop feeling compelled to fill the silence. Relax; let him take his time.

Slowly, Hank's lips twisted and his eyes narrowed with fierce concentration. 'Go.' As Harper smiled encouragingly, he forced another word. 'Home.'

Go. Home? Wait. What? He wanted her to go home? Stunned, Harper swallowed air, felt as if she'd been punched.

'You must be tired.' Harper kept her voice cheery. 'I'll go soon. I wanted to see you, but you should rest. I'll come back later.' She forced a smile, tried not to worry her hands.

Hank shook his head, no, and scowled. 'Not not not.' His fist tightened and he pounded the top of the dresser.

Not? Not what? Not come back later? Didn't he want her to visit at all? Why? What had happened? That morning, he'd seemed so positive and affectionate, happy with his oatmeal. 'Hank, what's wrong?' Harper frowned.

'He's just frustrated – I'm sure he doesn't mean it like it sounds.' The orderly took firm hold of Hank's arm to prevent more pounding. Then he led him to the reclining chair. 'Sit down, Mr Jennings. Relax, take a breath, and when you're ready, try again.' He looked at Harper. 'They get this way sometimes. Trying to talk gets them exhausted. He should rest.'

Harper nodded, hating that the orderly talked about her husband as if he weren't there. Then again, maybe Hank wasn't there. The man in the recliner had dark shadows under his eyes, and his thick curls needed trimming. His brows furrowed and he wasn't dashing. He didn't look very much like her Hank at all. Besides, her Hank would never have told her to go home and not come back. Missing the man he'd been, Harper closed her eyes, saw him sliding off the roof. No. Not again.

Hank's mouth contorted; he was working on more words. 'No,' or maybe, 'Now,' he finally formed. 'Go. Home.'

Home. She pictured the rambling half-gutted Victorian house with the steep slate roof. When – how – would she ever manage to stop replaying his fall? Harper went over to the chair, put her arms on Hank's wide shoulders, crouching so her eyes met his. 'It's not very hospitable, Hank, telling me to go home.'

He blinked at her urgently. 'Me. You. Not.'

Right. Harper regretted surprising him. She shouldn't have broken their routine, popping in when he wasn't expecting her. She stood again, determined to remain positive, searching for a light-hearted topic, hoping he'd stop ordering her to leave. Seeing a menu on the top of the dresser, she picked it up. 'What's for dinner tonight? Hmm. Breast of chicken with peach salsa. Balsamic rice. Asparagus. Peach pie. Yum.' Harper felt her face get hot, ashamed of her sing-song tone and feigned happiness. She was talking to Hank as if he were a child. Just because he talked like a toddler in small words and short phrases didn't mean he wasn't still an intelligent adult who probably understood perfectly well what was being said to him.

But it didn't seem to matter what Harper said because, apparently, Hank wasn't listening. He was working his mouth, trying to say something. She waited until, again, he insisted, 'Now. Hoppa. Go.'

She sighed, defeated. 'Fine. I'm going.' She studied his face, his eyes. 'Hank, I love you. I'll be back after dinner.' She kissed his mouth, then his stubbly cheek. She pressed her face

there, storing the smell of him and the sensation of his rough whiskers. Then she gathered up her bags and walked out before he could speak again.

But he spoke anyway, loudly. 'Hoppa. Home.' He struggled to form another sound, but Harper was gone and the orderly wasn't listening. 'Me.' Then, he shook his head, no, and added, 'With.'

When the elevator doors opened, they revealed one of Hank's doctors. Dr Ron Kendall's boyish face and fair hair made him look young enough to be a medical student, but, in fact, he was a world-renowned neurosurgeon and researcher. He carried himself accordingly, as if expecting mobs of manic fans to descend on him at any moment. Over the last several weeks, though, Harper had learned to look beyond his superstar attitudes. Dr Kendall was a genius, committed to his patients. His cutting-edge brain-injury work with his partner, Dr Steven Wyatt, was what had convinced her to bring Hank to the clinic.

Dr Kendall flashed a professional nano-smile. 'Harper. How's it going?'

It was merely a conventional greeting. Dr Kendall didn't expect an actual answer. When they arrived at ground level, he waved, 'Take care,' and began to stride away.

'Dr Kendall.' The words spilled out, surprising her. 'Do you have a minute?'

He paused, head tilted, eyebrows lifted, as if considering whether or not he did.

'It's . . . One of my students killed himself today.' Her face got hot. Why had she said that? What was he supposed to do about it?

'Really, that was you? Your class?' Dr Kendall stepped closer and took her arm, led her into a corner of the lobby, sat facing her. 'How awful. I heard about it on the radio. They said a student jumped out a window.'

Harper nodded. The story had spread quickly.

'What a shock, Harper. How are you doing?' He leaned forward, studying her with gentle, hazel eyes. Harper hoped she'd washed all the mud off her face. Dr Kendall put a hand on her arm, and the tenderness of his touch surprised her, particularly after Hank's blunt rejection. Suddenly, tears blurred her vision. Tears? Really? She was a war veteran; soldiers didn't cry. Even so, her eyes were wet. Dr Kendall handed her his handkerchief; she stared at it before taking it. Men still carried handkerchiefs?

'Thank you.' Harper dabbed her eyes.

'Did he say anything? Give a reason?'

'No. Nothing.' Harper was annoyed by her tears. Crying was a sign of weakness, a waste of time. It interfered with clear thinking, accomplished nothing. So, even as Hank's doctor tried to console her, she blew her nose, sat straight and changed her focus, asking about her husband's case.

Dr Kendall blinked, startled by the abrupt change of subject. He shifted his position, leaning back and crossing his legs, taking on a more professional demeanor. 'Sorry. What?'

'Is he making any progress?'

He cleared his throat. 'Harper. Both Dr Wyatt and I have discussed this with you—'

'Hank seems unhappy. Frankly, I need to remind myself why he's here. And why he has to go through all these procedures.'

'He's here because we might be able to help him. And, as you know, the procedures help us assess the damage to specific parts of his brain—'

'But how long will it all take? Shouldn't he be improving by now?'

Dr Kendall folded his arms, creating a physical barrier. 'Harper, the answer to your questions is the same as it's been all these weeks: we don't know. Your husband's aphasia affects his ability to form language. It might or might not improve. Meantime, we've started him on speech therapy, and art therapy to encourage alternate outlets for expression—'

'But those are conventional treatments. What about the experimental procedures you talked about. Like electronic stimulation?'

'We're evaluating his eligibility for a variety of experimental treatments.'

Still? How long did it take? Why weren't they moving faster? 'But couldn't you treat him as an outpatient, with him living at home?'

'Harper, we've already discussed this. Outpatient treatment is out of the question. We're dealing with your husband's *brain*.' Dr Kendall waited, letting his words sink in. 'Having him here is difficult for you, but be patient. We're studying Hank's frontal lobe injuries with varied functional MRIs. The process takes time. And we need to be thorough. You wouldn't tolerate anything less.'

No, she wouldn't. So why was she pestering him? Harper looked away, felt her neck flush.

'Meantime, who knows? Conventional therapies might help, or Hank might experience spontaneous recovery. In either of those cases, we might not need an experimental route.' Dr Kendall glanced at his watch. 'So, are we OK here?' He stood, guiding Harper to her feet. 'I was about to take off.'

'Thank you, Doctor.' She hefted her bags. 'Sorry to be a bother.'

'Not at all.' Dr Kendall gave her a brief, professional hug.

Harper had almost crossed the lobby when she heard him call, 'Harper? Again, deepest sympathies regarding your student.'

The words felt like an assault, reminding her of Graham. She saw him dangling from the window, the look in his eyes. No, she told herself. Stop. Focus on the moment. Don't worry about Hank. Don't think about Graham. Walk. Shoulders up, eyes ahead. She counted her steps: one, two, three, four. One, two, three, four. Ten more and she'd be out the door. Soon she'd meet the detective. Then she'd see Leslie. She'd get through the day. Somehow.

'Loot?'

Harper stopped. Had someone called to her?

She scanned the lobby. Two nurses waited at the elevators. An orderly pushed a wheelchair past the receptionist's desk. Against the far wall, a bunch of young people, maybe students, hung around the registration window. Wait, wasn't that Larry? And Esoso? And a woman in pink – she had to be Monique. What were they doing there? Was her whole recitation hanging out at the Neurological Center? Of course not. Just three. Still, it was odd. And none of the three had called to her; they were absorbed in conversation, not even looking her way.

'Loot – over here.' Harper turned to the waiting area on her right. Anna sat on a sofa, holding a magazine.

Harper smiled and walked over, aware that the girl had passed out at least twice that day. Maybe she was there to get checked out.

'I thought that was you, but I wasn't sure.' Anna smiled shyly. As always, she looked puffed-up and pasty, like unbaked white bread. She wore no make-up, and her thick eyebrows and black hair emphasized her paleness. Her nose and eyes were red, and she dabbed them with a wadded tissue. Probably she was crying about Graham. Harper couldn't remember Anna and Graham talking or even acknowledging each other; Anna always sat by herself. Still, the death had been a tragedy. A shock. 'I was surprised to see you, Loot. Are you volunteering here?'

Volunteering? 'No. I was visiting a patient.' Why be secretive? Why not say it? 'My husband.'

Anna blinked, surprised. 'Oh. Really? I just assumed. See, a lot of people from Cornell volunteer here. As subjects. For the research.' She nodded toward the students waiting against the wall. 'It's good money. Some of the experiments, all you have to do is sleep. I overheard Esoso saying he makes a hundred dollars a night.'

'Seriously?' Harper wondered if she made that much teaching, couldn't do the math. 'So, are you a volunteer?'

'Me?' Anna's eyes shifted, looked at the wall. 'Oh, no. I'm – I'm not eligible.' She wiped her eyes. More tears for Graham?

'Are you OK, Anna?'

'Sure,' she sniffed. 'I'm just narcoleptic.'

Harper blinked, confused.

'It's a sleeping disorder.'

Harper nodded. She'd heard of it, began to understand.

'Basically,' Anna went on, 'I fall asleep when I get upset or stressed.'

Narcolepsy. So that was why Anna often slept in class. And it was why she'd passed out on the quad.

Anna's eyes filled up. 'My doctor at home in Utica recommended this clinic. They have a whole sleep department. So my parents had me transfer.' She pressed the tissue to her nose, and her voice broke. 'God, Loot, what happened today? I don't get it. It was so . . . out of nowhere.'

'I know.'

'I had an episode. I passed out in class. Nervous about the quiz. I remember you handing it out. The next thing I knew, everyone was screaming. I couldn't open my eyes, but I could hear the commotion and the cries, and I didn't know what happened. Oh God. Why did he jump? Graham – he was so amazing.'

Amazing? Was he? Harper had no idea. In fact, after three weeks of class, other than their majors and faces, she didn't know much about her students. And she wondered how Anna did; from what she'd observed, Anna didn't have a single friend in the class.

'It's his birthday next week. He was going to be twenty. I was going to bake a cake and bring it to class. You know, as a surprise.' Anna's eyes filled with pain. 'Damn, Loot. I really liked him.'

Harper wasn't sure how to respond. Apparently, Anna had planned a birthday party for a guy who didn't even notice her. She'd had a secret crush on Graham. Poor Anna. She wasn't a pretty girl; had a swollen, unhealthy look. Didn't fit in. Kept to herself. Even so, maybe Graham had liked her. Maybe they'd been close, privately.

And, if they had been, maybe Anna would know about his gun.

Harper put a hand on Anna's shoulder, comforting her. 'Anna, I need to ask you something. Just between you and me, OK?'

Anna nodded.

'It's delicate. I don't want to start rumors or damage Graham's reputation.'

'I can keep a secret.'

'You knew Graham pretty well?'

'Yes.' Her eyes darted away. 'Very well.'

'OK.' Harper hesitated. Even if Anna were exaggerating, it wouldn't hurt to ask. 'Anna.' She lowered her voice. 'Do you think Graham might have been, well, involved in something he shouldn't have?'

Anna's eyebrows lifted. 'Like what?'

Harper's shoulders were aching from the weight of the bags; she set them down. 'I came across some stuff in his book bag. Medications. A lot of money. And a gun.'

'What?' Anna's eyes widened. 'A gun? Money? What are you saying? He was doing something illegal? No. Not Graham. Graham was—' Her eyes seemed to lose focus, and her words began to slur. 'He wuzzobyootif . . .'

She stopped mid-syllable. Harper watched gravity take hold of Anna's body, saw her begin to fold. This time, Harper wasn't going to let someone fall right in front of her. Belting out, 'No!' she lunged for Anna's waist, but found herself grabbing Anna by an armpit and a breast, barely catching her before she hit the floor, asleep.

*   *   *

'I need help here!' Harper called, lowering Anna gently on to the tiles. Across the lobby, the group at the registration window gaped at them, useless and confused. Harper looked around for medical staff, saw the receptionist motioning to a security guard and a guy in metallic yellow and blue Spandex, carrying a bike helmet, running towards her, an orderly trailing him.

'What happened?'

Wait. Harper blinked. Dr Kendall? It took Harper a moment to recognize him in biking clothes. His thighs were stronger, more developed than she'd have imagined. His shoulders more muscled. He knelt, taking Anna's pulse. Efficient. In command.

'She passed out. I managed to break her fall. She said she's narcoleptic—'

Magically, Dr Kendall produced a stethoscope and held it against Anna's chest. Without looking up, he asked, 'You know her?'

'She's my student.'

He glanced at Harper, spoke pointedly. 'You said something that upset her?'

'Me? No – she was upset about the suicide. We were—'

The orderly interrupted. 'Should I get a gurney?'

'Yeah, Greg. Take her to the sleep unit. Make sure Wyatt finds her a bed.' Dr Kendall punched a number into his cell phone. 'Flo? Ron. Anna Winters is coming in . . . Yep, cataplectic . . . Just now, in the lobby. When she wakes up, chart the details. And make sure she's taking her meds, will you? Thanks.' He hung up and looked at Harper.

'Wait. You're Anna's doctor, too?'

'One of them. Sleep's one of my sub-specialties.'

Harper thought his eyes had changed color. Earlier, they'd been a hazel green. Now, they reflected his Spandex shirt, a light, glowing yellow.

Dr Kendall extended his hand, helping her to her feet. Maybe it was his biking outfit, but he seemed relaxed, more personal. 'You're having a hell of a day, aren't you, Harper?'

Yes, she agreed. A hell of a day.

Greg reappeared with another orderly and, together, they lifted Anna on to a gurney.

'So – what now?' Harper watched them wheel her away.

'She'll be fine.' Dr Kendall picked up his bike helmet. 'Don't worry. She'll be up soon.'

Harper felt responsible. She shouldn't have gotten Anna upset. 'Should I stay? Until she wakes up?'

'Stay?' Dr Kendall's head tilted, as if viewing her from a different angle. 'Well, that depends.'

It depended? 'On what?'

Ron Kendall's face remained solemn, but his golden eyes warmed. 'On whether you'll have coffee with me while you wait.'

What? Coffee with Dr Kendall? Was he serious? He watched her, waiting for an answer. Why would Dr Kendall want to have coffee with her? Harper wasn't sure what to do; since the war, she avoided social situations where roles weren't clearly defined. She couldn't accept; wouldn't know how to behave, what was appropriate to say. They'd already talked about Graham and about Hank and his progress. What else could they possibly talk about?

Moments later, Harper was still trying to answer that question as she sat in a booth, staring at the coffee shop menu.

The tag on the waitress's shirt said 'Chelsea'. Chelsea wore rings on every finger and long burgundy acrylic nails sprinkled with tiny rhinestones. She held a pencil with some difficulty, her grip encumbered by her manicure, as she stood beside their booth, waiting for their order.

'Have you ever eaten here?'

Harper shook her head.

'Really? Well, then, get ready: you're about to experience the world's greatest pie. Home-made.'

Pie? She'd downed bonbons for lunch and now she was topping them off with pie? Oh well, it wasn't as if she did this every day. Besides, there was fruit in the pies – fruit was good for you, right? Harper slid further into the booth, trying to get comfortable. And knocking her leather bag off the seat, into the aisle, where her tissues, baby wipes, Tylenol, water bottle – she still packed those supplies – plus keys, phone, wallet, pens, students' work – everything spilled out on to the floor.

Mortified, bending over to pick things up, she smacked her head against the edge of the table. 'Damn.'

'You OK?' Ron moved across the booth to help her.

'I'm fine.' Harper rubbed her skull. 'It's OK – I've got this.' She leaned down again; this time, her arm brushed her place setting, sending her napkin and silverware clattering to the linoleum. Lord. Could she be clumsier?

'Let me get that.' Chelsea appeared, easily scooping the wallet, phone, keys and papers into the big leather sack.

Mortified, Harper thanked her and shoved the bag safely into the corner of the booth. Then, folding her hands, sitting straight, she tried to regain her composure.

Dr Kendall studied the menu, politely overlooking Harper's altercation with gravity. He read the list aloud. 'Rhubarb, sour apple, gooseberry, blackberry . . .' He stopped to lick his lips before naming the cream pies.

Chelsea poured coffee, and Dr Kendall ordered gooseberry à la mode, Harper blackberry. Ron smiled. His teeth were perfectly aligned, sparkling white. Patrician teeth.

Harper bit her lip. This was precisely why she kept to herself. She couldn't do polite conversation, didn't have the skill anymore. Didn't think the way civilians did, didn't have the knack. She searched for a topic, but all she could think about was Dr Kendall's skintight neon Spandex. The man didn't have a trace of fat. Not anywhere. Just defined, lean muscles rolling when he moved, biceps flexing as he lifted his coffee cup. And there it was: a topic. 'So, Dr Kendall, you bike a lot?'

'Ron.'

Ron?

'Every day, weather permitting. The hills are a great workout. Cycling's my escape. I get real Zen about it, you know, into the zone. It's my only break from work.'

'You're very devoted to the Center.'

'Devoted?' Ron chuckled. 'Most people who know me – especially my ex-wives – have used other terms. Like self-absorbed, obsessive, compulsive, ambitious, uncompromising. I like "devoted".'

Ex-wives? Plural? Harper picked up her cup, unable to think of a follow-up. She sipped. Damn. She shouldn't have come.

Dr Kendall – Ron – seemed completely comfortable with the silence. Unhurried, he regarded her wordlessly, warmly.

Say something, she told herself. Anything. Ask him another question. Ask about his work. 'So, Dr – I mean, Ron –' she stumbled over his name – 'why did you become a doctor?' Actually, it was a good question; she was curious.

'No choice,' he grinned. 'I'm a third-generation physician. It's in my blood. My two brothers, sister and I are all in medicine, various specialties. My grandfather was a surgeon; so was

my dad. It was never a question that we kids would follow. It
got pretty intense. Like – you know that song, "The leg bone's
connected to the knee bone"?' He sang it. 'We learned it this
way: "The fibula's connected to the patella . . ." All the way up
the body. And that was just preschool.' He smiled. 'What about
you? How did you get into – sorry, remind me what you teach?'

'Archeology.'

'Right. Why?'

Harper hesitated. Over the past weeks, she and Dr Kendall
had held frequent, often prolonged conversations, but he'd never
expressed the slightest interest in her or her career. Even now,
he was probably asking only to be polite.

'I got into it while I was in Iraq.'

'You were in Iraq?' His eyes were a startling shade of amber.

She sat straight, recited her name, rank and serial number.
'After my parents divorced, Mom couldn't afford tuition, so I
did ROTC. The army sent me to college.' Why had she said
that? He didn't need to know her life story.

'So what was it like? Iraq.'

Harper stiffened. Didn't want to discuss it.

'Sorry. I didn't mean to—'

'No problem.'

'You were wounded? Your leg?'

He was a doctor, had seen her limp. No need to be secretive.
'Suicide bomber.'

'I'm sorry.' Ron leaned on his elbows, watching her. His
arms were tanned, almost hairless. 'So what happened that got
you into Archeology?'

He seemed genuinely interested. Before she knew it, Harper
was telling him about small relics she'd found in the sand. Spent
bullets. Shards of broken glass and pottery. And how one day,
off duty, sifting sand through her fingers, she'd had an epiphany:
the sand swallowed everything. One day, it would swallow the
war and those fighting it, just as it had swallowed up generation
upon generation before them. It would cover their bodies, their
bombed-out ruins, their possessions, the finest of their cities.
The sand would take all of it, as it always had and always
would. She wanted to search for its secrets. To reclaim the past
that it held.

When she finished, Ron was quiet. Still watching her.

'I've bored you,' she apologized.

'Quite the contrary.' He leaned forward, eyes glowing. 'I was captivated. You become alive. You're radiant when you talk about your field.'

Harper looked down. Unsure how to respond.

'Here you go, guys.' Chelsea rescued her, delivering two generous pieces of pie.

Ice cream and whipped cream melted in thick white puddles around warm crust. Harper cut off a wedge, lifted it to her mouth. The filling was tart, the crust flaky. She closed her eyes, savoring.

When she opened them, Ron was grinning, licking a gooseberry off his lip. 'Good, huh?'

Her mouth full, Harper grinned. Yes. It was good.

Coffee with Ron was much easier than she'd expected.

He talked about his family, its tradition of competing to out-achieve each other, the summers of his youth filled with tennis matches and sailing regattas. 'But I'm boring,' he sighed. 'Let's talk about someone interesting. Tell me about Harper Jennings. Who is she, really?'

Harper blushed, swallowed pie. 'Just who you see.'

'Who I see? Then she's a beautiful, accomplished, intriguing woman.' He smiled; her neck got hot. 'Seriously. I've done all the talking. Tell me about you. Before the army.'

Oh dear. Harper told herself to relax; she could omit whatever she wanted. 'Not much to tell. I grew up outside Chicago, near the lake. One brother. Divorced parents.' There. That was enough, wasn't it?

'Did you sail, living near the lake?'

'When I was little, my dad had a boat, but . . . he left.' And the government took it, along with his antique cars, art collection and everything else of value. Even the house.

'What did your father do?'

For a moment, Harper thought he meant what crime. But, of course, he was only asking about his profession. She tried to sound casual. 'Accounting. Financial stuff.' She stopped herself. No need to elaborate. 'But he and my mom split up. And he left.' For fifteen to twenty. By now, he'd have been released, but Harper hadn't been in touch. Didn't plan to be, despite her bargains with God.

Ron swallowed coffee. 'How old were you when he left?'

'Twelve.' She fiddled with her fork. 'Overnight, we went from ostentatiously affluent to dirt poor.'

'Ouch.' Ron raised an eyebrow, probably wondering what happened to the money.

Enough. No more about her. Harper never talked about her family. Or Iraq. So why was she suddenly blabbing about both? She took a bite of pie.

Ron watched her chew.

'What?'

'Nothing.'

Oh God. 'Do I have blackberries on my mouth?' She lifted a napkin, wiped.

'No, no.' Ron laughed. 'I'm just enjoying myself. Actually taking a break.'

Harper reddened, lifted her cup, looked away. She changed the subject. 'How long will Anna sleep?'

Anna, after all, was the reason they'd gone for coffee, but so far neither had mentioned her.

Ron looked at his watch. 'Not long.'

'I should go let her know I'm here—'

'No rush. They need to talk to her when she gets up.'

Harper recalled the suddenness of Anna's fall. 'I've never known anyone with narcolepsy. I thought she just was bored and dozed off in class.'

'Bored?' Ron feigned disbelief. 'In *your* class?'

Harper grinned.

'Actually, Anna's falling asleep in class indicates the opposite of boredom. Narcoleptics tend to have episodes when they feel intense emotion.'

Intense emotion? As in a crush on a classmate? 'Anna said there's no cure.'

'No. But there are ways to ease symptoms. Napping regularly. Taking medications.' Maybe Anna hadn't been taking her pills.

Well, for that matter, neither had Harper. She hadn't taken her flashback medication for weeks. But talk of pills reminded Harper of the vial in Graham's book bag. Maybe Ron would know what it was.

'Let me ask you something.' She unzipped the bag, took it out.

'What's that?' Ron set his cup down.

'Graham – my student – had these with him when he died.' She held the bottle out. 'The label says they're from the

Neurology Center. There's a number, but no doctor or drug
name. Can you tell what they are?'

'These were with him when he died?' Ron frowned.

'Here in his book bag.'

The frown deepened. He opened the vial and looked inside.
'Is this the only bottle he had?'

She nodded. 'Why?'

Ron took a pill out, studied it. 'I just . . . I'm wondering how
he got hold of these.'

'Why? What are they?'

'I'm not sure. There's no pharmaceutical code on this. It
might be from a drug trial.'

A drug trial? Anna had said that her classmates were partici-
pating in drug research. 'So maybe Graham was taking part in
a trial? That would explain why he had them, right?'

Silence. Dr Kendall turned the pill in his hand.

Harper pressed on. 'Actually, I thought they might be medicine. For depression, maybe. Or some condition that would
explain what happened—'

'No. If your student did have a condition, these pills weren't
to treat it. The vial is labeled, see?' He pointed to the marking:
RKM93. 'It looks like the code number for a study.' Ron set
the pill on a napkin. 'So, what do you plan to do?'

To do? Oh, with the pills. Harper shrugged. 'I'll give them
to the police with the rest of his stuff.'

Ron folded his hands.

'Is there a problem?'

'No, of course not.' Ron looked from Harper to the pill, then
back to Harper. 'Look. Actually, Harper, I'd like to ask a favor—'

Chelsea appeared, refilling their cups. And Harper saw Ron
wrap the pill in a napkin and stuff it into the pocket of his bike
shorts.

'What's the favor?' Harper eyed his pocket, about to ask him
what he thought he was doing.

Ron leaned across the table, came close enough to whisper.
Reflexively, Harper backed away, unaccustomed to close contact
with men in Spandex. 'I want to take that pill with me, so I
can identify it.' He sat back, waiting for her answer.

What he said made sense. After all, the things needed to be
identified, and he was taking just one. She still had the rest of
the vial for the police.

'OK. Take it.' She didn't mention that he already had.

Ron didn't seem satisfied. He fidgeted with his spoon, scowling.

'What?'

He met her eyes. 'To be honest, I'm concerned about the police getting that vial. The suicide is all over the news, and the kid had the pills with him when he died. It's going to be a disaster if the media get a hold of that tidbit.'

'I don't follow.'

'Harper, the media blow everything out of proportion. It's what they do. Don't you see? If these pills are part of a drug trial, and a test subject suddenly kills himself, that means some real bad publicity.'

'You're worried about publicity?'

Ron's eyes were fiery. 'You bet I am. I have to be.' He drew a deep breath. 'Harper, this death was a terrible tragedy. And I'd like to avoid even the slightest implication that a drug from the Center had anything to do with it. We need to keep a low profile here.'

Harper was appalled. 'You're worried about public image? A student is dead—'

'Exactly. And if these pills in any way contributed to his death, then no question, that needs to be and will be addressed.' Ron folded his hands. 'But if, as I suspect, the pills are benign and completely unrelated, I'd prefer – I'd strongly prefer – to keep the Neurological Center out of the news entirely.'

Harper looked away, confused. Ron Kendall was the man she trusted with her husband's brain – with his life. But what kind of man was this ambitious third-generation doctor? What exactly was he asking her to do?

Harper looked directly at him. 'To be frank, Dr Kendall, it sounds like you care less about a student's life than the Center's reputation—'

'Now, hold on.' His voice was too loud. He stopped, lowered it, leaning close. 'You of all people know that isn't true. My entire career is about saving lives. Which is why, despite my sorrow about your student, I've got to look at the big picture.'

'The what?'

'The Center is privately funded, completely dependent on grants and donations. And our work is unparalleled. Our research – like that on frontal lobe injuries affecting your husband and

thousands of war veterans – our advances on learning and
memory – nobody in the country – nobody in the world does
what we do.'

He reached for his cup. Picked it up, put it back down.
'Harper, I might sound cold, but I'm assistant director of research
here. So, yes, I'm concerned, very concerned, about publicity
and its effects on our funding. And, frankly, with your husband
here, you should be, too. We'd both hate like hell to see the
Center's financing sabotaged and our work halted by misleading
bad press.' His eyes glowed gold.

Harper saw his point. But not what, if anything, he wanted
her to do about it.

They sat silently. Harper looked at pie crust, avoided his eyes.

'Sorry I got upset. But these are tough economic times, and
we depend entirely on—'

'Right. I get it,' Harper interrupted. 'You can't afford bad
press. But you can't expect me to hide the pills—'

'No, of course not.' Ron seemed startled by the thought. 'I
wouldn't ask you to. No. The only way to avoid bad press is
for me to hurry up and identify this.' He tapped his pocket. 'If
it played no role in your student's death, that'll be the end of
it. If it did, well, the Center will have to deal with it.' Ron's
eyes focused on Harper. 'I shouldn't have even bothered you
about this. It's not your problem.' He reached across the table,
touching her arm.

It was just a touch, but it brought goose bumps, jolted her.
She looked away, made herself think of Hank. Pictured him
upstairs in his sterile room, watching daytime television. Or
napping, awaiting his next procedure.

Ron gave her arm a squeeze; Hank's image fizzled away.

'Ready to go?' He released her arm. His hand retreated across
the table, picked up the check. She could still feel its warm imprint.

Stop it, she scolded herself. She'd been starved of male
companionship for too long. Ron's concern, his request to identify the medication – their coffee and conversation – were purely
professional. His touch had been a normal human gesture,
nothing more.

'Ready.' Harper gathered first her bulky bag, then Graham's,
and slid out of the booth, careful not to knock anything on to
the floor.

*   *   *

Paycheck in his pocket, Larry sat in the coffee shop, popped a couple of his remaining pills and thought about what he was going to do. Graham, the fuckhead, had really screwed him. Screwed them all. Right after the cops stopped asking questions, Larry had raced home and searched the apartment, turned Graham's toilet of a room upside down, hadn't found a thing. Dammit, where had Graham stashed them?

Larry rubbed his eyes, fought a headache while considering the chick in the corner booth. Long dark hair, tattoo on her ankle. Low-cut halter top. He could see a mole on the top of one tit. But then, while he was picturing what he'd do to that mole, to his sheer astonishment, in walked his Archeology teacher. And guess what?

She was carrying fucking Graham's fucking book bag.

His book bag. Shit. The asshole. He must have stuck the numbers in his book bag. Of course. Larry had looked every-place else and found zip; they had to be in the book bag.

Actually, the Loot looked pretty messed-up. Her clothes were muddy and her hair was all clumped. But she was so into the bike guy she was with that she walked right past Larry, didn't even notice him sitting just a couple of booths away. The babe in the corner didn't seem to notice him, either. Just as well. He didn't need anyone to remember him being there, not if he was going to get his hands on those numbers. Damn Graham. Couldn't he at least have handed them over before he took a leap?

Larry glanced at the Loot's back, wondering if she'd found them, if she had even a clue what they were, if there was a way to get the bag from her. Shit. Shit shit shit. He reached in his pocket, took another pill from an almost empty vial, popped it into his mouth, felt his anger building. The chick, meantime, was annoying him. She was the kind who knew she was hot, wearing tiny cut-offs and fancy jeweled flip-flops, leaving her long legs bare. Flaunting that damned tattoo. She was playing him, telling guys like him: Look at me, want me, but don't even think about getting close.

He was, though, thinking about doing exactly that. Getting close enough to bite off her little mole. The idea tickled him, and he was picturing it when the waitress came by, changing the other chick's entire future.

See, there was something about waitresses. He'd studied them, had become an unofficial expert, and he'd discovered that waitresses were like spiders, luring you into their fine, almost invisible traps. Supposedly, they were there to take care of you and bring you food, but *really* they were trying to entice you so you'd give them your money. They teased, wagging their hips, batting their eyelashes, pretending to be your friend. Until they got what they wanted.

'Hi, I'm Chelsea,' this one announced. 'I'll be your server.'

His server? He smiled, imagining it. Indeed, Chelsea, you will be my server, but not yet. Asking, 'What would you like?' with her eyes opened all round and innocent, as if she had no idea what he would like, even though she wore a tight black skirt with a shirt unbuttoned to her cleavage. She did it on purpose, using her tits to tease him so she'd get a big tip. Well, the teasing worked. He had a big tip, and he'd give it to her. But not now.

Now, he ordered a root beer float and took one more pill while he watched her waltz from booth to booth in her black leather sneakers. Her hair was the color of straw, and she had it pulled back off her face, maybe trying to keep cool. But forget being cool. This one generated steam, enough to power a factory. The idea amused him; he chuckled out loud as she put the float in front of him.

'Anything else, sir?'

See how she was messing with him? Calling him 'sir'. As if she were the cat and he the mouse, not the other way around. Her eyes were blue, her lashes blonde, almost white, so they glistened. Her lipstick was faint, almost worn off, and when her mouth moved, he could see the tiniest chip on her front tooth. She stood beside him, and he wanted her to stay there, so he pretended to be thinking about her question, but really he was smelling her, inhaling her. He took in a breath, analyzing it. What was in her scent? Something powdery. And vanilla? He shut his eyes briefly, concentrating, penetrating the superficial aroma, seeking her underlying, genuine scents. Finding them. Yes, there they were – dark, musky, sweaty – the smell of tired skin bound up in tight, confining clothes, of hot and aching feet snug inside black leather. Of private places, simmering, festering, never exposed to light.

Clearing his throat, stalling, he snuck a peak at her chest; it was right there at eye level, and he saw a swelling of flesh, a tiny edge of beige lace. Freckles. But he couldn't linger there, didn't want her to notice him yet. So quickly, deftly, he moved his eyes to her hands. She had long nails, probably fake, painted dark, decorated with rhinestones. Seriously? Rhinestones?

She was so close.

'So, you're all set?' She was taunting him.

Again, he cleared his throat, counting the gold rings on each of her fingers, even her thumbs, rings spattered with small colored stones that sparkled when her hands moved, flashing red, yellow, blue, purple, as she waited for him to answer.

She was, after all, his server.

Stop, he told himself. Be cool. He wanted to take her right then, but instead he raised his glass and took a long suck on his straw, reminding himself to stay invisible. Not to draw attention. So he gave her a casual, forgettable smile. 'Yup, Chelsea. That'll do it.'

'Thanks.' She scribbled on her notepad, ripped the page off and dropped his check on to his table. 'Have a great day now.' With that, she pivoted, showing him her backside, working it just a little as she approached a guy in the booth behind his teacher and the bike man. Seeing them made him think of his predicament. The problem of getting Graham's bag. Damn. He had to make a plan, had to get out of here and think. Teacher's back was to him; no chance she'd look his way. Time to move.

'Hi, I'm Chelsea,' he heard as he stood and moved behind her, unable to resist brushing her body lightly as he passed, feeling her heat, inhaling a final deep breath of her. 'What can I get you?'

Her body swayed slightly, sensing him, moving in response. Excellent. He lowered his head, walking swiftly, pretending he wasn't there. On the way to the cashier, he passed the dark babe in the corner and slowed, grabbing one final gander at her legs. Her skin was tawny, but by no means as tantalizing as Chelsea's. No contest. He'd made his choice.

Her smell was still in his nostrils as he left the coffee shop and walked across the lobby, invisible, blending in, waiting. Planning all the stuff he had to do.

Half an hour later, Harper sat at her desk in the cramped, tiny office she'd been assigned for the summer. Olive Tjaden Hall was on the corner of the Arts Quad; her small window on the top floor provided a skinny view of the hills, the edge of town and a sliver of Lake Cayuga. She gazed at the thin slice of calm water, thinking positive thoughts, imagining being out there, sailing away from suicide, narcolepsy, flashbacks and blistering heat. But she wasn't out there. She was here on the blistering fourth floor, and she had email to answer and a eulogy to prepare. Christ. A eulogy? Here? This wasn't a war zone. Kids weren't supposed to die in Ithaca.

Email was easier, so Harper started with that. Her adviser, Professor Schmerling, had written from Peru; he and the research team still regretted that she'd been unable to join them on the dig. He hoped her husband was recovering and that she could accompany him next time. Photographs and notes related to her dissertation were attached.

Lord. Her doctoral thesis? Was he serious? How was she supposed to do a dissertation? Dr Schmerling, the dig – her career plans – everything seemed out of reach. Harper closed her eyes, felt the rush of air from her office fan. Saw Graham's eyes locked on to hers as he hung from the ledge. Would that image ever fade? Would her flashbacks ever stop? Would life ever feel normal again?

Actually, for a little while that day, it had. In the coffee shop with Dr Kendall – Ron. Sitting in the booth having coffee, talking, tasting each other's pie, she'd felt almost normal. Like part of a couple. Harper felt a pang, missing Hank. She pictured him puttering in the kitchen, grinding beans for coffee so strong it had blasted her out of the house, made her talk fast and tremble for hours. Now, without it, she drank chai. Man, that had been good coffee.

But, today, coffee had been with someone else. Ron had been easy to talk to. Not just about Anna's narcolepsy or the pills in Graham's bag, but about anything –careers, sports, education. Good Lord, she'd even talked about her father. The only topic they hadn't touched on, actually, was the most obvious one, the one that linked them.

Well, of course they hadn't. They hadn't mentioned Hank because they had already discussed him a thousand times. It wasn't as if she'd done anything wrong. She'd had a piece of pie; that was all. OK, not all. She'd had whipped cream on top. But whipped cream wasn't the issue. The issue was that, for almost an hour, she hadn't had to struggle to be thankful or positive; she'd simply enjoyed herself. Was that so wrong?

No. Except enjoying herself wasn't the issue, either. The real issue was neither food nor fun; it was that she'd had both with a man. A man who wasn't Hank.

Ron wasn't even close to being Hank, didn't remotely resemble him. Yet, when he spoke, Ron's easy words underlined Hank's inability to speak. The lightness of his eyes brought to mind the darkness of Hank's, and his elegant, smooth hands emphasized the roughness of Hank's hairier, calloused ones. Everything about Ron was un-Hank-like, and his presence across the table from Harper screamed of Hank's absence. Sitting with him, chatting and eating pie, Harper had fought the heart-wrenching sense that she was glimpsing her future: going places Hank couldn't, doing things he couldn't. Without him.

Harper drew a breath. She needed to write a eulogy. To think about Graham's loss, its affect on her students. Anna, apparently, was OK; she'd awakened, been checked out and left the clinic before Harper had finally looked in on her. But what about the others? What should she say to them? Maybe she should consult Dr Michaels, the 101 lecturer. But, to him, Graham had been just one of a hundred students. He hadn't even known his name.

No, never mind Dr Michaels. She was on her own. She needed an opening sentence: Graham's life was . . . She searched for a metaphor. A glimmer of light? A breeze? A brief but gentle touch. She thought of Ron's hand on the small of her back, guiding her through the coffee shop. No, Graham's life wasn't like that. It was like something else – a tease, a riddle . . .

'Loot? You in there?' Someone knocked at the door. 'Loot? It's Larry.'

Larry? Good. Poor kid, seeing his room-mate kill himself. He probably wanted to talk. She hurried to the door. 'Larry. Come in.'

Larry didn't. He stood in the doorway, cracking his knuckles. The heat of the day hadn't improved his scent; sweat stained his T-shirt.

'Are you OK?'

He shrugged, eyes averted. 'Yeah. It's . . . weird.'

Harper agreed. Yes, it was.

He stood silent and awkward, looking past her into her tiny office.

'Come sit down.'

He stepped inside but didn't sit. His gaze darted around the room, scanning the shelves, her desk. 'I saw you before, coming in. I almost didn't come up, though.' He fidgeted, had a nervous twitch in his cheek.

'I'm glad you did. It might help to talk—'

'Oh. No, I don't want to talk. What's the point?' He paused, eyes darting. 'Actually, I came up because I saw you carrying Graham's book bag. Is it here?'

Yes, it was. Under her desk, ready to go to the police. But she didn't tell Larry that. Instead, she said, 'Why?'

Larry looked away. 'He was my room-mate.' As if that answered it. 'Do you have it?' He tried to sound casual. Failed.

'It's right here.' Harper reached under her desk, pulled the bag out.

'Oh, good – I have some stuff in there.' He eyed it, one hand a fist at his hip, the other against his flat belly. 'Can I look inside?'

'What stuff?' A gun maybe? Or money?

'Just stuff.' Larry stared at the bag. 'Actually, some money.'

'Money?'

'Yeah. Graham owed me for rent.' He met her eyes. 'Is it in there?'

'What's going on, Larry?'

'What? Nothing.' Larry watched her with unblinking, innocent eyes. 'He said he'd stop at the bank and bring it to class.'

'How much did he owe you?'

Larry rolled his eyes. 'Like, six hundred thirty.'

Bingo. The amount matched. Graham must have been carrying his rent money. Otherwise, how would Larry have known how much was there?

'What am I supposed to do, Loot? The rent's due, and I need his share.' He blinked at her with large, pleading eyes.

Harper studied Larry. Neither handsome nor homely, he was average in height, light in weight. A wiry, dark-haired, Brooklyn-raised kid with mild acne and eyes so sad they tore your heart. She glanced at the clock. Almost time to meet Detective Rivers.

'Problem is, Larry, I can't help you. I don't have the right to disperse Graham's possessions—'

'But Loot. The money was mine—'

'If you want something from the bag, you'll need to talk to the police. Meantime, talk to your landlords. With Graham's death, I'm sure they'll give you a break.'

Larry crossed his arms and gazed resolutely at the bag.

'Is there something else?'

'Not really.' Still, he lingered, didn't leave.

Poor kid, Harper thought. She should encourage him to talk about what happened. Maybe he had an idea about why Graham killed himself. Or why he was taking those pills.

'Larry, was Graham healthy?'

'Yeah, I guess. Why?'

'Was he taking any medication?'

'Medication?' Larry chewed his lip. Stalling? 'Well, just for work.'

'Work?'

'He worked on a drug trial at Cayuga. The Neuro Bureau. You get paid to test drugs. You take some pills, give some blood. Fill out some questionnaires. Graham and I are – were – subjects there. That's how I met him.'

'So you take the drugs, too?'

'For the trials. Sure. Lots of us do. It's easy money.' He scratched his head, dark eyes wavering. 'Loot. Here's the deal. Graham was our section leader. He kept all the pills and gave us our weekly doses. So it's not just the rent – I'm looking for the pills, too.'

Larry cracked his knuckles again. Loudly. Shifted his weight. Couldn't stay still. Harper wondered if the experimental drugs were addictive. If Larry needed a fix. But that was ridiculous; the Center wouldn't run drug trials that created addicts.

'So, did you find any pills in his bag? Or a record of where he kept them?' Larry's sorrowful eyes tugged at her. 'Because I've looked everywhere. You know, for the subjects in our group. So, we can continue to work. Did you—'

'Sorry. No.'

He glanced at the bag. 'Can you look again?'

'I need to leave everything as it is, Larry. For the police.'

'But you've already looked inside. What harm would it do?'

'Sorry.' Why was he so insistent?

'Man, Loot—' Larry ran a hand through his hair, stifling a curse.

'Look, I'm sure the Center will replace the pills. What study were you involved in?'

Larry's face went blank. 'Oh. They don't tell you. You're just divided into groups.'

'But you must have some identifying code numbers or something.'

'I don't know. I was in Graham's group. That's all I know. Graham was in charge of it.' Larry's weight moved from leg to leg, an edgy dance.

'Researchers keep records, Larry. They'll know what study Graham was working on and they'll decide how to proceed.'

Larry stiffened. 'Right. So . . . I'll just talk to them.'

'I think that's best.' Then she added, 'And also to the police.'

'The police?' His head cocked. 'Why the police?'

Harper paused. 'About your rent money?'

'Right.'

'And about the drugs Graham was taking when he died.'

'The drugs?' Larry popped his knuckles. 'Why? Wait. You think they had something to do—'

'No, of course not.' Damn. Why had she mentioned it? Rumors could get started – exactly what Ron was trying to avoid. 'But the Center will want to make sure—'

'No way. Loot, if those pills caused suicide, Graham wouldn't be the only one. Everyone in the our group would be jumping out windows.'

Larry had a point. 'Who else was in your group?'

'Like forty of us. Esoso. His room-mate. Monique and me. Graham. I don't know all the other names. But nobody's dead except Graham. We went to pick up our paychecks today, and everyone was still breathing.'

That was reassuring.

'So, you're sure you won't give me my rent money?'

Harper narrowed her eyes. 'Larry—'

'OK. I'll ask the police.' He turned to leave. 'Oh, wait –' he ran his hand through his hair – 'Did you find a list of numbers?'

A list of numbers? Yes, Harper had seen a piece of paper with numbers written on it. It had fallen off Graham's desk.

'I mean, it's no big deal. But Graham – he borrowed my study sheet. For Economics. It's just a list of pages to study. Was it in his bag?' Larry waited, working his knuckles.

'No. There was nothing like that in the book bag.' It wasn't a lie. The paper was in her leather sack. Harper wasn't sure why, but she wasn't going to tell him that.

Larry blinked rapidly, looking around as if something was still on his mind. But all he said was, 'OK. Later, Loot.'

Harper stood in the hall, watching Larry disappear into the stairwell, wondering why he was so charged up. Wondering about the pills. Unsettled, she checked the clock again. She was still early for her meeting with Detective Rivers, but she was too bothered to sit and write a eulogy. So, grabbing her leather sack, she hoisted Graham's hefty book bag on to her shoulder and headed out the door.

With time to spare, Harper took the scenic route, allowing herself a short detour to her favorite spot along the Suspension Bridge. Halfway across, resting her leg, she slowed to look down at the rocky walls and gurgling water, vaguely noticing a guy on a mountain bike coming up behind her. A couple of girls approached from the opposite side, chatting. T-shirts with tiger-striped letters that read 'Delta Gamma'. Sorority sisters.

'It doesn't matter why—'

'No. I agree.'

Harper had never pledged a sorority; she'd pledged ROTC. What would college have been like, going to frat parties and playing drinking games instead of repelling off rooftops and spit-shining shoes? Having sisters-in-play instead of brothers-in-arms? Who would she be now if she hadn't gone off to war? She wiped sweat from her forehead, nodded at the girls as they walked by and momentarily imagined spinning around and joining them. Going back in time. Starting over. The thought made her head hurt; Harper strolled on.

Looking down at the stream, she was again aware of the bike, sensed that something about it wasn't right. Glancing back, she saw what it was: in ninety-degree heat, the rider was wearing a hooded sweatshirt. With the hood up.

Instinctively, Harper picked up her pace. No one else was around, and she was suddenly aware that only a thin layer of swaying walkway separated her from an abyss of empty air.

Calm down, she told herself. There's no reason to think that guy intends any harm. She stopped walking to let him pass. But he didn't pass. He pedaled right behind her, moving at her pace. Maybe she knew him? Harper turned, looked directly at his face and saw a ski mask. A ski mask? In this heat?

Harper smelled smoke, heard warning shots, spun around and hurried ahead, her left leg unsteady. No mistake: the guy was following her. Who was he? What did he want? Was he a robber,

a rapist? Damn. Breaking into a run, Harper thought of the gun
in Graham's book bag. Could she unzip the bag and pull it out
in time? Maybe she'd be better off sticking her strong leg out,
knocking the bike over as it neared. Or rushing him, shoving
him off balance. Before she could decide, the bike caught up to
her; the rider's arm jutted out and grabbed the strap of Graham's
book bag, knocking Harper off her feet, dragging her.

Reflexively, Harper bent her arm, locking the bag against her
body, not letting go. The rider had underestimated her strength;
his bike jammed, bucking, and he half fell, half jumped off, his
face hidden under his woolen mask. He was taller than Harper,
more muscular, and he wrestled for the bag, shoving her against
the railing, pummeling her head. Harper fought back, ducking
his punches, kneeing him in the groin, pounding his gut even
as he landed several neat jabs to the sides of her skull. She kept
fighting as pain and light flashed in her head, and the tunnel
vision of war took over, focusing her completely on the battle,
blocking out all else. Except, oddly, for the smell of peppermint.
Peppermint? Her attacker was sucking a breath mint? She dodged
a fist and grabbed his arm, scratching deep under the sleeve,
tearing skin off, drawing blood. Harper hung on to the bag with
a death grip, trained never to separate from her gear.

But the guy would not stop. His arms closed around her waist
and, while she punched and kicked, he lifted her, hefting her
until her waist was level with the spikes of the bridge railing,
the gorge gaping hungrily below. She grabbed for the spikes as
a handhold, felt them dig into her belly, and her mind grappled
with the news that her feet were no longer in contact with the
bridge, that she was dangling in air. That her life was in the
hands of a masked, peppermint-scented mountain biker who
was wordlessly about to heave her off the bridge.

Harper opened her mouth to yell for help but swallowed air,
making no sound. She couldn't breathe, couldn't do anything
but swim frantically through air and grab hold of the railing,
letting go of Graham's book bag and her big leather sack. Of
everything but her life.

As soon as she released the book bag, the rider dropped her
and snatched it up, speeding away on the bike, leaving Harper
on her knees in the middle of the bridge, dazed, bruised and
indignant.

*   *   *

Slowly, cautiously, Harper got to her feet and took inventory, assessing the damage. Skin had been scraped off her knuckles, her head had been throttled, and her cheek bled where she'd been punched. She'd landed on knees and elbows when the guy had released her, and the jolt of impact reverberated through her bad leg. She felt off balance, dizzy with vertigo. Wiping a trickle of blood off her face, she decided her injuries were minor and stumbled back toward the campus side of the now-deserted bridge.

Explosives flashed in her peripheral vision, and she heard blasts of gunfire. Keep going, she told herself. Do not have another flashback. She was still alive, hadn't been dropped into the gorge. Her head throbbed, but she wasn't tottering off her feet. Even now, she had reasons, however feeble, to be thankful.

Clinging to the guard rail, dragging her leather bag, she moved cautiously, painfully, to the end of the bridge. Finally on solid ground, she took refuge under a cluster of trees, eyes closed, catching her breath, regaining her equilibrium. When she felt steadier, she looked around.

Not ten feet away along a wooded path, among a clump of weeds, was Graham's book bag.

Why would someone be willing to kill her for the bag, only to toss it seconds later?

Aching, wincing, Harper got to her feet and picked it up. Contents were strewn across the ground. Graham's papers, textbook. Phone, keys and snacks. No money. No gun. And no pill bottle.

No surprise.

Harper looked around; nothing else lay abandoned on the ground. Damn, her head hurt. So did her leg. So did the rest of her. Who the hell had been on the bike? Who had even known that she had Graham's book bag?

Larry knew. And, of course, Ron. But neither of them would attack her. Maybe Larry had told someone else that she had the bag. But who? And why? Who would try to kill her for six hundred dollars, a gun and a few pills?

Harper held her leather sack to her chest and looked around, searching the space between tree trunks and hedges, seeing not a single soul. Above her, tree branches shook. Harper dove behind a forsythia bush, peered out.

A squirrel, she told herself. It was just a squirrel jumping

branches. There was no one, nothing to fight. The guy on the
bike was gone. She was alone.

Harper limped past Balch and Ridley dorms toward Noyes Lodge
where she was to meet Detective Rivers, painfully aware that
she had no gun, no money. No pills. Nothing substantial to give
her. Harper was furious with herself. Somebody had attacked
her and, for all her combat experience and training, she hadn't
taken him down. She couldn't even identify him or his bike. All
she knew was that he'd been strong enough to lift a furious
five-foot-three-and-a-quarter-inch, hundred-thirty-pound woman
easily off her feet. And that he chewed breath mints.

Sore and bruised, she made it to the deck behind Noyes,
where Detective Rivers waited at an outdoor table.

Rivers got to her feet, open-mouthed. 'What the hell
happened?'

Harper stuffed the book bag into the detective's arms, plopped
on to a chair and told her.

Detective Rivers fished some cubes out of her iced coffee,
wrapped them in a tissue and pressed the wad against a cut on
Harper's cheek. She wanted Harper to go to the hospital.

'One pupil is dilated. You might have a concussion.'

'I do have a concussion. But I'm not going to the hospital.
They'll just tell me to rest.'

'I got to tell you, Mrs Jennings, you look awful.'

'I'll be OK. Really. I've been hurt a lot worse than this.'

Rivers shook her head.

'I'm a vet.'

'Yeah?' The detective looked surprised. 'Really? Where?'

'Iraq. Mostly north of Baghdad.'

'Huh. Interesting.' She smirked. 'You don't seem military.'

Whatever that meant. 'I've got the scars to prove it.' Harper
rubbed her aching leg.

'My whole family's army. Four generations. We were in the
First and Second Wars. Korea. Dad was Nam. I got a baby
brother in Afghanistan.'

'How's he doing?' Harper didn't know what else to say.

'Still breathing. At least he was on Saturday. He calls my
mom. So what were you? Army? Guard?'

'Army. I got out as first lieutenant. ROTC in college.'

Detective Rivers nodded. 'So I was right; you were never a

grunt.' She pulled on a pair of latex gloves, unzipped the book bag and began digging around. 'A vet, huh. Well, even for a seasoned war vet like you, Mrs Jennings, that scene today has to be tough. It sure is for me. In fact, for me, today is as bad as it gets. When I see a dead kid, especially a suicide, I wonder why I do this. There's got to be better ways to earn a buck.'

Harper agreed. Seeing dead kids sucked. She blinked, erasing the boy with no face.

'So. Why'd you look inside?'

Inside? Harper blinked, confused.

'You opened the book bag. Why?'

Oh, the book bag. 'I was looking for an ID. To make sure whose it was.' Actually, she couldn't remember.

Detective Rivers eyed her, all business, like an MP. 'And that's how you found the gun.' She sifted through textbooks, notepads, half-eaten snacks. 'So the guy who mugged you, he took the gun and the money. Anything else missing?'

'A bottle of pills. It was there earlier, but I didn't find it with the other stuff.' Harper put the ice against her temple, pressing on the pain.

'Pills?' Detective Rivers cocked her head. 'What kind of pills?'

'I don't know. The label didn't have a name. It just had a code on it. RKM . . . 93? Something like that.'

The detective's eyes riveted on Harper. 'You're sure. RKM93?'

Harper pictured the vial. 'No. Not positive.'

'Did the label have a pharmacy name?'

'No – just the name of the Neurological Center.'

Detective Rivers set the bag down, drew a deep breath. 'Who else knew about this bag? Did you tell anyone that you had it? Or what was in it?'

Harper hesitated. She'd already considered Ron and Larry and decided that neither would hurt her. Even so, she had to answer. 'I discussed the pills with my husband's doctor at the Neurological Center. And Graham's room-mate knew about the money. I don't know if he knew about the gun.'

'Forget the gun.' Detective Rivers snapped. 'I'm interested in the pills.'

'The pills?'

Detective Rivers pursed her lips. 'This isn't public information, Mrs Jennings, OK? Back in May, we had a coed jump into the gorge. A week later, a kid drove his Wrangler into the lake. Same weekend, we had a series of rapes; all four victims accused a student in College Town. And a few weeks later – you must remember – we had an arsonist setting residence fires along Dryden Road. An exchange student – an English kid – died in one. We're pretty sure he was the arsonist.'

Harper didn't remember the incidents; for the last several weeks, she'd been completely absorbed by Hank's condition. But she didn't see what the detective was getting at. The sad reality was that some students suffered depression and committed suicide by jumping off bridges. And students drove recklessly, sometimes drunk, and had terrible accidents. And, statistically speaking, out of the tens of thousands of people on campus, someone was sooner or later bound to be a rapist or an arsonist. So what was the point here? Why was Detective Rivers seemingly recounting every tragic incident that had occurred to students in Ithaca that spring?

'Thing is, it could be pure coincidence. But in investigating each of those events, we found bottles of pills from the Neurological Center. They had no name, just a code number. RKM93.'

Harper blinked, heard gunfire, hunkered down. What were those pills? Did Ron know about the other incidents? He must. The police would have told him. But why hadn't he told her about them? Maybe, she reasoned, because he knew the pills had nothing to do with them.

'Well, if you knew the pills came from the Center, why didn't you talk to people there? They'd tell you what they were.'

Charlene Rivers smiled. Her smile was a grim-looking thing, twisting downward at the sides. 'Good idea, Mrs Jennings. In fact, we did. I did. Personally.'

She paused, losing the smile. 'They told me the drug isn't related to the deaths. It's some new wonder drug, a miracle designed to enhance learning or improve memory. Something like that. They said a few thousand people had been testing it. It's actually in final trials, and the FDA is about to approve it.'

'Really?' If it were such a miracle drug, so widely tested, then wouldn't Ron have recognized its code on Graham's vial?

'Mrs Jennings, did you know they pay people to test experimental drugs? Kids here on campus, for example. If they're over eighteen years of age, kids can get paid to take drugs. Perfect, huh?'

Detective Rivers didn't expect and Harper didn't give an

answer. She was pondering why Dr Ron Kendall hadn't recognized the code on the vial. Or had pretended not to.

'So. Graham Reynolds. Another dead kid carrying RKM93. In two months, in addition to the fires and rapes, we've got, what, four bodies?' Detective Rivers zipped the book bag closed. 'Could be a coincidence.' She removed her gloves. 'Probably is. I mean, over the past six months, hundreds of people around here have been taking this drug, and we're talking about what – seven or eight incidents? Do the math. It's not all that high of a percentage. Still. It makes you think.'

But Harper couldn't think. Her head was bruised and her mind was tangled.

'Mrs Jennings, lots of violence is associated with those pills. Suicides, arsons, rapes. So those pills trouble me. We don't know for certain that they played a role in your attack. But just in case there's a connection, I think you should take extra precautions. For your safety.'

Precautions? Harper pictured firearms, helmets.

'For starters, don't wander around alone. In fact, don't be alone.'

Harper sighed. 'Don't worry, Detective. I'll be fine.'

Detective Rivers eyed her, unconvinced, and she took down Larry and Ron's names, mentioning that she'd already met Dr Kendall. She asked if Harper remembered anything else about her assault and filled out a report detailing what had happened on the bridge. Harper held on to melting ice cubes, focusing on their numbing coldness to ground herself in the present, resisting flickering images of Sameh and Marvin, ignoring explosions that threatened to storm her mind.

Detective Rivers had been reluctant to drop Harper at the parking lot; she'd wanted to take her to the hospital. But Harper had been adamant. She rode home on her Ninja and trudged into the house, dropping her heavy leather sack on to the kitchen counter, checking the clock. She had barely half an hour to clean up and get to her appointment with Leslie. Head pulsing, she plodded to the first-floor bathroom and ran the shower above the claw-footed tub.

Wincing as her wounds met water, Harper considered the possibility of ever again taking an actual bath. She pictured sinking into bubbles scented with jasmine, leaning back against

the porcelain, soaking until the water got cool. Someday she'd
do that. But not yet. For now, she'd stick to the comfort zone
of her combat shower. Habit and training allowed thirty seconds
to get wet, sixty to scrub, ninety to rinse. Rinsing, standing
under warm streaming water, Harper closed her eyes. Graham
stared up at her from the depths of the gorge. She turned off
the water, stepped out of the tub, wrapped herself tightly in
thick terry cloth.

Even later, when she was dry and dressed, she couldn't shake
the sensation that the ground beneath her was giving way and
that she faced an impending endless fall.

By the time Chelsea Johnson got off work, she'd almost
forgotten about the guy. He'd said he'd be waiting for her, but
lots of guys hit on her and she hadn't taken him seriously. Even
so, there he was, leaning against a blue Chrysler convertible,
gazing up at the sky.

She snuck up behind him, making her first mistake, and
covered his eyes with her hands.

'Guess who—'

He spun around before she finished asking, smacking her
head, yanking her by the hair. 'Jesus. Don't *ever* do that.' He
released her hair.

'Hell with you – I was just fooling around.' There were tears
in her eyes. She was done, turning, walking away.

'Hey, wait.' He put a hand on her arm. 'You all right? Chelsea?
Look, I didn't mean to snap. It was just – you know – a reflex.
Involuntary. You shouldn't sneak up on somebody.' Gently, he
led her back to the car, opened the passenger door. 'Come on.'

Chelsea hesitated. Her chin wobbled.

'Please?' He had a puppy-dog smile. Sad, pleading eyes. A
few zits, but he was buffed, and his eyes just wouldn't let go.
She got in, making her second mistake, and when he helped
with her seat belt, she let his arm brush against her breast.

'What's with the seat?' Green plastic lined the passenger side.

'Sorry. My buddy got drunk and tore up the leather. I'm
having it fixed, but meantime this'll do.' He popped a pill and
handed her a flask.

Chelsea sipped, tasted fruity punch.

'You like it?'

Chelsea drank some more, nodded. 'It's sweet. What's in it?'

Larry grinned. 'My specialty. A little of everything.

She took another long swig, her final mistake. 'So wh...
going?' She shouted to be heard over the music.

The top was down; his hair ruffled, dancing in the w...
'Buddy of mine has a place by the lake.' He reached over a...
gave her left breast a squeeze.

Chelsea smirked, pushing his hand away, shaking her pointer
finger. College boys were nothing new to her. She knew how
they liked to party. Fact was, Chelsea liked to party, too, but
she'd been around enough to know how to pace herself. If she
wanted Mr Chrysler to stick around, she'd have to be careful
about how hard and fast she played. She leaned back, drinking
some more. It had been a long day at the coffee shop, and, now
that she was sitting down, she felt it. Her feet throbbed; legs
ached. The wind in her face made her eyes burn; she shut them,
taking sips from the flask, listening to the music, the engine
and the wind. Drifting.

The truth was that Larry had planned to mess with her, not
necessarily to kill her. That part solidified when she fucking
snuck up on him, startling the shit out of him. What was she
– a moron? From then on, everything about her irritated him.
Her coarse, trailer-trash voice. Her cheap rhinestone nails. And
all those rings; did she think she could mesmerize men with
the motions of her fingers? Like a damn belly dancer? Even
her tits pissed him off. They were puffy round ones, and she
used them as a lure, pushing them up, showing them off. She
was so damned transparent. And so stupid. Even after he slapped
her, she got into the car, simply because he looked sad.

When she finally fell asleep from his drug-laden elixir, he
realized he'd had it in the back of his mind to kill her all along.
Prepared for it. Lined the passenger seat with plastic. Brought
equipment. So his conscious mind was moving slower than the
rest of it. Fascinating. His mind knew things before he did. He
chuckled at that and thought about the waitress slumped next to
him. From watching her in the coffee shop, he knew a lot about
her: how she moved; how she smelled; how her little nose
scrunched up in a pout she undoubtedly thought was cute; how
she repeated the same insipid stupid sing-song comments to
customers all day long, day after day; how she primped at her
reflection in the window when she thought no one was looking.
He knew, too, that she would have resisted when he tried to fuck

..ig to pressure him into more than a one-time hook-up.
.. idea of her resisting him – that made him mad. By the
..ney got to the lake, he was so angry and actually bored
her that he didn't even want to nail her anymore.
..nstead, he undertook a more ambitious project.

A while later, woozy and confused, Chelsea forced an eye
open. Saw darkness. Wait – where was she? Crickets were
chirping. In a car? The college boy – his car. She blinked,
swallowed. Drank something warm. Blood? What? Her mouth
felt swollen; she moved her tongue, felt a loose tooth. What
had happened? An accident? No, the car was parked, surrounded
by trees. And the dark, hazy sky. She couldn't get air, choked
on the razor sharp pain across her throat. Oh God. She tried to
move but couldn't; opened her mouth to cry out, but made only
bubbling, gurgling noises. Where was the college boy? He could
help her – take her to the hospital. She tried to look for him,
but couldn't turn her head. Had no strength.

When the car door opened, Chelsea Johnson was barely
conscious. If her throat hadn't been cut, she might have screamed
as her date gathered her in plastic and hoisted her over his
shoulder. If she hadn't been tied so tightly, she might have
clawed at him as he dumped her in the woods. But unable to
scream or to claw, Chelsea fell to the ground beside the lake,
dying silent and alone.

'Did you have your lemon with you? Did you bite it?'

Leslie's red hair glowed in the lamplight, and her brown eyes
held steady, as if nothing in the world were as important as
what Harper had to say. In Leslie's comfy office, together on
a pillow-laden green sofa, they sipped tea with honey, and
Harper talked about her day, working a twisted narrative backwards. She started with an explanation of her wounds and an
assurance that she was really OK; ended with a description of
the flashbacks that followed Graham's suicide. It was the flashbacks that Leslie wanted to discuss first.

'No lemon. But I had a pencil, and I pressed the point into
my hand until it just about impaled it.'

'But pain didn't help.'

No. 'Leslie, this wasn't an ordinary flashback. It was like –'
Good Lord, what had it been like? '– like channel surfing in my
head. One show changing to another every few seconds. Only

they weren't shows. They were real. Sniper fire. Hank falling. Graham falling. Marvin blowing up. Bam bam bam.' Harper held her head.

Leslie reached out, gently touched Harper's arm.

In the few months Harper had been off-and-on seeing her, she had come to trust Leslie, thought of her as not just a therapist but also a friend. The friendship, she knew, existed only within the walls of Leslie's candle-scented, plant-filled office. Even so, Harper relied on it. In some ways, she'd been more open with Leslie than with anyone ever, including Hank.

Leslie's voice was soft, validating. 'So, with the channels abruptly changing, you must have become disoriented. You couldn't possibly anticipate what would come next.'

'Well, yes, except—'

'Except that you knew how each episode would end?'

'Exactly.'

Leslie leaned close, watching Harper's eyes. 'So tell me how you felt.'

'How I felt?' What? Were there even words to describe it? 'I don't know. Frantic? Powerless? I couldn't change what I knew was coming. Couldn't help anyone.' But those words didn't even touch how she'd felt. Didn't address the urgency or the danger. Didn't include the tangibility – the sounds, the smells.

'It sounds terrifying.' Leslie released Harper's arm, sat back.

Terrifying? Yes, Harper supposed it had been. But that word didn't touch it, either. 'So what do I do, Leslie? Is this how I'm going to be? Is this my new normal?'

'You know I don't use that word, Harper.' A big, generous grin reminded Harper that they both knew there was no such thing as 'normal' in a complex, ever-changing world. 'But that type of multi-tiered flashback hasn't been typical for you. So, for you, no, I wouldn't consider it "normal".'

Leslie let Harper absorb the comment before continuing.

'Let's think about what set it off. The suicide of your student. An unthinkably violent and unexpected event. Completely out of nowhere. Maybe your reaction to something so atypical was similarly atypical?'

Harper smiled. Of course. Leave it to Leslie to make sense of what had happened: her mind had responded to sudden violence with its own sudden violence. It seemed obvious now; the morning's flashbacks were an aberration, a one-time deal.

Her shoulders released some tension. 'So I'm not necessarily getting worse?'

Leslie shook her head, no. But she shifted positions, sitting face to face with Harper. 'I don't like "better" or "worse" any more than I like "normal".'

'I know, but—'

'Because PTSD isn't about good or bad or sick or well.'

'I know.' Harper had heard this speech before. Many times. She continued it for Leslie, hoping to shorten it. 'Post Traumatic Stress Disorder is not a disease to be cured; it's a condition to be managed. And I'll probably have to live with it forever.'

Leslie nodded. 'Sadly, that's true. For now, the best we can do is manage it. Has the Effexor helped you?'

Harper shrugged. 'I haven't been taking them lately.' In fact, she'd stopped taking the pills weeks ago when her flashbacks had seemed to ease.

'Are you sleeping?'

Harper never slept through the night. Hadn't in years, not since Iraq. 'Same as usual.'

Leslie sipped tea, pressed her lips together, thinking. 'OK. Let's go back to this morning. You pressed on a pencil point to cause pain. But that didn't ground you.'

'Right.'

'Did you use any other techniques?'

Harper knew what Leslie was asking. The theory was that PTSD symptoms might be minimized or interrupted if, at the start of a flashback, sufferers grounded themselves in the present moment. Which meant sharply stimulating their senses. Leslie had recommended biting into a lemon, smelling intense scents like mint or cloves, clutching an ice cube (or, in a pinch, the point of a pencil), listening to music or even counting the number of chairs in a room or trees in a park. So far, Harper hadn't tried many of these techniques.

Leslie waited. 'You said you didn't have a lemon with you. How about your scents?'

'No. I carry drops in my bag, but it was up in the classroom, and I was outside.'

'So they were no good.'

'Leslie, if I'd eaten an entire lemon, it wouldn't have helped. This was powerful. I was in no condition to concentrate on smelling salts or counting by threes.'

'I get it.'

They were both silent. Leslie frowned.

'It wasn't your fault, you know.'

'What wasn't?'

'Any of it. The mugging. The suicide—'

Sudden tears blurred Harper's vision. 'Leslie, I was holding his arms. He fell out of my—'

'It's not your fault. Nor is what happened to Marvin and the others in Iraq. Nor is your father's fraud or your parents' divorce or Hank's fall. None of it's your fault. None of it.'

Now, Harper was angry. 'So? If none of it's my fault, why bring it all up?' She tensed, almost got to her feet. 'What's your point, Leslie? That things keep happening to me? That I'm some kind of perpetual helpless victim?'

'Yes, in a way—'

'What?' Harper stood, her face red, eyes bulging. 'Seriously? Me? A victim?'

'Yes. A victim.' Leslie remained unperturbed. 'But no more than anyone else. Harper, none of us – no matter how many push-ups we can do or how accurately we fire a rifle – none of us can control everyone and everything all the time. Once in a while, everyone – even the toughest of us – becomes a victim. Nobody can protect everyone—'

'And I don't expect to. But today – it was my job to run that recitation. Which implies to protect it. And, since you brought it up, I was in charge of the patrol, too. It was my job to take Marvin's back and secure that area—'

'Harper, you could not foresee what happened to Marvin.'

Harper didn't answer. She remained rigid, hands on hips. Leslie was trying to soothe her, and that was infuriating.

'Nobody could have prevented what happened to Marvin except the bombers.'

'You weren't there. You don't know.'

'I think I do, Harper, because I know you. If anything could have been done, you'd have done it. You weren't at fault. Not then. Not now.'

'No? Well, that's good news. I guess everything's just fine, then.'

Leslie scowled. 'Do you want it to be your fault, Harper? Is feeling guilty preferable to feeling powerless?'

Harper fumed. She pushed a hand through her hair, sat again.

Drank more tea. Didn't look at Leslie. How had the conversation turned to fault, anyhow? She'd never meant to discuss blame. People were gone. What did it matter whose fault it was? Marvin was gone. So were Sameh and the boy. And nine other soldiers, and seventeen civilians. And her father. And Graham. Even Hank was gone, in a way. Fault wasn't the issue, was it?

'Harper. Do you think you're still in danger?'

In danger? Of another flashback? 'Not really.'

'Because that mugging didn't seem random.'

Oh, the mugging. Leslie had changed the subject. 'No, it wasn't.'

Leslie put her mug on the coffee table. She met Harper's eyes. 'I've got to tell you, Harper, I'm concerned. The guy knew you and was specifically following you; he wasn't just coasting along until he saw a book bag he liked and decided to grab it. Am I right?'

She was.

'So what did he want? Six hundred dollars? A gun? A few pills?'

'What are you saying?'

'Harper, whoever attacked you is impulsive, violent. Willing to take risks, even in broad daylight. Look, I'm not a cop. But it's clear to me that you were targeted because somebody wanted something you had. If that something was in the bag, fine. He got it. Game over. But what if it wasn't?'

'Then he'll be back.' Harper hadn't articulated that possibility; she'd merely reacted to it, becoming super-watchful, alert, braced for an attack. 'And, next time, I won't be surprised. Next time, I'll break his effing neck.'

Leslie said nothing. Harper checked her watch. The hour was up. She gulped the last of her tea, set the mug down, stood to go.

'Hang on a second.' Leslie went to the tiny refrigerator in the corner. 'I can't help you fight off muggers, but at least I can give you this. Keep it handy.' She pressed a plump lemon into Harper's hand. 'You start to feel detached or fuzzy, chomp away.'

'Yum.' Harper stuck the lemon in her bag and gave Leslie a hug. 'This was good, Leslie. Thank you.'

'Be careful, Harper.'

Harper stepped into the hall, looked both ways, then paused to look back through the window of Leslie's office. Leslie was still standing there, brown eyes fixed on her as she walked away.

*   *   *

Harper strapped her bag on to the Ninja and took a long way home. The air was heavy, buggy, humid, but the motorcycle tore through it, carving its way down the road.

Home was on Hanshaw Street, about a mile north-west of campus. Harper parked her bike in the driveway, grabbed her bag, stopped on the front porch to look around. The grass was knee-high; the gazebo surrounded by weeds. Her flower garden overgrown, untended. Neglected. Sighing, she went into her empty, half-renovated house. Glanced into the dining room covered with drop cloths. Dropped her bag in the hall, headed for the kitchen. And heard her cell phone ring.

For half a nanosecond, she thought: maybe it's Hank. But then she remembered; of course it wasn't Hank. When would she accept reality? Hank wouldn't be calling any more; he couldn't call. Couldn't talk. Hank had Broca's aphasia. When would that sink in?

Reaching into her leather bag, Harper found her phone. Caller ID said CAYUGA NEUROLOGICAL. Wow, maybe it was Hank, after all? She answered, breathless.

'Harper?'

No, it wasn't Hank. Harper's eyes darted around the foyer, the walls stripped of paper. She smoothed her hair.

'Are you busy? Is this a bad time?'

'No. No. I – it's fine.' Why was Ron calling? Oh God, had something happened to Hank?

Hesitation. 'I enjoyed our coffee today.'

Harper bit her lip. Why was she so damned awkward? Ron was just being polite. Then again, his voice was muted, hushed. Why was he talking so softly? Never mind. It didn't matter. 'So did I.' She tried to sound chirpy.

He paused. Harper waited.

'So I said I'd call when I had news about that pill.'

Of course. That was why he was calling: the pill. She thought of Detective Rivers, what she'd said about the other deaths. 'You found out what it is?'

Another pause. 'The short answer is yes. But it's a long, rather complicated story—'

'So? Start.'

'Harper. Is something wrong? You sound – I don't know. Short?'

Short? She stood up straighter. 'I'm just tired. Tell me about the pill.'

'No, you've had a rough day. If you're tired, it can wait—'

'I'm fine. Tell me.'

He exhaled. 'It's a new drug, still experimental, but in final trials. About to be approved by the FDA. It has amazing properties; it stimulates parts of the frontal lobe, improves learning, enhances mental acuity and short-term memory. Its potential applications are boundless—'

'So why didn't you tell me this earlier?'

'How could I? I had to identify it.'

'Really?' Harper frowned. 'Because I saw Detective Rivers earlier. She knew what the pills were right away—'

'What?'

'She said that the same pills were found with other recent fatalities—'

'Wait.' She pictured Ron leaning back, covering his eyes. 'You discussed the pills with the police?'

Harper let out a breath. 'I didn't plan to discuss them, Ron. But she insisted, and . . . Look, I don't want to go into it. Like you said, it's been a rough day.'

'But, after our conversation earlier, I don't understand why you'd draw police attention—'

'Because after you and I had coffee, I got mugged—'

'Wait – what? Are you OK?'

'I'm fine—'

'Harper, my God. Why didn't you call me?'

Call him? Why would she have called him?

'I'm fine, really. But afterwards, I met with Detective Rivers—'

'No, don't go on. This is crazy. Tell me in person. Have you had dinner?'

Dinner?

'Look, I've got another hour or so here, then I'm going to grab a bite. How about joining me?'

Joining him? Harper looked up the empty steps. Then down the empty hall.

'I can't.' She couldn't.

'Tomorrow, then. We need to talk.'

'I don't know. I have a lot to do—'

'You've got to eat, Harper. And you come to the Clinic every evening, don't you? Why don't we meet tomorrow after visiting hours. Say, around eight thirty. We'll eat; you'll tell me what happened to you today, and I'll fill you in about the theft.'

Theft? 'What theft?'

'Oh, sorry, I didn't finish. I'll tell you tomorrow—'

'Tell me now.'

'OK.' He took a breath. 'Short version. At the Center, we store all experimental drugs in coded bins. This spring, there was a robbery. A bin was emptied out. And guess what? Graham's pills came from that bin.'

Really? 'They were stolen?'

'Hundreds of vials were taken. Gone. During final trials.'

'But they aren't harmful – I mean, you said they make people smarter.' She wondered about Graham's grades. Had his As been drug-induced?

'Harper, all drugs have side effects. And if taken in large doses, those side effects can increase.'

'What side effects?'

He sighed. 'How about I explain it all tomorrow at dinner?'

Fine. But a detail was bothering her, nagging in the corner of her mind. 'Today, in the coffee shop. When you saw the pills, you recognized them, didn't you?'

Ron hedged. 'I suspected, but I wanted to be sure before I said anything.'

'So what Detective Rivers said about them – is it true? Have those pills been associated with rapes and fires and other violence? Were there other deaths besides Graham's?'

His voice tightened. 'That whole idea is misleading.'

Misleading?

'In fact, it's completely erroneous. That drug is perfectly safe.' Ron was insistent. 'But this conversation is too important for the phone. Let's talk tomorrow. The lobby. Eight thirty.'

OK. Tomorrow. In the lobby. At eight thirty.

Wait. What was she doing? First having coffee, now dinner?

Well, why shouldn't she? They were going to talk about stolen pills, assaults and violent deaths; that was all. And, like the man said, she had to eat.

Which she ought to do now, and quickly; it was almost time to go see Hank.

Any hopes Harper had about not telling Hank about the mugging were smashed as soon as he laid eyes on her.

'What. You.' His eyebrows furrowed, his jaw tightened, and he tried to stand, but his ankles caught in the footrests of the wheelchair. Frustrated, he stumbled back into the seat and slammed the armrest with his fist, his eyes never leaving her face. 'Hoppa. You.'

She crouched at his side, wincing at the soreness of bruises and stiffness of her bad leg. 'I'm all right.' She kissed him, but he put his hands firmly on her shoulders and, scowling, examined her face.

'Cut.' He touched the wound on her cheek, the darkening lump beside her eye. 'Steak.'

Steak? Really? 'Does that work?' She smiled, pleased that she understood him. And amused that Hank would suggest slapping a hunk of meat on her eye to stop it from blackening. She pictured it. What should she use? Chuck? Sirloin? A nice fillet?

Hank didn't smile. His eyes darkened, angry. 'Say. Me. You. What.'

Hank wanted to know what had happened. She wasn't going to lie to him; she never had. But she would spare him the grisly and upsetting details. Harper took a seat beside his chair and took his hand. 'I'm OK, Hank. Really. But somebody mugged me.'

He scowled. 'Hurt.'

'I'm fine.'

He looked her over. 'No.' Again, he touched her cheek.

'It's nothing.'

'Killed?' His eyes sparkled.

Harper started to assure him that no one had been killed before she understood. Hank always teased her about being scary tough. She could lift a lot more than the 130 pounds she weighed – as much as strong, taller men. She could do push-ups and chin-ups all day long. So, his point was: how could someone mug her and live?

'Not yet.' She laughed. 'I'll get him, though.'

Hank became serious again, eyes burning, his hands tight around hers. His lips puckered, slowly forming a word. 'Who.'

'I don't know. I didn't see his face. But I'm OK. He just knocked me down and grabbed my bag.' And threatened to drop her into the gorge.

'Bag. Take. Your.'

'No, it wasn't my bag – it belonged to a student.' She didn't tell him which student, didn't talk about Graham or his suicide. Didn't want to upset him further.

Hank looked her over, gently touched the Band-Aid on her hand, eyed her arms, her shoulders. Her hair. 'Hoppa.'

Harper tried to make light of what happened. 'It was just some kid, Hank. He took me by surprise, but when I catch him, I'll scramble him. We'll have him for breakfast.'

Hank wasn't amused. 'Hoppa. You.'

'Yes?'

'O–K?'

'I am. Yes. Truly.'

'Both. Us. OK. Us. Two. Gr–reat.'

Wow. Hank was being sarcastic; the old Hank was resurfacing. His eyes twinkled, teasing, but the twinkle seemed muted, sad. 'Home. Want. Go. Us.'

Home? Us? He wanted to go home with her. Harper couldn't bear it. 'Come on. Let's take a walk.'

Silently, the pair walked along the corridor, Hank pushing a walker in case his right leg faltered. He had a definite limp, but then so did Harper; her left leg giving in when she was tired or, in this case, recovering from a mugging. The two of them ambled along, wobbling side to side, step by step, arm in arm. Clearly, Hank's overall strength was returning; his intense regime of physical therapy was working. After several laps around the unit, it was she, not he, who wanted to sit and rest. So they landed on a sofa in the lounge, drinking dreadful coffee from the vending machine. Harper massaged her thigh, hoping to keep the rest of the visit light.

'How was dinner?' The question was uncomplicated, requiring an uncomplicated answer. Fine. Awful. Great. OK. He should be able to manage it.

But Hank didn't respond. He looked at Harper with startling intensity, penetratingly, almost accusingly, and then, abruptly, turned away.

'Hank? Is something wrong?' What a stupid question, she scolded herself. Of course, something was wrong. The man couldn't talk, for one thing. And that was only the start.

Hank blinked soberly, absorbed in thought. Silent.

'I know this is hard for you.' Harper moved closer, taking his arm. 'It's hard for us both. But we've got a lot to be thankful for.'

Hank glanced at her, as if daring her to explain.

'You could have died in that fall, Hank. We're lucky. You're still here. We're together.'

Setting coffee down, Harper put her arms around her husband
and leaned her head on his shoulder. Hank rested his head
against hers, wrapped his strong left arm around her. They sat
that way, cradling each other without the need for words. Harper
ached for him, for the way he had been. Closing her eyes, she
remembered Hank, painting the dining room, wearing torn cut-
offs and a painter's hat, shoulders rippling as he lifted his brush.
When she'd passed, he'd dabbed her nose with Chinese red
enamel. She'd taken him down, and they'd ended up on the
drop cloth, paint spattered and naked, Meatloaf playing full
blast. '*I would do anything for love . . .*'

Absently, holding Hank, she hummed along to the memory.
I would do anything for love . . . She looked up, met Hank's
eyes, then his lips. Felt him quiver.

Other people came into the lounge, but Harper and Hank
didn't budge, even if people openly stared. When they finally
moved apart, visiting hours were over, and Harper's coffee was
cold. They kissed goodnight, as always.

Hank pursed his lips, struggling. 'H–honny.' His eyes laughed.

Honey? Was he calling her Honey? How dear. But, also, how
unlike Hank. He never used trite terms of endearment. 'Yes,
I'm your honey. And you're mine.'

He shook his head, no, and repeated. 'Ho. Nee.'

Harper felt him hold on to her, his reluctance to let her go.
And something else.

She was in the elevator, descending to the lobby, thinking
about that other something when she realized what Hank had
been trying to say. It wasn't 'Honey'. Since the accident, he'd
had trouble enunciating his Rs.

The only sound was the crickets. And the only light was the
moon. The air smelled moist and green, having cooled with the
dark. Harper parked the Ninja, but didn't go into the house.
Instead, she wandered out back to the new deck, thinking about
Hank's last remark: Hank was horny. He wanted sex.

The truth was she was probably horny, too, but hadn't
admitted it. Since Hank's accident, she'd suppressed all thoughts
of sex. Even when she fantasized about having a family, she
focused on the children, not on making them. But now that
Hank mentioned it, she couldn't stop thinking about sex. And
thinking about it made her nervous.

She told herself that her nerves were understandable. Inevitable. She'd been immersed in Hank's survival, then with his recovery, now with minuscule improvements. Over the last weeks, she'd measured every aspect of his physical being: his heart rate, blood pressure, brain functions, intake and output of liquids and solids, and, at some point, she had become his caretaker instead of his lover. At some point, she'd stopped thinking of him sexually. Now, suddenly, Hank was telling her, in his broken way, that he wanted sex again. And she wasn't prepared.

Harper stood on the deck, cloaked in darkness. Memories bubbled up, of precisely the things she'd worked to forget. His breath on her skin. His chest against hers. His rough stubbly face brushing her breast. Hank's lips nipping her neck, his thick fingers stroking . . .

She stepped over to the hot tub and sat on the edge. Imagining what it would be like now. Not like before, couldn't be. Weak on one side, Hank wouldn't move as he had. So, would she have to be on top? Or would they lie on their sides? Picturing it, mentally repositioning their bodies, she felt awkward. Reluctant. Hank was different now. His speech – it was so childlike. Did she regard him as a child? No, of course not. Hank was still Hank. Wasn't he? Oh God. She was so confused. What did she feel? Fear? Sorrow? No. More like grave, imminent danger.

Without warning, the screeching of crickets crescendoed, became ragged, anguished screams. The deck faded away. A bomb exploded so close that it seared the hairs on her arms. Somewhere close, men fired their weapons, darting for cover – no, damn it, she had to fight this. Where the hell was her lemon? In her bag. On the back of the Ninja. Too far away.

Dodging bullets, Harper looked around, saw rippling dark water. Holding her breath, she flung herself into the hot tub and its stagnant, unheated, not very chlorinated contents. Clothes and all, she sunk into cool, shockingly wet water, hiding under the surface, making no sound. Only when she was sure the gunfire had stopped and the flashback aborted did she let herself step on to the wooden deck. Then, sopping and cursing, she sloshed through brambles, bushes and trees back to her Ninja, retrieved her bag and headed into her big old Victorian house, not noticing the bicycle leaning against the shadowed wall.

Inside, Harper dropped her leather sack in the foyer and stripped off her clothes to protect the new hardwood flooring

from puddles. In her underwear, she was halfway up the stairs before it registered that, at the end of the downstairs hallway, the door to Hank's study was ajar.

Carrying her wet clothes, Harper backed down the stairs, careful to avoid the creaky spots, shifting her weight gently so as not to make a sound. She stopped at the bottom, listening to faint rustling noises coming from Hank's study, and quickly, silently, she searched for a weapon.

Kitchen knives were too far away; Hank's tools were out in the shed; her pistol up in the attic, and Hank's shotgun – was it in the broom closet? Harper wasn't sure, didn't have time to check. Sidestepping to the living room, she dropped her bundle of wet clothes and grabbed a poker from the stand beside the fireplace. It felt puny and unimpressive. Would it scare a prowler away? What if he grabbed it from her and slammed her with it? She thought of the guy on the bridge pounding her head – was this him again? Hell, it could be; she should call the police. Poker in hand, she started for her bag to search for her phone. But before she got there, something in Hank's study slammed.

Harper froze. Another slam, louder this time. Barefoot in wet underwear, Harper ran down the hall, poker raised overhead, poised to strike. At the door, she paused to steady herself. And then, with a warrior's fury, she charged.

'Jesus, Harper.' Trent Manning cowered. Staring first at the poker, then at her wet bra.

Trembling, Harper lowered the poker. 'Christ.' It was all she could manage.

'What the hell?' He forced a laugh and straightened up. Then he noticed her face. 'Good God. What happened to you?'

Harper ignored the question. 'My God, Trent – damn, I could have killed you.' She yanked Hank's corduroy blazer off the back of his desk chair and pulled it on, covering herself, awkwardly switching the poker from hand to hand.

'Seriously, kiddo. You look like a prizefighter.'

'I got mugged.'

'Right.' He chuckled, didn't believe her.

Harper was in no mood to explain. She stepped over to him, gave him a perfunctory peck on the cheek. 'Dammit, Trent. You scared me. What the hell are you doing in here?'

'I didn't realize I needed permission to come over.' Trent

seemed to think that his presence should be no surprise; after all, until the accident, he'd practically lived with them, coming and going at will. Often, she'd come home to find Trent in the kitchen, reading a journal, scrounging for a beer. Trent and Hank had been inseparable, consulting on projects, teaching together, collaborating on articles. Since Hank's accident, though, Trent hadn't been over much. Actually, at all.

'You should have called first,' she scolded. 'I live alone now.'

Trent raised his eyebrows, wounded. 'Of course. I understand.' He picked up a glass of Scotch that had been resting on Hank's desk.

'Sorry. You're always welcome, Trent. I just wasn't expecting you.' Harper was still shaken by how close she'd come to bashing in his skull.

There was an uncomfortable silence. Trent swallowed Scotch.

'You saw him tonight?'

'I see him every night.'

Trent nodded. 'Any change?'

Harper met Trent's eyes, saw a shadow of guilty sadness. 'You wouldn't need to ask if you'd visit him yourself.'

Trent smirked. 'I'm not the best company in this situation, Harper.'

'It wasn't your fault, Trent. He doesn't blame you. Nobody does.'

'Really? Well, then, I'm a lucky guy, don't you think?'

'You didn't make him fall. And he'd like to see you.'

'Would he?' Trent considered it. 'Yes, well, I bet he would.' His tone was odd.

Harper sighed. 'So?'

'So, I'll go see him.'

'Good. When?'

'Soon.'

Harper stared at him.

'I will. Really.'

The poker was still in her hand. She set it on the side of the desk, but it fell off, clattering to the hardwood floor. 'So, what were you doing?'

'Oh. Right. I was, um–looking for Hank's notes. Printouts. Or his laptop. You know how it is: publish or perish.'

Yes. Harper knew. Both Hank and Trent were up for tenure. With that in mind, Hank had written countless articles for

scientific journals, edited chapters for books, co-authored papers with Trent, which they'd presented at academic, geological and ecological conferences. This year, Hank probably would have been granted tenure. A permanent full professorship. Now, of course, his tenure was out of the question. Trent was still in the running, though; she hoped he'd get it.

'So, do you know where his laptop is?'

Harper didn't. She hadn't seen it, hadn't even thought about it. 'It's not here?'

'I don't see it. I'm guessing he printed out his notes, though. Mind if I keep looking?'

'Have at it.'

As Trent rifled through Hank's filing cabinet, Harper looked around the office. She hadn't been in there since the accident. The room hadn't been touched, looked as if Hank might at any second appear to dig into work. Books, papers, maps and folders scattered his desk. Post-it notes clung to every surface; yellow pads were everywhere. The trash can was full, and a dent marked where his fingers had last dipped into his bottomless bowl of M&Ms. In the corner, Hank's oversized, overused leather easy chair sagged in the middle, defining his shape. The hassock was scuffed where his heels had repeatedly dug in. She wandered over, smelled the worn leather, touched the place where his head had rested. She could see him there, looking up from his book when she came in. His eyes, as always, laughing.

'Any idea at all? Harper?'

'What?' Harper turned to Trent; when she looked back, Hank's image had vanished.

'The notes must be in his computer. Are you sure you haven't seen it?'

She shrugged, staring for a moment at the empty chair. Then, explaining that she needed to get some clothes on, hurried away, leaving Trent alone with ghosts of her husband's past.

But there were more ghosts upstairs. Hank's clothes greeted her from the closet, ready for duty. A tweed jacket, a pair of worn jeans. Shirts, slacks, a rack of shoes. A camping vest, drooping from a hook. She remembered Hank wearing it last spring when they'd hiked in the Smokies. Cooking out. Lying together in a tent in the middle of nowhere.

Harper grabbed a robe and closed the closet door. Back

downstairs, avoiding Trent, she went to the kitchen for something to eat. But the open bottle of Johnny Walker Black beckoned her. Food could wait. She took out a glass, poured. She shouldn't drink with a concussion, and booze wasn't prescribed for flashbacks. But one drink wouldn't hurt, and, Lord knew, she deserved one after today.

In one swallow, she downed the contents, shut her eyes as the smooth burn flowed to her gut. Sat at the table, poured another. Took a gulp, another. Closed her eyes. And saw Graham, watching her as he fell. Damn. Why had he jumped? She saw him again, doing a back stroke in the air. Hitting the ground. Was Detective Rivers right? Had his death been related to those pills?

Harper's head ached. She leaned back against the wall, eyes shut. Remembering Ron examining the pill, turning it with long, elegant fingers.

A glass clinked and liquid sloshed. Harper opened an eye, saw Trent refilling his glass.

'I couldn't find a damned thing.' Trent plopped on to a chair. 'No printouts, no laptop. Nothing.' He raised his glass. 'So, what do you say we get hammered?'

Harper managed a smile. She was halfway there and, clearly, Trent was way ahead of her.

Trent slammed down his drink, poured another.

'If you need his files, why not just ask Hank where they are?'

Trent froze. 'Seriously? He communicates?'

'Go see for yourself.'

'But you're saying . . . Hank can talk?'

'Simple sentences.'

'Really?' Trent seemed startled. 'I thought he spoke gibberish.'

'It's not gibberish.' Harper sounded defensive. 'He can say things like "Go home".' She didn't mention that he could also say he was horny.

Trent studied his fingernails. 'So. Does he remember . . . does he talk about . . . what happened?'

'He's never mentioned it. I don't know how much he remembers. But he doesn't blame you.' She swallowed more Scotch.

Trent nodded, unconvinced. 'Will he improve?'

'Maybe. Maybe not.'

Trent nodded again. They sat for a while, each drinking to

ease their own pain. Finally, Trent uncrossed his legs and leaned toward Harper. 'Nothing has been the same since that day. Nothing.'

Harper didn't answer.

'I keep reliving it. Over and over, I keep trying to catch him—'

'Trent. Please.' Harper saw Hank falling. Graham falling. Marvin blowing up. She clutched the drink in her hand, focused on its icy cold.

'He was right there. Within my reach. I should have grabbed him.'

'Look at me.' Harper waited until he did. She looked into his gray, unsteady gaze and enunciated each word slowly. 'It. Was. Not. Your. Fault.' She channeled Leslie's voice. 'I mean it, Trent. Guilt is uncalled for. It was an accident. Stop blaming yourself.'

Trent looked away.

Harper put a hand on his arm. But the arm was suddenly not Trent's; it was Graham's. Harper pulled her hand away, turned.

Trent poured another finger of Scotch. 'Have you talked to Vicki lately?'

Harper bit her lip. Shook her head, no.

'Poor Vicki.' Trent exhaled Scotch breath. 'I'm afraid she didn't marry well.'

Oh Lord. Trent was diving into drunken self-flagellation. Harper was in no mood for it. She was exhausted, more than a little inebriated. Her head throbbed.

'Fact is, since Hank's injury, I haven't been much of a husband.'

'You've been upset. I'm sure she understands.'

'Well, her head might. But others of her body parts are less inclined to reason.'

What? Time for Trent to stop talking. 'Speaking of Vicki, she must be wondering—'

'You know the parts I mean. The parts that don't do much thinking. But, truth be known, lately my dear wife's parts haven't had much interest in mine.'

Trent's eyes were glazed and he stared at her without seeing. Harper wanted him and his glassy stare to go home. Dear God, she'd been mugged and her student was dead, and now, to cap her day off, she had to listen to Trent whine about his sex life?

'Trent, Vicki's probably worried.' She stood, indicating that he should follow. Trent didn't move. The walls did, though. They shimmied and swayed; Harper held on to a kitchen chair, steadying herself.

'Yes,' Trent said into his glass. 'My Vicki has begun to set her fires in other hearths, I'm afraid.'

What? Harper sat again, dizzy and dumbfounded. 'Vicki wouldn't cheat.'

'Really? You underestimate our Vicki.' His smile was bitter. 'For example, did you know she had a thing for Hank?'

Harper was indignant. How dare he imply such a thing? Even with too much Scotch in him, there was no excuse.

He leaned closer. 'You're surprised?' He grinned morbidly. 'Hank Jennings, PhD. Mountain climber, spelunker, intellectual, hunk extraordinaire. The perfect male specimen. How can you feign surprise that other women would be drawn to him?'

'That's enough, Trent.' Harper leaned on the table and stood again. 'Go home.'

Trent stared at her breasts. 'You know, if two can play, so can four.' Suddenly, clumsily, he lurched, lips puckered. Harper stepped aside, yanked his shirt collar to break his fall, and, balancing carefully, dragged him out of the room.

Trent opened his mouth, raising a finger as if to spout profundities, but Harper kept moving, pulling him along. At the door, she shoved him on to the porch, turned on the outside lights and, minimally concerned about his lack of sobriety, watched as he staggered to the driveway, climbed on to his bike and pedaled unsteadily away.

Harper went back to the kitchen and downed the rest of her Scotch, washing away her encounter with Trent. Or trying to. She was depleted, needed to eat something. It was almost eleven, and she hadn't had anything since the pie. She opened the freezer, found half-empty ice cream containers, frozen lima beans and a few Lean Cuisines. Selected some kind of peanut noodle chicken thing. She'd eaten worse. Like cold MREs. Or even hot ones. Plopping the thing into the microwave, she set the timer and began shivering. Suddenly, she was icy cold, despite the warm night air.

Harper went to the hall closet and pulled out Hank's big down-filled winter jacket. It hung on her, oversized and thick,

and she snuggled inside it, trying to stop the shaking. She shouldn't have had all that Scotch. She recognized the symptoms, had seen them in others: she was in shock.

Keep moving, Harper told herself. Get your blood circulating. She paced the floors, the events of the day pacing with her. Graham's curls dropping from sight. The flashback of the war. The damned bike rider, the gaping mouth of the gorge. And Trent. Lord. Had Vicki – her best friend – really had a crush on Hank? No, not possible. It had just been Trent's inebriated insecurity talking. Nothing more.

Back in the kitchen, with cold, unsteady hands, Harper took out a can of soda, a fork and spoon. The spoon reminded her of pie and, unexpectedly, she saw Ron Kendall's golden eyes.

Ron Kendall. Why was she thinking of him?

She opened the soda can. Actually, it wasn't a surprise if Vicki had a crush on Hank. Who could blame her? Especially since – let's be honest – the poor woman was married to a drunken twit. And a crush didn't mean anything had actually happened between Hank and Vicki. Of course, it hadn't.

Harper sipped Dr Pepper. She was feeling vulnerable, having just been mugged and witnessed a suicide. But hell, she'd survived a war, wasn't about to be bothered by something as trivial as a crush. Even so, she wandered the house in Hank's parka, searching for his face in old photographs, staring at close-ups, wondering whether deceit would show in a person's eyes.

All she saw were Hank's familiar rugged features, his hearty, open smile. His laughing eyes held no hint of secrecy. She needed to forget about Trent and go to bed. She needed sleep. She needed this day to end.

But Harper didn't go up to bed. She stayed in the unfinished family room, studying photograph albums, revisiting the past with Hank. And, some twenty minutes later, that's what she was still doing when the doorbell rang.

Just before midnight on that hot summer night, Detective Charlene Rivers found Harper Jennings at home, bleary-eyed, wearing a huge down-filled winter jacket and reeking of Scotch.

'Evening, Mrs Jennings. Can I come in?'

'Of course.' Harper stepped aside.

Deep inside the house, something was beeping.

'What's that sound?'

'Sound?' Harper seemed unaware of it, cocked her head, listening. 'Oh – damn, I forgot.'

Together, they entered the kitchen, where they rescued an abandoned peanut noodly pre-packaged dinner from the microwave.

Detective Rivers was all business, observant. She scanned the room quickly: a tan corduroy jacket on a chair, a couple of used glasses and a mostly empty bottle of Scotch. She'd been in the room months earlier. It was emptier now, lacked fresh-cut flowers and the clutter of an active kitchen. She saw changes in Harper, too: the fatigue in her eyes, the gauntness of her face, the deep purple tones around the cut on her cheekbone.

Harper offered a soda; Detective Rivers declined.

'Are you all right, Mrs Jennings?'

'Harper. Please, call me Harper. Yes, I'm fine.' She thought she should record that sentence. 'Come sit down.'

Leaving the dinner on the counter, Harper led the detective to the living room. The place was a mess, the carpet rolled up and the furniture covered with drop cloths.

She yanked the cloth off a corner of the sofa and gestured for the detective to sit; didn't bother to uncover the matching easy chair, just sat on it.

For a moment, they were silent, watching each other.

'Kind of late for a visit, isn't it, Detective? What's on your mind?'

Detective Rivers studied her. 'I saw your lights on, took a chance you were up. I have some more questions for you.'

Harper wondered why the questions couldn't wait until morning.

'You said you had no idea what led to Graham Reynolds' suicide?'

'Not a clue.' She saw Ron holding the pill.

'What did you do after the suicide?'

'You mean, all day?'

'Yes. All day.'

Lord. Was this necessary? Why now? Slowly, Harper retraced her steps. When she finished, there was silence.

Detective Rivers didn't move. She watched Harper until Harper began to feel uneasy and shifted positions, crossing her aching left leg.

'Where did you say you had coffee with the doctor?'

Harper was losing patience. 'I'm sorry, Detective. But I don't see how a cup of coffee relates to Graham's suicide.'

Detective Rivers crossed her arms. 'Actually, Mrs Jennings – I mean, Harper – I'm not here about the suicide.'

Harper felt another chill and hunkered down into Hank's parka. 'Then, why are you here?'

'Because there's another body.'

Another body?

'A young woman. Murdered. She was found tonight, out near Taughannock Falls.'

Harper stopped breathing. A young woman? Oh God. Was another of her students dead? She pictured Anna or Shaundra or Gwen lying on the ground.

'Her throat was cut; in fact, she was sliced up pretty good. And raped.'

How awful. Harper's jaw clenched. 'Who was she?' She braced herself to hear.

'Her name was Chelsea Burns. She was a waitress.'

Harper released a breath, actually relieved that her students were apparently still alive and unhurt. But, if the victim wasn't one of her students, why was Detective Rivers here?

'But why are you telling me about this?'

'Good question.' Detective Rivers leaned forward, elbows on her knees, and looked into Harper's eyes. 'I wouldn't normally. But, I'm curious, Mrs Jen— sorry, I'm not good with first names. Mrs Jennings, how well did you know the victim?'

'Know her?' Harper started to answer that she didn't know her at all.

But the detective cut her off. 'See, the thing is, you might want to think about it before you answer. Because Chelsea Burns obviously knew you; she had your grade book in her purse.'

'My grade book?' That made no sense. Harper's grade book was with her students' papers, in her big leather sack.

But then she remembered. That morning in the coffee shop. Her sack had fallen, spilling its contents into the aisle. The waitress – had her name been Chelsea? Oh God – she was dead? The young woman who had helped her pick everything up? Harper recalled the long nails and ringed fingers gathering up her belongings – her keys, wallet, baby wipes, papers, markers, loose change. But her grade book? It must have landed

out of sight, and Chelsea must have found it later, Must have put it in her purse, intending to return it. But Harper should have noticed it missing. Why hadn't she? She remembered the spill; Ron sitting across from her, wearing Spandex.

'OK. When I was in the coffee shop, I dropped my bag. My grade book must have fallen out; the waitress must have found it.'

'That would explain it.' But the detective didn't seem satisfied. 'Mrs Jennings, I won't play games with you. I know a little bit about you.'

She did?

'You told me you were army, served in Iraq. I know you were wounded there.' She glanced at Harper's bad leg.

'That's right.' So? Why was her leg relevant?

'I also know about your husband and what happened to him.'

'Really.'

'I guess you don't remember. It's understandable; you were pretty distraught. But I took the call. In fact, I was here for quite a while after your husband's accident.'

Harper didn't remember, couldn't recall any faces other than Hank's. And there he was again, in the hedges, banged up and bloodied.

'How's he doing, by the way?'

'Hank?' Stupid question. What other husband did she have? 'He's coming along.'

Detective Rivers watched her, but not unkindly. 'You know, Mrs Jennings – Harper – Ithaca's a pretty small city. And, in the summer when most students are gone, it's generally quiet. But today, in twenty-four hours, we've had a suicide, a mugging, a murder.'

Harper huddled into the parka.

'We have two healthy young people dead. True, one's a suicide and one's a homicide. But both were violent. And both of the deceased are connected to you.'

Harper stiffened. 'What are you saying, Detect—'

'Relax.' Her tone softened. 'I'm not saying you're responsible.' She put her hands up as if to ward Harper off. 'I'm just saying that this is Ithaca. Oh, it's not Eden. We get our share of crimes: date rapes, kids driving under the influence, fights at bars, stolen IDs, drug overdoses. A few suicides every year. Once in a while, we get homicides. Matter of fact, you might

remember Jimmy Moran killing his wife and her boyfriend back in December. And I mentioned earlier the recent rapes, arsons and deaths associated with those pills you gave me.'

'That waitress – did she have pills on her, too?'

'No. At least, we didn't find any.' Detective Rivers tilted her head. 'But my point is, two violent deaths within a day? Not in Ithaca. That's not normal. And even less normal are two violent deaths and a mugging on the same day that both of the dead victims have spent time in the company of the mugging victim—'

'Now wait – I had nothing to do with that murder. I didn't even know that waitress—'

'Still.' Detective Rivers pursed her lips, nodding. 'It's odd, don't you think?'

Harper didn't answer. But yes, it was odd.

'Assuming that you had nothing to do with either death, here's my point. Given the unlikelihood that the victims' connections to you are coincidental, and given that you've already been attacked once, you might opt to exercise extreme caution.'

'Sorry?' Harper blinked.

'OK. Try this. These incidents are too close to you for comfort. I wish our department had spare officers to keep an eye on you, but we don't. The best I can do is have a car drive by now and then. But, until we figure this out, I don't think you should be alone. Do you have a friend you could stay with for a while?'

Harper sat speechless. Hours ago, Leslie had given her the same advice.

'Do you? A girlfriend maybe?'

Harper thought of Vicki. But she didn't want to go there. 'I don't know.'

Detective Rivers let out a sigh. 'Well, think about it, OK? I understand that, being a combat veteran, you probably assume you can take care of yourself. But that didn't work too well for you earlier today. If I were you, I'd avoid being alone. I'd keep my eyes open and my backside covered.'

'But I don't understand. Why would someone want to hurt me?' She pictured a hooded figure on a bicycle and felt the open-mouthed pull of the gorge.

'I don't know. But somebody already has. And we have to assume he'll try again.' Detective Rivers stood, put a card on

the coffee table. 'Harper, you think of anything, need anything, call me. I'll look in on you as frequently as I can. But, even with police drive-bys, you need to be careful. Lock your doors and windows when I leave.' The detective's eyes insisted on compliance.

Harper walked her to the door and double-locked it behind her. Then she went back to the kitchen and locked the door, threw the uneaten noodly peanut thing into the trash and downed another shot of Scotch.

In the morning, leather bag secured behind her, Harper was a bit hungover as she piloted the Ninja to visit Hank. She rode around campus along Thurston to East, over to Hoy, damp morning air clinging to her skin. The clouds had thickened; maybe it would finally rain, breaking the heatwave.

Harper left the cycle in the lot, following her usual routine as if it were just another hot summer day. As if she weren't looking around, eyeing strangers. Pedestrians. Drivers. Detective Rivers' warning had intensified Harper's state of alert. Why was that guy in jogging gear lingering at the corner? Was he really reading that magazine? And that woman in the Bimmer – was she staring?

Harper walked across the parking lot, braced for a fight, assuring herself that Detective Rivers was wrong. It was merely a coincidence that she'd seen both Graham and Chelsea shortly before their deaths. Nobody could reasonably think that the suicide and the murder were connected to each other, much less to her. Still, she was watchful. And bothered by something else.

Trent's insinuation plagued her. The idea of Hank and Vicki was absurd; Hank wouldn't cheat. And, if he would, it wouldn't be with Vicki, his best friend's wife and his wife's best friend. So why was she bothered?

Entering the building, her mind bounced from one troubling topic to another. Preoccupied, she signed in at reception, greeted Laurie and hurried to the elevator. When the doors opened on the third floor, she almost barreled into Ron Kendall's partner, Dr Steven Wyatt.

Dr Wyatt was the senior of the two, more heavily established in the medical community and a principal force in the establishment of Cayuga Neurological Center. Obviously, though, his

stature as a physician hadn't heightened his self-esteem. A tall, stout, socially inept man, Dr Wyatt struggled to conceal his baldness with an ill-fitting toupee, darker and straighter than the sideburns protruding from it.

'Mrs Jennings.' The line of Dr Wyatt's mouth barely moved when he spoke.

'Hello.' Harper tried to pass.

Dr Wyatt, though, didn't move aside or step into the elevator. He stood stiffly, eyeing her closely. 'Are you doing very fine today?' He cleared his throat, as if to erase his bungled phrasing.

Harper didn't want to discuss how she was doing. Stepping around him, she forced a smile and a 'yes, thanks, and you?' and kept moving, head down so she'd make eye contact with no one else. She didn't slow down until she got to Hank's room, but, even as she entered 307, she felt Dr Wyatt's probing gaze following her, piercing her back.

As soon as he saw her, Hank's eyes sparkled their usual affectionate light. His kiss felt the same as usual. And he wore his usual hearty grin, unmarred by guilt or deceit. Harper snuggled against him, fitting herself into the crevice between his torso and his undamaged arm, breathing in synchrony. She was with Hank – her Hank. And the troubles of the outside world faded – wars, suicides, murders. Cheating.

But there had been no cheating. Trent's ramblings had been merely boozy banter. Harper nuzzled, secure and hopeful. Soon Hank would be well enough to come home. The recent crimes would be solved. Life would resume where it had left off.

'News?'

News. Oh dear. He wanted to know what was going on. But it wasn't right to burden Hank with accounts of murder and suicide. There was one incident that she could tell him about, though.

'Trent came by.'

Hank frowned.

'He asked how you're doing.'

'Now. Why.'

'He's writing an article. He needs notes from your files.' She waited, slowing down, giving him time to respond.

'Trent.' That was it, Hank's entire comment. It had taken all that time for him to say one syllable.

'So, your notes – are they on a jump drive? Or did you print them out?'

Hank twisted his mouth, frowning, agitated. 'Not.'

Not. Not printed? Not in the computer? Or maybe he did not remember?

Hank moved away, pointing at her chest with his stronger hand. 'Notes. Trent. Not. No.' His voice was firm, his eyes steely. But why wouldn't he want Trent to have his notes? They'd worked together for years, shared credit on articles.

'Friend. Trent. Not.' Hank's eyes gleamed. Understandably, Hank would feel that way; Trent hadn't come to see him in weeks.

'He is your friend, Hank. He just can't face you.' Harper waited, choosing her words. 'Trent's been drinking a lot. He blames himself for your accident.'

Hank's expression didn't soften, and she wondered what he understood. The doctors couldn't be sure, and Harper worried that his comprehension wasn't much better than his speech. Hank glowered, his face dark with anger or frustration. Or something else. Fear? But fear of what?

'Vicki. Trent. Cheat.'

Cheat? Vicki? Trent? What? Cheat? Clearly, he'd used the word by chance. He wasn't – couldn't be – telling her that he'd had an affair with Vicki.

Hank nodded, emphatically. Somberly.

'You mean Trent cheated on Vicki?'

'No.' He shook his head. 'Me. Screw.'

Harper stopped breathing. She blinked, chest searing, not willing to decode any more of Hank's phrases. Had he just confessed to an affair? So casually, without a trace of shame? With no apology? Quite the contrary; he seemed earnest, eager to talk. He uttered a syllable, stopped mid-word, started again, sputtered with frustration.

Harper almost asked him – almost said, 'Hank, did you and Vicki have an affair?' She started to ask, but stopped at 'Hank', not ready to hear his answer. Instead of finishing the question, she looked at the door and stood. It was almost time to go anyway. But Hank grasped her arm.

'Hoppa. Wait. Hear.' Or here.

She sat again, eyes on the door.

'Not. Trent. Me. Push.'

Harper's mouth went dry. For the first time, Hank was talking

about his fall. She spoke slowly. 'I know Trent didn't push you. It was an accident.'

Hank tried again. 'Screwed Vicki. Push me. Trent new.' Or knew? He was breathing hard, watching her urgently, but Harper didn't want to understand what he meant. In fact, she tried not to grasp his apparent assertion that Trent had pushed Hank off the roof because Hank had screwed Vicki.

'Not let. Trent. Hoppa look. You find. Why.' Hank was insistent. He slapped the armrest as punctuation. Or frustration. 'You see.'

He was combining words. Another sign of progress. First, Hank had talked about his fall; then he was making phrases. Harper should be elated, but she wasn't. She wanted to slug him.

Hank watched her, his expression open and guileless. Clearly, she was misinterpreting his meaning. She must be. There were other explanations for 'screwed Vicki'; had to be. Even if she couldn't imagine what they might be.

'Not Trent. You find.' Hank resisted her embrace, hell bent on telling her something, twisting his tongue to form a sound. 'Ah. Coo. Mal.'

Had Hank just said Acumal? 'Acumal?'

Hank nodded. Acumal. The town in the Yucatan where they'd spent their honeymoon.

'Trent. Not. You see. You. Ah coo mal.'

Harper had no idea what he meant. Unless it was that he didn't want Trent to know about their honeymoon? 'Hank, I don't understand.'

Hank kept trying. Repeating, 'Ah. Coo. Mal. Save.'

Finally, she couldn't stand it any more. 'Enough. Please, Hank. Stop.'

Questions filled his eyes. 'Hoppa?'

'I'm sorry. I don't get what you're trying to say.' Go on, she told herself. Get it over with. Ask him if he cheated. But Hank's eyes were concerned, full of affection. Her question got stuck, wouldn't come out. And the words that did surprised her.

'Dammit, Hank. Dammit, dammit.' Tears swelled in her eyes; she turned away.

Hank put a hand on her cheek, guiding it back so she'd face him. 'Mad. You?' He wiped a tear.

'No, I'm fine.'

'Me, Hoppa. What. Tell.' He waited.

'Tell? OK.' Her tone was sharp, her mind on Vicki. 'Hank, you're not the only one who got hurt when you fell. We both did. This is a struggle for me, too.'

Hank looked down, shoulders sagging, jaw muscles tight. He didn't try to speak, simply sat.

Harper felt as if she'd slapped him. 'I'm sorry.' She hesitated to touch him. 'I just meant this has been tough on us both.'

Hank sat still for another moment. Then slowly, he put a hand out and gently moved Harper's head to his shoulder. They stayed that way, wordlessly holding each other until the orderly came to take Hank to physical therapy.

Harper's entire body felt bruised, and her leg was so stiff that, even though she despised the haze caused by medication, she allowed herself a pain pill. She popped one with a gulp of to-go iced chai from the coffee shop, where she avoided the eyes of the cashier, afraid to see grief for Chelsea, the murdered waitress. Then, with time to spare before her recitation, she parked the Ninja down the hill from campus and climbed, listing the good things in her life. Her chai. The panorama. Air that was free of dust and smoke. Her survival, and Hank's.

At the top of the hill, she didn't stop to enjoy the view; she detoured to Hank's office in Snee Hall, hoping to find his laptop and notes. And to figure out why Hank didn't want Trent to have them.

The office was locked, so she had to find Marcia, the department secretary, and ask for a key. By the time she finally got the door opened, the pill had started to kick in; she was tempted to curl up on the reclining chair and nap. Instead, she opened the blinds, letting in daylight, and looked around. Dust floated in the sunbeams, coated every surface. The room hadn't been touched; the desk calendar was still opened to April. A pile of phone messages still waited to be answered. A Cubs hat hung on the coat rack, ready for Hank's head. Photos dotted the walls: Hank on geologic studies with Trent; Hank with grad students. There were shots with Harper, too, snorkeling on their honeymoon, camping in the mountains, building their deck, soaking in the hot tub. From all corners of the office, pre-accident Hank beamed at her, sturdy and confident, without the faintest idea of what was to come.

Harper couldn't breathe, had to leave. Without even looking

for the notes, she located Hank's laptop, stuffed it into her sack and fled the office, leaving it to the dust.

About forty minutes until recitation. She still hadn't finished her remarks about Graham, and the dean was coming. She'd have to introduce him. Harper walked to her office, trying to come up with appropriate words.

Nothing.

The air was hot and breezeless again, the sky filled with dark swollen clouds. Harper looked up, wishing for a storm.

Oh, get on with it, she told herself. Just begin. OK. 'Good morning.' Excellent. She was on a roll. 'We have a guest today.' Brilliant.

Harper climbed the steps to her office without a clue what to say. Apparently, the pill she'd taken had numbed her brain more than her pain; her leg still throbbed, but she couldn't think. Maybe she'd just say, 'Dean Van Arsdale is here to talk to us.' Was that too blunt? Did his ego require more fanfare?

'Loot?'

Harper turned to the voice. Anna was waiting outside her office door. She covered her mouth, gaped at Harper's face. 'God. What happened?'

'Just an accident.'

'On your motorcycle? Did you crash?'

Harper smiled at Anna's earnestness. 'No. Not on my motorcycle.'

'But you're OK?'

'Yes. Fine. What's up?'

Anna glanced at the office. 'Do you have a minute?'

'Two even.' Harper didn't; she had to prepare a eulogy and an introduction, but Anna seemed nervous, her plump fingers tugging the strap of her book bag. She unlocked her office door. 'Come sit down.'

Anna came in but didn't sit. She stepped closer to Harper, whispering. She looked out the door. 'Loot, I'm scared.'

'It's OK, Anna – don't be scared.' Harper had no idea what was wrong, but she didn't want the girl to collapse again.

Anna chewed a thumbnail, eyes darting.

'Have a seat.'

Anna wouldn't. She paced in small agitated circles, wringing her hands.

'What's on your mind?' Harper glanced at her watch. Thirty minutes until class.

'I heard stuff,' Anna fretted. 'At the clinic.' Her breath was shorter, her voice thinner.

'Anna, calm down. You don't want to go narcoleptic.'

Anna still didn't sit, but she stopped pacing, took long deep breaths.

'Now. Calmly. Explain.'

'I was in the Sleep Clinic, having an episode. And when I have episodes, people forget I'm there. They think I'm asleep, so I become like furniture. Or a potted plant.'

'I'm sure they don't forget—'

'It's called cataplexy. It's like you're stuck somewhere in between awake and asleep. You can't move, no matter how you try. You can't talk or call out. Can't make a sound. You're paralyzed, but you're aware. You're not actually asleep.'

Harper couldn't imagine it.

'But the thing is, you can still hear. During cataplexy, I can't even blink my eyes. I can't make a peep. But I hear everything perfectly.'

'How horrific.' Oops, she probably shouldn't have said that.

'I'm used to it. I've learned to just wait it out.' Anna kept twisting the strap of her book bag.

'So you heard something?'

Anna nodded, eyes wide. 'About Graham.'

Really? 'Go on.'

'Two men were talking. One said Graham died because of stolen drugs.'

Wait. Stolen drugs? 'What?'

'That's what he said. Clear as day. Loot, something bad is going on over there—'

'Anna, don't jump to conclusions. Those drugs didn't necessarily cause his—'

'Wait – you mean it's true? He had stolen drugs on him?'

Lord, why had she said that? 'No, I didn't say—'

'Are you sure, Loot? Because Graham wouldn't do drugs. And he definitely wouldn't steal them.' Anna was beyond pale, her face translucent. Like a big oval moonstone.

Harper grabbed a bottle of water from her mini-fridge. 'Here. Drink this.' She opened the bottle, handed it to Anna. 'Who were the men you heard, Anna? Do you know?'

She swallowed water. 'One was the head of the Sleep Clinic – Dr Wyatt.'

Dr Wyatt? 'Are you sure?'

'Very. I know his voice. He said Graham stole drugs and overdosed on them, and that's why he killed himself.'

'Well. The autopsy will show if that's true.' Harper didn't know what to think. Maybe Anna misheard; hadn't Ron said the drugs were benign? She glanced at her watch. Twenty minutes until recitation.

'There's more, Loot.' Anna paused, scrunched her lips. 'They didn't just talk about Graham; they talked about you.'

Harper blinked. 'Me?'

'Dr Wyatt called you "that Jennings woman". He said you knew too much about the "situation" and might make trouble. The other man told him not to worry. He said you'd even help find the stolen drugs.'

What? 'Anna, are you sure that's what they said?'

'Very. Dr Wyatt got mad. "You know what this means? Another dead kid – how many more will there be? It's out of control." The other one tried to calm him down. He said, "Steven, those deaths are not on us. Those kids popped whatever pills they got their hands on. If not on this, they'd have OD'd on something else." He said he'd take care of everything, including you. Dr Wyatt said, "I hope so. Because every minute those pills are out there is a minute too long"—'

'Wait, hold on a second.' Harper couldn't absorb what she was hearing.

'But, Loot, why did he say Graham stole drugs? Or that you'd help find them? Do you know where those drugs are?'

'Of course not.' But she was pretty positive that she knew something else: that the second man in the conversation was Ron Kendall.

Anna's eyes were wide. 'Loot, that man said he'd "take care of you". Don't you get what that means?'

Harper had to smile. 'Anna. This isn't the movies. "Taking care of" somebody doesn't mean feeding them to the fish—'

'But they think you have Graham's stolen drugs. Or that you're able to get them. Don't you see? Dr Wyatt said more people will die . . .' Her eyes rolled.

'Anna.' Harper put her hands on Anna's shoulders, gently shaking her. 'Stay with me here—'

'I can't . . . go back there.' Anna spoke in spurts. 'I have an . . . appointment later. What if they . . . figure out what I . . . know—'

'Sit, Anna. Please. Before you fall.' Harper stood ready to catch her.

Finally, Anna sat.

'Listen. Those men have no idea that you heard their conversation. But even if they did, it's all right. They aren't villains. The second man you heard – he does research at the Center. He's my friend.' But Anna must have misunderstood. Why would Ron tell Wyatt that she could help find the stolen drugs? Or that he'd 'take care of her'. He'd said on the phone that he had a lot to talk to her about, that it was complicated. Clearly, he did, and it was.

But something else nagged at Harper: Larry. When he'd come to her office, he'd said that Graham had been dispensing the drug dosages for his research group. That Graham's drugs were part of their study. But the vial in Graham's bag had been stolen, not part of a study. So which was it? Was Larry trying to find legitimate test drugs or stolen ones? Harper had suspicions but not facts. And there were five minutes until class; the dean would be waiting. She had to leave. 'Anna? We have to go.'

Anna blinked rapidly. 'Loot, I swear. Those people at the Neurology Center –they did something to Graham. I know it. He never would have jumped—'

'Anna.' Harper looked into her eyes. 'Your doctors at the Center are excellent. They aren't going to hurt you.' She was pretty sure she was right.

'OK. Don't believe me. But I'm telling you, something's going on there, and if they find out what I know, I could end up like Graham.' Upset, Anna stood too quickly.

Harper caught her as she fell and held her up, positioning her comfortably on the couch. She was late for class, but, as she hurried down the steps to the Arts Quad, she called Ron on her cell. She had a lot of questions, but Ron wasn't available. Harper got his voicemail, left a message and ran into White Hall, climbed four flights of stairs and rushed into the hallway where the dean waited, scowling.

Class was a jumble of harrumphing by the dean, a brief talk by a grief counselor from Health Services and an unsuccessful

attempt by Harper to open a discussion about Graham and his suicide. Despite her assignment, no one had prepared anything and no one volunteered to talk.

'Nothing? Not one of you wants to say anything?'

Fourteen students had shown up; fourteen pairs of eyes diverted from Harper's.

Gwen squirmed. 'It's too personal.'

Pam nodded agreement.

'OK. Then write it down. Use the rest of the hour to write about what happened.'

Shuffling. Chairs scraping the floor. Students settling down to work.

Harper sat at her desk beside the fan. The assignment had nothing to do with Archeology; still, it was important. The group needed to acknowledge their own pain as well as their fallen comrade.

Esoso stared out the window, writing nothing, finally scrawling on his paper, 'Dead is dead. I have nothing to say,' and walking out.

Larry left next. On the way out, he leaned too close. 'Hey, Loot.' His voice was low. 'I wonder if you found that study sheet? You know, the page numbers Graham had?'

'Sorry.' Harper shook her head and took his paper, a jagged, almost illegible composition.

Monique had trouble writing; she said she'd hurt her arm in a fall. The gauze of her bandage was, no surprise, bright pink, matching the rest of her outfit. Monique wrote about a different color, though – the color of blood; about how deep crimson now permeated her visions, even her dreams.

Shaundra's piece described a classroom haunted by the spirit of a troubled, hovering soul. Jeremy's detailed the moment in which Graham's body made impact with the concrete below, describing in graphic detail what occurred to each of Graham's individual body parts. Pam wrote about the incident from a grasshopper's point of view; it was, he'd thought, the end of days.

Kevin was the last to hand in his paper. It was a pencil drawing of an agonized face.

Back in her office, Harper found Anna just as she'd left her. Harper sat at her desk, staring out the window at the heavy clouds blanketing the sky. Even in the middle of the day, the

light was dim and bleak. Like her mood. Get up, she told herself. Go out. But she wanted company. No, not just company; she wanted Hank, the pre-accident Hank.

Her office phone startled her.

'You called?' Ron sounded warm and untroubled. Not like a man about to feed her to the fish. 'Everything OK? You're not canceling tonight, are you?'

Tonight? Oh right. Dinner. 'No, nothing that serious.'

'What's up?'

'Not much. Just that I've learned I'm in grave danger because of some stolen drugs.'

'No, really. Why did you call?' Ron sounded impatient.

'I'm serious. Did you by any chance tell Dr Wyatt I'd help you get the drugs back?'

A sigh. 'Harper, you're not making sense. Look, we said we'd talk over dinner. Why don't we wait till then and I'll explain everything.'

'But Graham's pills – they'd definitely been stolen, right?'

'Yes. An entire bin was taken. They were from that bin.'

'And the drug is supposed to help people learn, right?'

Another sigh. 'Yes. It enhances learning and memory, stimulates the frontal lobe.'

'So the pills couldn't cause someone to kill himself, right?'

'What?' Ron stopped to cough. 'Where did you get that—'

'Could they?'

'Of course not. In proper doses, the drug is completely benign. With minimal side effects.'

Harper released a breath. 'And Graham Reynolds – was he a suspect in the theft?'

'Harper, I really don't want to go into this now—'

'I need to know.'

'Yes. He was a suspect. He had knowledge of and access to the bins. But he wasn't the only—'

'He had access because he dispensed the drugs?'

'I'm sorry. What?'

'Graham was the guy who gave his test group their pills—'

'No, no. Our staff gives out the doses, individually. No student dispenses drugs under any circumstances. Where did you get that idea?'

Where? Well, from Larry. Who'd obviously lied. Which probably meant that the drugs in Graham's bag – and the drugs

Larry had been looking for – weren't being tested in some study; they were, in fact, the drugs that had been stolen. Which meant that both Graham and Larry had some part in the theft.

'Look, Harper, you understand how sensitive this is, don't you?'

Harper didn't answer. Ron continued talking, but she wasn't listening. She was thinking, staring at the papers stacked on her desk. Larry's illegible scrawl was near the top. She pulled it out, looked at it. Was Larry a drug thief? Just like Graham, he'd had opportunity – he was involved with the trials, had access to the bin. Maybe Larry, not Graham, was the thief. Maybe he'd been selling the pills. And Graham had been a customer, and the money in his book bag hadn't been for rent but for drugs. Or maybe they'd been stealing and dealing together, room-mates and business partners? Harper recalled the brash way Larry had leaned across her desk, breathing into her face, asking for those numbers, even though she'd already told him she didn't have them.

The numbers. Why were they so important?

'Hey, Ron.' She interrupted, had no idea what he'd been talking about. 'Do you know anything about a list of numbers?'

'Numbers?'

'I found a page of numbers with Graham's things. I've still got it – I was going to toss it. I mean, it's just scrap paper, but a student has been looking for it. Thing is, that student is also involved in your drug trials. And he was Graham's room-mate. Do you think the numbers could be related to the theft?'

'Numbers? Related how?' Obviously, he didn't.

'I guess I'm over-thinking.'

'Harper, look. I'm late for a meeting. Try to put all this aside until we talk later, OK? Eight thirty.'

Harper hung up, confused. She leaned on her arms, trying to piece together murders, rapes, arson, suicide and stolen pills. When she stood to go, she noticed Anna, lying on her sofa, unmoving. Damn – even if she couldn't move, Anna had heard everything Harper had just said. She tried to replay her part of the conversation, couldn't remember it exactly. But she knew she'd asked Ron about the stolen drugs. And about Graham being a suspect in the theft. And about the possible connection between the drug and the deaths. Oh Lord. This wasn't good. Anna would draw inferences and worry even more. Harper had forgotten the

girl was even in the room. Like Anna had said, when cataplectic, she blended into the background, like furniture.

Harper's cell phone rang as she was watching Anna, wondering how much longer she'd lie there.

'Where have you been?' It was Vicki. 'You never return my calls.'

Harper didn't offer excuses. 'Sorry.'

'Don't apologize. It won't work. But I just had a double cancellation.' Vicki was a dentist. 'So drop what you're doing and come to lunch.'

Harper hesitated. She had nothing to do and, truth was, despite Trent's assertions, she missed Vicki.

'Good. Lost Dog. Fifteen minutes?'

Harper couldn't just leave Anna there. She turned, checking on her. Anna's eyes were open. When she saw Harper looking at her, she sat up, smoothed her hair and grabbed her book bag.

'Give me twenty.' Harper motioned Anna to wait; she was getting off the phone.

But Anna didn't wait. She mouthed, 'Thanks, Loot,' and dashed out the door.

'Anna? Just a second—' Phone in hand, Harper hurried after her. But Anna was already gone.

Ron knew she couldn't be home, but he knocked the knocker and rapped on the door repeatedly, loudly, just in case. Then he looked over his shoulder, making sure no one was around.

No one was.

Cautiously, he tried the door. Locked. So, as if looking for Harper, he strolled around to the back of the house. Casually, in case somebody passed, he stepped over knee-high weeds and unmowed grass. The place was neglected, almost dilapidated. He liked Victorian homes, appreciated the classic lines in this one. But, Christ, it was a heap. It needed a monumental amount of work. What had Harper been thinking when she'd bought it? It had to have been her husband's idea; he looked the burly construction-worker type. After all, wasn't that how he'd gotten hurt? Repairing the roof? Ron glanced up at the steep-sloped shingles from which Hank must have fallen, saw the height of the drop. Whew. It was a miracle he'd survived.

Ron kept walking, passed a gazebo, made his way to the

back of the place where, surprisingly, there was a modern, newly constructed deck, complete with a hot tub. The thing was sturdy and probably useful, but bizarrely out of place on this elegant old house. Like Air Jordans on a dowager. At least it was in the back where nobody would see it. And, even better, it led to a back entrance.

Ron crossed the yard to the deck, eager to get this visit over with. He wasn't comfortable breaking into Harper's home, especially because he was certain he wouldn't find anything there. But Wyatt held the purse strings, and Wyatt had insisted. In fact, he'd threatened to search the house himself, and, given Wyatt's jitters, Ron couldn't allow that. In fact, Wyatt was too nervous. A liability to their work. When this was over, Ron would have to make some changes. But one crisis at a time. First, he'd look through Harper's house for the pills, although he couldn't imagine that she'd have them. Obviously, she wasn't a dealer or a user. But what had Wyatt said? 'Statistically, she's got to be part of it. Too many roads lead to her for it to be mere coincidence.'

Wyatt. He knew zip about women. Harper was the kind whose neck got blotchy. She blushed. Women like her couldn't hide their emotions, couldn't lie. No, the only way Harper had the drugs was if she didn't know she had them. Maybe holding boxes for a student. But deliberately stashing them? Not possible. When he'd told her about the stolen drugs, she'd had no idea. She wasn't involved. He knew women. He could tell.

He skipped up the steps to the deck, thinking about the kind of woman Harper was, her direct gaze, her lack of deception. No question, she had an allure. He hadn't expected to be attracted to her; she wasn't like other women in his life – definitely not his ex-wives. Harper was unconcerned with appearances, couldn't be bothered to fuss with her hair, wore it short. No make-up, no nail polish. She wasn't girlie. Didn't play games. Harper was – what was the word? Wholesome? No, edgier than that. Stubborn? Feisty? And her limp? Well, on her, with that taut body and defined muscles, the limp was incredibly sexy. No question, Ron was in this for more than business. He pictured her limping toward him, naked, swaying as she moved, and he was so absorbed that he didn't notice the broken glass on the wood of the deck until he was standing on it.

'Damn.' Ron looked around, saw a broken pane on the half-opened kitchen door.

Had someone broken in? Stiffening, he looked over his shoulder at the yard, saw no one.

'Harper?'

He didn't expect or get an answer. Cautiously, he swung the door open, peered inside, saw no one in the kitchen.

'Hello? Anybody here?'

He stood, listening. Cautiously, he moved through the house, forgetting, for a moment, that he was there to look for the drugs. And then it occurred to him. Maybe someone had already come looking for them. Maybe that was what the broken glass was about.

But the glass might have nothing to do with the drugs. Harper had just been mugged; her attacker might have come after her again. Damn, when he'd talked to her not half an hour ago, she'd been in her office on campus. But what if she'd come home afterwards? And someone had followed her?

Harper was a combat vet. She could protect herself, might even be armed. Ron froze at that idea, but decided that if she discovered him in the house, he'd simply explain that he'd come inside because he'd seen the broken window and been concerned about her. Which wasn't entirely false.

Then again, she might not discover him, might not be able to. Ron stood still, struck by the realization that Harper might be hurt. Might even be dead.

Above him, the ceiling creaked. Again. Then again. Footsteps? Was it Harper?

Ron dashed out of the kitchen, looking for the stairway. If Harper was up there, why hadn't she answered the door or called back when he'd yelled her name?

Probably because the person upstairs wasn't Harper. Ron stopped at the bottom of the steps. Damn. Forget Wyatt, and forget searching the house; the shadows and creaks were getting to him. But now there were more noises, this time from outside. Someone was fiddling with the front door. Christ. Someone was upstairs and someone else was downstairs. Where was Harper? Why was the world converging on her house? He looked into the foyer, saw a silhouette on a shade of a dining-room window. Someone was messing with the windows, looking for a way in.

Ron flew, took the stairs two at a time, seeking a place to

hide. At the top of the steps, he saw a sunlit, unpainted room with a crib and a rocking chair. Nothing big enough to hide behind. Wait – whoa. A crib? Was Harper expecting? He blinked, considering that possibility as harsh whispers rose from downstairs. Jesus. People were in the house, walking around. Ron rushed down the hall, opened a door, found not a room but a tiny overstuffed closet bursting with khakis and grays. Harper's clothes, the colors of shadows. Not enough space for him. Looking over his shoulder, he ran on and found the bedroom, considered scooting under the bed, but stepped instead into what turned out to be a gutted bathroom. Fine. It would do. Locking the door behind him, Ron crouched where the bathtub used to be, grabbed his cell phone and called Wyatt, got his voicemail, left a whispered but spirited message. Damn, what if the intruders saw his bike outside? Would they come looking for him? No, they'd assume it belonged to Harper. Even so, he couldn't afford to be found. His back to the wall, Ron grabbed a rusted piece of a water pipe for defense and waited, listening to angry voices and unexplained thumps. And thinking of creative ways to strangle Wyatt.

Monique didn't like the idea, but Larry insisted. To tell the truth, even though he was two inches shorter than she was, he scared her a little. Ever since he'd started taking those pills, his moods had been unpredictable, all over the place. Playful one minute; brutal the next. And bossy. Lately, they argued about everything. And now, on the way to the house, he was driving too fast. Monique had to say something. He could kill them both.

'Slow down.'

Larry sped up. He ran a stop light, going sixty miles an hour up Buffalo. A twenty-five zone.

'Larry. Slow the fuck down.'

He accelerated again. Larry was scaring her. Something was definitely wrong with him. She clung to the armrests and kept her mouth shut. When had Larry gone from a Cuddly Monkey to Controlling Ape? Was it when Graham jumped? No, before that. But when didn't matter. Monique sat pinned to her seat, held her breath and braced for the impact of sudden death.

But they didn't die. They made it around town and across campus to the Loot's house and parked in some bushes. Hanshaw

Street was too quiet, too creepy, closed in by overgrown shady trees.

'Sit there.' Larry pointed to a swinging bench on the front porch. 'Keep watch. If anybody comes, warn me.'

Oh, really? She was supposed to stay outside with all the spiderwebs and bugs? 'No way.'

Larry stopped and looked at her. 'What the hell, Monique?'

'I'm not staying here by myself.' Who did he think he was, ordering her around?

'Don't piss me off, Monique. I'm warning you—'

'Fuck you, Larry. You're nobody.'

As soon as she said he was nobody, Monique knew she shouldn't have. Larry seemed to inflate, Hulk-like. His eyes got weird, his gaze got dull; even though he was looking at her, it seemed like he didn't see her anymore.

Monique backed away from him and kept talking as if she'd never said it. Changing the subject. 'What if she comes home? What'll we do?' It seemed to work; Larry's eyes came back into focus. 'What if she walks in on us?'

Larry thought that if Monique asked one more question, he'd bash her skull in.

He glared, but Monique chattered on, oblivious.

'She might, you know. She might show up. How do you know she won't? What if she sees your car in the bushes? What if—'

She stopped mid-question, gasping as Larry yanked her hair, pulling tight.

'I told you to shut up.'

Monique's eyes teared with pain, but she wasn't going to let Larry push her around. She clawed her fingers, reached her unbandaged hand around and grabbed at his crotch, squeezing as hard as she could. Larry yowled, released her hair and stomped up the path, staggering just a little. Popping a pill as he went. Monique rubbed her sore scalp. She was mostly positive that Larry had been cheating on her. His touch was different – rougher, as if he was pretending she was somebody else. He even kissed different. And since Graham's jump, Larry had been a complete ass. It was as if the guy's death didn't even bother him; all he talked about were the pills and the money. He had to find the pills. He needed the money. Meantime, Larry was swallowing whatever pills he had, doing things that were risky

and rash and made no sense. He pushed her into helping him, made her do things. Shit, her arm still hurt from that last thing. And now this. Suddenly, he'd decided they had to break into the Loot's house.

She reached into her pocket for a Lifesaver, sucked on one as she looked around. The place was old, rambling. Kind of crumbling, although someone was working to fix it up. The front porch and latticework were new, painted a cheerful sky-blue. Even so, the building looked unfinished and off balance. Haunted. Monique had a bad feeling about being there. She wanted to leave and hurried to catch up to Larry as he stepped on to the porch.

'How do we even know the Loot has them?'

'Graham had them with him in class. But they weren't there when I went back up to get them because she took his book bag. She must have them.'

'But how do we know they're here in the house?'

'Because they aren't anyplace else.'

'But you haven't looked everywhere else—'

'No, Monique.' Lord, she was annoying. He faced her, determined to stop her infernal blithering. 'You're correct. I personally have not looked literally everywhere else. But I checked out our apartment. I tore his room apart looking for a copy. There was nothing remotely resembling numbers. Nothing. Zip.'

'But that doesn't mean—'

'Between the three of us, we've looked all over. In her office. In Graham's book bag. Nothing. So that leaves her house. They must be here somewhere.'

'Not necessarily – not if she threw them out. I mean, she doesn't know what they are. She might have thought they were just a list of random numbers and tossed them in the trash. Or maybe she gave them to the police—'

'Shut up, Monique. I swear, I'll break your fucking neck.'

He meant it, too. He was real tired of Monique. He thought of that waitress. The fire he felt with her. The things he'd done to her. Just remembering got him pumped. The fact was that Monique was boring. Screwing her wasn't even interesting anymore, didn't do it for him. Once he got this pill thing taken care of, he'd dump her. Meantime, he had work to do. He tried the door. Locked. No big deal; he checked out the porch windows. Because of the heat, they were open, covered only

with screens. One of which came loose as he jimmied it and, just like that, they were in the dining room, standing in dim light, looking around. The wallpaper had been completely peeled off; the hutch and table were covered with drop cloths. The Loot was redecorating.

'Shh—' Monique grabbed his arm. 'Listen – did you hear that?'

He listened, heard nothing. Started for the hallway, but she wouldn't let go of him.

'Wait. Larry, did you hear that? Like footsteps.'

'Get off me, Monique.' Larry shoved her, walked away. 'Go outside. Keep watch like I told you to.'

'No, I'm serious.' Monique ran after him, clinging. Whispering. 'I think somebody's here.'

Christ, he wanted to kill her right here. Strangle her and watch her fat pink tongue pop out. Damn Monique. But to shut her up, he stood still for a few seconds, listening. 'I don't hear anything.' Peeling her hand off his arm once again, he started across the room. The floor creaked under his feet, and Monique gasped, grabbing Larry yet again.

'Jesus Christ, Monique. Calm the fuck down.'

Monique was breathless. 'Where are you going?'

'Why are you fucking whispering?'

Whispering? She hadn't realized it. It was the place. Too dark. Too crooked. They shouldn't be there. 'I don't like it here, Larry. Let's just go.'

'You know what, Monique? Nobody asked you to come with me. You insisted. Or doesn't your idiot brain remember that? Whatever. Just wait right here. Just fucking let me do what I came here to do.' Larry stormed off, leaving Monique alone.

Sunlight didn't penetrate the dining room, and oddly shaped shadows lurked all around, made her skin prickle despite the heat. Wait right there? Uh uh. No way was she going to stay in that room. Instead, she climbed back out the window on to the porch where at least there was light and she could sit on the bench and wait.

The bench was one of those rocking things; she swung back and forth, wondering how long Larry would be. Man, she was sick of him, his moods, his pimples, his pills, his short height and his huge temper. The things he made her do. Her head still smarted where he'd pulled her hair. It was time to break up

with him. But, for now, she waited in the heat, swaying back and forth, lulled by the motion, relaxing, closing her eyes.

She opened them as the knife penetrated her throat, and she recognized the person holding it. While her blood spurted, she tried to ask, 'What are you doing here?' and, 'Why are you cutting me?' But, with her neck so deeply sliced, Monique couldn't speak, so she died with her eyes still open, her questions unanswered. Even unasked.

Vicki's jaw dropped. 'What the hell happened to your face? Bar fight?'

'You should see the other guy.' Harper smiled. 'I like your hair.'

Vicki had dyed it again. Auburn this time. And she'd cut off about five inches; now it was short, spiky. Funky. Like Harper's.

'Do you? It's the new me.'

They hugged a greeting, Vicki, taller than Harper, slouching to embrace. Harper was surprisingly glad to see her. She'd missed Vicki, her broad grin, her painted red nails and bright red lipstick that often clashed with her clothes. Vicki, despite her new do, remained rock solid, unchanged.

'So really. What happened to your face?'

Apparently, Trent hadn't told her about the mugging. Maybe he'd been too hungover.

'Not a big deal.' Harper didn't want to go into it yet again. 'Somebody mugged me.'

'You got mugged, but it's no big deal? Oh God, that guy sure picked the wrong victim. Did you go after him? Of course you did. How bad did you hurt him?'

'Let's go inside.' Harper led the way into the Lost Dog Café, where a young guy in jeans seated them and recommended the special veggie chili.

Harper picked up a menu; Vicki took it from Harper's hands, dropped it on to the table. 'Uh uh. You're not looking at the menu until you tell me why you haven't returned my calls.'

Harper's neck got hot. 'Sorry. No excuses. It's just the same old, same old.' The same old suicides, muggings, murdered waitresses, stolen drugs. Oh, and husband with a damaged brain.

Vicki didn't back off. 'How's Hank?'

Vicki's eyes probed, genuinely concerned. And familiar. And comforting. It was good to see her again. Harper had missed

eir daily breakfasts and walks, their easy companionship.
Vicki had been with her when Hank had fallen, had spent long
hours with her in the emergency room, had stayed by her side
as the doctors gave her the news. Vicki had been a steadfast,
reassuring presence during the onset of Hank's ordeal. So what
had happened? How had they lost touch, not talking for weeks?

In the back of her mind, Trent piped up, answering her questions, elaborating on Vicki's 'thing' for Hank. Harper began
talking, drowning Trent out.

'He's doing OK.' She stopped herself from urging Vicki to
visit him. Not that she believed Trent, but just in case. 'Little
by little.'

'So back up. When were you mugged?' Vicki's voice had its
usual creamy tone. 'Why didn't you call me?'

Harper hesitated. Where should she start? With the mugging?
Graham's suicide? The horrid flashbacks? Chelsea's murder?
Or Trent's drunken assertion that Vicki was attracted to Hank
who, by the way, had recently mentioned that he was horny?

'Ready, ladies?' The waiter appeared out of nowhere. He
looked exotic, multi-ethnic. His wrist bore a Chinese character
tattoo.

Vicki ordered a tofu burger and iced tea. Harper still hadn't
looked at the menu, ordered the chili. They sat silent for a
while. Out of sync.

'We should go shopping,' Vicki tried. 'Get massages.
Pedicures – no, makeovers.'

Harper didn't respond. The suggestions were ludicrous.

'Makeovers would be fun. And, honestly, you could use a
new look. Enough military drab, Harper. Get some clothes with
bright, cheerful colors. You'll feel better.'

Harper said nothing.

'What?' Vicki persisted. 'You think that's superficial?'

'I don't need a makeover. New clothes won't change anything,
and, besides, I don't—'

'You don't wear bright colors. I know all about your camouflage chic. But that's nonsense. You should. You'd look spunky
in red or yellow.'

Harper didn't answer, had explained to Vicki about her wardrobe many times.

'Come on. This is Ithaca, not Iraq. Bright colors won't draw
the attention of snipers.'

'You never know.' Harper closed her eyes, saw the boy with no face. 'So what's new with you?' she changed the subject. 'Pulled any wisdom teeth lately?'

'Don't be like that, Harper. It was just an idea, a way to have fun.'

More awkward silence.

'OK, cut the crap, Harper. Something's eating at you, and it isn't just Hank's condition. I can see it on your face.'

She saw it on her face? Reflexively, Harper's hand went to her cheek, feeling for the something.

'Dammit, Harper. Talk to me. I ask how Hank is; you say, "OK." I say, "Let's go do something to cheer ourselves up"; you say, "No." That's it, the whole extent of our conversation, after all these weeks? And don't blame it on the war and how you don't feel comfortable around people. I'm not "people". Our friendship is deeper than that. But since the accident, you've – I don't know. Withdrawn. Disappeared.'

She had withdrawn? *She* had disappeared? Harper stiffened. No way, it had been Vicki who'd done the disappearing, never visiting Hank. Not stopping by. Calling only rarely when she knew Harper would be out. Not that Harper had returned those calls. 'What do you want from me, Vicki?' Her voice was chilly.

'I knew you'd react like that, all pissy and defensive—'

'I am not all pissy—'

'Listen, Harper. Here's some news: you weren't the only one affected by Hank's fall. Trent and I – things haven't been easy for us, either. And I want my friend back. I want to drop by with scones and share bottles of wine. I want to be the way we were.'

Harper remained quiet, hearing echoes of her own voice in Vicki's. She wanted their old lives back, too. And Vicki was right; lately, she had been too self-absorbed. But, hell, what did Vicki expect? That, with Hank so badly injured, Harper would still meet her for ladies' lunches or trips to the farmer's market? Why didn't Vicki understand? Harper stared at Vicki, saw thin spidery lines around her eyes, vulnerability all over her face. And suddenly, she understood: Vicki needed a friend. They both did.

So, hesitantly at first, Harper listed the events of the last few days, omitting only the conversation with Trent. Vicki sat riveted, not speaking until Anna finally woke up in Harper's office.

Jow.' Vicki reached across the table and squeezed Harper's
d. 'My God. It's a good thing you're Superwoman. Nobody
e could deal with all that.'
Two huge glasses of iced tea landed on the table. 'Your
Junches are coming right up.'
Vicki gazed into her drink, diddled with her straw.
'What? You OK?'
'Me? Sure.' Vicki took extra napkins from the container and
passed a few to Harper. 'Compared to you, anyhow.'
'Compared to me? Why? What's going on?'
'Harper, I can't complain, not after hearing what you've been
through. Suicide, murder, a mugging – not to mention Hank.
No, everything's peachy with me.'
'Go to hell.'
'How did our lives become such disasters?'
'What's your disaster?'
Vicki sucked on her straw. 'Trent. He's a mess. A drunk.
Hasn't been sober since the accident.'
Harper remembered Trent gulping Scotch in her kitchen.
'You know how pumped Trent and Hank were, being up for
tenure?'
Of course she did. Before the accident, Hank and Trent had
constantly razzed each other, trying to make light of the
competition. But they'd known that only one of them would
receive tenure; the other would probably have to move on.
'Well, that was nothing. Now, Trent's obsessed with tenure.
It's all he talks about. And he doesn't mention Hank. Ever. If
Hank's name comes up, Trent dives into the liquor cabinet.'
'Tofu burger.' The plates slid on to the table. 'Chili. Anything
else, ladies? Enjoy.'
The place was filling up. Four men sat across from them; a
couple ate behind them. Somewhere, a baby cried. People waited
in line for tables to open up.
'You know –' Harper waited until the waiter walked away
– 'what happened to Hank wasn't Trent's fault. I've told him
that.'
'So have I. Don't you think I've told him that? But . . .' She
shifted on the seat to better face her friend. 'Harper, this is
beyond guilt. Trent's changed. He's not the same man.'
'Of course he is—'
'No. It's not just the tenure thing.' Vicki sipped her tea. 'This

goes way beyond work. He wakes up and has a beer for bre
fast. He's bitter and depressed, and, frankly, I'm scared.'
    'You're scared. Of Trent?' The idea seemed preposterous.
Harper exhaled on him, he'd fall.
    'Of him. For him. Whatever.'
    'As in, you think he might hurt himself?'
    Vicki shook her head. 'I don't think so; dead men don't get
tenure.' She smiled sadly. 'Trent and I – we have no relationship
anymore. We don't talk. Don't have sex. He's not the guy I married.
Poof. First Hank. Now Trent. In a way, they're both gone.'
    Harper closed her eyes, heard distant gunfire. Vicki took a
bite of her burger and chomped.
    'Trent's not gone, Vicki. Maybe it's a phase. I mean he had
a bad trauma.' Harper lifted a spoonful of chili to her mouth,
wondering if Trent had flashbacks, too. Maybe he drank to stop
them.
    Vicki said something, but her voice was muffled, full of
French fries.
    'Sorry?'
    'I can't, Harper. I can't live with him anymore.'
    'What?' It was all Harper could manage to say. Trent and
Vicki had been married for – what? Fourteen years? More?
They'd been part of her life since she'd met Hank, were Hank's
best friends, a single unit. 'You're not serious.'
    'He's unbearable. He gets drunk and belligerent and accuses
me of all kinds of stuff.'
    'Like what?' Like having a crush on my husband? Harper
crushed crackers into her chili bowl.
    'Like anything. He gets so mad, the veins pop out in his
head, and I'm scared he'll have a stroke.'
    'What's he mad about?'
    'Here's one: he insists I'm having an affair.' Vicki chewed
as she talked.
    'An affair?' Harper swallowed chili too fast, almost choked.
Was Vicki going to confess to a relationship with Hank? She
remembered him insisting, 'Vicki. Screwed.'
    'He's absolutely convinced. He doesn't believe anything I
say—'
    'Well, are you?'
    'What? Having an affair? Are you kidding?' Vicki dodged.
    'Because, if you are, you can't blame him for suspecting—'

. I'm not.' Her tone was forced. 'Of course I'm not.' She
.d away, nipping off the tip of another French fry. 'Not
.ore.'

Harper froze, spoon in the air.

Vicki crossed her legs, toyed with an earring. 'Last winter.
had a thing with somebody. Trent knows about it. It didn't
last long – a few months. It's over.'

Harper told herself not to jump to conclusions or out of her
chair to yank Vicki's hair out. There were lots of men in the
world besides Hank. And if it wasn't Hank, it wasn't her business. Even so, she wanted to grab Vicki by her auburn spikes
and demand that she tell her whether the 'somebody' she'd had
a 'thing' with had been her husband.

Instead, she maintained a calm, as if she were barely curious.
'Who was it?'

Vicki met her eyes. Her mouth opened, then closed. She
grabbed her glass of iced tea. 'I can't tell you.'

Harper clenched her jaw, deciding whether or not to choke
her.

'It wouldn't be right.'

'Why not?'

'Because – well, because you know him.'

Oh God. It was true?

'And I don't want to mess up his reputation. There'd be . . .
repercussions.'

'What, you think I'll put it on the six o'clock news?'

'It's just . . . I better not say, OK?' Vicki sipped.

So. Harper knew him. Was Vicki playing with her, hinting
that her affair had been with Hank, making her squirm?

'How well do I know him?'

'What?'

Eyes drilling into Vicki's, she repeated the question slowly,
enunciating clearly.

'Oh. Not very.' She sounded cautious. Lying?

Go ahead. Ask her, Harper told herself. Just come out and
ask. But to ask would be to admit that Harper didn't trust her
husband. That he'd given her reason to doubt him and suspect
that he might cheat. And, especially if Vicki had betrayed her,
Harper didn't want to give her that satisfaction. She formed the
question, but stopped herself.

'Anyhow, Trent thinks I'm cheating again. He interrogates

me every time I go out. Where were you? Who were you
He calls my beautician to see if I really had an appointn
He checks the mileage in my car to see if it matches with wh
I said I went.'
'That's freaky.'
'Oh, but that's nothing. Listen to this. He smells me. I'm
serious. He pretends he's hugging me, but really he's smelling
me to see if I've taken an unexplained shower. You know, to
wash away some guy's scent.'
Yikes. Harper pictured Trent sniffing at Vicki for traces of
another man.
'I can't live this way.'
Of course she couldn't, not with Trent's nose at her neck.
Maybe his comments about Vicki and Hank were just part of
a larger obsession, an invention of Trent's jealous mind. He
must have had some kind of breakdown after the accident.
Hank's fall seemed like the first in a row of dominoes. Hank,
Trent, Vicki. Who'd topple next? Oh, right: Harper. Her head
ached. She smelled ashes.
Maybe they all needed makeovers.
Vicki took a breath. 'Anyhow, I needed to tell you . . .' She
picked up another fry, bit its head off.
'Of course, you did.' Harper touched her friend's arm, noticed
the softness of Vicki's skin. And pictured Hank touching it,
Hank noticing its softness. She heard him again: 'Screwed.
Vicki.' Stop it, she told herself. Nothing happened. The whole
idea of Vicki and Hank was a creation of post-breakdown Trent,
without merit or substance. Even so, the image nagged at her,
buzzing like a rabid mosquito.
After lunch, Vicki and Harper hugged goodbye, promising
not to lose touch again. Vicki waved from her Mini Cooper and
drove off to fill cavities. Harper lingered on Aurora Street before
climbing on to her Ninja. The air was perfectly still, suspended.
Not a car drove by. Clouds still hovered above, darkening the
sky, but the air didn't smell like rain.

Harper stuffed her bag and Hank's computer into the storage
case, straddled her Ninja and looked around. The street, Ithaca,
the world – everything was altered, off kilter. Nothing was
stable. Even Trent and Vicki were breaking up. Harper didn't
feel ready to start her bike, didn't want to take her feet off the

ground yet. While she hesitated, centering herself, her cell phone
rang. LESLIE.
'You didn't call me. You were supposed to check in.'
She was? Harper didn't remember.
'I'm fine.' She reminded herself that Leslie was her shrink. She
didn't need to say she was fine. 'Nothing big. Murmurs mostly.
Distant gunfire.' But no more freshly warm pieces of Marvin on
her belly. No visits from Sameh or the boy without a face. 'They're
not gone. But on the perimeter, not right in my face.'
'Hmm.'
Hmm?
'Harper, I want to try something with you.'
Harper waited.
'It's called Rapid Eye Movement Therapy.'
Harper had heard of Rapid Eye Movement. 'Wait. REM.
Does that have something to do with sleep?'
'Yes, REM occurs when people dream. But we'd do this
while you're awake. It sometimes helps PTSD symptoms.'
Leslie had a cancellation the next afternoon, wanted Harper
to come and talk about it. Maybe, Harper dared to think, just
maybe there was hope for ending her flashbacks. And if there
was hope for her flashbacks, maybe there was hope for other
things, too. Like for Hank. Their future. Harper started her bike
and rode home, humming oldies, resting her mind, focusing on
the open road.
Halfway through her rendition of 'Stand By Me', Harper
pulled into the driveway, parked her Ninja, hung her helmet on
the bike and her sack on her shoulder. Walking to the house,
she glanced at the porch and was surprised to see someone
there, sitting on the swing. Wearing all pink. Monique? But
what was Monique doing there? As far as she knew, her students
didn't know where she lived, let alone feel free to drop by
uninvited.
'Monique? Is that you?' Harper called from the path.
Monique didn't answer. She didn't seem to hear.
Harper continued toward the house, watching the person in
pink, seeing the bandage on her arm. Yes, it was definitely
Monique. She was slouching, asleep.
'Monique?' Harper called gently, not wanting to startle her.
It wasn't until she climbed the steps to the porch that she noticed
a puddle clotting on the blue wooden slats, not until she rounded

the banister that she saw a large dark stain along the neckline of Monique's no longer pink shirt.

'Monique—' Harper dashed over, trying to rouse the tall, muscular girl, feeling for a pulse. Then, backing away, she tripped down her porch steps into the overgrown grass, pawing through her bag for her phone even though Monique was beyond help. Monique was dead. Murdered, and the killer might still be around.

Harper rooted around in her bag, fumbling under students' papers and Hank's computer while she scanned the property, the copse of trees beside the house. Was someone lurking there? Across the street, in those hedges – did something just move? Harper spun around, braced for ambush, hearing sniper fire, smelling blood.

But where was her damned phone? Frustrated, Harper dumped her entire sack on to the ground. Out came Hank's computer, student papers, faculty memos, Graham's list of numbers, baby wipes, cloves, keys, wallet, the lemon. And half hidden by a water bottle, her cell phone. Her throat tight, heart pounding, she dialed 911, eyeing Monique, seeing Hank unconscious on the hedges. Harper blinked to make him go away. But he didn't. He stayed there, his body splayed atop the dogwoods.

No, she insisted, and she reached into the weeds for something yellow, picked it up, but by then Sameh was crossing the road, walking toward Marvin. Lemon in one hand, phone in the other, Harper ran to warn them, dodging sniper fire. But where were they? Oh God. She smelled burnt flesh, felt stickiness on her belly.

'Nine–one–one. What is your emergency?'

What was her emergency? Seriously?

'I need help—' Harper crouched for cover, had no breath.

'Tell me your name? Where are you, ma'am?'

Where? Rapid gunfire, swarms of flies and smoky dust concealed her exact location. But she was holding a lemon. A lemon? Where was her gun? Why was she holding a lemon? Bite it, Leslie's voice urged. What? Bite the lemon? What for? But she did. She opened her mouth and shoved the thing in, skin and all. And bit down, hard.

Sour juice and bitter rind jolted her taste buds, shocked her

into the moment. Harper blinked, looking around. Christ, how had she gotten behind the hedges?

The voice called out. 'Ma'am? Are you there?'

Harper's lips puckered from the lemon; her words were distorted. 'My student – someone killed her.'

Dazed, Harper emerged from the bushes and stood, recovering, before deliberately approaching Monique. Making sure she was really dead.

'Where are you, ma'am?'

Climbing on to the porch, Harper started to give her address, but didn't finish. She couldn't. She saw a sudden white flash, felt the impact of something slamming her head, but she didn't have time to process either before everything went dark.

'Ma'am?'

Harper had been conscious for a while, but she hadn't let on. She'd stayed flat on the porch with her eyes half shut, playing possum, assessing her situation. Was she a prisoner of war? Was the enemy still there, watching her? The person talking to her – was he really an American? If so, why didn't he address her by rank and title? Cautiously, she opened an eye, looking for a weapon. Seeing only a doormat and blood-spattered blue paint.

Blue paint? Wait. She remembered something about blue paint. Something . . .

'Mrs Jennings? Can you hear me?'

A shoulder descended into view. Wearing a white shirt. With a red cross on it. A paramedic?

Harper blinked. Took a breath. Tried to sit up, thought better of it. Grunted.

'Don't get up. Stay still.'

Harper stared.

'It looks like somebody slammed you with a two by four.'

A what? 'Where?'

'You're at home, ma'am. On your porch.'

The answer confused her. She'd meant where on her body. She hadn't yet located a source of pain; everything hurt. Somewhere, her cell phone was playing a jingle, announcing a call.

'Just lie still. We'll take care of you.'

'No. I'm fine,' Harper tried to say, but her voice was muffled, her words lacked form. Like Hank's, she thought. Hank? Was

Hank calling? No, she remembered; he couldn't be. Oh God, would she be like him now, brain-damaged, unable to talk? What a perfect couple, talking nonsense to each other. The medic messed with her, shining a light in her eyes. When he turned away, Harper tried again to sit, wriggled up, made it this time.

'Ma'am, you need to lie down.'

But Harper wouldn't. She looked around, orienting herself. Remembering. Someone had killed her student. On her front porch. And then they must have attacked her. In just a couple of days – within heartbeats of each other – two of her students had died. Who was doing this? And why? Harper lifted a hand to the side of her head, found a lump. OK, she thought; it's not so bad. She struggled to her feet; the paramedic tried to force her back down.

'Please, ma'am. Stay still. You have a concussion.'

Another one? How many could she get in a week? Was there a limit? A world record?

'But I have to go—'

'No, ma'am.' He interrupted, pressing on her. 'You don't need to go anywhere.'

The guy was pissing her off.

'Yes, I do.' Harper pushed him away.

He took a stance as if he might actually try to overpower her. Wobbly, she faced him, preparing to take him down. Somewhere, her phone was ringing again.

'Mrs Jennings?'

Harper turned too quickly, sent her brain spinning, She nearly fell over.

'What are you doing on your feet?' For a moment, Detective Rivers appeared to have two heads, both of which glared. 'You need to lie down. At least sit.' Detective Rivers – both of her – took Harper by the elbow.

'I told her to lie down. Her skull might be cracked.' The paramedic tried to redeem himself. There were two of him, as well. 'I advised her not to move—'

'I got this. Give us a sec.' The Detectives Rivers led Harper to the steps, sat her down.

Harper looked out at the overgrown yard, covered with police cars and ambulances. Cops, medical workers and crime scene investigators scurried around; a gaggle of gapers stood at the curb; a television crew or two had set up near the street. It was just like

the commotion after Graham's suicide, except that this time it was her front yard. And everything was blurry. Harper shivered, cold. In shock.

Detective Rivers handed Harper her phone. 'You were holding this.'

Harper remembered a lemon. 'I was calling the police—'

'You called nine–one–one. It seems you got knocked out in the middle of the call.'

A man whose Yankees T-shirt was tucked into his jeans walked over, and Rivers introduced Detective Boschi. He was chewing gum.

'I'm cold.' Harper's teeth chattered. 'Can I go inside for a sweater?'

Rivers asked the paramedic for a blanket. Detective Boschi led her to the gazebo beside the house, away from the commotion. The gazebo hadn't been used all year, though, and spiders had taken over. The detectives swung sticks around, clearing away webs, and, finally, they led Harper in, sitting with her on the benches inside.

Shivering despite the blanket and the heat, Harper told them how she'd come home to find Monique dead on the porch, how she had no idea why the young woman was there. She omitted the parts about the suicide bombers and the lemon. As she talked, the detectives made occasional side comments, drawing comparisons, making references to other cases. Harper tried to follow but couldn't. Maybe the spider webs had penetrated her head. Why was it so hard to think?

The detectives huddled together, conferring, and the paramedic came back and checked her pulse, speaking in a soft slow voice as if she were a child. 'Try to relax, ma'am.'

Harper obeyed. Trying to relax, she watched television crews filming reports from the curb and police investigating on her porch. And while the paramedic studied her scalp, she listened in on the detectives.

'. . . wounds are similar,' Rivers said. 'She was slashed like the waitress.'

'Yeah,' Boschi agreed. 'But this doesn't look like a rape. And there's no mutilation or signs of struggle.'

Harper's arm tickled; she looked down, saw a brown spider. Brushed it off. Looked down to see where it landed. And saw spiders everywhere. Red, black, brown, yellow. All shapes, all

sizes. She looked up, found dozens, hundreds more, crawling. Spinning webs. Harper was on her feet, slapping her clothes, shaking the blanket, jumping into the grass.

'Harper?' Rivers called.

'Spiders!'

Knee high in weeds, with double vision, Harper watched four detectives leap out of the gazebo, joining her.

Boschi brushed off his arms. 'Porch is free now.'

Blood still pooled near the swinging bench, but Monique's body had been removed. The detectives sat Harper on a wicker love seat at the other end of the porch, away from the blood.

Boschi leaned against a window frame. Harper noticed that the screen was loose; another thing she'd have to fix.

'You already know,' Detective Rivers began, 'this isn't the first murder of its kind around here.'

Harper tried to ignore the tickling along her back and between her breasts. No spiders, she assured herself, had crept under her clothes.

'But, more to the point, it's not the first connected to you.'

Or inside her thighs. Harper pressed her legs together, trying to smash anything walking there.

'First there was the waitress,' Rivers prompted. 'Chelsea, remember?'

Did she think Harper could forget?

'Now there's this young woman. Monique.' Detective Rivers frowned. 'And again, the victim knew you.'

Harper shivered.

'So. Three deaths in two days. And, as a bonus, you got mugged twice in the same time period. So, it's not rocket science to conclude that you and/or people you know are being targeted.' She paused for emphasis.

Harper repeated the last sentence in her mind. And couldn't quite grasp it.

'Frankly –' Rivers crossed her arms – 'we're not sure yet what we're dealing with. But you should be aware that many serial killers follow patterns in choosing their victims.'

Whoa – serial killers? Harper looked up; the trees, the sky, everything – even her thoughts – were floating clockwise. Was someone she knew a serial killer? Who? Larry popped to mind. After all, Monique had been his girlfriend, Graham his

room-mate. Maybe he'd known Chelsea, too. He volunteered at the Neurology Center, probably went to the coffee shop there. Larry might be connected to all three of the dead.

Harper pictured him – a wiry kid with shaggy hair, bad skin, big eyes. He'd been looking for Graham's book bag, his money and pills. But could he kill? She didn't want to think so. And Monique had been inches taller, had bigger bones; in a fight with Larry, she'd probably win. Besides, Larry couldn't be the only one with connections to the victims – lots of students must have known all three.

But Detective Rivers wasn't finished. '. . . whoever the killer is, he knows you. You are clearly on his radar.'

Without warning, something came up Harper's throat, acidy sweet. And she smelled something metallic and overpowering. Monique's clotting blood? Harper needed to get to the bathroom, fast. She stood and took a step, but tottered unsteadily. No way she'd make it inside. Instead, she turned and thrust herself against the railing, letting half-digested chili fly into the grass. Sweating profusely, she felt less shivery as the paramedic reminded her that nausea was a symptom typical of concussions.

Harper sank back on to the wicker seat, asking again if she could go into the house, wash her face, lie down. Rivers looked at Boschi.

Boschi shrugged. 'The house has been checked out; it's safe. But before you go in, you need to know. Somebody's been in there.'

What did that mean? Had she been robbed? Vandalized?

Boschi chomped on his gum. 'I'll go in with you. You'll need to make sure nothing's missing. Make a list of things that are gone—'

'Harper! Harper!' Vicki stood at the curb, yelling. She'd seen live coverage of the murder on the television in her office waiting room and sped over; now she was annoying police, shouting across their barricade. At Harper's insistence, Detective Rivers let her through. She ran over, hugging Harper, asking questions.

'What happened? Are you all right? Christ. Look at all the blood—'

'Mrs Jennings? Are you ready?' Impatient, Boschi held the door open.

Harper brushed away another invisible spider and took hold

of Vicki's arm. 'Come with me? They said someone's been inside.' She stepped to the door.

'Who did this?' Vicki whispered. 'Do you have any idea?'

Harper shook her head, but again thought of Larry. How he'd pressed her for Graham's money and pills. And for that list of numbers, whatever it was. She ought to look at it more closely, still had it in her bag.

Harper was distracted, thinking about Larry. So she was startled when Vicki gasped, 'What the hell happened?'

Then, looking around her living room, Harper had a pretty clear idea.

The house was a shambles. Drop cloths had been removed and thrown about, cushions tossed off the sofa and chairs upended. Harper moved slowly from room to room, still off balance, holding Vicki's arm and the walls for support.

The hutch in the dining room had been emptied out; china dinner plates and long-stemmed wine glasses, some broken, littered the floor. The kitchen was a mess. The freezer had been emptied. Her stash of rum-raisin ice cream, Dove and Snickers bars dotted the floor, defrosting alongside frozen lima beans and packages of Lean Cuisine. The shelves of the cupboard held only a few cans of soup or beans; everything else – pasta, cake mixes, jars of spaghetti sauce – lay helter-skelter on countertops. Canisters of flour and sugar had been dumped on to the floor.

Harper felt as if she'd been sucker-punched. Who had done this? And why? Her den was topsy-turvy like the living room. Completely ransacked. Down the hall, she opened the door to Hank's office and stopped, gawking.

Every drawer had been pulled from the desk and emptied on to the floor. Every book had been removed from the shelves. Papers were strewn everywhere – files, journals. The desk chair was upside down, the couch overturned. Artwork, paintings and photographs had been ripped from the wall. The room – the only finished room in the house – had literally been torn apart.

Harper cursed, livid, holding on to the wall. Her head throbbed, leg ached, stomach churned; even so, the feeling she was most aware of was rage. Police were still in the house; she heard them upstairs in her bedroom. Oh God. Had the intruders gone through her clothes? Her lingerie? Her old uniforms? Hank's things? Had they opened her jewelry box, stolen his

grandmother's pearl-and-emerald engagement ring? Outraged, she headed for the stairs, but stopped, dizzy. About to be sick again.

'Mrs Jennings?'

'Harper?'

Vicki and the police were calling her. Harper didn't answer – didn't dare open her mouth. As fast as she could, she ran to the bathroom across from Hank's office, trying to make it to the toilet. Realizing that, if she didn't, it didn't much matter; the house was already a catastrophe.

Hand over her mouth, Harper lunged over the bowl just in time. It wasn't until she stood up, wiping her face with a wash-cloth, seeing cough medicine, toothpaste, the entire contents of the medicine cabinet, strewn everywhere, that she looked in the mirror and realized, without making a sound or even a flinch, that she wasn't alone.

In the mirror, she saw someone huddled in corner by the laundry basket, hiding behind the bathroom door.

Harper held the washcloth at her face, not even breathing, watching the dark sneakers in the mirror. For a few measured heartbeats, she stood that way, waiting, watching. If he moved, she'd tackle him, flatten him. Put him in a headlock. Yell for the police; they were right across the hall. But what good were the police? They'd obviously failed to notice this rather signifi-cant detail in the bathroom. Never mind. For now, she had to be cool; she had the advantage of surprise, didn't want to blow it. The guy was behind the door, unaware that she'd seen him. Even so, she shouldn't be too confident; if he'd killed Monique, who was large and formidable, he must be strong. And he might still have the knife. Probably, she shouldn't attack. Probably, she should pretend she hadn't seen him, leave and tell the police he was in there.

Yes, that was the best idea. Walk away. Quickly. And send in the cops.

OK. On the count of three, she'd leave. She counted, making no sudden movements. One. She put the washcloth down, leaving Hank's shaving cream, razor and deodorant in the sink. Slowly, checking the mirror one last time, she turned toward the door. Two. Her bad leg felt like cement, but she stepped forward, keeping the sneakers in her peripheral vision. When

they didn't move, she dared another glance at them, saw blue jeans above them. And something else on the tile floor beside the jeans. Something wet. And red.

Harper didn't get to three. She swung the door back, and there was Larry, propped up against the wall, Harper's nail file protruding from his neck.

Harper and Vicki sat at the kitchen table opposite the two detectives, who, in Harper's vision, occasionally split into four. The boy with no face appeared and disappeared as pieces of Marvin sporadically decorated the walls. Harper pressed an ice bag against her lump, focusing on the cold, not only to ease her pain but also to push away flashbacks. Other people – police, people from the coroner's office, investigators, insurgents, suicide bombers and God knew who else – wandered in and out of the house.

Detective Rivers had blasted two uniformed officers for not finding the body, had apologized profusely to Harper for the inexcusable oversight, had offered again to have her taken to the hospital. When Harper again refused, Boschi asked if any of her possessions had been stolen. Harper blinked mutely. How the hell was she supposed to know if anything had been stolen? She'd only been in the house for a couple of minutes, and every single one of her possessions had been turned upside down or tossed on to the floor.

But the detective asked again.

'I don't know.' Harper knew she was in shock. She'd stopped shivering, but all of her, even her blood, was cold. Her thoughts were muddled and slow.

Detective Rivers asked another question: Did Harper have any idea what Monique or Larry had been doing at her house?

Harper imagined the two of them, Monique waiting on the porch as Larry snuck around, searching. But, suddenly, it wasn't Larry prowling around in the house; it was Trent Manning. After all, just a couple of days ago, she'd caught Trent rifling thought Hank's office. Maybe Trent had come back, desperate to find Hank's papers. Maybe Trent had found the students at the house and confronted them . . .

No. Trent couldn't have killed anyone. Certainly, not over Hank's notes. And if he were going to, it wouldn't be by stabbing; he'd probably pass out if he saw blood. But if not Trent, who could have been there?

Harper didn't get it. Why would Larry and Monique come over? It had to connect with Graham. Again, she replayed Larry's visit to her office, asking her for Graham's book bag. Larry and Monique must have thought she had something of Graham's – something to do with the stolen drugs. And they'd come looking for it. But what was it? And why would they look in her house? Larry had known she'd given Graham's things to the police.

The detective touched Harper's arm. 'Harper? Are you all right?' She was attractive, Detective Rivers. Chocolate skin, round eyes. She was trying to be patient.

Vicki took Harper's hand. 'Would you like a drink, Harper? Some Scotch?'

Harper shook her head.

'She really should go to the hospital.' Boschi chewed. 'She's not right.'

'I agree, Harper. You should get looked at.'

Harper put a hand on her thigh, remembering the pain of her operations. And the terror of the vigil she'd spent beside Hank's bed. No, no hospital.

'Well, then? Do you know why?'

Why? Why what? What was the question? Rivers repeated it. Did she know why the kids had been at her house? Oh, right. That question.

'No,' she answered. 'But I think it was about Graham. The stolen pills.'

'How did you know about that?' Boschi's tone was pointed.

'About what?'

'That they had pills on them.' Rivers' gaze zeroed in on Harper.

'We found a vial in Larry's pants pocket, another in Monique's bag.' Boschi frowned. 'How did you know that?'

'I didn't.' But now that she did, Harper was certain that the pills were at the root of the deaths, and she told the detectives about Larry.

Boschi frowned, chewed hard on his gum. Maybe he didn't believe her. Maybe he thought she was a thief, a drug dealer, a killer. Harper's head hurt; she closed her eyes and saw Monique on the swing and Larry slumped against her bathroom wall. Damn. Why were they dead? They were just kids.

Just kids. But Graham, Monique and Larry weren't typical.

All three had participated in research studies at the clinic, and all three had been in possession of stolen pills. Harper tried to remember who else she'd seen at the clinic. Larry and Monique. Jeremy. And Esoso and his room-mate . . .

Wait. Maybe Larry and Monique hadn't been at the house alone. Maybe a whole swarm of students – a gang including Esoso and Jeremy – had been there. Certainly, the place looked like an entire horde had invaded it. Maybe something had gone wrong, and the gang killed Monique and Larry? But what about Chelsea? Would they have killed her, too?

Harper's head pounded. She was making up scenarios based on nothing. Her students weren't killers. But who else had a reason to ransack her house and kill Monique and Larry? Who else even knew about the drugs? She could think of no one. Well, except Ron. And Dr Wyatt. And the other researchers at the clinic. And, of course, the FDA.

Eyes open again, she clutched an ice bag, refusing to duck for cover even when Marvin exploded right next to her. Think of the coldness, the ice, she ordered herself. You're in the kitchen. Count the tiles on the floor, or the dishes tossed there.

Detective Rivers was watching her. 'Is it?'

Apparently, Harper had missed yet another chunk of conversation. 'Sorry?'

'Your phone? Is that your phone?'

Harper hadn't heard it. Anyhow, it had stopped. It was probably her mother. Or Leslie. It didn't matter.

The detective leaned closer, studying Harper's pupils. The boy with no face kicked her hard under the table, but she didn't react. Harper sat stoic and unmoving, her face inscrutable, watching bodies fall, hearing men scream.

Trent was out cold, reeking of booze on his living room sofa. Harper sank on to an adjacent easy chair, listening to him snore. Her house was a crime scene, and Detective Rivers had positively forbidden her to stay anywhere alone, had even threatened to put her into protective custody. She'd avoided that by agreeing to let rotating cruisers keep an eye on her, packing a small bag and promising to stay at Trent and Vicki's. The snoring, though, amounted to torture, and Harper couldn't decide which was worse – a serial killer or Trent's snoring – when Vicki rescued her, taking her by the hand into the kitchen.

'Hungry?' Vicki asked. 'I need to eat.'

Eat? Harper's stomach had been empty since she'd lost her lunch hours ago, but she hadn't even thought about food. Suddenly, though, she saw a cake on the table and was voracious. 'What's that?'

'Red velvet cake. I baked this morning.' Vicki baked when she was upset. 'Ham sandwich OK?'

Harper nodded, eyes on the cake.

Vicki set an empty glass in front of Harper and poured a few fingers of Scotch. 'Drink.'

Harper already had double vision and a double concussion. Scotch wasn't a good idea.

'Go on. Drink.' Vicki sounded like a drill sergeant.

Harper didn't.

But Vicki did. She lifted her glass. 'To better days.' She drained it.

What the hell, Harper thought. 'Amen.'

The booze burned her throat but warmed her insides. Vicki topped off the glass and refilled her own, gulping most of it before getting out the bread and ham. Leaving Harper alone with the cake.

Her stomach was empty. And cutting seemed like a waste of time and clean knives. She reached out a finger.

'Harper, wait – I'll cut you a piece—'

'Don't bother.' Harper's mouth was full. She gouged out another piece, moist and rich and gently chocolate. Vicki's baking was always perfect. In fact, everything Vicki did was perfect. Her home was immaculate. Her clothes high fashion, her red nails flawless. Did Hank think so, too? Had he been impressed by Vicki's perfectness? The idea infuriated Harper, and she dug her unmanicured fingers back into the cake, withdrawing a shapeless blob of reddish brown and ivory, shoving it into her mouth. She chased the cake with Scotch. Yum. When she set her glass down, she realized that she saw only one hand holding a single glass – no doubles. Good. She was recovering. Maybe liquor was helping.

At any rate, she was calming down, had stopped shivering. Vicki brought their sandwiches and sat, eyeing the damaged cake, swallowing Scotch. 'Really, Harper? Taking your frustration out on baked goods?'

Harper bit into her sandwich.

'Well, if it helps, have at it. Because, I mean, two murders? At your house? Oh God, what a horror.'

Harper chewed, saw Monique on the porch, Larry on the bathroom floor. Graham on the Arts Quad. Her eyes welled up. The food clogged her throat, so she washed it down with Scotch. And then she let go and sobbed.

The tears wouldn't stop.

'The shock is wearing off.' Vicki hugged her. She spoke with authority, as if she knew about shock. 'Reality is hitting you.'

Vicki was right. Except that reality wasn't just hitting her, it was beating her to a pulp. Harper used a mustard-stained napkin to smear tears off her face. She needed to get hold of herself and think. Why had Larry and Monique been killed? How were their murders connected to the stolen drugs? Why had they been at her house? And what had the guy on the bike and whoever had ransacked her house been looking for? Did they think she had the drugs?

She put down the napkin, unable to figure anything out. All she knew for sure was that, for all her training and military expertise, she'd failed to protect anyone. Not Marvin, Sameh, the boy or the others in Iraq. Not her husband, her students or herself here at home.

'Go ahead, Harper. Cry. You have every reason to feel sorry for yourself.'

Wait. What? To feel sorry for herself? Harper stiffened, stunned at the thought.

Vicki offered a box of tissues. Harper pulled one out, blew her nose and swallowed the tears.

'I'm fine.'

'Oh, please, Harper. Stop pretending. As far as I know, you haven't let go since Hank's accident. Frankly, sorry as I am about those poor kids, it's a relief to see you fall apart.'

To see her *what*? Harper bristled, squared her shoulders. She was army strong, didn't fall apart, never had. Well, not since middle school. Never would. At least not in front of others. Unless she was having a flashback. Or dampening Ron Kendall's handkerchief. No, even at her worst, Harper kept on, dependably, reliably responsible, functioning regardless of her personal feelings, keeping them to herself. She didn't fall apart; wasn't even now. Why didn't Vicki know that?

Harper took another bite of honeyed ham, chewed with a stuffed nose and washed down her mouthful with yet another gulp of Scotch.

'Why don't you let go, Harper? It's just me here. Don't you trust me?'

Harper thought about it, hesitated too long, recalling Trent's suspicions. And Hank's declaration: 'Vicki. Screwed.'

'Oh God, you don't.' Vicki's hand covered her chest, wounded. 'Really? Why not? What did I do?'

'Vicki, please.' Harper was in no condition to discuss it.

'I care about you, Harper. I'm here for you. But once again you're shutting me out—'

'You're right. Sorry.' Harper cut her off. 'Look, we talked about it at lunch. I haven't been much of a friend. I just don't have the energy right now.'

'OK. I get it.' Vicki sighed, pouting. 'I don't want to guilt-trip you.'

Silence. Except for the snores resonating in the adjacent room.

'Listen to him.' Vicki swished her drink around in her glass. The walls were shaking. 'Even when things were good, I couldn't take that snoring. I moved him into the guest room years ago. It's one thing I won't miss when he moves out.' She didn't sound happy.

'You're really splitting up?' Harper blew her nose. 'After so many years?'

'Yup. We are.' Vicki swallowed more Scotch. 'It's not a marriage anymore. Especially since Hank's accident.' She chewed her lip. 'I started to tell you before. Trent can't even . . . perform.'

'Depression maybe?' Harper offered. 'I've heard that can happen when men get depressed.'

'Maybe.' Vicki's eyes were glazed now. 'But Trent's just . . . It's like I'm invisible to him.'

They sat for a while, listening to him. Harper held more ice against the lump on her head and considered Vicki's situation, feeling invisible in a sexless marriage. 'So that's why you had your affair?'

Vicki's mouth opened. She looked surprised. 'Uh–well, no. That – the affair – was before Hank's accident, back when Trent was still . . . functional.' Her eyes drifted, staring into the air. Troubled.

'So? Did you love him?'

The question jangled Vicki. 'Who? Trent?' She poured more booze.

'The guy you had the affair with,' Harper persisted. 'Did you love him?'

Vicki's lips curled into a kind of grimace. 'I did, yes. Still do, in a way.'

Harper's hands tightened around her glass. Was it Hank? Was Vicki in love with Hank? She looked at the remainder of the red velvet cake, considered what it would look like smeared across Vicki's face. Stop, she told herself. You don't know for sure.

'How did it start?'

'Uh uh, Harper.' Vicki suddenly slurred her words, sounded hammered. 'I don' wanna talk about it.'

Harper clenched her jaw, deciding it was better not to hear the details. 'But it's over?'

Vicki took yet another swig. 'Yup. Over.'

Of course it was over. Hank was in the clinic, unable to talk, much less romance anyone. Still, Harper couldn't stop herself. She needed to know. 'Who was he, Vicki?'

Vicki raised her manicured pointer finger, scolding, her voice a sing-song. 'Uh uh. No, no. Can't tell you.'

'Why not?' Harper's tone had a razor edge.

'Because,' Vicki's eyes watered boozily, 'he's married.'

Harper felt the blood drain from her face. 'So?'

Vicki shook her head, no. 'It'd be bad if I told.' She met Harper's eyes. 'Very bad. Cuz you know him.'

Confront her, Harper told herself. Ask if it was Hank. 'I know him?'

Vicki nodded slowly. 'Yep, you do.'

Harper watched Vicki drain the rest of her drink. 'Was it Hank?'

Vicki coughed, choking, spitting out Scotch. 'What?'

'Was it?' Harper's voice was surprisingly matter-of-fact, but she wasn't going to back down. 'Did you have an affair with my husband?'

'With Hank?' Vicki's mouth hung open. Then she began to laugh, maybe too hard. 'Wait – zat what you think? Oh my God. How could you think that?' It wasn't an answer.

'Well?' Harper persisted, a little less calmly.

Vicki's eyes floated from her empty glass to the bottle to Harper. 'Me. With Hank? God, Harper. That's ridiclus. Doesn't d'serve 'nanswer. Hank thinksh . . . He thinksh yer th'only woman in th'world. Th'sun rises and setsh on you. B'sides, I'm your friend.'

Vicki went on, vehemently, drunkenly denying the charge. Harper had finally managed to ask the question, and now she wasn't sure she believed the answer.

Abruptly, Harper cleared her plate and said her head hurt; she wanted to lie down. In fact, she suspected Vicki of lying about Hank and couldn't bear to look at her. So, even though it wasn't yet eight o'clock, she thanked Vicki for feeding her and letting her sleep over, and said goodnight.

Leaving Trent to the family-room sofa, she moved into the guest room he normally occupied. Vicki trailed after her, offering to help her change the sheets or run a bath, but Harper insisted that she just needed to rest, could take care of herself.

The guest room smelled like air freshener. Harper opened a window and sat beside it, inhaling the summer evening air, aching with every breath. She had three dead students, a battered head and an aphasic, possibly adulterous husband. And she couldn't even go home because her ransacked house was a crime scene that she couldn't enter. Harper hurt all over – her skull, her cheek, her leg. Her heart. She wished she could cry but couldn't, especially after Vicki had accused her of feeling sorry for herself. So, dry-eyed, she stared into the darkening sky and realized that she'd missed her nightly visit to Hank. Who might have had an affair with Vicki. She thought of calling, asking the nurse to tell him she had a cold.

Then again, it wasn't that late. She could still get there before nine, the end of visiting hours. Quickly, a little dizzily, Harper took a shower, changed her clothes, grabbed her leather bag and headed outside. She didn't bother to tell Vicki she was leaving, didn't want to explain. Silently, avoiding the police cruiser idling protectively across the street, Harper snuck out of the house into the screaming of crickets and the shadows of oncoming night. She might not be able to bring back her dead students, but at least she could find out the truth about her husband, for better or worse.

*   *   *

She didn't take the Ninja. Partly because she'd been drinking, partly because its noise would announce her departure, mostly because she'd left it back home in her driveway. Besides, Vicki's house on Fairmount Avenue was above College Town, less than a mile from the clinic; it would be tight, but she could make it in time if she walked fast.

On the way, she rehearsed what she'd say to Hank. She'd keep it simple, asking questions with yes or no answers. Just a blunt: 'Did you and Vicki have an affair?' No. Too polite. 'Were you screwing Vicki?' Better.

The streets were duskier, more deserted than usual. Clouds hid the moon, and the red sunset bled across the sky. Breezes brushed her shoulders, tickled her neck as she hurried through the wooded, undeveloped area near the clinic. She felt off balance and dizzy. Too much Scotch, too many head injuries. She leaned against a tree, steadying herself, listening to rustling leaves, then to stillness.

What was she doing? Nobody – not a single person – knew where she was. And the killer was still out there; someone who knew her, who knew where she lived. What if the killer were watching her now? Following her? What had she been thinking? Why had she ventured out alone?

Her phone rang, startling her. Harper started walking again, reaching inside her bag, pulling it out. Distracted, she didn't watch where she was going, didn't see the root of an oak in her path. She went down hard, slamming the dirt and dropping the phone, which smacked something solid and stopped ringing on impact. Damn. Now what had she done? On her knees in dirt, head throbbing, her bad leg protesting, she scrambled in the dusk to find her lost, probably broken phone. She rooted around inside her leather sack for a penlight that she was almost certain was in there somewhere, wrapped her fingers around a thing that felt right – no, it was a ballpoint. Finally, after fingering countless pens, highlighters, pencils and tampons, she found it and flashed a feeble beam of light around, hunting, annoyed with herself for stumbling. Searching, she decided that the call had probably been Vicki, looking for her. That she'd better hurry if she wanted to get to the clinic before nine.

Wait – was that her phone, under that tree? She reached for it, touched a rough, square stone. Hard and cold, covered with slimy moss. She looked again, felt more dirt, fingered snaky

vines and stems. Where was the damned thing? It had to be there. Shadows surrounded her. And noises. Sounds of night creatures that normally calmed her alarmed her now. Branches cracked. Something screeched; something scurried. Was that a breeze on her neck? Or was someone behind her? Harper whirled around, aiming the light into the shadows, stabbing the darkness with a frail beam. Was someone there? Had someone moved in the thicket? She remembered Monique, the stains on her pink shirt; Larry, the nail file in his neck.

'Who's there?' Her voice sounded raspy and thread-like, not as she'd intended.

There, behind the tree. Something had definitely moved. She stiffened, kept perfectly still. Nothing. A limb rattled above her head. Harper jumped to her feet, took a fighting stance, legs tensed. But the limb was silent again. It was nothing, she told herself. A bat or an owl. Behind her, something swished in the bushes. A fox, she reasoned. Or raccoon looking for dinner. Nothing lethal. Even so, she waved the light with anxious hands, looking for a murderer.

Cut it out, Harper told herself. Get on with it and find the damned phone. Rotating, trying not to lose her balance, she cast the frail beam in a circle around her feet. And there it was. Not a yard away, at the edge of the path. She scooped it up, brushed it off, tested it for a dial tone and, without taking the time to see who'd called, dropped it back into her bag, hurrying ahead. As she walked, Harper looked around to see if anyone was behind her. On a bike to grab her, or on foot to bash her on the head. She watched, making sure that the sounds she heard were merely those of the woods at night, but saw no one.

Except for Sameh and the boy with no face, Harper was alone.

Eight twenty-seven. Limping and winded, Harper waved at the guard and stopped at reception to scribble her name in the visitor's book. And then, without catching her breath, she hurried to Hank's room. By clinic time, it was late. He'd be in bed, probably watching television. Probably wondering where she was. The closer she got, the more anxious she was to find out the truth. No matter what it was, she told herself to give him a chance. If he admitted his mistake and begged for forgiveness, she might not strangle him.

When the elevator reached his floor, she dashed past the nursing station, not even slowing down when a nurse called out. 'Harper? Wait. He's been waiting for you—'

'I know. Thanks.' Harper hurried down the hall to his door, dizzy, head pounding. Just a few more steps. Finally, she grabbed the handle, flung the door open.

'Hank,' she began. 'I have something to—'

She stopped mid-sentence. Hank wasn't in the bed. The bed lamp was the only light on, so the room was dim. Hank was standing at the window, looking out at the driveway below.

He turned, scowling. 'Waiting.'

He walked toward her slowly, on his own. No walker. Not even a cane. He wobbled unevenly, but then so did she.

'Hank.' Her jaw dropped. 'Look at you, how you're walking—'

'No. Look. You.'

He glowered so darkly that, as he neared her, Harper took an unintended step back.

'Tell.'

Tell? 'Tell what?'

'Not.' He pointed to the television. 'Killed.'

What? This wasn't the conversation she'd planned.

'Killed. Saw. Home. You.'

Oh God.

'Tell. Me. Hoppa. Killed.' He put his hands on her shoulders and faced her, studying her severely, waiting. 'What.' His gaze held her eyes, seared her face.

Harper stood dumbstruck. Hank had seen the news. The story about Larry and Monique must have been the lead; the reporters had been standing in front of their house. Understandably, Hank was upset. More than upset. His eyes were on fire. Why hadn't she anticipated his reaction? It hadn't even occurred to her that, of course, he would watch television, find out about the murders. And that when she'd been late for their nightly visit, he must have become frantic about her safety, unable to ask anyone how or where she was.

Harper didn't know how to answer him. Didn't have the energy to explain. Instead, she threw her arms around him, pressed herself against him, tried to hold on. But Hank would have none of it. He moved her away, resisting the embrace.

'Tell.'

'Hank. Don't worry. Everything's OK—'

He leaned over, glowering. 'Stew. Not.' He shook his head, frustrated. 'Pid. Me.'

Harper juggled the syllables, felt a pang. 'No, you're not stupid.'

'Else. What.' He glared, unforgiving.

What else? He wanted to know everything? Oh God.

'Lies. Tell. Hoppa.' He took her head in his hands, pressing on her lump, radiating pain. Harper refused to wince, hoped he couldn't feel the swelling.

'No, Hank. That's not fair. I haven't lied to you.'

'Jump.'

What? He knew about Graham? How?

'What jump?' She played dumb. Maybe she was misunderstanding him.

'Dead. Jump. Him.' Again, he pointed to the television. Damn. He knew about Graham. And who knew what else. What had they said on the news? Had they connected Graham's suicide to the murders? They must have. Larry and Graham were roommates, both dead within days. Both her students.

Hank waited; her skin sizzled from his glare.

'Can we sit down?'

He didn't move, didn't sit, but at least he released her head.

'Hank, I haven't lied to you. But you're right. I haven't told you everything that's happened. I didn't want to upset you.'

His jaw clenched, but he said nothing.

'I thought you needed to concentrate on your recuperation. I didn't want to distract you. What would be the point? Why trouble you with things that . . .'

She stopped. They both knew what she'd been about to ask: Why trouble him with things that he couldn't do anything about? Essentially saying that Hank couldn't function the way he used to. That Hank couldn't protect her or their home. That he was too damaged even to handle the truth.

Her aborted sentence and its unspoken ending jarred him, and he moved away, sat slumped on the side of the bed, not looking at her.

Harper didn't go to him. 'Hank—'

He put up a hand, stopping her. 'Get. It.'

'I didn't mean—'

'Now. Not. Say.'

She regretted her words, understood his lonely frustration.

128   Merry Jones

And she ached, physically ached, for the comfort of his body, his strong familiar arms. Pained, unable to give or receive solace, she watched him for a while. Then, without a kiss, without even mentioning Vicki, she went to the door, her throat too tight even to say goodnight.

Again, passing the nursing station, Harper heard her name.

'Was he OK?' one of the nurses, Linda, called from the desk. 'I tried to warn you; Mr Jennings has been inconsolable ever since he watched the news. Usually, we think it's good for the patients to watch, you know, to keep in touch with what's going on, but we had no idea.'

Harper was in no mood for conversation. She kept moving, but the nurse kept talking.

'It's sounded awful, what happened. On the news, they said those kids were your students. Do they know who did it?'

'I'm sorry.' Harper hurried to the stairway, avoiding the wait for the elevator. She made it to the lobby at about the same time she realized that she didn't have the stomach to go back to Vicki's or the ability to go home. That's when she saw Ron, sitting on the sign-in desk, watching her. Frowning.

'I thought I'd been stood up.'

What? Harper was baffled.

'It's after nine. We were supposed to meet at eight thirty.'

They were? Oh God – yes, they were. She'd completely forgotten. She'd agreed to have dinner with him. He had something to explain to her. Something about the drugs.

'Oh Lord, Ron. I'm sorry—'

'I've been calling, but you didn't pick up.' His eyes were strained. Tired? 'And when you didn't show, given all that's happened, I figured—'

'Sorry.'

'No, don't apologize. Are you all right? After what you've been through, it's amazing you're even standing.'

Ron knew what had happened? Oh, of course, he did: the news. That's how Hank knew. That's how, apparently, everybody knew.

'I figured you'd come to see your husband, so I checked the sign-in book and saw your name. So I waited. Thought you might need to eat.' He studied her face, knitting his eyebrows. Looking her over, head to toe.

Harper looked down, saw the knees of her khaki capris covered with dirt and moss stains from her fall. Her nails were filled with soil from crawling in the woods, searching for her phone. And who knew what her face looked like? She'd showered before leaving Vicki's, but no one would guess. She was a disaster.

But Ron didn't seem to notice. He was concerned about the murdered students and the upheaval at her home. And most of all, about her state of mind. His arm coiled around her, leading her to his car, and, before she knew it, they were seated at a corner table in a restaurant where the lights were so low nobody could see what a mess she was. Especially not Ron.

Ron listened attentively, and Harper didn't hold back. Words spilled; sentences poured. She repeated her theory that Larry had stolen the drugs. That Graham might have been his partner. Or maybe Monique. Or both. She reeled at the number of students who were dead, but kept control, swallowing her emotions with hot tea.

As she spoke, though, control became more difficult. When her voice wavered, Ron took her hand and assured her that the crimes would be solved. 'This will work out,' he promised. 'The murderer will get caught.'

Harper tilted her head. 'How can you be sure?'

'Think about it. The guy is out of control, killing too many too fast. In just a couple of days, he's murdered a waitress and two students. He's losing it; he'll make mistakes. They'll catch him.'

'You think it's just one guy?'

Ron hesitated. 'Yes, of course.'

Harper wasn't sure. 'Well, he better pray the cops find him before I do. The dude went into my house. He killed my students. On my property. This is personal; between him and me, it's war.' Harper spoke too loud. A man at a nearby table twisted his neck, looking at her.

Ron peered at her through the candlelight. 'Harper, I'm worried about you.'

He was? Really? Harper swallowed more tea. 'Don't be. I'm fine.' But she was still off balance, and her pulse was racing.

'How's your head?'

How did he know about her head injury? Had she told him?

She couldn't remember. Maybe it had been on the news. Or maybe he meant her old head injury, from the mugging. 'It's OK. No big deal.'

Silence while she sipped tea.

Ron watched her, grim-faced.

'Really. Thanks for caring. I'm fine.'

Ron looked away. Sipped his Martini. 'So. Any idea who the guy is?'

'Not who.' Harper lowered her voice. 'But I think I know why.'

'Really?' Ron's eyes riveted hers.

She leaned forward, closer to him. 'Those drugs. It has to be. First, the guy mugged me. He must have thought they were in Graham's bag. But he didn't find them there, so he searched my house. And, again, he found nothing. So he still thinks I have them—'

'But Harper, a whole bin of drugs was stolen. They wouldn't fit in a book bag.'

Harper was unfazed. 'But some of them would.'

Ron looked doubtful.

'OK, I don't know exactly what he wanted – the actual pills or money for them or what. But it was something to do with the drugs. I'm sure of it.'

Ron pursed his lips, thinking. 'Except for one thing.'

'What?'

'Let's say you're right, and Larry, Graham and Monique stole the drugs. Graham was already dead. So who killed Larry and Monique?'

Good point. Someone else had to be involved.

Ron cleared his throat. 'Harper. Leave it alone. There's more to this than you're aware of.'

More? Harper's pulse picked up. She heard a bang and looked up, expecting to see pieces of Marvin. But all she saw was Ron, his liquid, golden eyes.

As if on cue, the waiter appeared to take their orders.

'How about a steak?' They hadn't even glanced at the menus.

Harper shrugged. She wasn't hungry, didn't care about food. She wanted to hear what Ron had to say.

Ron ordered. The waiter left, and Harper waited for Ron to pick up where he'd left off. He didn't. She had to ask. When she did, Ron took a swig of his Martini before answering.

'I'm trying to decide how to phrase it. But I can't think of

a delicate way, so I'll just say it. Our research indicates that, in extremely rare and unlikely circumstances, the missing drugs can have unanticipated adverse side effects.'

Harper sifted through syllables to grasp Ron's meaning. Side effects? 'But you said the pills were benign.'

'Absolutely. In proper dosages. But—'

'What kind of side effects?' In the dim light, Ron seemed fuzzy, as if his skin lacked definition; as if he might fade into darkness.

Ron drew an audible breath. 'Let me explain. This drug works by stimulating specific parts of the frontal lobe. In trials, that stimulation has significantly enhanced memory and facilitated several processes involved in learning. In short, it's proved to be a miracle drug.'

He paused.

Harper waited. Bottom line, the drug helped memory and learning. She'd already known that. 'The side effects. Tell me.'

'Well, that's just it. In normal dosages, when the drug is taken for limited durations, there don't appear to be any side effects at all. It's only when it's taken in large doses or over extended time periods that undesired effects might arise. Mind you, they don't *always* arise. But testing has shown that the drug can over-stimulate the hippocampus.'

The hippocampus? Harper tried to call up fifteen-year-old information from her undergraduate psychology classes. No luck. She had no idea what a hippocampus did. But she didn't want to sound stupid, so she didn't ask.

Instead, she asked, 'Causing what to happen?'

'Let me repeat.' Ron leaned across the table; his voice was hushed. 'The side effects appeared only rarely when the drug was taken in large dosages or over an extended period of time.'

Harper waited. 'What are they?' Why wouldn't he just tell her? Were they so horrible?

Ron faced her, met her eyes. 'The hippocampus. Do you know anything about it?'

'Just that it's part of the brain.'

'Well, in part, the hippocampus is known to regulate impulsive behavior.'

He waited, watched Harper's face, making sure she was following.

'Normally, the mature brain engages many processes to evaluate

behavior, envision consequences and overcome impulsive drives. But abnormally high activity in the hippocampus can override those processes, resulting in excessive impulsive behavior, even violence.'

He paused again, letting the information sink in.

'For example, mapping the brains of serial killers typically shows extremely high activity in the hippocampus.'

Oh dear. 'So, if some thrill-seeking kids steal it and pop a handful at a time, thinking that if a little is good, a lot will be better, then—'

Ron nodded. 'Exactly.'

Harper didn't finish. They both knew what she'd been about to say: those thrill-seeking kids would be at risk of side effects causing impulsive, possibly violent behavior. 'Oh God.'

'Now, Harper.' Ron leaned on his elbows. 'Let's keep a perspective. This drug isn't unusual; large dosages of many common FDA-approved drugs can be harmful.'

'Harmful, in that they cause impulsive violent behavior?'

'Even worse. Some – like common sleeping and pain pills – can kill people.'

'So can impulsive violent behavior like jumping out a window.'

Ron didn't answer. He examined his fingernails, avoiding her eyes.

'And how about what happened to the waitress? Could those drugs cause someone to commit rape and murder? You think that's what happened? Someone took too many pills and killed the waitress, and Larry and Monique?'

Harper fired questions at Ron, but his gaze remained fixed on his hands, and she wasn't surprised when he didn't answer.

Harper's eyes were on Ron but she wasn't seeing him. She was seeing Graham impulsively and violently flinging himself out the window. He'd had an open vial of the experimental drug in his book bag. Who knew how many he'd taken? Maybe he'd swallowed a handful, thinking they'd help him with his quiz.

Instead, the pills had caused impulsive violence. In the form of his suicide.

Harper leaned back in the booth, her shoulders suddenly less tight, her breathing slower. Oddly, she felt relieved. But why? Nothing had changed: Graham was still dead, the waitress still

a victim of rape and murder, and Larry and Monique still lying on slabs in the morgue. The missing pills were still out there for other unsuspecting people to swallow. Even so, Harper felt lighter, more optimistic than she had all week. The violence erupting all around her wasn't the work of some depraved, deliberate serial killer. It was accidental, the result of a drug-induced chemical imbalance in someone's brain. It was synthetic, stoppable. Not truly evil. And her reaction was palpable; a ripple, something like giddiness, rose inside her. When the steaks arrived, Harper dug in, suddenly starving, slicing through tender meat, soaking up blood-red juice with potatoes au gratin.

'So you can see –' Ron chewed – 'it's imperative that we find the missing drugs.'

Right. It was very imperative.

'We can't let any more of these mishaps occur, especially not at this late stage in the trials.'

Wait. 'You're continuing the trials? With what you know?'

'Of course we are. Harper. Used as directed, this drug will help patients with learning disabilities, brain injuries, certain forms of dementia. It will dramatically enhance memory and learning capabilities. Its benefits are broad and significant—'

'Unless someone takes too much and kills somebody?'

'If you took too much aspirin, you'd die, too. Too much anything can kill you.'

He was right. Too much anything, including red meat. Harper cut another chunk, savored the texture, the richness of prime beef. The waiter brought a bottle of red wine. Candles flickered, cast a golden glow on to the palette of Ron's face; darkness and light impishly danced on skin. What was she doing here with him? Couldn't he have told her about the pills on the phone?

She watched his fingers deftly working his utensils, his jaw flexing as he chewed. Rippling his cheek muscles. He smiled, suddenly, aware of her stare. 'What?'

'Nothing.' She looked away.

Ron put down his fork, studying her. Then, reaching across the table, he touched her arm, held it. 'This has been an ordeal for you. But, from what I've seen, you've handled it with incredible grace and strength. Thank God that, in spite of everything, you're all right. Except for that nasty lump.'

The lump again. Harper couldn't remember telling him about it. She must have, though.

'. . . you can think of?'

She'd missed the first part of his question.

'Think for a minute,' he went on. 'Do you still have anything of Graham's at all?'

Of course she didn't. 'Nothing.' Well, except for that scrap of paper with scribbled numbers on it. Larry had said that it was a study guide. The numbers probably weren't important. Still, maybe she should mention it. Maybe Ron would know what they were. 'All I can think of is that list of numbers.'

He released her arm. 'I should take a look at it. Just in case.'

Harper stiffened; the timbre of Ron's voice had changed. 'Just in case?'

'In case it's important. Look, I don't mean to be an alarmist, Harper. Whatever the guy who tossed your house is looking for, he's killed people trying to get it.'

Ron was warning her that she could be next. That she was in danger. Sameh entered the restaurant, approaching them, smiling. Oh God. Not now. Harper looked for a lemon, grabbed the twist from Ron's empty Martini glass and shoved it into her mouth.

'Harper?'

Eyes closed, she munched on the lemon rind, concentrating on the tang. The intensely sour, bitter flavor.

When she opened her eyes, Ron was watching her. Thank God, Sameh was nowhere in sight.

Ron finished his last bite of steak, put his fork down and leaned back. He looked worn out. 'Who'd have thought a wonder drug could cause so much trouble?'

Harper had no answer. In her experience, trouble popped up all over the place. Why not from a pill bottle? She swallowed the last of her potatoes.

Ron sighed. 'Well. There's no option anymore. I'll issue a press release about the theft. Give the serial numbers of the missing pills and vials. Warn people not to buy or take them. It might ruin our trials, but I don't see any way around it.' His mouth formed an unconvincing smile.

This time, Harper touched his hand. It was smooth, strong. Her fingers felt comfortable there, wanting to remain. 'People have died, Ron. Others are in danger. It's the right thing to do.'

He met her eyes and the skin of Harper's fingers tingled.

'It's late,' Harper made herself say. 'We'd better go.'
He didn't say anything, just kept looking at her. Harper looked
back. His stare was intense, probing. She returned it, oddly
engrossed, examining his features. They were symmetrical,
delicate but still manly. And his lips – oh dear. They looked
soft and plump. Probably, he was a slow and tender kisser, the
kind who slides and slips, gently pressing and releasing. She
could almost feel it. But Ron stood, offering not his lips but
his arm to escort her out of the restaurant. Wow! Where was
her mind going? She needed to get out of there, to get a grip.

Harper didn't look at Ron or speak until they got to his car
and drove off. And, then, all she said was that her house was
a crime scene, so she wasn't going home. She'd begun giving
him directions to Vicki's when Ron pulled off the road and
stopped.

'Come to my place.' His eyes pierced hers, and his voice
was throaty, like sex. 'Stay with me.'

'What?' Stay with him? Really? 'I can't.'

'Of course you can. Look, this is serious, Harper. I'm not
propositioning you; I know you're married. But your husband
isn't able to be there for you, and you shouldn't be alone.
There's a killer out there, and I . . . Hell, I want you to be safe.'

Ron's gaze was warm. Or something was; Harper felt heat
welling up around her. He smelled of spice and booze and work
and musk, and he covered her hand with his. His touch was no
longer strange.

'I promise, I won't make a pass.' His eyes twinkled softly and
his lips teased with a playful smirk. 'Unless you want me to.'

God forgive me, Harper thought. Because, at that moment,
she wanted him to, very badly. Her skin throbbed where he
touched it. And where she imagined him touching it. Even so,
something held her back. No matter how intoxicating Ron's
scent, no matter how seductive his touch, the man simply was
not Hank.

But Hank might have cheated on her. And he wasn't able to
be with her. And he might not ever be able to, no matter how
badly she needed him or how much she wished otherwise. Ron,
on the other hand, was right there. With his gentle caring hands
and thick voice and knowing, glowing eyes and smooth, smooth
skin. He was there.

But no. No.

Later, as she lay down on sheets perfumed with fabric softener in a room filled with air freshener, Harper replayed the scene again and again, hearing Ron inviting her to stay with him. And no matter how hard she tried to stop, no matter how she tried to replace his image with thoughts of Hank, Harper lay awake, tossing, wondering what would have happened if she'd agreed and gone.

Sleep simply wasn't going to happen. Harper fluffed pillows, turned from one side to the other. Tried to read a *TIME* magazine she found on the nightstand, but couldn't focus on the page. Switched on the television, found the noise, the commercials irritating.

Finally, she got out of bed and wandered around Vicki's guest room, feeling trapped and edgy. She looked out the window. The police cruiser had gone, and she gazed into the trees, wondering if the killer might be watching her, still convinced that she had some connection to the stolen drugs. Nothing moved outside; the night air was still and undisturbed, revealing no sign of a trespasser. Harper moved away from the window, sat on the bed. Saw her bag on the dresser beside Hank's computer. And remembered the page of numbers. She'd forgotten to show it to Ron.

Maybe, if she looked at it again, she could figure out if they stood for anything. Assuming they weren't a study guide, maybe they were some kind of code. Opening her bag, she felt around for loose papers, found some receipts for groceries and stamps, to-do lists she'd made and abandoned. But no page of numbers.

Damn. It was in there, somewhere. It had to be. She dumped her bag out on to the bed. Found the usual: keys, extension cord, change purse, wallet, pens, notebooks, folders, grade book, flashlight, textbook, tampons, hairbrush, baby wipes, chap stick, tweezers, toothbrush, forms for the copy machine, candy bars, water bottle, antibiotic cream, lip balm, Swiss army knife, sunglasses, stapler, Tylenol, plastic spoon, corkscrew – Lord, was there no end to the stuff this bag could carry? Paper clips. Nail clipper. Two Tide sticks. Sewing kit. Sun screen. Memo about a department meeting. Baseball cap. More baby wipes. Band-Aids. Out-of-date coupons for shampoo, toilet tissue and Parmesan cheese. Old birthday card from her mother. Receipt from her last physical.

But no sheet of paper with numbers written on it.

Harper sat on the bed, puzzled, staring at the small mountain beside her. It had to be here. It had been there earlier; she'd seen it when she'd called for help. Damn. Where was it? Had she inadvertently stuck it in a folder? She rifled through them, the textbooks, the grade book. Nothing. She knew she hadn't tossed it out. But had she accidentally dropped it? Not noticed it floating to the ground?

Impossible. She distinctly remembered stuffing it into her bag.

Well, probably it was nothing, anyhow. But, then, maybe it was. Either way, it bothered her that she couldn't find it. So why couldn't she?

Probably, it was right in front of her. Probably, she couldn't see it because she was looking so hard for it. That happened a lot, didn't it? Things turned up when you weren't searching for them. What she needed to do was think about something else. Do something different. And that's when, looking around the room, her gaze landed on Hank's computer.

Harper shoveled her things back into her bag. She'd look for the numbers later, with fresh eyes. Meantime, she'd log on to Hank's computer and find out why Hank didn't want Trent to use his notes.

Problem was, though, she didn't know Hank's password. She stared at the blank box on the screen, resenting it. Hank was her husband. Under the circumstances, she should have access to all his files, shouldn't need a damned password. The computer, however, was unimpressed with her opinion; it waited, not letting her in.

Harper wouldn't give up. She was entitled; Hank was her husband. She knew him better than anyone and ought to be able to figure out his password. It wouldn't be their address or his middle name; too obvious. Harper watched the screen, realizing that she had no idea where to start. She needed sustenance. Chocolate.

She found a mini Snickers bar in her sack, nibbled at it as she typed in Hank's Alma Mater: S T A N F O R D. Nope. She tried his mother's maiden name, his father's first and middle. She tried her birthday, their wedding anniversary; was unsurprised when neither worked.

OK, she told herself: think like Hank. She popped the last of the Snickers into her mouth and focused on her husband's past, his passions. The mutt he'd had as a child – she typed 'Ralph'. No luck. His first car – Mustang. Nope. OK. Maybe his first sweetheart – what was her name? Suzanne? No. Probably it was something about his work. About geology. She tried earthsci, geology, geodoc, earthdoc, earthman, earthling. Mountain, stalactite, stalagmite, volcano, seismic, striation, crystal, geode, rocks, petroleum, oilfield – every related term she could think of. Still nothing.

Harper leaned back, crossing her arms, frustrated. And in a furious burst, typed in Vicki, then VickiManning. Smiling when neither worked.

She thought back to Hank's insistence that Trent shouldn't get hold of his notes. Harper couldn't imagine why. What would Hank need to keep from Trent? And then she remembered Hank saying something else.

Harper typed it into the computer. A C U M A L. She was in.

Harper browsed the files, finding page after page of notes, lectures and articles, with no idea what she was looking for. Finally, she decided to stop. The simple fact was that Hank didn't want Trent to have access to his notes. It didn't matter why or which ones. She shouldn't even have begun the search.

Yawning, she was about to shut down the computer when she noticed the envelope icon. Hank had mail. She sat for a while, looking at it. She shouldn't open it. Email was private. But in her case, as Hank's wife, she had to handle his affairs; something important might be there.

Gingerly, as if the mouse might bite, she clicked the icon. Two hundred seventy-four emails. Lord. Most of them had arrived after the accident. Faculty memos, student messages. Spam. Calls for papers and publication submissions. Invitations to conferences. Departmental announcements. But there were other messages, too. Older, from before the accident. Most were from Trent. A few were from clients; some from journal editors, one in particular.

Randomly, Harper opened one. The editor thanked Hank for his submission and asked for clarification on a few specific points. She opened another, from Trent, and found a list of citations. Opened another.

'What the fuck, man? Do NOT go that route. I promise it will end badly.'

Harper read it again, stunned. She pictured Trent sputtering as he wrote it. What had he been so mad about? She searched sent mail, trying to match the date of Trent's message with email from Hank, but she found nothing from Hank to Trent on that date. She tried the preceding day and the one before that. Nothing had been sent from Hank to Trent that whole week. Whatever had angered Trent must have transpired by phone or in person.

Harper went back to incoming mail and found more email from Trent. All normal stuff. Nothing that indicated anger. Whatever the dispute had been, they must have worked it out. After all, right up until the accident, the two had been inseparable. And Hank had never mentioned any trouble. She thought of Vicki. Had she been the issue?

But then Harper opened a message from Trent sent in April, just days before Hank fell: 'Congratulations, Pal. You win. Do whatever you want. No doubt, you'll get it. But what goes around comes around. It's your karma now.'

Harper reread it, relieved; Vicki wasn't an 'it'. So the conflict wasn't about her. In fact, she was pretty sure that Trent's 'it' meant tenure. But there was something disturbing in his email, almost a premonition. As if Trent were warning Hank. But no. Trent had been bitter about some professional issue, nothing more. Partnerships, after all, were like marriages, full of ups and downs, high drama, complex emotions. And, sometimes, betrayal.

Harper moved on, scanning email until her eyes burned, finally tired. It was after two a.m. Time to shut down the computer, try to fall asleep.

But she didn't close it down. She started to, but stopped when she saw another block of email. From Vicki.

'Honestly, I understand how you feel,' Vicki had written. 'But while you're both up for tenure, it would be unfair of you to expose this thing. For now, can't we please keep it *entre nous*?'

Harper let out a breath. What 'thing' was Vicki asking Hank not to expose? Was it the same 'thing' Trent had talked about, Vicki's 'thing' for Hank? And why had Hank saved the email?

Harper massaged her temples. There were lots of possibilities other than an affair. The email could be about Trent and Hank's

professional rivalry, something that, if revealed, would give
Hank an edge. Still, she pictured Hank and Vicki in a seedy
motel room, neon lights reflecting on the sheets. Stop it, she
told herself; suspicion was destructive. She needed to stop spying
on her husband. And she would. As soon as she finished reading
Vicki's emails.

One had been sent a week before Hank's accident. 'Hank,
I'm begging you not to say anything. Trent has no idea. He's
not as strong as you and wouldn't recover. I mean it, Hank;
he'd be destroyed. It's not too late to fix it so he'll never know.
Whatever you decide, I love you and always will.'

Harper reread the message several times. Especially the last
line: Vicki loved him and always would. The words seared
Harper's eyes, inflamed her brain. Her stomach knotted and her
lump throbbed.

Vicki and Hank had had an affair. And Vicki had begged
Hank not to tell Trent about it.

The air in the bedroom was suddenly thin; Harper's stomach
churned. Even so, she opened another email, written a few days
before Hank's fall.

'Trent knows. I don't know how. He won't talk to me. He's
moping. Drunk.'

Drunk and moping? Just because his wife was having an
affair with his best friend? Shocking.

Vicki's next email sounded frantic. 'Trent's self-destructing.
He says whatever I did was your fault, that it was all because
of you. He says I'd never have done it otherwise. He swears
you're ruining his life, and he's going to make you pay. You've
got to talk to him before he does something crazy.'

Harper stared at the screen, her mouth dry, her hands cold.
Stop reading, she told herself. None of these messages will
help; they'll only hurt you more. But she read on.

Vicki's messages – at least the ones Hank had saved – began
with Vicki's plea to protect Trent from the truth and ended, just
before the accident, with her plea to help Trent deal with it.
She wrote that he was drinking himself into stupors, talking
about leaving the university, swearing he'd never write another
article or trust another soul. He'd moved into the guest room.
He'd asked for a divorce. He was going to talk to Dr Hayden,
the department chair, about what had happened.

Good God. Trent was going to the department head about

Vicki and Hank? Well, that capped it. Absolutely everybody except Harper had known.

Harper held her wrenching stomach. Why hadn't she seen it? She replayed their shared beers and dinners, looking for clues. Hank and Vicki might have had a few side conversations, maybe some eye contact. But nothing to indicate an affair. They'd been awfully discreet. Or she'd been awfully blind.

'Damn it. Damn you, Hank.' Her fist pounded the mouse, closing the window that held his mail. Harper stood, pacing and cursing. Seething. What a chump she'd been. Her lungs felt raw, her eyes burned, her leg ached, and the lump on her head pulsed with pain.

'OK,' she heard her voice repeating. 'OK. No more drama. Calm down.' The affair was over; Vicki had said so herself – that whoring, two-faced, slime-ball bitch. And Hank's cheating days, like his conversations, were over, too.

Finally, Harper obeyed herself and sat, making herself breathe evenly until her pulse slowed. And then she began to think. Not about murders or stolen drugs. Not about the killer who might be watching her. No, all she thought about was her husband's infidelity. Right up until the accident, Vicki had been emailing him about their affair, worrying about Trent's reaction. Harper closed her eyes, saw Hank sliding off the roof, falling. And behind him, she saw Trent, his arms out, reaching for Hank . . .

Or pushing him?

No. Not possible. Even though they were both up for tenure and Hank was likely to get it? Even though Trent had learned that Hank was banging his wife?

Oh God. But Trent was no killer. His only weapon was his sharp tongue. Besides, Hank was much more agile and athletic. Trent could never have overpowered him.

Unless Hank had been taken by surprise. Shoved while he was off balance. And it might not have been premeditated. It might have been a spontaneous act of rage.

Harper envisioned it again and again. Hank kneeling, maybe checking a shingle; Trent watching as he began to stand, coming at him with the full force of his body, knocking him over, watching Hank fall.

It was possible. It would explain why Trent never visited Hank, and why Hank was so insistent: 'Trent. No.'

Enough uncertainty. Harper had to know for sure. This time,

she wouldn't let Hank change the subject, blindsiding her with questions. This time, the only questions would be hers.

Once again, Harper headed outside. She didn't care about darkness, danger, pain or exhaustion. She cared only about Hank. About getting the truth.

The room was dark, the curtains closed. It was way past visiting hours, but Harper told the night guard that she'd left her phone in Hank's room. Hank was asleep, breathing evenly. Harper stood at his bed, imagining him sneaking around with Vicki. When had they done it? Late at night? Early morning? And what about their pillow talk? Had they invented pet names for each other? Was Hank her Snookums or Teddy Bear? Damn. Vicki deserved to smolder in hell. And how could Hank look so innocent, lying there, dreaming peacefully without a single pang of regret?

'Hank. Wake up.' Harper nudged him without tenderness.

His eyes opened, and he grunted, confused. She nudged him again, and he squinted up, identifying her. 'Hoppa?' He looked surprised, then happy, then concerned.

'Wake up.' Still no affection in her voice.

He sat, rubbed his eyes. Looked at her blankly, with no clue why she was there. God, she wanted to throttle him. Or maybe to jump into bed with him, reclaim him, feel his body next to hers. Half asleep, he looked mussed and cuddly. Strong. Damn, who was this man? What did she know about him?

Do not be sidetracked, she told herself. Make him admit the truth. He watched her, eyebrows knitted, yawning, no doubt wondering why she'd awakened him.

'You have some explaining to do.' Her tone was harsh, unforgiving; she took a seat on the side of the bed.

He blinked, waiting. 'Do?'

'Yes, you do. Tell me about Vicki.'

'Vicki. No.' Or, maybe, Vicki know.

Harper tried again. 'What's your relationship with her?'

'Vicki? Why. Hoppa?'

Good. They were having a conversation. And it was Harper's turn to talk. 'Why? Because I want – no – I deserve to know.'

Hank's head tilted, puppy-like, confused.

'I was looking in your computer for the notes Trent's been looking for—'

'Trent. No.'

'And guess what? While I was looking for the notes, I found Vicki's emails.'

Hank scowled. 'Snoop. Mad.'

'Mad? You bet I am. Damn you, Hank. I know about you and Vicki.' Harper's eyes welled up. 'I know what you did.' Her words came out too fast and shrill, accompanied by unanticipated angry tears.

Hank looked stricken. He put his hand on her back. She squirmed at his touch, pushed it away.

'No. Hoppa. Not. Wrong.'

Harper was stunned, humiliated by his denial. Apparently Hank felt no need to admit his behavior.

'Why, Hank? Just tell me why.'

Hank didn't respond. He sat, silent, staring at her.

'Stop pretending you can't talk, Hank. I know you can if you want. You can tell me why you cheated. Go on. Tell me how you screwed your best friend's wife.'

Nothing.

'Fine. Just sit there. You know what? I lost three students this week. Three kids. Dead. But I'm not able to mourn them or help my other students because all I can think about is my cheating husband and how he was fucking my best friend.' On its own, Harper's fist rose and took a dive, landing hard, right in Hank's solar plexus.

His mouth opened and he grunted, air blasting from his lungs. Harper kept slugging, shouting at him until Hank managed to block her with his weak arm and grab one of her wrists with the strong one.

'Hoppa,' he gulped. 'Stop.' He squeezed her wrist, letting her carry on until she finally got tired of smacking at him and quieted down, still stiff with anger.

'Dead.' He repeated it, reminding her of the gravity. 'Three. Safe. Not.'

'Don't change the subject. Tell me about Vicki.'

Hank frowned, still panting. 'Hoppa. Rife. Ell. My. Take.'

His rifle. He was dodging. 'Answer me, Hank.'

'Shoot.' His eyes were worried.

'I don't need the fucking rifle—'

'House. Take. Shoot.'

'Hank. Forget your rifle. Tell me about Vicki.'

He watched her severely, his eyes insisting that she heed his advice.

'Tell me.'

'Not.' Hank's jaw set, hard and angry.

'Did you have an affair?'

Hank's eyes were steely, unwavering. 'Not. No.'

What was he saying? Was he denying the affair?

'Hank.' Harper wasn't convinced. 'What were the notes Trent wanted—'

'Notes. Cheat. Tell. She.' His answer confused her, frustrated him.

What?

'Write.' Or right? His nod was emphatic. 'Not.'

Not write? Or not right. Harper thought for a second. 'You mean Trent didn't write an article? He cheated?'

'No.' Hank's hands tightened into fists. 'She. For. Trent. Ten. Cheat. Yure.'

That might have been the most complex statement Hank had made since his fall. Harper tried to make sense of it. Vicki cheated? Trent cheated? One of them cheated somehow to get Trent tenure? Maybe Hank had found out, had proof of their cheating in his computer – and the proof was those 'notes' Trent wanted? But Harper didn't know what the proof was or even that it existed; she had no evidence that Trent had done anything unethical or dishonest. She was making up the whole story. Even so, when she closed her eyes, she saw Trent standing on the roof, arms reaching out as Hank fell.

And, once again, Hank was diverting her attention. 'Tell me about you and Vicki.'

'Not. Her.' His eyes softened, became puppy-like. He reached out with his strong arm. 'No. Not. Hoppa. You. Me.'

Hank's good hand stroked her arm, knowing just how to touch her, giving her goose flesh. She closed her eyes, her body recognizing his touch, reacting. Lord, she missed him. But no. She wasn't going to be so easily won over.

'Hank. I read Vicki's emails.'

His eyes darted away and he released her arm. Was that a confession?

'What went on, Hank?' Harper insisted. 'I deserve to know.'

Hank stared into air for a long moment before meeting her gaze. When he did, his eyes seemed wounded. And the slightest

bit altered, as if belonging to a Hank impersonator. Someone
who was almost but not quite Hank. 'Hoppa.' He shook his
head. 'Mail not. Write.' Or male not right? 'Hay. Den.'

Hayden. Dr Hayden, head of the Geology Department? What
about him? Hank's mouth twisted, forming another word. 'Bee
leave?'

Harper didn't know what he was saying or what she believed.
She wanted to trust him. But trust was beyond her. Hank held
her shoulder with his good hand, tightening his grip until it began
to hurt. She tried to pull away, but he wouldn't release her.

'Hoppa. Bee leave.' His tone was grave. 'Oowife. My.' For
once, his eyes were not laughing. They held on to hers, much
as a cat's might hold on to its prey's. Hank's grip tightened.
For a heartbeat, Harper felt afraid.

She sat still, a captive of her husband's eyes. Finally, Hank
released her, and they sat silently, watching first each other,
then the walls, each knowing that something between them had
shifted and that there was nothing either of them could do about
it. Harper got up and told Hank she'd be back in the morning,
but he didn't respond; he stared stubbornly at the wall.

For the second time that night, Harper left without a kiss.
When she passed the guard, he called to her, 'Did you find it?'
Find what? 'Oh, yes.' She nodded, but didn't remember – had
no idea – what he meant.

A sunbeam carved its way through the crack in the curtains
and landed on her forehead, spotlighting her eyes. Harper
moaned and opened one of them. The drapes were unfamiliar.
So was the wallpaper. Harper closed her eyes again. Maybe she
was dreaming. But when she opened her eyes again, the drapes
and wallpaper had not changed. For a few confused eye blinks,
Harper couldn't figure out where she was.

Slowly, though, with a wave of disgust, she remembered. In
the middle of the night, she'd gone back to the bitch-slut's house
and finally fallen asleep. The clock on the nightstand said eleven
forty-nine. What – almost noon? In a heartbeat, Harper was on
her feet, limping on her sore leg, cursing, looking for clothing,
grabbing her bag, rotating without efficiency and without being
fully awake until she remembered that, oh – hadn't the day
before been Wednesday? Yes. Bloody Wednesday. The day of
the murders. Of dinner with Ron. Of discovering her husband's

affair. Which meant today must be Thursday. Which meant she had no recitation. Which meant she hadn't overslept.

Harper stood in the middle of Vicki's guest room, checking the clock, the window. Seeing another police car parked in front of the house. Feeling a sickness in her bones: her encounter with Hank, his lack of repentance. How was she supposed to deal with that? What did people do when they found out their husbands had had affairs with their best friends? Murder was far too mild. She was thinking of other alternatives when her phone rang.

Caller ID announced MOTHER. Damn, not now. She couldn't talk to her mother now, couldn't put on a front and pretend that she was fine. She let it ring; her mother must have heard the story of her dead students on national news, must be worried. Mom would smother her with well-intended but useless advice full of irrelevant tangents about a neighbor's son who'd known somebody in college who'd taken drugs, or a distant relative of a friend who'd killed himself. She would ramble on, sharing stories. It was how she expressed affection. Suddenly, Harper missed her, needed to hear her voice. She grabbed the phone.

'Mom?' Harper listened for her mother's smoky voice, which over the years had descended in pitch to a throaty baritone. But there was only empty air. Her mother had hung up.

Harper closed her eyes, felt alone. Never mind, she told herself; it's OK. You'll talk to her later. Meantime, she needed to collect herself. She'd survived worse things than an affair. She was tough. Army tough. She'd be fine.

She limped to the shower, turned on the water, stepped inside. Beginning her day. Afterwards, she'd dress, go assure the policeman in the cruiser that she was fine, and later see Leslie. She'd function. Even so, washcloth in hand, she stood with her face up, directly under the shower nozzle. That way, with water cascading over her face, Harper wouldn't have to admit even to herself that some of the stream was salty, coming from her eyes.

The Sleep Clinic was almost empty when Wyatt caught up with Ron and pulled him into a corner, demanding to know what had happened at Harper's house. Ron dodged. He didn't want to deal with Wyatt.

'You saw it on the news. What more do you need to know? It was a mess.'

'But you were there?'

'Don't act surprised, Steven. You sent me there.'

Wyatt sputtered. 'Damn it, Kendall. What the hell were you thinking? What if somebody had seen you? You could have been charged with murder. This whole thing would be exposed, the trials cancelled. Forget the trials – the entire Center could have been brought down, our careers with it.'

Ron kept his voice calm. 'How was I supposed to know people were going to be murdered there? Steven, you yourself insisted that I find out how she's involved.' He had anticipated Wyatt's reaction, had resolved not to get riled. He'd prepared what he would say, how he'd say it.

'But I didn't tell you to break into her house—'

'I didn't break in. The back door was open.'

Wyatt crossed his arms, scanning the mostly empty Sleep Clinic. Just three occupied cubicles. Two sleep apnea patients, one narcoleptic. He was fuming; Kendall was too impulsive, had become a liability. When this crisis resolved, he'd have to deal with him.

'Did you see what happened?'

Was Wyatt kidding? 'Of course not. When I heard people coming in, I hid. When things got quiet, I left. The dead girl was on the porch.'

Wyatt drew a breath, eyed Ron pointedly. 'Did you kill her, Kendall?'

Ron remained calm. 'If I did, Wyatt, do you think I would tell you?'

They glared at each other. 'Assuming you weren't seen, then. What did you find?'

'Nothing. Not a thing.'

Silence, except for Wyatt's wheezy breath. 'She's involved in this, Ron. It's obvious. Everything connects to her. Even if the drugs aren't in her house, she must know where they're stashed. Maybe she's got a key to the place. Or maybe they're up in her attic. Did you check her attic?'

'No. I didn't check her attic. I figured it was time to leave when I saw the dead kid.'

'Well, then, how do you know she doesn't have the drugs? Stop thinking with your dick, Kendall. That woman has something or knows something. Why else did those kids go to her place? Why was the killer there? All of them were there for the same reason you were. To find the goddamned drugs.'

Ron didn't reply.

Wyatt faced the door. 'Christ. This is out of control.'

He was right.

'And it's only going to get worse until we recover the pills. Too much is at stake.'

Ron still didn't answer. What was the point? Wyatt was stating the obvious.

'So. You're convinced she doesn't know anything.'

'I am.'

'Well, how about this?' Wyatt squinted, thinking. 'Maybe she does know something, but she doesn't know that she knows it.'

'What the hell does that mean?'

'Maybe that kid who committed suicide said something to her before he jumped. Or maybe he had a key, like I said, and slipped it to her without her noticing. And maybe those kids found it, but whoever killed them took it from them. In which case, the killer has access to the pills—'

Ron rubbed his eyes, fatigued. A key? Harper would certainly have told him about it; after all, she told him about finding a scrap of paper. Ron interrupted, 'So bottom line, Steven, what do we do now?'

Wyatt hissed, inhaling sharply. 'If I'm right, the killer has what we want. So, we find the killer, we find the drugs.'

Great. 'And how do we do that?'

'Dammit, Ron. I don't know. Ask your lady friend what she had that's missing, so we'll know what to look for. And find out who those dead kids hung out with. We'd better find this guy before he starts selling those drugs. Or, God help us, who knows what will happen.'

Wyatt was right. There was nothing else to say. Ron started for the door.

'And, Ron? If we want to save the trials – let alone our jobs – we'd better find him – and the drugs – before the police do.'

Ron kept moving, furious with Wyatt. The man seemed to hold him responsible for everything – the theft, even the murders. Which stunk, since Wyatt had seniority over him. So, unless he could somehow come out the hero in this mess, his status at the clinic – hell, his entire career – was in jeopardy.

Wyatt remained in the hallway, rubbing his forehead. His head ached, and he was feeling the effects of high blood

pressure. The stress was making him ill, but he had to keep up appearances, behave normally. He ought to check on the narcoleptic. She should be waking up any time now, and she needed a scolding for not taking her medications.

For the first morning since he'd been at the clinic, Harper didn't visit Hank. Even if she hadn't overslept, she wouldn't have gone. She needed time. Wasn't ready to see him. Leaving Vicki's, she saw a note with her name on it in the kitchen, but she didn't read it, didn't even touch it. She asked the policeman to drive her back home to get her Ninja. Then, promising to be careful, she got on her motorcycle and escaped. Harper rode randomly through sticky hot air until it was time for her appointment with Leslie.

She arrived early, but Leslie was ready for her, handed her a mug of sweet chai.

'You've been crying.'

She had been. More in the last few days than in the last decade. But she shook her head, no. 'Just allergies.'

Leslie smiled. 'Don't lie to your shrink.'

Harper sipped chai to hide a wobbly chin. When she was able, she answered. 'Hank.' But her throat closed, unwilling to let her speak. So she paused, started again. 'Hank was having an affair. With Vicki.'

Leslie didn't react. Holding her mug in both hands, she settled into the big green leather sofa. 'How do you know this?'

'Email. On his computer.'

Leslie waited. 'And you're sure?'

Harper nodded, choosing anger over grief. 'God, Leslie. After everything we've been through. His accident. And all the hell that's happened these last few days – all that's not enough? I also have to find out my husband was fucking my so-called best friend? Really?' She paused, nostrils flaring, jaw tightening. 'So I guess I must be real superficial and self-centered, because here I am, worrying about their affair, obsessing on it. A waitress was murdered. A student killed himself, and two others got murdered right in my own fucking house, and what am I doing? I'm picturing my husband in bed with my friend—'

'Harper. Stop right there.' Leslie's tone was firm. She waited for Harper to catch her breath.

'Let's put this in perspective. You've had one shock after another, not just these last few days, but over a period of years. You've suffered significant traumas, which is why you came to me.'

'What's your point?'

'Finding out that Hank cheated is another trauma. But this one isn't like the others.'

'You're right. Nobody died. So why am I fixated on it when so many worse things have happened?'

'Harper, in its way, Hank being unfaithful – if indeed he has been – would be more traumatic to you than anything you've been through. It would hit you right in the gut, and not because you're selfish or superficial, but because, unlike the other events, it involves not physical but emotional injury. And not just any emotional injury. It involves betrayal. Betrayal by the people closest to you, the people you've trusted.'

Harper replayed that idea in her head. It seemed obvious. Betrayal by someone she loved was worse than a bomb set off by a stranger.

Leslie gave her time before continuing. 'Harper, we've talked about how you feel responsible for others. How, consciously or not, you blame yourself for what happened in Iraq, your parents' divorce, Hank's accident, even your students' deaths.'

Another pause, waiting for the concept to settle. 'But Harper, as we talked about last time, the flip side of guilt is powerlessness. Being guilty implies that you had control; that it was in your power to prevent an event. But if your husband had an affair – and I mean *if* – then you had no power. No control. No ability to prevent it. And, for you, Harper, powerlessness is the worst of all scenarios. Being powerless, being a victim – it's unacceptable. Intolerable.'

Harper's head hurt, partly from her wounds, partly from trying to grasp what Leslie was saying. She didn't quite get it, didn't try. Instead, she changed the subject to her latest trauma: finding Larry and Monique.

Leslie checked Harper's eyes and the newest injuries to her head. 'You should have gone to the hospital.'

'And you should know why I didn't.'

Leslie sighed. Sipped chai. Asked Harper to repeat what had happened at the house. When Harper finished, Leslie was still waiting, expecting more.

'And?'

And? Harper blinked. And what? Wasn't the murder of two students enough?

'Flashbacks?' Leslie persisted. 'In all of this violence and mayhem, didn't you have flashbacks?'

Actually, she'd barely avoided some. She recalled grabbing the twist out of Ron's Martini glass. 'I used a lemon a few times. It helped. Ice, too. I was able to ground myself.'

'Good. That's good.'

Silence. Leslie watched her, sipped. 'Harper, I mentioned that I want to try something new today. Grounding techniques like lemons can help you manage flashbacks, but there's a technique that some say has actually helped reduce them. Even stop them.'

Harper put her mug down. 'I thought PTSD was permanent.'

'So far. But every day there are new discoveries about how the brain works.'

Indeed, Harper thought. Drugs were being developed that could help brains learn. Or cause them to commit suicidal rapist serial killings.

'Is this a drug?'

'No – oh, no. It's based on eye movement. Let me explain.'

The technique was called EMDR, for Eye Movement Desensitization and Reprocessing. The theory was that PTSD arose because the brain had inadequately processed the memories of traumatic experiences, and that stimulation of both sides of the brain through rapid eye movement, coupled with other processes, could help the brain fully process and integrate those memories, thus easing or even eradicating symptoms.

'Rapid eye movement?'

'It's a normal process that happens in sleep. When we dream.'

'So this is like hypnosis?' Harper was skeptical.

'No. You'll be fully conscious, aware of your location and of your safety.'

'Sorry. I don't get how it works.'

Leslie smiled. 'The idea is that PTSD is linked to a dysfunctional memory. Simply put, your memories got incompletely or inaccurately recorded, so your brain got stuck on them. We're going to help you retrieve the missing parts of those memories. Parts that haven't appeared in flashbacks. For example, think of a car crash. The driver is too freaked out during the crash

to record every detail. But, revisiting the crash in a relaxed situation, he might recall details, such as the color of the other car or what was on the radio during impact. By retrieving more details, you'll attain a broader view of what happened. Get it?'

Sort of. 'But won't remembering details only bring on more flashbacks?'

'Doubtful. Your flashbacks are triggered by feelings of imminent danger and specific sensations – smells, sounds and sights that you associate with what happened in Iraq. Here, you're in no danger. You won't hear explosions or smell fire. There's no sun or sand or flies or guns or screams. No triggers, no flashbacks.'

Harper shifted, folded her arms. 'I'm not sure it will work.'

Again, Leslie smiled. 'Well, we won't know unless we try.'

And so they began. First, Leslie asked Harper to identify a place where she felt safe, and to relax and think about it. If she had to, during the therapy, she could always return to that place. Harper thought of her grandmother's kitchen, the aroma of mince pies baking, and allowed herself to drift.

Then Leslie used her hands to direct Harper's eye movements from side to side, quickly. And she asked her to return to Iraq, to the morning of the explosion that had wounded her. Leslie guided Harper to the checkpoint where she and Marvin had been on patrol. And Harper's memories began. Marvin was talking about a movie. The morning was hot. Dry. She had cramps. Felt sore and bloated. Wasn't really listening to Marvin. The others on patrol were in the intersection by the orange cones, facing away. A local boy came along, waving. The woman, Sameh, approached, heading for the market. For about twenty seconds, Harper pictured the scene. The boy hanging around the soldiers, the sun glaring through the dusty haze, buildings the color of sand, conversational clatter from the market. Her cramps so bad that she didn't notice a car approaching from the north.

And – bang – the sensation of flying.

Leslie told her to relax and stop moving her eyes. 'Tell me what comes to mind. Any thoughts?'

Harper bit her lip. 'I should have prevented it. It was my job. They all died because I fucked up.'

'Tell me what was new. What do you notice about the memory?'

'The car. I should have seen it.' She was holding her stomach.

Leslie pointed to Harper's hands. 'What's with your tummy?'

'Oh. I had cramps that morning. Bad ones. I've never remembered that before.'

Leslie beamed. 'See that? You recalled things that your mind never processed. New details.'

'So this is working?' Harper let go of her belly. 'Remembering cramps will stop my flashbacks?'

'It's a start.' Leslie finished her tea. 'Let's begin again.'

Again, Leslie directed Harper's eye movement, asking her to focus on the approaching car. Harper saw it in the periphery of her vision. She stood beside Marvin, nodded 'good morning' to the boy and to Sameh. The car approached, trailing a cloud of dust. Leslie asked who was driving the car. Were there passengers?

Harper stood on the corner, peering at the car, trying to make out the person inside. Her eyes darted rapidly from side to side. Who was driving? A man? Yes, a man. But there was a second person beside him. So, two young men? And an arm hanging out the open back window. Three?

Leslie told her to relax, stopped directing her eyes. 'What do you think?'

'There were three. At least three in the car.'

'Good. Anything else?'

Harper thought. The car full of suicide bombers was coming straight down the road. Headed for the soldiers at the checkpoint, Sameh, the boy – all of them unaware that in seconds they'd be dead. Because Harper had been too distracted to stop the car.

For the rest of the session, they repeated the pattern: half a minute of rapid eye movement with memory, then a short discussion about it.

Again and again, Harper faced the unbearable fact that she was responsible for the carnage that morning. She had seen the car, should have stopped it. Again and again, she saw the boy with no face and felt her body soar on to the top of a parked car, covered with bits of Marvin. But, at the end of the session, even though she tried, she still couldn't locate the remains of the other soldiers, and she had no idea what had happened to Sameh.

Leslie was excited by Harper's progress and made an appointment for the next day, urging her to jot down any related thoughts

or memories that might arise. As Harper was leaving, she touched her arm. 'One more thing, Harper. Remember: an affair doesn't have to mean the end of a marriage.'

Really? It didn't? Harper walked out of Leslie's office, unable to imagine trusting Hank ever again. Or any man. Or woman. Did she trust Leslie? Who knew? Harper felt drained. Except for her skull, which felt full of goose down, fuzzy and soft, unable to function. Her limbs ached, sore to the touch. She needed sleep; thought of her room, her bed, her home. She wondered if she could go back. Even if the police were done with it, could she go back there? Could she sleep where Monique had been murdered, where Larry had sucked his last breath with a nail file stuck in his larynx? There would be blood on the porch, on the bathroom floor.

Still, she'd have to go back some time; ought to call Detective Rivers and find out when she'd be allowed. She pulled her phone out of her bag, saw that she had missed calls. Two from her mother, wanting Harper to call. Two from Vicki, explaining that Harper had been asleep when she'd left that morning and she wanted to know how she was; would she please call. One from Detective Rivers, reporting that her house was no longer a crime scene, so Harper could go home. And one from Ron, asking how she was.

Ron had called. Just to ask how she was.

Harper got on to her Ninja, thinking about Ron. About their dinner the night before. And about going back to Vicki's, turning down his invitation to stay with him. She'd been unable to sleep afterwards, imagining it. Not just staying there, but actually sleeping with him. Having sex with him. She hadn't done it, of course, but she'd thought about it. So, how different was that from Hank?

Very different. Because, even if she'd considered it, she hadn't done it. She had spurned the offer and lain awake, feeling lonely, needy, guilty and cranky, staring at the television, turning, pacing and, eventually, going through Hank's computer. To find out that he had slept with Vicki.

If only she hadn't logged on to that damned computer. Everything would be different. She wouldn't be furious with Hank, wouldn't want to tear out Vicki's hair. The affair, the cheating and lying still would have happened, but at least she'd be blissfully unaware.

In her head, Leslie repeated, 'An affair doesn't have to mean the end of a marriage.'

Really? What did Leslie know about it? Had Leslie's husband ever cheated? With her friend? Harper doubted it. She'd only seen him once, from a distance. His shorts had been too short; his legs pale and skinny, his knees knobby. Not a cheater.

Starting the Ninja, she stopped to make sure her bag was secured behind her seat. Man the thing was bulky. She carried too much stuff with her – all that junk she'd dumped on to Vicki's guest bed, looking for that missing paper. And what about that missing paper? She took her bag out again, peeked inside, half expected to see it lying right on top. No luck.

She poked around, but it simply wasn't there. So where the hell was it? She'd promised to give it to Ron. Now she'd have to tell him she'd lost it. Embarrassing. Even so, she picked up her phone, returned his call. And minutes later pulled into the Ithaca Bakery's parking lot, feeling flushed.

Ron was waiting at a table with her iced chai and some banana walnut bread. When Harper approached, he stood, brushed her cheek with a kiss. A kiss? Just a peck, Harper told herself. A greeting, nothing more. In France, she'd have gotten two of them. She took a seat, her cheek tickling from the bristles of his chin.

The place was empty. Two o'clock: quiet time. Ron reached over and took her hand. His grasp was confident. Entitled.

'I'm glad you called.' His eyes glowed, golden. 'I've got to say it even if it offends you: I thought about you all night.'

He had? Harper looked away. Then she looked back. 'You didn't need to worry. I was fine—'

'I wasn't worrying.' Ron grinned, his teeth white against his tan. 'The fact is, you were on my mind.'

Harper's free hand tightened around her drink, a smile pasted on her face. Awkward.

'You're not offended?'

She laughed nervously, dared to meet his eyes. 'No. You were on mine, too.'

'Seriously?' He grinned, leaned forward. 'Harper, I don't know what's happening here. And I shouldn't say this. But . . . honestly, I'm kind of smitten.' He watched her. 'I should be at work now, but I had to see you.'

Harper watched his lips move. He had to see her?

'I know it's bizarre. Fact is, aside from the Center, we barely know each other. And you're married, for Christ's sake. And the circumstances. Murders and drug thefts? Not exactly a good prognosis for a relationship.' His eyes gleamed. 'But here I am. Here we are. I mean, are we?'

Were they?

Harper stalled, crushed a napkin. 'We are.' Well, they were. What to do about it was a different issue. But, for the moment, she didn't need to do anything. It felt good just to be there.

They left together, in his car. Going to her house, presumably so she wouldn't have to face the mess alone. As he drove, he held her hand with a comfortable grip. She thought only sporadically of Hank.

There were no police cars at the house, but yellow police tape still draped the porch. She dreaded going inside. Her belongings would be scattered. Blood would have crusted on the bathroom floor. When Ron parked the car, she turned to thank him; silently, gently, he lowered his mouth to hers.

The kiss was softer than she'd imagined. Like mousse. Or meringue. She lingered, making it last, wanting to sink into it.

'I'll be right beside you.' His voice was gravelly. Not like the kiss.

Was he hoping to have sex? Another kiss. His tongue flicked across her lips. Harper's chest throbbed, and her body awoke, remembering it was female. Parts she'd tried to forget about began to demand attention. It had been too long. And remembering that too-long-ago time, she thought of Hank. Her Hank. Her lying, cheating, vow-breaking, deceitful Hank.

Ron whispered. His breath tickled her face. 'What's wrong?'

Not for the first time, he responded to her feelings before she'd said a word.

'Is it about your husband? Because, if it is, I understand. But –' he caressed her face with a finger – 'your husband isn't here now.' His lips brushed her forehead. 'And you shouldn't have to be alone.' Her cheek. 'And you've been through a lot.' Her neck. 'And you're so damned adorable.' And settled on her mouth.

This is wrong, Harper thought. Even so, she returned Ron's kisses. His smell was intriguing and new, like his taste. And his touch. But being touched kept reminding her of Hank and his

familiar, much more substantial, more solid body. Which she pictured humping Vicki. And she silently cursed him, telling herself that Hank, with all his secrets and deceits, had no right to expect his wife to be faithful.

'Want to move this inside?' Ron whispered.

Inside? Oh. To her bedroom? Hank's bedroom? Their bed? Harper hesitated, pulled away. Oh God.

'Harper?'

'This isn't . . . I can't do this, at least not here.' She held herself rigid.

'Someplace else then?'

When she didn't respond, Ron took a deep breath. 'Are you sure?'

No, Harper wasn't, but she nodded, yes. She pictured ripping his clothes off, wondered what his chest would look like. Was it rippled? Skinny? Freckled? Sprinkled with soft hairs?

Ron leaned against the window, an arm on the steering wheel, instantly composed. 'OK.' Harper thought she heard a trace of annoyance in his voice. 'Let's just go check the place out.'

They got out of the car, Harper wondering why he'd given up so easily. He could have suggested going to his house. Or a motel. But he hadn't; he'd just given up. Which left her and her body feeling rejected. Maybe, she thought, Ron felt rejected, too. After all, she'd been the one who'd called the halt, and she hadn't done it gently. She thought of his kiss, its tenderness, the way he'd anticipated her thoughts. Oh God, what was she doing?

Together, they walked to the porch where the puddle of blood had long since congealed and dried. Harper didn't look at it. Instead, she stood tall, bracing herself to face the mess inside, and realized that she really should – no, really had to – deal with the house alone. This wasn't just her home; it was also Hank's. Just as Ron didn't belong in their bed, he didn't belong inside their cabinets or dresser drawers. She shouldn't have let him come over. Her lips still pulsed from the pressure of his, and she could smell him on her skin. Dammit, why had he just given up? Why hadn't he asked her to his place? Why had the panting and petting stopped and everything fallen apart?

Ron stood in the foyer, looking around. In the dining room, drop cloths lay in bunches, the contents of the hutch scattered

on top. The living room furniture was upside down, cushions thrown every which way.

'Cool house.'

Was he serious? 'It is. We think so, anyhow.'

'You're renovating.'

'We were.' Harper didn't want to talk about that. 'Anyhow, I can manage from here. Thanks for . . . you know.'

Ron's stared at the mess. 'Don't be ridiculous. At least let me pick up the heavy stuff—'

'No. I can manage. Really.'

He didn't move. Didn't seem to know what to say.

'I kind of need to do this alone.'

'But you shouldn't. Be alone, I mean.'

'I'll be fine. The police keep driving by.'

Ron moved close, kissed her again briefly. 'I'll call you tomorrow.'

Harper nodded, ready for him to go. Wanting him to stay. She watched through the dining-room window as he walked to his car. Even if Hank had cheated on her, she was better than that. She was angry, but she wasn't going to have sex with Ron just to get revenge. She wasn't.

Bracing herself, Harper walked into the living room, turned over a chair. Replaced a cushion. Bent over for another when, suddenly, she dropped it, turned and ran to the door, hoping she wasn't too late to catch Ron.

Grabbing her bag, she flew out the front door, calling to Ron, catching him before he drove off, reminding him that her Ninja was still parked at the bakery. They laughed foolishly, and Harper got back in the car.

For several miles, they were silent.

'I hope you don't—'

'Look, I don't want to—'

They both began at once. And stopped at once. And laughed again, uncomfortably.

'Go on. What were you going to say?'

'No, nothing. You go ahead.'

Ron drove. 'I like you, Harper. That's all.'

'I like you, too. Really.'

Ron smiled. 'Good.'

Harper wasn't sure. 'Is it?'

'Yes. It is.'

Silence. Only, this time, it wasn't uncomfortable; something had been understood.

After a while, Ron sighed.

'What?'

'Nothing. Well, not nothing. Fact is, I don't want to go back to work. Wyatt's been a pain. He's obsessed about the drugs, putting pressure on me because he doesn't know what to do.' Ron stopped at a red light, turned to look at her. 'The problem's serious, but he's so freaking uptight. He's making it worse.'

'Dr Wyatt has always seemed . . . strung tight.'

Ron nodded, smirking. 'He's a genius; geniuses tend to be quirky.' He watched the road. 'Wyatt thinks you're involved in all this, Harper.'

Harper tensed. 'What? Why?'

'Think about it. You knew the murdered kids, the suicide, even the waitress.'

Detective Rivers had said the same thing.

'So far, you're the common thread. Plus, you've been mugged, your house has been tossed. It's obvious Wyatt's not the only one who thinks you're connected.'

'But how, Ron? How could I be connected? Does he think I masterminded the theft? I never even knew those pills existed—'

'No, no. He thinks you're an unwitting participant. That you fell into it by accident. That you must have something, maybe something you don't know you have. Or you know something you don't consider significant.' Ron stopped at a red light, turned to face her.

'But I've already told you—' Harper stopped mid-sentence, remembering that she hadn't told him about the paper. She'd met him for coffee to tell him, but they'd gotten sidetracked by their flirtation. 'Could it be that piece of paper? With the numbers?'

'Let me take a look at it.'

Harper swallowed. 'But it wasn't anything – just scrap paper with numbers—'

'Wasn't?'

She winced.

'What?' Ron waited. 'You lost it?' The light turned green. A car behind them honked. Ron drove, eyes still on Harper.

'It was in my bag – now it's not.'

'You're sure?'

She nodded. 'I dumped everything out. Twice.'

Ron paused, thinking. 'OK. Can you remember what was on the paper?'

'Just numbers.'

'What numbers?'

'I don't know. There were a lot – at least a dozen.' She shut her eyes, picturing them. 'The first was one.'

'Phone numbers start with one. Was it a phone number?'

'Maybe. I thought it might be a student ID number, but there were too many digits.'

'OK. IDs have eight digits, so we know there were more than eight. And we know the first one. That's a start.'

The air conditioning blew cold air into in Harper's face, made her eyes burn. 'Who else knew about the numbers?'

She thought. Remembered. 'Larry.'

'Larry? As in dead Larry?'

Harper nodded. 'He came to my office, looking for it. He said the paper was a study guide. A list of page numbers.'

'Well, obviously, that was bull. Did you tell him you had it?' Ron turned a corner too fast. A vein stuck out in his forehead.

'Not exactly. I told him that all Graham's belongings would go to the police, and if he wanted anything – even a piece of paper – he'd have to talk to them—'

'Which sounds like an admission that you had it.' Ron's eyes narrowed; he ran a red light. 'Damn, Harper. Why didn't you give it to me right away?' His tone was harsh, accusatory.

Harper bristled. Did he think she'd lost the page deliberately? 'Hold on a sec, Ron. Who knows if the numbers even relate to your stolen drugs? Maybe the paper's a cheat sheet for a quiz or a list of lucky lottery numbers. I don't know. But as soon as I thought of it, I contacted you.'

Ron took a breath, looked ahead at the road. 'You're right; you did. I'm sorry.' The words sounded forced.

Harper waited a few beats. In anger, Ron's eyes had become snake-like. 'Apology accepted.' Kind of.

Ron reached for her hand; he no longer resembled a reptile. 'Don't lie. You're mad at me, rightfully so. I was wrong to snap. Fact is, I'm annoyed at myself, not you. Because lives are in danger, and time is critical.'

Harper understood that time was critical. Lives were in danger. She'd messed up, and, once again, people were dying.

'So.' He started over. Calmly. 'About the numbers. When did you last have them?'

Harper stared at the dashboard, remembering. 'When I found Monique's body. It was in my bag when I grabbed my phone to call nine–one–one.' But what had she done with it? Ron was right; she should have given him the paper right away. If she had, he might have found the drugs. Monique and Larry might still be alive. She looked out the window; Marvin stood in the street, a car speeding toward him, trailing a cloud of dust.

Harper knew better than to react as it passed. Without a wince or even a cough, she endured the dry exhaust fumes, the rush of sandy wind and the acrid smell of explosives. She didn't blink as an unattached hand whizzed by, or cry out as she left the ground and flew, or cringe as she anticipated the merciless slam of her body against the rusted-out car.

Harper didn't resist, didn't let on what was happening, didn't even try to find her lemon. She simply shook her head again and said, 'I'm sorry.'

Ron didn't notice her flashback. He was pulling over, parking and putting on a CD, something monotonous and calming, and, calmly, he asked monotonous questions, trying to help Harper recall what was on the paper, what she'd done with it.

'Relax,' he told her. His voice was soft, but she sensed tension underneath. 'Close your eyes, Harper. Breathe deeply. Let air in and push it out slowly. Picture yourself back at the moment when you first found the paper. Let the memories surface.'

'What are you trying to do, hypnotize me?'

'If I have to.'

Was he serious? 'Don't bother. I can't be hypnotized. It won't work on me.'

'Fine, don't be hypnotized. Just relax and try to remember.'

Harper thought of her rapid eye movement therapy, wondered if it would help. She tried looking back and forth on her own. Left right. Left right.

'What are you doing?'

'Trying to remember stuff I haven't processed.'

Ron chuckled. 'You know about that? You're trying EMDR?' He rolled his eyes.

'What?' Harper stopped moving her eyes. 'What's funny?'

'Nothing. Sorry. I just think it's crap. Particularly when it's self-administered.'

Harper's face reddened. EMDR was crap? Really? Why would he say that? Never mind. She stopped moving her eyes and leaned back, simply trying to remember. Ron talked to her softly, coaxing her to let the tension out of her shoulders, back, legs.

Harper straightened up, shook her head. 'Sorry. I just can't remember.'

'That's OK. You did your best.' Ron grinned and started the car.

He seemed in a hurry. Harper looked at the dashboard clock; twenty minutes had passed since they'd pulled off the road. What? It seemed like only a couple. Five at most. How had she lost track of time?

'Ron? How long were we sitting there—'

His grin was smug. 'You know, you weren't entirely right. About not being able to be hypnotized.'

What? 'You hypnotized me?' Harper was astounded. She sat up, ran her hands through her hair. Appalled. Could somebody hypnotize her without her knowing it? Without her permission?

'Would I do that?' Feigned innocence. A smarmy smile.

Obviously, he would. But how? She knew how to resist suggestion.

'You must have wanted to be hypnotized, or it wouldn't have happened.'

Harper frowned, uncertain. 'Well? Did you learn anything?'

'You remembered a few details.' He stopped at a light. 'Some more numbers.'

'Seriously?' She had no recollection. 'Did you write them down? Let's go over them—'

'You've been through enough for now, Harper. Just relax. Breathe.'

Oddly, she did. His voice relaxed her. His tone. She didn't need to worry about the numbers; she could trust Ron. He'd tell her whatever she needed to know. When they pulled into the bakery parking lot, Harper picked up her bag and opened the door. Ron leaned over and kissed her. And a surprising sense of calm and optimism washed over her.

'Tomorrow,' he said. 'I'll call you.'

*   *   *

Riding home, Harper felt refreshed, light. Almost weightless. But she was perplexed: how had Ron been able to hypnotize her? And when? She'd been trying to remember details about the scrap of paper, to envision the digits. And then Ron started the car. She'd lost track of time, remembered nothing of the interim.

So what was that damned piece of paper, anyhow? A map – like a treasure map? The numbers counting out footsteps from a starting point to a secret hiding place? Or did each digit represent a letter, so the number was a code? Or was it simply a phone number?

She rode down the steep hill into Ithaca, passing tall trees and Victorian homes, trying to figure out when she'd last seen the paper, where she'd lost it. She'd had it in her bag continuously, hadn't taken it out – of that she was certain. And it had been there when she'd found Monique's body. So when could it have gone missing? Objects didn't just walk away. So . . .

Someone must have taken it out of her bag.

But how? It had been with her; she hadn't left it unattended. Then again, maybe she'd been unable to attend it.

As in maybe she'd been unconscious on her front porch beside Monique's body.

Of course. Whoever had killed Larry and Monique had knocked Harper out and taken the paper from her bag. Which meant that the numbers on the paper were probably what everyone had been searching for.

And that whoever had them was the killer.

As soon as she arrived home, Harper noticed the change. The house had always felt welcoming, its intricate Victorian design genteel and proud. But not now. Now, it felt altered, sinister. People had been killed here. Someone had ripped through the place, tearing apart its insides. Its charming nooks huddled shadowed and menacing; the creaking of its ageing wooden joints sounded like groans of pain.

Nonsense, Harper told herself. Places didn't change, at least not that suddenly. The house would feel comfy again once the mess was cleaned up. And she'd begin right away, right after she called Detective Rivers.

When Rivers answered, Harper excitedly explained her news: that Graham's list of numbers had gone missing from her bag

while she'd been unconscious, so the killer must have taken it. If they found the list, they'd find the killer.

Instead of appreciating the information, Detective Rivers reacted with confusion and anger. What numbers? What piece of paper? Why hadn't Harper mentioned it before? Why hadn't she turned it over to the police with the rest of Graham's property? What exactly were the numbers? What did Harper think they signified?

Harper righted a dining-room chair and sat, answering questions, feeling chastised. And afterward, she kept sitting, feeling that everything she did was wrong. Losing the numbers. Trusting Vicki. Reading Hank's email. Kissing Ron. Not stopping the bombers. Surviving the explosion. But guilt, she knew, was a paralyzing force. If she let it, it would hold her in the chair, immobilizing her permanently. And she had work to do. A ransacked house to clean.

Righting the living room sofa, she realized she should call Ron; he'd want to know what she'd figured out about the paper. But, surrounded by Hank's refinished floors, his books and photos, she couldn't call Ron. Ron could wait. For now, she needed to concentrate on rebuilding her home, and she immersed herself in the physicality of cleaning.

Harper went around front, turned on the hose and washed down the front porch, swabbing off caked blood. Inside, she donned rubber gloves and cleaned every item before replacing it, not wanting a single trace of a killer's touch to linger on a serving plate or wine glass, or even on a tin can. Throwing out shards of shattered porcelain, dumping thawed frozen foods, she numbed herself to the casualties of her kitchen, sweeping and mopping, refilling the broom closet. Finding Hank's rifle there.

She worked in silence, sweating. Occasionally, thoughts intruded. Questions about what the numbers might mean, or why someone would kill to obtain them. Visual images of the page itself, or a fleeting snapshot of scrawled digits – first a one and after that – a six? Again, she thought of calling Ron, telling him about the six.

But no. Instead, she threw herself into scrubbing, dusting, polishing, disinfecting – washing away thoughts of Ron. Of risks she couldn't afford to take, needs she couldn't afford to acknowledge. Besides, she wasn't sure she could trust Ron. He had,

after all, hypnotized her. Had taken from her memory without her knowledge. No, she needed to take control, figure out what was happening between them. What she wanted to happen. Why she'd kissed him, why thinking about him made her knees dissolve. No, she wasn't going to call him, at least for a while.

When she took a break from cleaning, she made a can of soup. Opened a bag of chips. Went up to the nursery and rocked for a while. Then, dutifully, she went to see Hank, staying for a mutually tense and conflicted, mostly silent, half-hour before she escaped back home. Inside, she avoided the computer but checked her phone messages. Her mom had called again, and Vicki, twice. Harper didn't answer Vicki, but she returned her mother's call, and, though she took pains to sound cheerful and light, her mother relentlessly questioned her about the deaths on campus and advised her to take vitamins, as she'd heard that depression was related to a lack of the Bs.

Finally, just before ten, Harper took another three-minute combat shower in the downstairs bathroom, wondering if she'd ever use the one upstairs; if she and Hank would stay together long enough to finish remodeling it. Scrubbing out her anger at him, counting the seconds, again she contemplated actual baths, relaxing and soaking like a civilian. She began to rinse off with forty seconds left to go and, as hot water cascaded over her head and shoulders, unexpectedly, she again thought of Ron.

In his office at the Neurological Center, Ron stared at the digits Harper had recited under hypnosis; 1671922072. He counted the digits. Ten, like a phone number. Maybe it was that simple. He picked up the phone and called it, got a computerized 'The number you have dialed is not in service'.

OK. So it wasn't a phone number. What the hell was it?

He leaned back in his desk chair, feet up, eyes closed, thinking. Probably it was a code, the numbers each standing for something. And probably the code wouldn't be too compli-cated; after all, it had been put together by undergraduates. The key would be relatively obvious. Simple. He tried substituting letters for the numbers – A for '1', B for '2' and so on. '1671922072' would be afgaibb . . .

Ron stopped transposing. Maybe the first letter wasn't '1' and '6', but '16'? Then it would be 'P'. Followed by 'G'. Then either 'S' or 'A'? OK. Neither combination spelled anything. Maybe

the code was more sophisticated than mere substitution. Maybe the '1's symbolized stops, like punctuation? Or maybe some of the numbers were dummies, meaningless fillers. He tried grouping the digits in clusters of three and fours, ignoring first the '2's, then the '0's, finally the '1's. And got gibberish again.

He backed up, tried rearranging the letters as puzzle pieces. Figgbbgb? Pabbfigb? No luck. He began again, arranging the letters as written, substituting others as if they were a cryptogram. Impossible. He paused, reconsidered the way he'd transferred the digits into letters, and tried different ways of combining them: '1' and '9' could be '19' or 'S'; '2' and '0' could be '20' or 'T.' P-F-S-V-G-B. Or A-F-S-T-G-B.

It wasn't working. The cryptogram – if it was a cryptogram – escaped him. He simply couldn't identify enough letters to make a clear pattern for decoding it.

Frustrated, Ron went down the hall to the vending machine, got himself a cup of awful coffee, filled it with too much awful non-dairy creamer and came back to his office. He stood, paced, sat, stood again, sat again. Sipped coffee. Looked at the original number again.

Maybe he could find help online. He logged on, Googled 'codes' and 'cryptology'. He was still searching when Wyatt came in, frazzled. 'So? Anything?'

Ron welcomed the help of another brain, even if it was Wyatt's. 'Wyatt. Good. Come take a look. I got this number when I hypnotized Harper Jennings. Maybe you can help me figure out what the hell it means.'

Friday morning, Harper stopped in to see Hank, but only briefly. He was walking with a walker, on his own, in the hall. A nurse watched from the station, waved as Harper passed. 'He's getting stronger every day, Mrs Jennings.'

'Great.' Harper forced a smile, continued down the hall.

Hank watched her approach and slowly stepped towards her. She greeted him with a hurried peck.

'Mad. You.' His eyes were wounded.

'What would you expect?'

'No. Hoppa. You.'

She didn't even try to figure out his meaning. What was the point?

'Look, let's deal with one issue at a time. For now, that issue

is your recovery. The rest, even the thing with Vicki, will wait.'
If only she meant that. If only she could wrap up her anger and
hurt, and stuff them into a storage bin.

'No. You. I.' Or know you I?

Harper managed to meet his eyes. They were almost black,
shining, twinkling at her. How could they twinkle, even now?
Did he think their situation was funny? Or maybe it wasn't a
twinkle of laughter. Maybe it was something else, a glower?

'You're walking well.' She changed the subject.

'Go. Three. Times. Hall.'

'Really? Three times?'

He nodded. 'Now. Six. Will.'

Wow. Ten days ago, he could barely make it to the nursing
station. 'Soon you won't need the walker.'

'Now. Not. Need.' It was true. He was gliding the thing along
with his good arm, not leaning on it at all.

'Use it anyhow. Just in case.'

'Soon. Hoppa. Home. Come.'

Together, they walked up and down the hall three more times,
each limping slightly on opposite sides. They talked politely
about neutral topics. The endlessly hot weather. Hank's need for
a haircut. No mention of dead students or marital infidelity. The
conversation continued tentatively, and Harper was so intent on
keeping it neutral that she was out of the clinic and on her way
to class before it occurred to her how much Hank was talking
or how easy it was to understand what he was trying to say.

And she was climbing the stairs before what he'd said actually hit her: soon, Hank intended to come home.

A cop car coasted behind her. Annoying. The cruisers appeared
at random times, watching her, making Harper feel invaded, maybe
like Iraqis had felt, being watched by her security patrol. She
resented the presence of the police. She wasn't a suspect, didn't
need to be followed. And she was army, able to defend herself.
Detective Rivers, though, thought differently, and the cop watched
her, making sure she was safe as she made her way to class.

Class, of course, was pretty empty. Three weren't there due
to death. Only a handful showed. Anna was among the absent.
Harper wondered how she was dealing with the news of more
dead classmates. She pictured her lying somewhere, trapped in
cataplexy.

'Are we having class, Loot?' Terence raised a muscled arm. 'Nobody's here.'

Wait. Hadn't he heard? Didn't he know? Harper drew a breath.

But Jeremy spoke before she could. 'We're all that's left. Everybody else is fuckin' dead.'

'Yeah.' Esoso's eyes widened. 'I swear, this class is cursed.'

'We need to talk.' Harper sat on her desk. 'But, first, let's make sure everyone knows what's happened. Has everyone seen the paper or watched the news?'

'The university sent out an email—'

Terence's face was blank. 'I didn't look at mine. Not in a couple days. What's going—'

'Larry and Monique. They're dead,' Shaundra wailed.

'Whoa, not funny, Shaun—' Terence stopped in the middle of her name. He'd turned, was silenced by the stricken look on her face. 'Damn. For real? They're dead?'

'First Graham; now them.' Esoso shook his head. 'I told you. It's a curse.'

Terence looked from classmate to classmate, saw their identical morose expressions. 'What – they killed themselves, too?'

As gently as she could, Harper explained that they'd been murdered, omitting any mention of her house. Some students would know that, but she didn't need to advertise the fact. She did, however, give more information than they'd have heard on the news.

'What I'm about to tell you is not public knowledge yet.' She'd seen Esoso and Jeremy with Larry at the clinic, so she kept her eyes on them as she continued. 'The deaths of your three classmates may have been connected to the theft of some experimental drugs from Cayuga Neurological Center, where some of you are research subjects.'

Esoso's gaze fell to his desk; Jeremy's moved slowly to Esoso.

'Whoever took the drugs probably thinks they can be sold and used for recreational purposes. But I've learned from a doctor at the Center that the drugs are dangerous. They can have serious, deadly side effects. So if any of you know anything about them – anything about how to get them back – please let me or the police or Dr Kendall at the Center know. You won't get in trouble. You can make an anonymous call—'

'Hang on a minute, Loot,' Dustin interrupted, eyes narrowed. 'What makes you think any of us would know about stolen drugs?'

Harper paused. 'I don't. But Graham's death and Larry and Monique's murders seem connected to the drugs. And since some of you were close to them, it makes sense that some of you might know something.' She didn't look at Esoso or Jeremy.

'What? Being close? That doesn't mean I'd know anything.' Terence crossed his arms. 'I liked to look at Miss Pinkie's backside, but that doesn't mean—'

'No, it doesn't.' Harper ran a hand across her hair. 'No one's accusing anybody of anything. But this is serious. Whoever wants those drugs isn't messing around. People have been killed. And I don't want anyone else to get hurt.'

Silence. Someone shifted in a chair. Someone coughed.

Someone burst through the door. 'Sorry I'm late.' Anna stood in the doorway, breathless and harried, carrying a lopsided white-frosted cake. 'I wanted to bring this.'

She rushed in, setting the cake on Harper's desk. Blue icing spelled out 'Happy Twentieth Birthday, Graham'.

'What's that?' Terence was on his feet, eyeing the plate.

Anna cleared her throat. 'Today is Graham's birthday. So my dorm has a kitchen. I baked him a cake.' She was elated, a bit hyper. She pulled plastic wrap off the cake and the aroma of chocolate and sugar wafted through the room.

Nobody said anything; they stared at Anna. Or at the cake.

'Well, it's his birthday. Somebody should remember it.'

Harper was worried that Anna might collapse; she was breathing shallowly and fast. 'That was thoughtful of you, Anna.'

'I brought plates.' Anna reached into her book bag and pulled out a steak knife, paper plates, napkins, even plastic forks. Harper watched, half expecting favors and party hats, too.

Terence eyed the cake, licking his lips. 'What is it – vanilla? I love vanilla.'

Anna shook her head. 'White chocolate. Graham's favorite.'

Harper spoke cautiously. 'I suppose it's fitting that, especially on his birthday, we take time to remember Graham. To celebrate his life. And, given what else has happened, we should take some time to think about our other lost classmates, too.'

Anna paused, crumpling plastic wrap. 'Other lost classmates?'

'Girl, haven't you heard?' Shaundra was amazed. 'You don't know about the murders?'

Anna turned to Shaundra, then to Harper. Then to the cake. 'Murders?'

Oh God, Harper thought. Anna didn't know.

Shaundra replied, 'Monique and Larry? They're dead.'

Harper stepped to Anna's side, ready to catch her. Anna's eyes drifted slowly.

'Terence, come over here. Now.' Harper used her best command voice, and Terence hopped to attention, not questioning why. Anna's pale skin had become ashen; her eyes rolled upward.

As the other students gaped, Harper grabbed hold of Anna's arm.

'Somebody killed them,' Shaundra continued.

'Damn.' Anna frowned. Then she keeled over into Terence's arms.

'Oh God. Is she dead, too?' Cathy gasped.

'I told you – it's a curse.' Esoso's eyes widened.

'Should I call nine–one–one?'

'Everyone relax,' Harper ordered. 'Anna's fine. She just passes out easily.'

The class gawked as Terence helped Harper carry Anna to a seat, positioning her head gently on to the pillow of her book bag.

'Don't worry,' Harper continued. 'Anna has a condition. Narcolepsy. She falls asleep when she's upset. She'll be up again in a little bit.'

The little class settled down, but the mood remained gloomy.

'Look, everyone. Remember what I said before. If you know anything about those stolen drugs, tell the authorities. And, whatever you do, if you come across unidentified pills, do not take them.'

Blank eyes watched her, needy, waiting. She recognized the look, had seen it before, in the war. The kids needed guidance.

'So. Let's take a moment. Does anyone have some words to say about Graham, Monique or Larry?'

A sniffle. A cough. A throat being cleared.

Finally, Terence spoke. 'They died too young, man.' He shook his head.

'That girl really liked pink,' Jeremy offered.

Dustin stood, pivoting, angry. 'This whole thing's messed up. What's the point of saying anything? They're dead. I mean, DEAD. What the fuck is happening? This is supposed to be college, not some slasher movie. It's frickin' fucked up.' He started toward the open window. Oh God.

Harper moved, positioning herself between him and the sill. Silence.

'May they rest in peace,' Esoso said gently, head bent.

'Amen.' Terence began to hum 'Amazing Grace'. A few others joined him, standing in a loose semicircle, Shaundra leading with a stirring soprano. After that, nobody said anything. Gwen was crying. Dustin stared out at the quad.

When Harper was sure that Dustin wasn't going anywhere, she went back to her desk.

'You're right to be confused. And angry. And sad. I wish I had an explanation or something wise and comforting to say. But I don't.'

More silence.

'Can we have some cake?' Terence's voice was sheepish.

Harper smiled. That was exactly what they needed to do. 'In honor of our lost classmates and Graham's birthday. Yes, let's have some cake.'

Picking up Anna's knife, she began to cut.

In seconds, most of the cake had been devoured. Sugar and buttery icing revived the class, distracted them from the tragedies.

'Do we have an assignment?' somebody asked.

An assignment? Harper had to remind herself what the class was actually supposed to be about. Oh, right. Archeology. She hadn't been following the lectures. Hadn't even thought about them. 'Yes. Review Chapter Six. Somehow, next week, we're going to get back on track.'

Before she could tell her students to take care over the weekend, before she could even dismiss them, the room erupted with the scraping of chairs and desks on the old wooden floor. Then they were gone, paper plates and plastic forks dumped haphazardly into or near the trash can. Harper wished that Esoso or Jeremy would come back and confide something about the stolen pills, but they didn't. For a while, Harper sat alone with the remains of the cake, watching Anna sleep, listening to the inept rattling of the fan.

The minutes dragged on. Harper couldn't leave Anna there, propped up on her book bag. But neither could she sit there and do nothing. The room made her uncomfortable with its empty chairs and stuffy heat. Its yawning window. If she looked at it, she would still see Graham, climbing over the sill. She didn't want to revisit his death, so, diverting herself, she picked at crumbs of cake. Fingered dollops of white icing off the edge of the plate. Yum. Maybe she'd have a small slice.

The cake was moist, fresh. Incredibly rich. Cream cheese icing? Clearly not a mix. Harper had never had white chocolate cake before. It was too sweet for her. But Anna had clearly put some effort into making it. Obviously, she'd had serious feelings for Graham, remembering his birthday, baking him a cake. Poor girl wasn't dealing well with his death. When she woke up, Harper would advise her to discuss Graham's death with her doctors at the clinic so they could help her cope with the trauma. Then again, in Harper's experience, doctors didn't have incredible success in that area.

Harper checked her watch. Anna had been out for a little over ten minutes, probably wouldn't wake up for another fifteen or twenty. Harper had to fill time. She checked her phone. Saw that Vicki had called yet again. Deleted the message. Went next door to the ladies' room, dawdled at the mirror, frowned at the stress in her eyes. Came back to the room and saw Anna still sleeping. And the remnants of the cake still sitting there. Cut herself another sliver, then another. She was considering shaving off a wad of frosting when Anna woke up.

'Oh God.' She lifted her head.

'No – wait. Don't sit up too fast.' Licking frosting off her finger, Harper went to Anna's side. 'Take it easy.'

'They're really dead?' Anna picked up the conversation where it had stopped half an hour earlier. 'Larry and Monique?'

Harper nodded. 'Yes.'

Anna's oval face became somber. 'What happened?'

Harper didn't want to go into it, didn't want Anna to pass out again.

'I heard you talking about the drugs.'

Oh, of course she had – during episodes, Anna could hear perfectly.

'Were they the same drugs, Loot? The stolen ones we talked about? Did they overdose or something?'

'Anna, really, I don't want to upset you—'

'I won't collapse. I promise.'

Harper explained carefully that, while the drugs themselves hadn't killed Monique or Larry, they might well have been the reason for their murders. And she mentioned that the stolen drugs could have dangerous side effects.

'What kind of side effects? Like headaches?'

No, not like headaches. 'The drugs can over-stimulate part of the brain, causing unpredictable behavior. Impulsiveness. Even violence.'

Anna's eyes lost focus. She began to swoon. Dear God, Harper thought. Was the girl passing out again?

'Anna?' Harper cursed herself for upsetting her.

Anna blinked several times and stood, steadying herself. 'No, I'm fine. It's just too much to think about. You were right; we shouldn't talk about it. It's so hot in here. There's no air. I'd better go.' She grabbed her book bag, explaining that she had to get to the clinic for her appointment, and Loot shouldn't worry about her. She'd see her on Monday.

Before Harper could respond, Anna was out the door, leaving her alone with the empty chairs, the rattling fan, the open window. And the remainder of the cake.

There really wasn't very much left. Besides, Harper had a lunchtime appointment with Leslie, wouldn't have time to eat. And it would be a shame to throw it out.

Wyatt was convinced that Ron's numbers had nothing whatever to do with the stolen drugs. He was certain the Jennings woman had sent him down a blind alley, and Ron was, frankly, too turned on by her to see it. Wyatt would have to take charge and somehow find the drugs himself before more people died. If the cause of this mess were discovered, the Neurological Center, its research and his own career would be destroyed. For over an hour, he sat at his desk, making lists. One list of employees, patients and others who'd had access to the drugs. And another of people who'd known about the drug's effect on learning and memory. A third of women Ron Kendall had been involved with since his latest divorce. Who knew what he'd told them?

The list was long. Too long. Subjects in the study, for example. They didn't know if they were taking placebos or the real medication. Or what dosages they were getting. Or what the

drugs were supposed to do. But they knew the drugs were there, being tested. And some of them felt smarter and more alert after taking them. Due to lax security, any of the subjects – and there were currently hundreds – could have stolen them.

Wyatt crumpled up the list, tossed it into the trash. Finally, frustrated, he checked his reflection in the mirror, repositioned his hairpiece and wandered to the Sleep Clinic to do his rounds.

A nurse interrupted his reverie. 'Beds three and seven are apnea. Four is somnambulism; six is insomnia. Two is narcolepsy.' She handed him a stack of files.

Wyatt stared at them. Wondering how long he could keep up the facade of business as usual. How could Ron Kendall remain so unperturbed? Bodies were piling up. In the space of a week, there had been four. And, if the drugs continued to be taken in excess, their side effects would only increase in intensity. Four bodies this week could mean ten next, or twelve, and thirty the week after that. The only hope was that the imbeciles taking them killed each other off, with the last of them flushing the extra drugs. Fatigue washed through him. Good God, what was happening? He could barely breathe. He hadn't slept, hadn't eaten. Needed to. Couldn't. But Ron Kendall – poring over his list of numbers as if they contained the damned secrets of the universe – Kendall seemed well rested, composed. And more than a little bit smug. Why? What was he up to? What did he know that he wasn't sharing? Something about the drugs? About that Jennings woman?

He was porking her. Had to be. And those random numbers – it was possible they were just a ruse, a construct by Kendall to keep attention off the woman. In fact, Kendall and the woman might be conspiring, hiding the drugs to bring him down, so Kendall could take over the research and the clinic . . .

Well, he'd see to it that he didn't go down alone. Kendall would go with him. He was as much at fault as anyone.

Oh God. Oh God. Wyatt put his head down on the nursing-station desk. How could this be happening?

'Dr Wyatt? Are you all right?' The damned nurse hovered over him. 'Can I get you anything?'

He sighed and sat up, stretched his neck. 'No, no. Please just carry on with your duties.'

Good God, couldn't a man have some privacy?

Wyatt stared at the pile of folders in front of him. Of course,

catastrophe wasn't a given; there was always the possibility that Kendall had killed those two kids because he'd learned that they'd actually been the thieves. That they and they alone had known where the drugs were hidden. That no one else would find them. That the trials could continue and be completed without further ado.

Those were definite possibilities. Even probabilities. So, probably, nothing else would go wrong. The drugs would be approved. The clinic's funding would continue. No, it would increase. Exponentially. As would its reputation. His reputation. His career.

Gradually relaxing, Wyatt became aware of phones ringing around him and banks of monitors recording patients' brainwaves and heart rates. That nurse, asking an aide to check the man in bed four. The living bustle of the clinic. He straightened up, inhaled deeply and opened a file. He knew the case; she'd been here almost every day. It was that young woman, that narcoleptic.

'So.' Leslie rearranged her legs, curling them under her on the sofa. 'Anything you want to talk about first?'

Harper shook her head, no. Not her marriage, not her childhood, not the murders, not the stolen drugs or the havoc in her house. Nothing.

'Well, then, why don't we begin?'

Leslie guided Harper's vision rapidly from side to side as she instructed her to revisit the street corner in Baghdad, the morning of the explosion. Once again, Harper was there in the glaring sun and dusty, hot air. Her equipment weighed heavy, and she had bad cramps, but wouldn't complain. Marvin chattered, Sameh approached with a smile. The boy dawdled, toying with a sack. The car came speeding toward them. Sameh stopped in the middle of the road, hesitating, looking back. Meeting Harper's eyes.

Leslie stopped the memory before the oncoming explosion. 'Well, two things are new. You never mentioned Sameh stopping before. Or said that the boy had a sack.'

Harper closed her eyes. She could still see them. If Harper had paid more attention to the car charging the checkpoint and ordered her patrol to fire at it, Sameh and the boy would still be alive.

'What are you thinking?'

'I should have stopped the car.'

'OK, maybe you should have. But what about the others? You blame yourself, but you weren't alone on duty that day. None of the others stopped it either. Why didn't they?'

Harper had no idea.

'What were the others doing?'

'I don't know. I don't remember—'

'OK. Go back again. Look.'

Again, Leslie helped Harper's eyes dart from side to side.

'Try to see what the other soldiers are doing.'

Harper moved her eyes, following Leslie's direction, and, suddenly, Marvin was beside her. The boy lingered nearby, his feet dusty but his shirt crisp and white. Sameh sashayed by, smelling of dusk. The car sped toward them.

Harper looked around. Two in her patrol stood on guard across the road. Two others – Cooper and Joe – were positioned by the orange cones that blocked the road. The rest were clustered near the Hummers, watching the car race their way.

'Excellent.' Leslie signaled for Harper to relax and digest what she'd said.

'They saw it. They watched it coming.' Harper frowned, confused. If the others had seen the car, why hadn't they stopped it? Why had they let it pass the checkpoint and blow everyone up?

Leslie talked about the significance of her memory. The new details she'd recovered proved that Harper was not solely responsible for what had happened.

'But I don't understand. Why did they let the car pass?'

'What was protocol?'

'Any vehicle approaching our security checkpoint was to be stopped and searched. Access to the area had to be approved.'

'And you had the street blocked off.'

'Yes. We did. I don't know. The car must have rammed us. They were suicide bombers, so they had nothing to lose. I guess they just kept coming.'

'Did they?' Leslie waited. 'Harper, you're remembering a lot of new details.'

So? What difference did it make? How was remembering going to change anything? 'Leslie, I'm sorry. I don't see the point—'

'OK.' Leslie nodded. 'That's OK. Indulge me one more time.

Go back. This time, focus on the car.' She began her hand motions, guiding Harper's eyes.

Somebody's arm was out the open window. The car old, dusty, dark green. A Taurus? She saw it coming, trailing its cloud of dust. Marvin stopped talking and spun around to look. Hummers and orange cones blocked the road; Joe and Cooper stepped up to the checkpoint, signaling the car to stop. The others readied their weapons. The boy froze, gaping. The car sped toward them and, at the last moment, brakes screeching, slid to a stop. Sameh turned, looked at Harper. And Harper left the ground, flying.

The patient in bed number two was no stranger to Dr Wyatt. He'd been treating her for months. When he entered the room, she was deep in cataplexy, perfectly motionless, corpse-like. Her chart indicated increasingly frequent episodes over the last several days, to the point that the young woman was unable to function, subject to collapse at almost any time. It also indicated that he'd prescribed medication for her.

'Nurse?' The woman kept closer to him than his shadow. 'Do we know that Anna has actually been taking the Effexor?'

'She says it doesn't work.'

'She told you? When was that?'

'Today. Before she passed out.'

'Why isn't that in her chart?' He couldn't tolerate incompetence.

'Excuse me?'

Wyatt simmered. 'Nothing in the chart indicates non-compliance to prescribed medication regimen.'

The nurse remained unapologetic. 'I suppose I was too busy recording everything else she told me before she collapsed. Such as the terrible stress she's been under with so many of her friends dying.'

Her friends dying? Wyatt blinked rapidly, thinking. His eyes darted from the patient to the nurse. 'And? Where did you bury those records?'

The nurse took the chart and pointed to lengthy notes inserted at the front, right where they were supposed to be, marked for his attention.

Wyatt grumbled, annoyed that he'd missed them, and began to read. The patient, it seemed, had been present at the suicide

of Graham Reynolds. She was a classmate of the two students murdered at the Jennings home, was in Harper Jennings' Archeology class with them. Her narcolepsy had gone haywire with the emotional upheaval she was experiencing.

Wyatt looked at the patient. Anna was hardly a woman, more of a girl. Although he'd been treating her for months, he'd never paid her particular attention. Porcelain, almost bluish skin; oval face lined with thick, frizzy black hair. Plump, bulging body stuffed into too-tight clothes. A pea-sized dark mole on her throat. Exceedingly plain. Probably a loner, the kind who'd spend Saturday night alone, reading Romantic poetry. Not likely to be part of a drug-taking, pill-popping, anything-for-kicks party crowd. Not likely to have much social life at all. Even so, she had proximity to the players. The girl might have over-heard the drug thieves, might know something about who took the pills, where they'd stashed them.

Anna's case was his new top priority. He checked her chart again, noting that she'd been lying there for almost forty minutes, and he took a seat beside her bed. Any minute now, the cata-plexy would pass, and he'd be able to interview her.

Harper was confused. The car had stopped at the checkpoint. If its occupants were going to blow themselves up anyway, why would they stop to be searched and risk their mission? Why not just keep going?

She replayed the memory, heard the screech of brakes, smelled the diesel exhaust, saw the car in the periphery of her vision. Her patrol had stopped them. She was certain.

'Sounds like you've been blaming yourself for no reason, Harper. Your patrol followed protocol and stopped the car. The bomb went off anyway, but that was beyond your control.'

Harper wasn't convinced. 'I should have prevented it.'

'But how? Think about it, Harper. There was a whole squad there. Not just you. Why do you single yourself out for blame?' Leslie's brow furrowed. 'You're going back.'

'Not again.'

'One more time.' Leslie directed her eye movement.

Harper resisted for a few seconds, tired and full of dread. But, then, there she was, at the corner with Marvin, suffering cramps, watching the boy, seeing the car skid to a halt, turning. Seeing Sameh. Meeting her eyes.

And then a blinding flash, a gust of heat forcing her off the ground, flying.

Harper covered her face. 'Sameh!' Her legs bent and came up, dodging an unseen blow. Or explosion. She stopped moving her eyes, letting them rest on Leslie's.

Leslie waited.

Harper was panting, heart pumping. She closed her eyes, aware, finally, of the source of her guilt. She was the only woman in the patrol unit. The only one who would have been allowed to stop and search a female civilian. But because her friendly greeting had become routine, Harper had never suspected, had never even considered stopping Sameh.

And for that a boy had lost both his face and his life; Marvin, the rest of the squad and civilians had died.

Harper slowly leaned back against the cushion on Leslie's sofa. 'Oh God. It was all my fault.'

'No, Harper. Even if you'd have stopped her, she'd have set the bomb off, and the only difference is that you'd be dead, too. Listen to me. You didn't blow everyone up. Sameh did.'

Harper didn't say anything for a long moment. She allowed Leslie's words to repeat themselves in her mind, letting a mantra take hold: it hadn't been her fault. She hadn't killed everyone on the street. Sameh had. Sameh had. Sameh had.

Wyatt looked at his watch. The wall clock was two minutes off; his watch was accurate to one hundredth of a second. He thought again of Ron Kendall, sitting at his desk, playing with number puzzles. Wasting time. But this girl, this Anna, might know something substantive. If she did, he'd have to use some finesse to get her to open up to him. Kendall might be better at that than he was; Kendall had charm, knew how to manage women. That would be the plan. If, upon assessing her, he thought Anna knew anything about the drugs, he'd fetch Kendall and let him work his magic.

Anna, meantime, showed no signs of life, and Wyatt was getting impatient. He looked around the cubicle that served as a sleep room, saw her book bag hanging on a hook. Maybe there would be something helpful inside it. For lack of anything else to do, he got up, took it off the hook, unzipped it. And backed away from the stench.

The bag reeked of bologna. Indeed, half a sandwich, wrapped

in waxed paper, was smashed inside against some books. Who used wax paper anymore? Wyatt glanced at the girl. She hadn't moved, so he dug deeper. Almost laughed out loud when he found a book of English Romantic poems. Lord Byron. Shelley. Keats. Good God. He'd had her pegged.

What else? Her Archeology text. A spiral notebook. Pens, the usual. A stapler. A bunch of rumpled-up loose papers. A to-do list with items already checked off: Bake cake. Buy plates. Arch recit. Storage. Drop off. Clinic.

'What are you doing?'

Damn, the girl was awake. Caught him with his hands in her bag.

'Who said you could go through my stuff?' She pulled the wires off her body, getting out of bed.

'Anna, don't stand up so fast.' Wyatt stuck the wad of papers into the pocket of his lab coat, wrapping his fingers around one of the syringes he carried there, deftly popping off the protective cap.

But Anna was on her feet, coming at him, furious. 'What did you take? I saw you take something from my bag. Give it back.' She reached for his pocket.

Damn. For such a homely girl, Anna was surprisingly assertive, and she was making a racket, drawing unaffordable attention.

Wyatt smiled to reassure her. 'Calm down, Anna, dear.' He reached an arm out for her and, before she could see it coming, withdrew his other hand from his pocket, emptying the syringe into her shoulder.

Anna yelped and began to pull away, but the sedative worked quickly. She sunk deep into sleep, and Wyatt dragged her back to the bed, replacing the wires that monitored her brainwaves and vital signs, covering her with a blanket. Wheezing and cursing, he made notes on her chart that would discredit her in case she awoke and started talking. Anna had been delusional, paranoid; he'd had to sedate her. She might be having a breakdown. Might be abusing drugs. He wrote an order for her arms to be secured to the bed. After all, no one wanted her to fall.

Before he left, certain that she'd been trying to hide something, he looked in her bag again but found nothing of interest. A good luck charm. Some keys. A few dollars. A phone. Nothing. Not even cigarettes or pot. Damn. Wyatt still wanted

to question her, but she'd be out cold for a while, and he'd already spent too much time. Other patients were waiting. Best to carry on as if nothing had happened.

Dabbing sweat off his forehead, rechecking his toupee, Wyatt brought the chart back to the nursing station. He had a bad feeling about Anna, the aggressive way she'd come at him. The way he'd had to subdue her. Most definitely, when the medication wore off, he and Anna Winters would have to chat.

If she'd been guilty of anything, Harper understood, it hadn't been of failing at her duty. It had been of trusting the wrong people. She'd trusted Sameh, had let her pass.

Leslie had promised that they'd talk about the trust issue next time they met. But, after she left, as Harper rode down the hill to town, she decided that the trust problem wasn't always her fault. People had deliberately deceived her. Not just her father, who'd deceived everyone. Or Sameh, who was a terrorist. But also Hank and Vicki, who were the people closest to her. If she couldn't trust them, how could she trust anyone? Why should she try?

She accelerated, speeding out Route 89 toward the lake, the wind in her face. No helmet, not today. Who cared if she crashed? Today, she took the little Ninja to its limits, riding through the heat, reliving the moment when she'd realized that Sameh, not the men in the car, had set off the bomb. That Sameh had carried the explosives on her body. Hidden beneath her smile.

Harper seethed. She wanted to pound Sameh, shake the grin off her face. But Sameh was long dead, her final, satisfied smile forever frozen in Harper's head. Harper raced, trying to outpace her mind, but the fact was that she'd been a chump, had greeted a murderer every morning, considering her, in those faraway, barren times, almost a friend.

Well, Harper Jennings was finished being taken for a fool by people who posed as her 'friends'. Even if there was nothing she could do about Sameh, she sure as hell could express herself to the live ones.

Before she realized she was going there, Harper doubled back through Ithaca and College Town, ending up on Fairmount Avenue in Vicki's driveway, then in her kitchen. And before Vicki could greet her or ask why her calls had gone unanswered,

Harper balled her hand into a fist and landed a solid punch directly on to Vicki's lightly powdered nose.

Vicki landed on the parquet floor about the same time Harper landed on the seat of her Ninja and sped away, glad that, for once, no cops were following her around. All right, she thought. She hadn't undone what had happened with Hank, hadn't saved her students' or her fellow soldiers' lives. She hadn't changed a thing. But damn, she thought, decking Vicki sure felt good.

Gwen Summers fought tears as she stomped down the hill. She couldn't make sense of what was happening. Kids were dying all around her. It was scary. She wanted to go home, but summer session was short, tuition was too high to drop out, and home was all the way in La Crosse, Wisconsin, a bus ride and two plane trips away, too far to travel for just a weekend. So, upset and lonely, she called a classmate, Shaundra. Maybe she'd meet her in town.

'I can't.' Her nose was stuffed. She'd been crying. 'I messed up, Gwen. I don't know what came over me. I've never been in trouble before. Not even a detention in high school.'

'It can't be that bad.' Oh God. Was Shaundra pregnant?

'I didn't mean to take the stuff – I just – at the last minute grabbed it.'

Grabbed what? 'What stuff?'

'I'm in big trouble, Gwen. My room-mate had to pay two hundred and fifty dollars to bail me out of jail.'

Jail?

'I needed some of those sticky things, you know, to hang posters, so I went to the hardware store. Next thing I know, a cop is looking in my bag, and I'm handcuffed, and I have all kinds of shit in there. Tape and a screwdriver and tools I don't even know what they're for, let alone how they got there. I'm in so much trouble, Gwen. If my parents find out, I swear I'm dead.'

Gwen didn't know what to say. Shoplifting? Really? Shaundra was sophisticated, glamorous, dramatic and very cool. Who'd have guessed she was a shoplifter?

'And did you hear about Jeremy and Esoso?'

Gwen's mouth was dry. She almost didn't want to hear.

'They got arrested, too. I saw them at the station. Jeremy's nose is broken, and Esoso's got a huge black eye. They were

in College Town outside Johnny's Big Red and started some kind of brawl. I don't know anything else.'

Again, Gwen ached for La Crosse where nobody she knew ever brawled or stole. Or jumped out of windows. Or got murdered. She missed her golden retriever, Athena.

Alone, Gwen wandered through town. It was hot; suddenly, she realized she'd feel a lot better if she had a cold beer. She'd rarely been to a bar, never by herself. And, while she'd had her share of liquor at fraternity parties, she'd never had a drink so early in the day. Even so, she really craved a tall one, could almost taste it. Throat parched, she hunted for a bar, finally smelled one from half a block away and stepped inside.

Willy's was dark, air-conditioned. It had an old-fashioned juke box, a dartboard, a pool table. But Gwen didn't care about any of that; she just wanted a beer. Cold clean beer would wash away the sweltering heat and her morbid mood. Maybe she'd get wasted. All by herself.

She climbed on to a stool; rows of well-lit booze bottles greeted her from the wall behind the bar, offering themselves in consolation and partnership. Gwen was tempted, but she didn't have enough cash for hard liquor. Beer would have to do.

The bar was empty except for a shapeless middle-aged guy with frameless glasses who was jawing with the bartender. She sat for a while as they both ignored her. Finally, she called out, 'Hey, can anybody get a beer in here?'

The bartender eyed her and slowly ambled over. 'ID?' He had slick dark hair and a toothpick in his mouth.

Gwen handed him her ID. He took it with thick, stubby fingers, turned it around and over, smirked, looked at her and shook his head, wiggling his toothpick.

'I don't think so, baby girl.' He tossed it on to the bar, returning to the middle-aged guy who was watching her now with open contempt. Who did he think he was? Did they think they were better than her just because they were old? Look at them. Lardy old turds.

Two guys sauntered in, biker wannabes. Tattoos and piercings; one with a shaved head, the other with a mullet and obscene little goatee. Tank tops.

'It's a valid ID.' Gwen didn't give up. 'What's your problem?'

Without even looking at her, the bartender answered, 'You ain't the babe in the photo. You got red hair and freckles. She don't.'

Well, he was right. The photo in the ID was her cousin. But
they looked alike. 'I dyed my hair and wore make-up in the
picture. You're blind. Look again.'

'Honey, you want a drink? I'll get you a glass of milk. Otherwise,
take a hike.' He turned to the new guys. 'What'll it be?'

Gwen wasn't going to be dismissed. She wanted a beer and
she was going to get it. Maybe the bikers would help. She
approached them; the bald one checked her out over his shoulder.
The other got up to put money in the jukebox; music blared, loud
and electrifying. Country? He chose Johnny Cash? But Johnny
Cash moved her; she'd never noticed how deeply. She started to
dance. Couldn't help it; the music pulled her from inside, moved
her body without her help. The mullet guy watched her.

'She's a minor,' the barkeep warned.

'No, I'm not,' Gwen insisted. She was, after all, eighteen.
And a half.

Mullet put an arm around her, led her to a booth in the corner.
The bald one brought the pitcher. Gwen didn't mind sharing a
glass. Before long, she drank straight from the pitcher.

And not long after that, only mildly amazed at herself, she
was on a table in the back room, bones vibrating to the music,
her hair flying, spirit soaring. She hooted along with the small
appreciative crowd, spinning, twirling, tossing her bra into the
air, reveling first in the cheers, then in the arms of her enthu-
siastic fans.

Vicki was still moaning on the kitchen floor when Harper headed
toward the clinic to see Hank, determined to confront him, as
well. She felt energized, empowered. She didn't know if Leslie's
eye movement techniques had ended her flashbacks, but they
certainly seemed to have restored her self-confidence. She
thought about what she'd do when she got to the clinic. Burst
into Hank's room and pop him in the nose, too? What would
he do? But picturing the clinic made her think of Ron. Of
running into him there. Of kissing him.

Wait. Didn't she need to talk to Ron? Yes. She still needed
to tell him about the numbers, that whoever had them was the
killer. She pulled the Ninja to the side of the road, pulled out
her phone to call him, but by the time he answered, she'd realized it would be better to tell him about the numbers in person,
at her house, and she told him to meet her there. Right away.

He asked why she sounded so urgent. Was she all right? Had she found out something about the drugs? Harper gave no answers. She simply told him to meet her and turned her Ninja toward home.

When she got there, she whooshed around, straightening the bedroom, changing into some loose lounging pajamas, spraying herself with jasmine body scent, going downstairs to brush her teeth and check herself in the mirror, putting on lip gloss for the first time in half a year. Finally, Ron's car pulled into the driveway.

Harper met him at the front door. Without a word, she pulled him to her, pressing her mouth against his, wrapping her limbs around him, taking him by surprise.

Except that Ron didn't seem all that surprised. He half-carried Harper up the steps to the bedroom, his shoes abandoned at the front door, his shirt on the stairs, his khakis on the floor beside the bed. He let her claw at him, marking his back, chewing his lips, and he responded in kind, tossing her roughly on to the mattress.

Harper climbed on to him, rolled on top and under him, nipping and clutching, releasing weeks of pent-up frustration, allowing stifled needs and suppressed desires to erupt. For Harper, reality blurred; her life seemed far away, out of reach. Unimportant. This moment and this man were all that mattered; the rest faded, and she held Ron tightly as if he were her only tether to the world. Her entire body yearned; each cell ached to connect with Ron. Her legs encircled him, her arms clung, her torso pressed, attempting to merge. Sex had never felt as desperate, as consuming. As dangerous.

Afterward, Ron slept instantly, noiselessly. He didn't snore the way Hank did, didn't toss. He just slept. Harper lay still, listening to his silence, thinking. Parts of her body that had been dormant for months still tingled from Ron's touch. And his scent was now everywhere, on her skin, her sheets. In her mouth. Oh God. His skin was smooth, almost hairless. The whole time they'd made love, his eyes had been open, watching her. Conscious of her every reaction, each pant or moan. Sex with Ron had been athletic. Tensions had been wrested from her body; she was lighter, freer. And afterwards, lying beside him in the bed that belonged to Hank, she wondered at how easy it had been to break her vows.

Did she feel guilty? Was she sorry? She wasn't sure. After all, Hank had cheated on her, hadn't he? And, until now, she'd been a celibate, faithful chump. Ron's arm lifted, rearranged itself, landing on her belly. He'd told her he cared for her. That it was easy for him to be with her. That he could look at her face forever. He wasn't shy about expressing his feelings. Unlike Hank. Even before the accident, he hadn't often articulated his affection. No, Ron wasn't like Hank. Not his easy words or his agile movements. Not his silent climax.

Oh God. What was she doing, rolling around in bed with this man, comparing him to her husband? Sorrow washed over her; she missed Hank, longed for him. Stop it, she scolded. Don't punish yourself. Hank isn't here. Can't be here. Hank is not available. He probably never will be.

No, she had nothing to feel guilty about; she'd done nothing wrong. She'd only tried to find some comfort so she could survive. Harper turned over and propped herself on an elbow, watching Ron sleep, confronting the undeniable truth that another man's head was on her husband's pillow. No question, the man was beautiful. Not just handsome; he was aesthetically exquisite. His features were symmetrical, chiseled. Not quite strange to her anymore. Becoming familiar.

Harper lay back again, but the movement disturbed him. His eyes opened, and he turned to look at her. Smiled.

'You OK?' He touched her face.

Harper smiled back, kissed his fingers. Yes, she was fine. He sat up, getting out of bed, pulling on his khakis. Harper sat up, blinking. Was he leaving? All of a sudden?

'Going to the john.' He headed into the hall and down the stairs.

Oh, just going to the john. No big deal. Wondering vaguely why he needed pants for that, Harper fluffed her pillow, turned over, snuggled down. And then, suddenly, her eyes opened.

Wide.

Before she could fully process the reasons, she dashed out of bed, pulling on a T-shirt, stepping into panties. Oh God. Ron had gone downstairs to the john. Oh God.

Cool down, she told herself. You're overreacting. There had to be a reasonable explanation. But, if there was, she couldn't think of it.

How, on the first time she'd invited him into her home, had Ron known not to use the bathroom adjacent to the bedroom? How come he hadn't even glanced inside to see that it was being renovated? And how had he known where the other bathroom was?

There was only one explanation: Ron had been there before. Inside her house. Without Harper's knowledge.

But when? And why? Obviously, to look for the stolen drugs. Had it been Ron who'd ransacked her home? And if so, had Ron killed Monique and Larry? She pictured it. Ron prowling the house; Larry and Monique finding him. A confrontation. Murders.

Heart pounding, jabbing her legs into cut-offs, she told herself that she was wrong. Ron was not – could not be – a murderer; even so, she hurried down the hall to the stairway. She took the steps gently, avoiding the creaky parts, trying to balance on her weaker leg, the scarred one that, just minutes ago, Ron had kissed. Damn. Ron's touch still echoed on her skin, tingling like the shadow of a killer.

At the foot of the stairs, Harper glanced down the hall at the bathroom, hoping Ron wouldn't hear her. That he wouldn't realize his mistake until she was gone. What would happen when he found out she knew? Would he kill her, too?

Harper wasn't going to risk it. She edged toward the front door. Before Ron got out of the bathroom, she needed to get out of the house. Just a few seconds and she'd be on her Ninja, riding away.

'Hey, Harper?'

She froze. His voice was close. Not coming from the bathroom down the hall, but from the kitchen. He'd heard her, knew she was downstairs. Maybe she could bolt past the kitchen to the front door and get out before he caught her. Maybe. She crept to the kitchen doorway, peeked in. The refrigerator was open. Ron was leaning inside, looking for something.

'Hey, got any beer?'

Harper held her breath, still considering a dash to the front door. 'Bottom shelf. Way in the back.' She edged toward the front door.

'Want one?'

'No, I'm good.' Her voice sounded thin, and she moved unsteadily, off balance, her weak leg wobbling.

Ron stepped out of the kitchen. 'Harper? What's up? Where are you going?' He moved toward her, holding a bottle of beer. His smile was baffled, kind of wounded.

Harper kept moving back, watching him; he matched his steps with hers. 'Don't come closer, Ron.'

Or what? She'd cry? She had no weapon.

'"Don't come closer"? Seriously?' His free hand rumpled his hair. 'Wait, sorry. I must have missed something. Are you the same lady who was upstairs with me? Because I don't think there *is* any closer than we just got.'

He moved towards her, still hadn't realized his error.

'I figured it out, Ron. What you did. So step back.'

But he didn't. He kept coming. 'What I did? What did I do?'

'You used the bathroom.'

Ron tilted his head, not getting it. 'You're mad that I took a leak?'

'How did you know where my bathroom was, Ron?'

A jolt of realization flickered in Ron's eyes. He glanced toward the bathroom and drew a breath, wincing, taking yet another step. And another. Forgetting that Harper had been trained for combat.

'Come on, Harper. What's the big deal?' Another step. A charming smile.

'When were you here before, Ron? Was it when Larry and Monique were in the house? Did they see you here? Is that why you had to kill them?'

'Kill them? Come on, Harper. You can't be serious.' He began to reach for her.

Quickly, Harper turned, twisting her torso, balancing on her damaged leg just long enough to launch a sidekick with her strong one. Her heel landed on Ron's chest, knocking him, stunned, to the ground, his bottle of beer clattering, rolling, spilling on to the wooden floor.

His smile vanished as he scrambled to his feet, coming after Harper. 'Damn,' he coughed.

Harper's weak leg had collapsed with the kick. Pushing herself up, she ran for the door, had her hand on the knob when Ron lunged, grabbing her ankle from behind, pulling her down. She reached out to break her fall, but her knees slammed the floor. Jagged pain roared through her, reverberated in her head, the shock of the impact momentarily blinding her. Even so, she

kept moving, trying to crawl, but Ron had her ankle, so she spun around to face him, snarling.

'Christ, Harper. Stop. What are you doing?' Ron was winded, his eyes glowing and angry. He pounced and knocked her back to the floor, leaned on her shoulders, holding her down.

Harper lay still, panting. Noticing the beer bottle lying at her side.

'Are you crazy? All this is because I knew where your bathroom was? Do you really believe I killed those kids? Really?' His eyes riveted hers, intense and golden. Reminding her of sex. 'Come on. You've got to trust me at least a little bit. If I let you up, will you stop fighting?'

Ron leaned over her, watching her, panting on her face. Moments ago – maybe five minutes – she'd have reached up and caressed his cheek, inhaled his breath. Now she tightened her hands into fists and searched his eyes for lies. At the very least, Ron had trespassed and hidden the truth. At the worst, he'd committed a double murder. And he wanted her to trust him? His eyes showed no signs of guilt or remorse, only fiery indignation, and he glared at her, waiting for an answer.

Harper waited, too. But not to answer. As soon as she could move her arm, she reached for the beer bottle, quietly closed her fingers around its neck.

Ron's eyes narrowed, and he started to lower his face to hers, probably to kiss her. But he never had a chance; as soon as he was off balance, Harper struck as hard as she could, shattering the bottle against the back of his head.

The warm night air ruffled Harper's hair as she sped across campus and north to the clinic. No way was she going to let Hank stay at a place run by Ron, not one more night, not one more hour. The faster she rode, the faster her mind worked, and she reached conclusions with unaccustomed speed and clarity. She was convinced that Ron had a hand in the deaths of her students – might have killed two of them himself. All three – Larry, Monique and Graham – had been research subjects at the Neurological Center and must have been involved with the drug theft. It was obvious: Ron had worked his way into her life just after Graham's suicide; that couldn't be a coincidence. He'd been using her to find the drugs.

A light turned red; Harper saw no cross traffic, kept going.

She wondered how long Ron would be unconscious, how badly she'd hurt him. His gash had bled a lot. She thought of him lying in the hallway, out cold. When she'd rolled him off of her, his face had been relaxed, his chiseled features no longer beautiful, but sharp and predatory. Oh God. What had she done? She'd cheated on Hank. She'd jumped into bed with another man. And then, minutes later, she'd bashed that same man in the head. When had she become so rash? And so violent?

Well, it didn't matter. She was done with the damned drugs, the damned Neurological Center and its damned clinic. She was going to rescue her husband from those crooked, shady doctors and their crooked, shady drug trials. She'd been wrong to entrust Hank to the care of strangers. He'd happier at home; might make more progress there.

She continued uphill. Ran another red light. Rounded the corner on to Dryden Avenue. Couldn't stop thinking of Ron, the feeling of climbing on top of him, bodies linked. Of rolling on to her back and feeling his lips tracing the scars of her knee, her thigh. What had come over her? She was no better than Vicki now. Oh God – Vicki. Harper wondered if her nose had stopped bleeding. If it was broken. If she'd press charges.

Never mind. The task at hand was to rescue Hank. Harper turned on to Hoy and pulled into the clinic parking lot, realizing that Hank might not be able to ride the Ninja. She might need a car. Damn. But one thing at a time. She hurried into the building, signed in, greeting the receptionist who gawked at her. Uh oh. What now? Was she bleeding? Never mind. Harper kept going, past the coffee shop, the Sleep Clinic. Up the elevator, along the hall, past nursing stations and patient rooms, until finally, she thrust open the door and ran straight to the only person in the world with whom, God help them both, she truly felt safe.

Wordlessly, Harper went to the bed and climbed in beside him. Hank opened his eyes, turned his head. He didn't seem surprised to see her. Not even a little.

'Hoppa.' He smiled, kissing her forehead, apparently not noticing the scent of another man. He stroked her hair with his strong arm, waking up, focusing. Then, squinting under the night-light, he looked at her more closely.

'Face hurt?' He frowned, waiting, while Harper realized the cut she'd gotten on the Suspension Bridge had opened, probably

in her fall. It was bleeding. Must be why the receptionist had gaped at her. Well, no matter. She wiped it with Hank's sheet, smearing blood across her face.

Harper wanted to stay there, clinging to Hank. Hiding behind his broad shoulders and beefy body, escaping the truth of what she'd done. She'd hit Vicki, then Ron. Soon, the police would come for her. Would they believe that she'd hit Ron in self-defense? Lord, why had she hit him so hard? And then she remembered why: Ron had known about the upstairs bathroom. He had snuck into her house to search for his damned stolen drugs, had likely killed her students. But, the fact was, she couldn't prove any of that. She had not one iota of evidence. Which meant she was in big trouble.

'Hoppa?'

They had to go. Now. But Harper held on to Hank, kissed his shoulder, allowing herself just one more moment in his arms. She pressed against him, wanting to dissolve into his body. Hank. Her Hank. What had happened to their lives?

But she couldn't afford the luxury of cuddling. Any minute, the police might rush in. She and Hank had to move. Fast.

'Happened?' Hank asked again. He touched her face, still waiting for her to explain.

'It's OK.' She pulled away, sitting up. There was no time for explanations. 'Hank, get up. We've got to go.'

Hank scowled. 'Face. Happened. Blood.'

Oh my God, Harper thought. Of all times, Hank had picked this moment to hold an actual conversation. She got out of bed, pulled the sheets off of him, turned on the light. 'Get up. Hurry.' She tugged at him.

Hank sat up, puzzled. 'Because?' Slowly, he swung his weak leg over the side of the bed.

'Because we're leaving.'

Hank's eyebrows lifted, eyes twinkling. 'Home?'

Well, not exactly. 'Let's go.' She guided him toward the door. He wore only underwear. 'My.' Hank pointed to his jockeys.

Oh God. Harper didn't have time to go through closets and dressers, find his clothes, help him into them.

'We'll get your clothes later. Tomorrow.'

Hank stood still, refusing to move. 'Man.'

Man?

'Pants. I. Man.'

Hank was refusing to go out in his underpants? Well, he was right. He was a man and deserved his dignity.

'Hank, look.' Harper opened the closet and pulled out his robe, trying not to act frantic. 'It's important that we leave now.' She wrapped the robe around his shoulders. He looked like a heavyweight on his way to the ring. Rocky escaping from the Neurological Center. She led him to the door. 'We'll get your stuff later.'

'Hoppa. What.' He repeated her name, unable to articulate all his questions. But he followed. Slowly, limping, leaning on her, Hank made it to the wheelchair, and Harper whirled it around and shoved it toward the open door.

They were almost there when a tall, familiar-looking man with lopsided hair walked up, greeting them with a crooked, skinny smile.

'Going somewhere?' Steven Wyatt stepped in front of the door, blocking their way. Harper stepped back into the room. Wyatt made her uneasy. Especially after Anna reported what he'd said about her to Ron.

'It's awfully late for a stroll, don't you think?'

'Hank couldn't sleep.'

Dr Wyatt sighed, eyeing the blood on her cheek, raising an eyebrow. 'Forgive me for being blunt, Mrs Jennings. Didn't you see Dr Kendall this evening?'

What? How did he know that? Obviously, Ron had told him. But why? And why had Wyatt mentioned that she'd been with Ron right in front of her husband? Harper's neck got hot. She glanced down at Hank, saw the unmoving back of his head. He didn't seem suspicious. Or at least the back of his head didn't.

'Ronald Kendall.' Dr Wyatt repeated. 'You met him earlier, did you not?'

'Um.' It was the best answer Harper could come up with. She wanted to run and began turning the wheelchair, hoping to get away before Wyatt could say more, but he stepped forward, still blocking the door.

'The problem, Mrs Jennings, is that Dr Kendall is unaccounted for. He's not here and doesn't answer his cell. You saw him last. So. Where is he?'

What was she supposed to say? That Ron was out cold, his skull crushed on her hallway floor?

'Maybe he's busy.' Maybe. If being in a coma or bleeding to death qualified as busy. She shrugged, tried an innocent smile, felt her lips quiver. 'I'm not in charge of Dr Kendall's schedule. Can you excuse us, Dr Wyatt?'

But Dr Wyatt didn't excuse them. In fact, he moved closer, looming over Hank's feet, smelling like peppermint. Like breath mints. Harper's memory stirred, flashing to the Suspension Bridge, the man holding her over the edge, the terror of dangling. The scent of peppermint. Had it been Dr Wyatt? He was as tall as the mugger, but was he sturdy enough to lift her? Alarm bells rang out; she pictured Dr Wyatt in a hooded sweatshirt and ski mask.

'Where is he, Mrs Jennings? Did you explain the numbers to him?'

Wait. Dr Wyatt knew about the numbers? Obviously, Ron had told him. Harper lost the smile, fumbled for an answer. 'What numbers?'

'Hoppa.' Hank twisted to look up at her. 'What?' He worked on another word, but Dr Wyatt's voice drowned out Hank's.

'We need to talk, Mrs Jennings.'

'Sorry.' Harper had no intention of staying there. 'We're on our way—'

'It won't take long.'

'Not,' Hank objected, raising an arm, pointing to the door. 'Go. Now.'

'Five minutes. That's all.' Dr Wyatt was long and lean, his face hollow, his limbs wiry like her assailant's. In the struggle on the bridge, she'd dug her nails deep into the guy's flesh. Subtly, she glanced at Dr Wyatt's hands. One was in his pocket; the other hung by his side, facing away; she couldn't see if either had deep scratches.

'Hoppa?' Hank was annoyed. 'Now. Out go.'

'OK. We're going.' But she didn't move, couldn't with Wyatt in the way.

Dr Wyatt leaned closer, lowering his voice. His warm peppermint breath hit her face, turned her stomach. 'Mrs Jennings. I don't care about blame or punishment. I simply want the drugs back. The Center needs them. Dr Kendall and I are under significant pressure to recover them. And I'm convinced you have information about where they are.'

'I told Dr Kendall everything I know.' Harper turned the wheelchair; Dr Wyatt stepped sideways, obstructing them.

'Where is Dr Kendall?' he growled. 'And where are the missing drugs?'

Harper sized him up. Could she take him down?

'You'd be wise to cooperate, Mrs Jennings.'

Really? He was threatening her? Harper's nostrils flared. 'Dr Wyatt. Can I see your arms?'

Wyatt blinked rapidly, his head tilted. 'What?'

'It was you, wasn't it? On the Suspension Bridge—'

'On the what? Mrs Jennings. Just tell me what I need to know.' Dr Wyatt wheezed. He waited.

'I don't know anything.'

Wyatt sighed deeply. Watched the ceiling. Didn't step out of the way. 'You know, every doctor in the country considered your husband beyond hope, but our Center accepted him, because our experimental procedures could help him. When he came in, he could barely form a syllable. Now, after just a few weeks, he's conducting basic conversations.'

'What's that got to do with the stolen drugs?'

'Research, Mrs Jennings. It's all about research. Our work is cutting edge. But no advances occur without risk. Wouldn't it be a shame if, say, your husband's case, which started out so promisingly, were to take a sudden, unfortunate turn?'

Harper met his eyes. 'Dr Wyatt, I'm taking my husband home. You can't touch him. Do not threaten us.'

The snaky smile wriggled across Dr Wyatt's face. 'I'm not threatening; I'm stating fact. If you take him away now, in the early stages of his course of treatment –who knows? He might revert to his former state. Or worse. You don't want to terminate his care so abruptly. You need us.'

Glaring, Harper warned, 'Get out of our way.' She shoved the wheelchair forward, rolling it into Wyatt's leg.

Dr Wyatt didn't flinch; his voice was controlled, deep. 'Tell me where the pills are.'

'Or what?' Harper blinked. 'You'll throw me off a bridge? Oh, wait – you already tried that.'

Dr Wyatt moved closer, his fist digging into his pocket. 'Ron Kendall and I have disagreed all along on how to handle this situation, but make no mistake: our work and the Center must and will prevail. We will not let our efforts be eradicated by a few college kids and a paltry teaching assistant.'

'Get out of the way—'

'OK, Mrs Jennings. Go.' Dr Wyatt's tone feigned resignation. 'But if more people get their hands on those drugs, the results will be on your shoulders. If they are taken in uncontrolled dosages, you can't – you don't want to imagine what will happen. You think a few deaths are upsetting? We could have hundreds of them. Mrs Jennings, we could have mayhem.'

Dr Wyatt glowered; his voice rumbled.

'I've lost sleep over this, Mrs Jennings. I don't have a shred more energy or patience. The Board delegated our committee to take care of this, but, frankly, I can't rely on Kendall. He's a philanderer, as you know, distracted by his libido.'

'Hoppa?' Oh God. Did Hank suspect?

'And I suspect that same libido is what has led you here tonight, trying to remove your husband from the Center.'

'Hoppa.' Hank repeated.

'No.' She didn't sound convincing, even to herself. 'Ron Kendall has nothing to do with this—'

'Hoppa.' Hank insisted, waving, pointing to the door.

Finally, Dr Wyatt and then Harper turned to look. And froze.

Ron Kendall teetered in the doorway, holding an ice pack to his still bleeding head.

Wyatt gaped at him. 'Mother of God, Kendall.'

Harper stood, wordless and not moving. The man's head was caked with crusting blood, and he could barely stand.

'Help. Call.' With his strong arm, Hank wheeled his chair to the side of the bed, reached for the call button.

'Did you find the pills? What happened to you?' Dr Wyatt sputtered.

Ron nodded toward Harper. 'She . . . hit me.'

'May I help you?' The wall speaker squawked.

'Blood. Help,' Hank yelled. 'Hurt. Now.'

'No. It's OK.' Wyatt quickly contradicted Hank, his voice full of authority. 'This is Dr Steven Wyatt. I have everything under control.'

'Help,' Hank argued.

'Never mind. I have it.' Dr Wyatt prevailed. 'Thank you.'

'No,' Hank insisted, glaring into Wyatt's eyes, but the call light was off; help was not to come.

'OK, Kendall.' Dr Wyatt put his arm around Ron, helping

him to the easy chair. 'Let's think. Quickly. Before we get you treated, we have to agree on a story. What should we say?'

'Say?' Ron had no wind. His voice was faint.

Dr Wyatt helped him to the easy chair. 'Problem is, if we tell them Mrs Jennings did this, they'll investigate and the whole sorry situation – her role with the drugs, and the drugs' role in the killings – all of it could come out.' He lifted the ice pack and examined the wound on Ron's head. 'Christ. That's quite a wound. She really clobbered you.'

Ron didn't answer, looked dazed.

'OK – how's this? We'll take you to the hospital. The ER. We'll say you got mugged. Didn't see the assailants. Random crime.'

Ron was covered with blood smears and sweat; his eyes were dull, his skin pasty. His breathing was ragged. 'She knew. And uh . . . about the drugs . . . and uh, knew the dead kids.'

Wait. What?

His voice was faint. 'She did it. All. Must have killed them.'

Wait. What was Ron saying? That Harper had killed her students? What? He was accusing her of murder?

'Really?' Dr Wyatt turned toward Harper, glowering. 'Mrs Jennings? Well, no surprise. I always thought you were behind this—'

'That's absurd.'

'Too late, Mrs Jennings. You know, two minutes ago, I might have been willing to forget about the deaths of your students in return for the drugs—'

'You're nuts.' Harper was aghast.

'But, frankly, you're too dangerous a woman. Bashing in Ron's head? Killing your students? You pose a major threat to all of us. And I'm tired. I need to clean up this mess.'

He stepped closer. Harper backed up, positioning her body to jab his gut and land a knee in his groin. She would have, too, if she hadn't stumbled over a wheel of the hospital bed, tripping backwards on to the mattress. Dr Wyatt smiled his snake grin, grabbing her arm with one hand, removing a syringe from his pocket in the other. No scratches or gouges, Harper noticed as she kicked. The flesh of his lower arms was unmarked.

'Wait.' Ron's voice was a weak rasp. 'Wyatt—'

Squirming, off balance, Harper glanced at Ron, saw him struggling to stand, unsteadily dropping back on to the chair.

Wyatt twisted her arm behind her back and stood over her; Harper swung her free hand, clawing, flailing to get free. But Wyatt was surprisingly strong, and his knee was lodged on her scarred thigh, his long fingers tightened above her elbow, holding firm. Harper wiggled, punched, yanked, bucked to no avail. Spring at him, she thought. Just arch and slam your head right into his face. But unable to get leverage, she lurched without momentum. As the needle touched her flesh, Harper stiffened her biceps, resisting, aware that she would be injected with something lethal, that she was about to die.

Hank, she thought. She needed his face, to see it one more time. She looked around, searching for him, finding his wheel-chair, empty. Oh God. Hank? Where was he? She couldn't die without seeing him. The tip of the needle pricked her arm, and she drew a deep breath, twisting her back, still fighting when, inexplicably, Dr Wyatt released her. His mouth flinched, his eyes fluttered and his body crumbled to the floor.

Harper scrambled up off the bed, staring. The syringe rolled slowly from Wyatt's limp hand.

Dr Wyatt had almost killed her. But Hank – Hank had decked him?

Hank stood over Wyatt, rubbing the fist of his strong arm. 'Now. Go,' he urged. Just like that, as if it were no big deal. Hank had saved her life.

He stood off balance, his weight on his stronger leg, and Harper ran to him so fast that she almost knocked him over, hugging, holding on. Kisses peppered the top of her head, forehead and mouth. Then he reminded her, 'Help. Now.' He pointed to Ron, who had slipped backwards, half-conscious, muttering in the chair.

'And uh . . . She stole the pills . . .' Ron blithered. 'And uh . . . must have killed them.'

'He. Needs.'

Damn. They needed to move. Ron might bleed to death while she canoodled with Hank right in front of him. She hurried Hank back into his wheelchair. Wyatt stirred, regaining consciousness, his fingers groping the floor.

Where was the syringe? She saw it, kicked it under the bed, but realized that he probably had dozens more of them. Kneeling on her sore leg, she pushed him down and reached into his

pocket, found a bunch of syringes, loose papers and prescription pads. Harper kept the needles but let the papers fall, pushing Hank's chair to the door. They were almost out of the room when she stopped and turned.

On the floor beside Wyatt, among the contents of his pocket, were some scraps of paper. Including a tattered list of numbers, written in Graham Reynolds' loopy scrawl.

Harper shook her head, trying to grasp what she saw. Wyatt had had the numbers all along? If so, it must have been Wyatt who'd knocked her out. Wyatt who'd taken the numbers from her bag. Wyatt who had killed Monique and Larry?

But that made no sense. Why would Wyatt kill to get the numbers if he didn't know what they meant? Never mind. She didn't need to understand his reasons. She needed to leave. Now.

Quickly, Harper scooped up the papers, stuffed them into her bag and raced down the hall with Hank in the wheelchair. This was no good. Hank wasn't strong enough to take the stairs, but they had no time to wait for the elevator. Any second, someone would find Ron, and Wyatt would recover and say that she'd attacked Ron and stolen drugs and murdered her students. In seconds, security and half the clinic staff would be chasing them. No, she and Hank had to get out of sight, fast. But where? And how?

Harper looked up and down the hall and, watching over her shoulder, she swerved suddenly, aiming the chair into a room directly opposite the elevators.

The man on the bed was unconscious; he wouldn't mind if they hung out there for a bit. Dumping the syringes into the trash, she picked up his phone and made her almost routine phone call: 911.

It would take a while for police to arrive. Meantime, Harper kept her eyes on the hallway and the elevator. Commotion rumbled in and around Hank's room; apparently, Ron and Dr Wyatt had been discovered. An orderly ran by, pushing a gurney. Two security officers rushed down the hall, a phalanx of nurses behind them. Hank sat alert, silent, watching the elevators. When the doors opened to let someone out, he pointed, and Harper dashed, shoving the wheelchair out the door, across the hall, into the car, where she punched the button for the first floor.

Finally, she let herself exhale. In a few seconds, they'd be in the lobby. Then out the front door, on to the Ninja – somehow, she'd get Hank on to it – and they'd ride to safety.

Except that the elevator doors didn't close. They stood gaping, exposing the two passengers, inviting anyone – including Dr Wyatt and a new syringe – to step inside.

'Go.' Hank directed the door. Harper pounded the 'door close' button, repeatedly pushed 'L' for lobby. She looked out, saw a throng of agitated staff rushing toward them. Come on. She pushed the buttons again. Suddenly, the elevator buzzed a loud, cloying electronic complaint. And, finally, excruciatingly slowly, just as the men and women in powder-blue coats descended on them, the doors edged together and slammed shut.

The elevator jerked, descending, three, two, one, lobby. The car jolted to a stop. The doors slid open. Cautiously, Harper wheeled Hank out. The first floor, so far, was quiet. No doctors with dripping needles. No nurses in pursuit. Nothing obstructing the front door. Escape was seconds away; the Ninja waited in the lot, just outside. Almost within view. All they had to do was keep moving past the Sleep Clinic and the coffee shop and they'd be safely outside, trying to balance on the back of the bike.

Harper tried to look normal, not to move too fast. Not to draw attention. She started across the lobby as a phone rang. The security guard at the reception desk answered. Getting the call to stop them? Damn. Before he could look around, Harper thrust the chair into a side corridor and sped ahead, looking for another way out.

The door was unlocked; Harper wheeled Hank inside without thinking about where it led. The lights were low; the space divided into cubicles where patients lay sleeping, their heads and bodies wired, their brain and other functions being monitored on remote computer screens. Harper slowed, recognizing the Sleep Clinic, Dr Wyatt's turf. Quietly, she peered around the corner, located the nursing station. Avoiding it, she steered in the opposite direction, wheeling Hank along the row of cubicles, peeking behind curtain after curtain, letting the bluish glow of night-lights spill on to her face, looking for an empty spot where they might hide.

Nothing. Every bed, every cubicle was filled with sleep patients. Pushing Hank, she hurried along but stopped suddenly

at cubicle four and doubled back to cubicle two, as her mind registered what she'd seen there: the patient in two was Anna. She was asleep. And strapped to the bed.

Explaining that she'd be right back, she left Hank's wheelchair by Anna's curtain and rushed to the girl's side. She was too still, her skin too gray, her arms bound too tightly. Harper touched her neck, felt for a pulse, found a surprisingly strong one.

'Anna, it's Loot.' Even if she couldn't move, Anna could hear her. 'They've got you tied up. I'm going to loosen the restraints.'

Harper tried, but had trouble untying the knots. Why were they tied so tightly?

'Psst—'

Harper jumped, spun around before realizing who'd made the sound.

'Loot, there's scissors in that drawer.'

'Anna. I thought you were slee –'

'I didn't know who was coming, so I pretended.' Her whisper was quick, impatient. 'Quick. Before someone comes. Can you find them?'

Harper moved fast, opening the drawer, taking out the slender scissors, snipping.

'Dr Wyatt drugged me, Loot. He's nuts.'

'Don't worry. We'll get you out of here.' Harper began cutting. The straps were thick; the scissors small.

'He said I knew too much. About the drugs—'

'You'll be OK.' She had one of Anna's arms freed, was working on the other.

'Hoppa? Go.' Oh great. Hank was shouting, letting the whole clinic know they were there. 'Hoppa.'

'Hank! Shh! One minute.' Harper kept her voice low, working the scissors, making little progress.

'Loot,' Anna whispered, nodding at Harper's shoulder.

Harper stopped cutting, stopped breathing. Her bones got cold.

'Mrs Jennings, why didn't you come when your husband called?'

Slowly, Harper turned to face Dr Wyatt. Fully recovered from Hank's knockout punch, he casually dropped a syringe into a biological waste container, and brushed off his hands. Oh no! Hank!

'What did you do?' Harper charged, ramming full force into him.

Dr Wyatt, almost a foot taller, doubled over, winded, his hairpiece askew. But he held on to her. 'Settle down—'

She thrust herself back toward Anna, who lay with her eyes closed, again feigning cataplexy. Dr Wyatt stepped forward, reached into his pocket. How had he replaced the syringes so quickly? How many did he have? Harper backed away, moving around Anna's bed.

'There's really no point in resisting, Mrs Jennings.' Dr Wyatt moved closer, following her. 'The police already know about your attack on Dr Kendall and your drug ring with your students. Until they arrive, I have no choice but to hold you here.'

Harper's back was to the wall. She had nowhere to go. Dr Wyatt stood between her and Anna's bed, and, this time, Hank couldn't rescue her. She was cornered, had no room for a kick; Wyatt was going to inject her. Harper looked at the needle, planning. She could duck at the last moment. Or cold-cock him. Or grab his arm and flip him, put him in a headlock, even bite him. Maybe butt him with her head. But before she decided on her final moves, Dr Wyatt yowled. His mouth opened, contorted with unpleasant surprise, and he spun around, turning his back.

From which protruded the handles of a small, fairly dull, but nonetheless effective pair of scissors.

The police arrived, and, in moments, ambulances scooped up Ron, who was barely conscious, and Dr Wyatt, who was barely alive. Hank was out cold on a gurney, sedated, his mouth hanging slack. Anna refused to go to the hospital. She huddled close to Harper, sipping a Cherry Coke someone had given her. Harper was concerned about Anna, had seen her hovering over Dr Wyatt after stabbing him, patting his torso, as if to comfort him. She hoped Anna wouldn't agonize over what she'd done; the man had clearly intended to harm them both.

Detective Rivers' eyes were bloodshot and tired. 'You're a walking crime scene,' she greeted Harper.

'Sorry, Detective.' Harper steeled herself, ready to be hand-cuffed for attacking Ron. 'It was self-defense, but I admit it. I hit him.'

'You hit someone?' Anna sat up, eyes wide.

Oh no. Was the girl going to pass out yet again? Harper

patted Anna's arm. 'It's all right. Not to worry.' Not to worry? Really?

Detective Rivers watched Harper, nodding slowly. 'I know you hit him. He told me.'

He did? 'So he's conscious?'

'Kind of. He's said a lot of things. He's in and out, rambling.' Anna gaped, confused.

'He seems to be saying that you had a primary role in the drug theft.'

'You did?' Anna gasped.

'That's not true.' Harper wondered how she'd defend herself.

Detective Rivers watched her warily. 'But you'll be glad to hear that Dr Wyatt isn't going to press assault charges. He was very weak, but he insisted on letting both incidents go.' She nodded at Anna. 'He said your sleep disorder makes you subject to hallucinations, so you weren't responsible for stabbing him. Of course, if he dies, we'll have to revisit that decision.'

Anna didn't speak; she tilted her head as if considering the information.

'And as for your husband's assault on him—'

Her husband's what? 'My husband didn't assault—'

'Mrs Jennings, please.' The detective took a breath and began again. 'Dr Wyatt could barely speak, but he said your husband's aggressive behavior was probably caused by his brain injury—'

'Bullshit—'

'OK.' Detective Rivers blinked rapidly, irritated. 'You might not want to say anything further. Because, if he survives, Dr Wyatt can change his mind and press charges. And if he doesn't, the state will decide how to proceed. Be advised: despite Dr Wyatt's leniency, your husband's outburst might indicate that he poses imminent danger to others. Which could be grounds for involuntary commitment—'

'No goddamn way.' Harper was on her feet. 'My husband did not have an outburst, Detective. Nor did he attack Dr Wyatt. The truth is that Dr Wyatt attacked me. My husband stopped him—'

'Odd. On what might be his deathbed, Dr Wyatt gave essentially opposite information. And his statement fits with that of the other victim.'

The other victim? Oh. Ron. Oh dear. 'What did Ron – Dr Kendall – say?'

'Here's the situation, Mrs Jennings.' Detective Rivers sighed. 'We have two statements indicating that you led your students to steal drugs. Something went wrong, so you had to eliminate a couple of your recruits—'

'That's absurd.'

'When Dr Kendall found out, you attacked and tried to kill him. He managed to get away, and you followed him to the Center—'

'No! It's the other way around. I was trying to get away from Ron – from Dr Kendall. I figured out that he'd been in my house before. He already knew where the bathroom was—'

'Really, you shouldn't say any more just now.' Detective Rivers looked sad. 'You probably should have a lawyer present before you talk to me.'

A lawyer. Oh God. What Detective Rivers had heard was all twisted. Harper needed to explain, set the facts straight. But how? What could she say? Her story contradicted the others. Why would anyone believe her?

No question, Harper was in serious trouble. And she wasn't the only one; if people swallowed the stolen pills, more lives would be at risk – lots of them. But where were the drugs? Had Larry or Graham already sold them? Had Graham hidden them someplace? Or did her other students have them – Jeremy or Esoso? Shaundra? Terence? Gwen? Were they going to kill themselves or commit other violence? Become murderers, too?

Harper covered her face with her hands and closed her eyes. Furious with herself. A couple of hours ago, she'd been rolling around in bed, cheating on her husband with a smooth, deceitful cad who was now accusing her of drug trafficking and murder. She'd betrayed Hank, the sweet bear of a man who'd tried to protect her and now lay slumped unconscious on a gurney. She deserved whatever happened to her.

'Am I going to be arrested?' She pictured her father, his years behind bars.

Detective Rivers sighed, assessing her. 'We're still trying to piece together what happened. We'll take statements, then we'll see about what to do with you.'

The detective again advised her to call a lawyer and stepped away, conferring with other officers. Harper watched her, questions swirling in her head. Why had Dr Wyatt mentioned the stolen drugs to the police? He'd been hell-bent on keeping them

secret. What had changed his mind? Was it that pills had been found on the victims? And what about the numbers she'd found in his pocket? Weren't they proof that Wyatt himself had killed Monique and Larry? She reached for her bag, pulled out the wad of papers she'd stuffed there.

'What's that?' Anna stiffened. 'Where did you get those?'

Harper didn't answer. She looked at the numbers, then at the other pages she'd grabbed along with them. A to-do list. And a recipe for a white chocolate cake.

When Harper looked up, she saw Sameh curled into the chair beside her. No. Harper shook her head, blinked. Anna sat gaping at her, holding her knees to her chest, ashen pale.

'Anna?' Harper controlled her voice, kept it quiet. 'Is this your cake recipe?'

Anna blinked. 'Where did you get that?'

In the corner of the lobby behind Harper, a sniper fired. The odor of explosives soured the air. Marvin started chattering. Damn. Not now. Closing her eyes, she lifted an arm to her mouth and bit down hard, grounding herself with pain.

'Loot? What are you doing?'

Harper heard the faraway voice and struggled to fend off the flashback. She needed to stay centered, to fit the pieces together. Her arm screamed with pain, and she looked for it, realizing it was in her mouth. Oh dear. Anna gasped, alarmed.

'Loot?'

Harper made herself smile. 'It's OK.' Her arm had purple bite marks, but, for now, the flashback and the gunfire were gone.

Anna reached for the papers in Harper's fist. 'Those are mine. Can I have them back?'

Harper didn't release them. She held on, trying to figure out how the page with Graham's numbers had gotten wadded up with Anna's cake recipe. How the numbers had traveled from her bag to Dr Wyatt's pocket, picking up Anna's recipe along the way.

Sameh was back. She swayed past the elevators, eyeing Harper coyly from a safe distance. Harper looked away, refusing to be distracted. Someone had knocked her out and searched her bag, removing the numbers. That person must have known that she'd had them. So, who had known? Ron, of course. She'd

told him about them herself, on the phone in her office. And Ron had told Wyatt. But neither of them had known what the numbers meant. Besides, if they'd wanted them, they could have just asked her for them; they didn't have to slug her. So it had to be somebody else. But who else could have known? Nobody.

Except for one person.

'Loot, please. Can I have those back?' Anna again reached for the papers.

Harper moved them away, out of Anna's reach.

'But I need to bake another cake—'

'Anna, stop.' Harper didn't let go of them. She spoke softly. 'I know.'

'Huh?'

'Stop pretending.' Harper met her student's gaze. 'I know.'

Anna swooned and rolled her eyes, collapsing.

'Don't even bother. I know you fake it half the time.' At least, she suspected.

Anna opened her eyes and gazed across the lobby at Detective Rivers. 'How long have you known?'

'Not long. And I haven't told anyone yet. It would be better if you told them yourself.'

'Seriously, Loot. I have no idea what—'

'Oh, spare me. I know everything.' But she didn't. The pieces didn't quite fit together. All she knew for sure was that Anna had been lying on her office sofa during Harper's phone conversation with Ron. Anna, in the throes of real or faked narcolepsy, hadn't moved. But she'd heard everything Harper had said, including that Harper had found a paper of Graham's with numbers on it. And, unless Anna had told anyone else about them, Anna was the only other person who'd known that. The only one who would have thought to look for them in Harper's bag. Which meant Anna must have been at her house, must have slugged her. And, no matter how inconceivable it seemed, Anna must have killed Larry and Monique.

Anna sat back, pouting. Then, suddenly, she burst into a giggle. 'Well, it was worth it. Did you hear what happened? Did you?' Her giggles were girlish. Silly.

Harper had no idea what she was talking about.

'Gwen stripped! That stuck-up snob got completely butt

naked.' More giggles. 'She took off everything, in a townie bar. Can you believe it? Goodie two-shoes, I'm-smarter-than-anybody Gwen? She got arrested for lewd behavior.'

What?

'Shaundra got arrested, too. For shoplifting. In a *hardware* store. Stealing, like what, a sledge hammer? And Jeremy and Esoso got in a fist fight – black eyes, bloody noses, the whole nine yards. And wait, this is great: Terence? He got his privates pierced.' Anna squealed with laughter. 'I tried to keep track. Don't know about Pam yet, but everybody – our whole recitation – went crazy today.'

Was any of this true? Why would all her students suddenly act so bizarrely?

'What about you, Loot? Did you do anything crazy today?'

Of course not. No. Well, except for punching out an old friend. And having rough, passionate, uninhibited sex with one of her husband's doctors, and then slugging him with a beer bottle. And kidnapping her husband from the Neurological Center. Actually, over the last several hours, her actions had been not just crazy but extraordinarily impulsive and violent.

And, suddenly, Harper knew why.

'The birthday cake.' Obviously, Anna had drugged it.

'Nobody seemed to notice it tasting funny.' Anna smiled. 'But it was only right, taking Graham's drugs on Graham's birthday. Celebrating in his honor.'

Harper had a sudden urge to choke the girl; probably the drugs had not yet worn off. 'God, Anna. Somebody could have gotten killed. Do you know what you've done?'

Anna cocked her head, thinking. 'The cake? It was no big deal.'

Havoc reigned. But it was no big deal? 'So you put pills in the batter. Where did you get them?'

'I told you. Graham had them—'

'So Graham stole them?'

'Well, not by himself. But he stashed them for us.'

Us? 'Where are they now?'

'Now?' Anna shrugged. 'I don't know.'

Harper thrust the page with the number in front of Anna's nose. 'What are these numbers, Anna?'

Anna glanced at it, then at Harper. 'Seriously? You don't know?' She smirked as if the answer were obvious. 'That's

where Graham kept the drugs. His storage unit number and the combination for his lock.' She reached an arm out. 'So can I have my recipe back now?'

The digits represented the area number, the row, the locker number, and the lock combination of Graham's unit in U Stash It, a storage company located just outside of town on Route 79. While Detective Rivers dispatched a couple of officers to search the locker, Harper and Anna waited with uniformed officers standing over them.

Anna pulled on the straw of her Coke. 'Don't look at me like that, Loot. It's not like I planned to kill anybody. It just . . . happened.' She cocked her head. 'Look, I was the one who thought up the whole thing. I was the one who found out about the drugs. I was the one who figured out how to take them. And after Graham jumped, I was the one who found out that you had Graham's combination numbers. The whole thing was me. But those two – after Graham was dead, all of a sudden they shut me out. Like I wasn't even part of it. Behind my back, they snuck off to your place to look for the locker combination? To get the drugs by themselves? Like I'm nobody? No, that wasn't going to happen, Loot. I wasn't going to be shut out. Not this time.'

Harper stared. The girl talked about the crimes coldly, with nonchalance. Anna didn't look like a drug thief or a murderer. A cat hoarder, maybe. Or someone with a secret, unrequited crush on her English Lit professor. 'We're going to have to tell all of this to Detective Rivers.'

Anna looked down. 'I don't think so, Loot. You already told the cops I knew what the numbers meant. If you say anything else, I'll have to deny it. And with what the detective said about Dr Wyatt and Dr Kendall blaming you for everything, think about how it would look if I admit I heard you and Graham talking about some deal you had, something involving pills.'

Anna was threatening her.

'Think about it, Loot. I'm a weak, sickly girl. Severely narcoleptic. Nobody will believe I had any part in any of this.'

She might be right. People overlooked Anna. Harper pictured her lying unnoticed on a bed in the Sleep Clinic, listening as doctors discussed drug trials. Noticing an opportunity, plotting a crime.

'Why did you do this?'

'Why?' Anna leaned back, gazing into air. 'Hmm. Must be my poor unhappy childhood. Isn't that what hardened criminals say? Poor me. I was never popular. Always falling asleep. Narcoleptic. If the cool kids noticed me at all, it was to make fun of me. For kicks, they tried to make me pass out. Or they'd mimic me, collapsing, rolling their eyes.'

Harper had little sympathy. She'd seen kids' arms and legs blown off. Being teased didn't seem so bad.

'As I got older, it didn't change. Those guys – Larry and Graham? I was invisible to them. I've had three classes with Graham. I sat right across from him in two of them, but you know what? He didn't even recognize me when I tried to talk to him this summer.'

'So you thought stealing drugs would get his attention?'

'I wanted him to notice me.'

'Oh, Anna.' Harper shook her head. 'You stole life-threatening drugs just to get a guy's attention?'

'No one knew they were so bad. We thought they were like steroids or uppers. Something like that.'

Detective Rivers came toward them, cell phone in hand, shoulders sagging. 'So. We sent officers to search Graham's storage unit. I just got the call.' She paused, eyeing them.

Her voice was grim. 'They found an old love seat, a guitar, a spare tire, books and posters. Stuff like that.'

'No pills?'

Detective Rivers scowled and folded her arms. 'Not even an aspirin.'

'You call a lawyer yet? We're ready for your statement.' Rivers' phone rang again, and she turned away to take the call.

'So where are the pills, Anna?'

Anna's eyes didn't waiver. 'No one will believe you if you accuse me, Loot. I'll deny having any part in this, and I'm the only one left. The others are all dead, so they can't say anything.' Anna's whisper was gentle, matter of fact.

'Tell me where they are. Look, Anna. This isn't over. If more people take them, more might die.'

'I know. It's terrible.' She sighed.

'So where are they?'

'I told you. I don't know. I kept some for myself, used some in the cake, and I delivered the others. Larry made a connection.

A guy from New York. That's why we freaked so bad – Graham died before giving us the numbers, and we had to deliver.'

'Who's the guy?'

'Who knows? I did what Larry said and left them in a pile of duffel bags on the quad. By Andrew Dixon White's statue. Guy picked them up, I guess. I have no idea who he is. He knew us, but I never saw him, never heard his name.'

'So you just gave them away to a stranger?'

'Of course not.' Anna bristled. 'We're not stupid. The guy paid in advance. Six hundred thirty-five dollars. Apiece.'

The money in Graham's book bag. His share of the payment. Harper closed her eyes, doing the math. Six hundred thirty-five dollars times four kids. About twenty-five hundred dollars for thousands of potentially lethal pills.

Harper studied Anna, saw no signs of malice or concern, no indication of sorrow. She seemed truthful. In fact, she seemed to be the same ivory-skinned, lonely, shy, vulnerable girl that Harper had imagined her to be. Except that she had no conscience whatsoever.

'Stupid Graham.' Anna wiped an eye.

Was Anna crying? Maybe she wasn't as emotionless as she seemed; at least she had feelings for Graham.

'It was the drugs, Anna. Like you said, he never would have jumped otherwise.'

Anna smiled sadly. She watched a police officer, making sure he was out of hearing range. 'But if he was going to jump, couldn't he have given us the numbers first? No, he was too fucking stupid.'

Harper was speechless.

'The asshole couldn't think ahead, so he just left them on his desk where you found them. Which is why everything got so fucked up. Larry asked you politely, but you wouldn't give him Graham's stuff, so Monique had to go chase you down and grab it—'

'Monique?' Anna had to be mistaken.

'She borrowed a bike and took after you to get Graham's book bag.'

Monique? Not Wyatt? Monique had been tall, athletic. Strong like her assailant. Might have liked peppermints. Harper remembered gouging the skin off the mugger's arm with her nails. And the bandage on Monique's arm the next day.

'And,' Anna went on, 'if we'd had the numbers, Larry and Monique wouldn't have gone behind my back to your house, and I wouldn't have caught them there. And I wouldn't be sitting here waiting for the police to give me the third degree. Well, hell with that. I'm not getting in trouble because of a moron like Graham. Frickin' freak. All his damned poetry and music, but he couldn't even follow a simple plan.'

Anna sat back, taking a long drink of Cherry Coke.

Detective Rivers was frowning. Before Harper could say anything, Anna swooned, leaning against her.

'Anna—' The detective knelt, catching Anna, not letting her fall.

Anna swayed and rolled her eyes, faking. Harper moved away and watched, thinking about what to say in her statement to the police.

'Sorry. I feel so weak,' Anna breathed. 'Maybe it's because I haven't eaten all day. They just left me tied to the bed.'

In seconds, a policeman was dispatched to get Anna some food. Meantime, someone went to the vending machine for another Cherry Coke. When she thought no one was looking, Anna took a couple of pills from her pocket, popped them into her mouth.

Harper saw. She moved closer. 'What did you just take?'

Anna swallowed. 'Narcolepsy meds.' She smiled. 'What did you think? I was taking Graham's pills?'

Yes. That was precisely what Harper thought.

'We're ready, Mrs Jennings. You're sure you don't want a lawyer?' Detective Rivers waited.

Harper stood. 'I don't need one.' At least not yet.

As they walked away, Anna called, 'Hey, Loot, good luck. I'll be thinking about you.'

Threatening her.

Detective Rivers led Harper to an office where a bald detective named Stenson recorded her statements. With the door closed, the room was small and windowless, suffocating. Harper spoke quickly, refusing an attorney, volunteering information, and, with the exception of her intimacy with Ron, telling everything she knew, starting with Graham's suicide and ending with this evening in the lobby with Anna. She raced through information, talking until her mouth was dry, desperate to get the process

over with so that she could get out of the airless, fluorescent-lit room. Hank would wake up soon, and, if they'd let her, she'd take him away from the Center and its experimental procedures, drug trials and subterfuge. Home.

Or no, not home. The place was still a mess from the ransacking. And, worse: the bed sheets were still rumpled from her romp with Ron. Ron? Oh God. Had she really had sex with him? Bashed his head with a beer bottle? Been consumed by overpowering rage? Even in combat, she'd never felt fury that intense.

But, then, she'd never taken those drugs before. And she'd eaten not just one but several slices of Anna's cake, must have taken quite a dose. But she was lucky; it could have been worse. At least she hadn't jumped out the window like Graham. Or stripped at a bar. Ron would recover; the harm she'd done would reverse itself. She hoped.

No use thinking about it. She needed to tell the police about Anna and get back to Hank. Take him somewhere safe – somewhere besides home.

'OK. That'll do it for now.' Detective Rivers folded her hands on the desk.

'I can go?'

The detectives watched her, not nodding, not shaking their heads. The entire time she'd talked, they'd shown no indications of belief or doubt, hadn't let on what they thought even as she told them about Anna.

Harper stood.

'Mrs Jennings, one more thing.'

'Are you sure?' Detective Stenson frowned. 'We should wait—'

'It won't matter. Either way, she'll find out.'

'Find out what?' Harper sank back on to the cushioned office chair. Her eyes moved back and forth from one detective to the other, reminding her of REM therapy, of flashbacks, of Marvin and the burning dust of Iraq. She blinked, biting her lip, causing pain.

Detective Rivers' hands remained clasped. Harper noticed, for the first time, that she wore a simple gold wedding band. 'Remember the waitress? Chelsea? She had your grade book with her when she was killed?'

Of course Harper remembered.

'The phone call I just took? Seems Chelsea knew Larry. The young man found on your porch.'

So? 'I don't understand.'

'Chelsea's purse and some of her jewelry were in the back of Larry's car. As was a plastic sheet covered with her blood.'

Harper swallowed. Larry had killed Chelsea?

He'd taken the drugs. Instead of getting pierced like Terence or dancing naked like Gwen, Larry's impulsive acts had been raping and murdering someone. Damn.

Detective Rivers unfolded her hands, standing, walking Harper out of the room. 'According to your statement, the stolen drugs are being peddled now in New York. Think about it. Before this is over, how many more Chelseas do you think there will be?'

She opened the door, letting Harper wander into the hall. 'You can go, but don't go far. I'll be in touch.'

Darker and darker. Harper knew exactly what had driven Larry to kill Chelsea. She had felt the darkness swell, feeding urges until they erupted, snuffing out all else. She'd felt rage boiling inside her as she'd lunged at Vicki, clawed at Ron's flesh in bed, then tried to crush his skull with unrestricted force.

Oh, yes. Harper knew how the pills could take over a person's judgment and will. And, suddenly, she knew something else, too: the pills Anna had taken earlier hadn't been for narcolepsy.

Harper headed for the lobby where Anna sat quietly near the elevators, chewing a turkey sub, perfectly calm. An officer sat beside her, holding a coffee cup. Harper caught her breath, relieved, and looked around for Hank. Vaguely, she noticed Detective Rivers entering the lobby, approaching Anna.

But where was Hank? She headed into a hallway; someone had pushed his gurney into a quiet corner. Ahead, in the shadows, she saw it, but the gurney was empty. No Hank? Maybe this was a different gurney. Or maybe he'd awakened and wandered somewhere.

'Hank?' she called, but instead of an answer, she heard a scuffle behind her. Furniture scraped; people yelled. Harper spun around. The air filled with dust and smoke; gunfire erupted in the distance.

'Believe me.' It was a woman's voice. 'You don't want to do this.'

Harper squinted through the haze. A police officer was down,

on the ground. And Sameh was standing on a chair, holding a gun to a young man's head.

But, of course, it wasn't – couldn't be – Sameh.

Harper had no lemon, no flashback-fighting tools. She smelled smoke, heard flies buzzing even as she told herself that neither was there. Stop it, she commanded; focus on the present. Count something. Quickly, she counted the people in the lobby who were holding guns. Two uniformed officers. Two detectives. Plus the woman who wasn't Sameh. That made five people with weapons, all raised and ready to fire.

'Nobody move. I swear I'll kill him,' Sameh shouted. No, not Sameh. Anna. The voice belonged to Anna. And Anna sounded confident, in control.

'Drop the gun, Anna.' Detective Rivers, on the other hand, sounded loud, rash. Not in control.

A third uniformed policeman lay on the floor beside Anna, limp and unmoving, his holster empty. Harper crept forward, assessing the scene. The hostage was young, dressed in scrubs, maybe an orderly. He was the only civilian visible; the receptionist and others must have fled. The police stood in a row like toy soldiers, all facing Anna, not spread out across the open space, not positioned effectively.

But what about the officer on the ground? Harper saw no blood, had heard no gunshots. Keeping out of Anna's sight, she stepped closer, peered around the corner. Saw a syringe lying beside the body. A syringe. Harper blinked at the improbable object. Until she remembered. Wyatt. Of course. Anna had lifted his syringes when she'd stabbed him. She'd injected the policeman. Taken his weapon, the weapon she now held against a young man whose face was white with fear. But who at least, Harper noted, had a face.

Anna nodded at Detective Rivers. 'Loot talked to you about me, didn't she?'

'Anna, put down the gun.'

'Did she tell you I put Graham's pills in that cake? Because I only put in some of them.'

'Let the man go. We'll talk.'

'No. See, I kept a bunch of the pills. For fun. I wonder what went on today at that alumni picnic on the quad—'

'What? Are you saying you drugged the food?'

Oh God. Harper pictured alumni erupting in random violence, unpredictable impulsiveness.

'Oh, and a coffee urn right here at the Center.'

Not just alumni . . .

'And a tray of cupcakes for sale on a table outside the Straight.' Anna giggled. 'They probably thought the icing had sprinkles.'

. . . but people all over campus.

'Anna—'

'Sorry, I can't remember all the other spots. It'll be fun to see what happens, right? But I didn't give out all the pills. I saved a few for myself. Actually, I just took some with my Coke.'

Harper exhaled, felt her adrenalin surge.

Rivers muttered something to an officer who scooted off, talking into his cell. 'Listen, Anna. I know you never meant to hurt anyone. It was the drugs – they altered your thinking. None of this is really your fault.'

The gun seemed huge in Anna's hands. Oversized. Like the eyes of her hostage.

'Really?' she called back. 'So you know what I meant or didn't mean. You've been in my head?'

'Let your hostage go, Anna.' Rivers spoke too fast. 'No one will blame you for what's happened—'

'Fuck off.'

'You're way outnumbered—'

'No. It's equal, one on one. You against me and me against him.' She jabbed her hostage in the head. 'If one dies, we both die.' Anna squinted, her eyes slits. The hostage cowered.

Across the lobby, a couple of orderlies suddenly went at it, shouting. Shoving. A cop struggled to separate them, but, apparently, the scattered pills were taking effect. The police had lost control, couldn't regain it.

Still unnoticed, Harper eased her way backwards, away from the scene. It was a stand-off. Harper could smell the outcome: blood would spill, and soon. Unless she stopped it. Old instincts, training kicked in. In combat mode, she moved across the hall to get a better view of the lobby. Direct access to Anna was impossible; any frontal or lateral approach would be seen and resisted, causing casualties. Her only choice was to move in from the rear.

Silently, she slipped back down the hall, searching for

makeshift supplies, finding nothing. Just empty polished floors.
And the gurney without Hank on it. It would have to do.
Releasing the brakes, she pushed down narrow pathways, around
corners, past the coffee shop, the gift shop, the Sleep Clinic
entrance, until, finally, approaching the lobby, she slowed,
emerging stealthily into the hallway just behind and to the right
of the elevators where Anna held the young man.

'This doesn't have to go bad.' Rivers' voice had become
ragged, discouraged.

Anna wasn't convinced. She nodded toward the still-belligerent
orderlies. 'Look around, lady. It's already gone bad.'

Hugging the wall, Harper stepped forward enough to catch
Rivers' eye. Rivers cocked her head subtly, no, but Harper
insisted, yes, motioning that she was about to create a commotion. A diversionary tactic. Again, Rivers twitched her head, no.
But Harper, in command, indicated that Rivers should draw
Anna's attention away, distracting her. Then, she rushed back
behind the gurney, measured the distance to her target and
waited for Rivers to comply.

And Rivers did. She moved across the lobby talking, taking
Anna's attention with her. When Anna's back was turned, Harper
shoved the gurney with all her body weight, propelling it
forward, sending it suddenly careening, clattering into a cluster
of chairs near the reception desk.

Anna spun toward it, instinctively aiming the gun away from
the hostage and toward the noise.

Harper pounced from behind, shoving the hostage away,
taking Anna to the ground, grabbing for the gun.

Anna fell, slamming the tiles, but she held on to the weapon.
In fact, she rebounded, hurling herself forward, using the
momentum of her fall to roll on top of Harper and flatten her
against the unconscious cop lying on the floor. Harper's damaged
leg twisted under Anna's weight and, as she shuddered in pain,
Anna firmed her grip on the gun, struggling to aim it at Harper's
temple.

Harper could hardly breathe, and her leg was on fire, but she
pushed back, turning the muzzle away from her head, toward
the wall. Then, thrusting her torso forward, she threw Anna off
balance, closed her arm around Anna's neck. Twisting the arm
that held the gun, she faced Anna, eye to eye.

'This is over,' Harper panted.

Anna grunted, rolling her eyes. Harper reached for the gun, wrapped her fingers around the barrel. Pushing against each other, they fought for control until, suddenly, Anna stopped struggling. Her eyes faded, her gaze turning inward. Was she giving up? Feigning narcolepsy? For a nanosecond, Harper shifted her weight, reacting, and in that briefest of moments, Anna lurched, flicked her wrist, aimed at Sameh's head. And fired.

Warm bits of brain, blood and bone sprayed all over Harper's face. For an eternity, she sat on the floor, cradling the body that had been Anna's – or Sameh's – oblivious to the commotion around her, only vaguely aware of the bustle, until someone approached her with a warm, wet towel and started gently cleaning her face.

'Hoppa.'

Harper turned. Hank took her hand and lifted her into his arms. Where had he come from?

'Men's. Room. In. Not. Hear.' Or not here.

Limping, even with one weak arm, he carried her past the gawking police to a cushioned chair, where he washed the reopened cut on her cheek. Gradually, Hank's touch and kisses grounded her. Her flashback faded, and she was staring not at Sameh but at yet another dead student.

'Ma'am?'

Harper looked up to see the hostage. The boy with a face.

'Thank you.' He held out a hand. He was sweating, shaking. His name was Myles. He was an orderly, a pre-med student at Cornell. 'You saved my life—'

'But only because she was lucky,' Detective Rivers interrupted. 'What were you thinking? You almost got yourself and the rest of us killed.'

Stenson wanted to arrest her. 'If not for you, Mrs Jennings, we'd have followed procedure, retrieved the weapon and freed the hostage without anybody, including the suspect, getting shot—'

'With all due respect,' Myles interrupted, arguing that Harper had been the only one to do anything to help him. That she'd risked her life for him and actually saved him. 'If not for this lady, that lunatic would have killed me.'

Stenson and Rivers ignored him, indignant that Harper had

overstepped, insisting that she'd had no business interfering. Stenson listed charges. 'Reckless endangerment, interfering with police procedures . . . and, oh yeah, that girl is dead, possibly because of your actions. How about manslaughter or negligent homicide—'

'Stop.' A new voice rumbled into the discussion, a thunderous voice that caused Stenson and Rivers to shut up. 'Hero.' Hank glowered. 'Hoppa. Saved him. You. Shame on.'

The detectives stared at the large man holding a bloody towel. And, suddenly, both detectives found other issues to attend to.

Myles shook her hand and headed off. Somebody taped up Harper's cut. Somebody else took a brief statement and told her she and her husband could go.

But they didn't go, not yet. First, Harper watched the police take eleven more pills from Anna's pocket, along with another sedative-filled syringe. And she watched them zip Anna into a body bag and carry her out. Then she sat, looking out the window into the darkness, an air-conditioned chill creeping beneath her clothing. She shivered even when Hank wrapped her in his arms.

When she finally got up to leave, her body dragged, her weak leg stiff and sore, her muscles out of sync. Her burst of adrenalin had faded, leaving her depleted.

'Hoppa. Go. Ride. Bike.' The cycle was right outside the door. Hank cradled her hand, teetering beside her under the moonlight.

Somehow, despite their various limitations, they managed to climb on, Harper fitting easily between Hank's thighs as she started the motor. In moments, they were blasting down the highway, hair flying without helmets, engine roaring through thick, moist air that smelled of summer and night.

Hank held on to her, his arms tight around her breasts, his robe billowing in the wind. 'YEEEHAAAAA!' His howl was primal. Joyful. Free.

Harper didn't respond to the scream. She sped into the night, watching for random impulsive violence, without the vaguest idea where they were headed.

The Ramada Inn on Route 13 smelled of cleaning products and stale air, and the windows didn't open. The worst part wasn't staying there, though; it was explaining to Hank why they

couldn't go home. Telling him about the various crimes and violence that had converted their house into a multiple crime scene. Omitting the part about the escapade in their bedroom. Feeling like slime.

Hank listened attentively. He touched Harper's face, took her hand. Sometimes, his jaw tightened, frustrated or angry at what she said. When she told him about Anna killing Larry and Monique, he glowered.

'Not,' he remarked. 'No.' Or know? He shook his head. 'Killed. She. Why.' They were talking.

It was after four o'clock when they got to bed. Harper had to help him out of the chair, but, after that, he was able to walk and take care of himself. He moved slowly, favoring his strong side, but he got undressed and into bed, watching Harper with laughing eyes, waiting.

Suddenly, Harper was shy. She felt embarrassed to get undressed in front of Hank. He's your husband, she told herself. But she felt self-conscious, and more than a little unclean, as if Ron's touch might show on her flesh. Beyond that, she was nervous. What would happen when she got into bed? It had been so long since they'd slept together. Hank had told her that he was horny. What if it was a disaster?

'Give me a minute.' She stalled, slipping into the bathroom for a shower, trying to scrub away both her deceit and her hesitancy. Reminding herself that she was with Hank again, that there was nothing to worry about. That she should be jubilant.

Finally, still hesitant, wrapped in a towel, she came out. The only light came from the flickering television; Hank had turned down the audio. The only sounds were the hum of the air conditioner and the steady drone of soft snoring. Hank was asleep.

Surprisingly disappointed, Harper climbed in beside him and lay back on the pillow, suddenly tired. Beyond tired. Paralyzed. Too exhausted to move. Without opening his eyes, Hank turned over, enfolding her in his arms as she rested her head against his chest. They were still in that position six hours later when Harper woke up.

Making love was effortless. It happened spontaneously, without any of the awkwardness or self-consciousness Harper had feared.

Hank's speech might still have been strained, but his kisses, his touch spoke eloquently. For a while, Harper believed she was dreaming. She smelled Hank's scent, licked his shoulder to taste him. Rubbed her face along his stubble to feel the scrape. Details like these were too specific for dreams, weren't they? Finally, she decided, it didn't matter; if it was a dream, she refused to wake up. In fact, she wanted to stay asleep all morning. Or forever.

Soon, they were lying together, comfortable, familiar, as if it were a normal morning. As if they hadn't been apart at all.

Hank's eyes danced as he looked at her. 'Missed. You.'

'I missed you, too.'

'Want. Coffee. Go. Eat.'

Oh. Hank was hungry. Amazingly, Harper hadn't even thought of food. She sat up and looked at the clock. Almost eleven. Checkout time. Their tired clothes watched them from the chair where Harper had let them fall. Hank's robe. Her T-shirt and shorts. First stop, after eating, would be to get some new stuff.

As Hank limped to the shower, Harper thought about how long she could manage to stay away from the house. Not long. But before she took Hank there, she'd have to get the place in shape. Sterilize it. Fine. She would call a cleaning crew to scrub their entire house. Get rid of every trace of Larry and Monique and Anna and Ron; wash away the blood, replace every uprooted possession.

'Some. Pants. Need. And. Food.'

Hank put on his robe, and Harper took out her phone, got the number of a cleaning service and made an appointment for that very day. Relieved that the house was taken care of, she leaned back, resting.

'Hoppa.' Hank pointed out the window. 'Rain. Soon.'

Dark clouds promised a thunderstorm. Great. Finally, the heat was going to break, but the downpour would catch them on a motorcycle.

'Go. Now.'

Hank didn't need a wheelchair. In his robe, he walked upright to the coffee shop, where he ordered by pointing to the menu items. A stack of pancakes, a side of bacon, fried eggs, juice and coffee. The waitress didn't even blink at Hank's attire; she simply poured their coffee.

Maybe it was going to be all right, Harper thought. Maybe they would have a new kind of normal. She reached across the table for Hank's hand.

'I love you.' She smiled, happier, more hopeful than she'd been since his fall.

Hank didn't smile back. His face was somber; his eyes aimed above her head. Harper turned; Detective Rivers was coming their way. She wasn't smiling, either.

'You two weren't easy to find.' Detective Rivers glowered, taking a seat in the booth beside Hank.

'We couldn't go home. The place is—'

'Mrs Jennings, I've been up all night. I didn't appreciate having to search for you. I made it clear that you should be where I could reach you. We called your house and your cell and five hotels before we located you.'

Harper's cell battery must have run out. Why were they looking for her? Was she going to be arrested? 'Well, it isn't like we were trying to hide—'

'Nevertheless. Before I go off duty, I thought I ought to advise you of some news.'

'News?' Hank sounded normal, like any guy asking a one-syllable question.

Detective Rivers eyed him. 'Yes. Ron Kendall's made a formal statement.'

Oh God. Harper held her breath.

'His statement was fascinating. At first, we thought he was saying you had killed your students. But he wasn't. Actually, he was trying to name someone. It sounded like he kept repeating, "And uh, and uh . . ."'

'Anna.'

Rivers nodded. 'Dr Kendall admits going to your house to look for the drugs. While there, he heard someone walking around and hid. Next thing he knows, he hears Larry arguing with a woman, but not you. Not your voice. She's accusing Larry of cheating her. Finally, the house gets quiet again. Dr Kendall comes out of hiding, sees Monique's body and splits.'

Harper blinked, allowing herself to exhale. Ron had told the truth. 'That agrees with what I told you. That Anna killed them.'

'People tell me all kinds of things. In this case, though,

despite what we thought earlier, Dr Kendall's account supports yours.' She gazed at Hank, then at Harper, who silently prayed that the detective would say nothing more about Ron or how he'd come to be injured in the house. She didn't want to think of what she'd done, even if it had been under the influence of the drug. 'For now, it looks like you're off the hook. I thought you'd want to know.'

For now?

'Thank you, Detective. That was thoughtful.'

Hank tapped Harper's arm, imitating a needle. 'Stuck Doc. Drug. How?'

'Oh. Hank's asking about Dr Wyatt.'

Detective Rivers shifted in her seat. 'Dr Wyatt will live, but he has some questions to answer. At the very least, he injected your husband and restrained Anna. But there are undoubtedly other issues – obstruction, conspiracy, reckless endangerment, negligence. Fraud. He's got problems.' She stood. 'OK, then. Enjoy your pancakes—'

'What about Anna? And the policeman she injected?'

The detective frowned, sat down again. 'We've notified Anna's family. And, except for his ego, Officer Manning is OK. We're still picking up complaints, though. A bunch of alumni looted the donut shop, and there was apparently an orgy of sorts down in the gorge. So far, no one else has died.'

So far.

'OK. Will be,' Hank reassured her.

'Between you and me,' Rivers confided, 'I never bought Anna's wide-eyed I-didn't-mean-for-any-of-this-to-happen act. She planned the drug heist; she killed two of her partners; she delivered the goods to the contact. She managed to do all that just fine. Don't you think it was a little too convenient that she just fell asleep every time things got hairy or she wanted to listen in? Not to speak ill of the dead, but there was something just plain scary about that girl.'

'Hairy? How?'

'I'll leave the explaining to you, Mrs Jennings – I mean, Harper.' Detective Rivers stood, mock-saluting a goodbye. 'It's been a long shift. I'm heading home before it storms.'

'Bye.' Hank turned to Harper. 'Now. Tell. Hairy.' He wanted to hear everything.

Harper picked up her cup and took a gulp of cold coffee.

'First, let's eat.' As thunder rumbled outside, she lifted her fork and stuffed her mouth with cold eggs.

That afternoon, thunder kept rolling, but it didn't rain. The cleaners arrived. Harper spent her time directing their work or on the phone. She answered weeks of email, mostly from Professor Schmerling, who'd sent updates daily from the dig site and worried that she wasn't responding. She talked with her mother, telling her little more than that Hank was home and doing well. And she arranged for outpatient physical therapy for Hank through his former internist's office.

For most of the afternoon, Hank wandered around the property or sat peacefully on the newly scrubbed and polished front porch swing, reading the newspaper, watching the dark, cloudy sky. By evening, the house was sparkling, and they were alone at home for the first time in months.

Harper cooked. There wasn't much in the house, but she fixed tuna salad and a can of vegetable soup. At night, Hank made it up the steps, one at a time. Slowly, carefully, holding the railing. They went to bed, their own bed. Neither could stop smiling as they lay in each other's arms, listening to the rain on the roof as the thunderstorm finally broke, falling asleep to the music of the pounding rain.

Days streamed along, sun-drenched and warm. Dr Steven Wyatt, fired by the Center, faced a medley of criminal charges, including assault and kidnapping. Dr Ron Kendall avoided significant legal troubles by abruptly resigning his position and, according to one rumor, accepting a position at a teaching hospital in San Salvador.

Summer session ended with fewer than half of Harper's students finishing the course. Harper's mother threatened to visit, insisting that Harper couldn't care for an invalid on her own; Harper assured her that Hank, although still having trouble with his speech, was hardly an invalid.

Determined to pick up where he'd left off with renovations, Hank stained the deck out back, installed the new tub and toilet upstairs, put wallpaper up in the dining room and redid the floors in the nursery, which Harper finally finished painting. With time, the physical labor increased his strength. His limp became less pronounced, and his arms moved more evenly.

There were setbacks, too. With Hank unable to teach for the foreseeable future, the Geology department passed him over for tenure and offered the position to Trent. Their letter to Hank guaranteed him a teaching position when he was ready and promised that when he did return to work, he'd be reconsidered for tenure. Hank seemed indifferent to academics. In fact, he seemed uninterested in life outside their small property, content for now to spend his time with a paintbrush or spackling and putty.

Harper, by contrast, focused much of her attention elsewhere. For weeks, she scoured the Internet, scanning newspapers across New York State and into New England, looking for sudden odd suicides or random murders. Almost every day, she found one or more such incident, wondered if it was related to the missing drugs. Finally, she realized that there was no way to connect any of the crimes to the drugs and abandoned the effort, consoling herself with the knowledge that not all impulsive acts would involve violence or crime. Some might be impulsive acts of kindness or generosity. Either way, the supply of pills was limited and the number of acts they inspired would be finite.

Harper continued to meet with Leslie, but Sameh, the face-less boy and Marvin still showed up, and occasionally she heard explosions or bursts of gunfire. Now, though, she was able to distinguish these intrusions from reality, enduring them without panicking or running for cover.

By August, life for Harper and Hank had become routine and quiet; the drama of early summer faded, seeming almost unreal. Harper resumed preliminary research for her dissertation, met often with Professor Schmerling and assisted him with data analysis from the Peruvian dig, became immersed in her studies.

Hank's speech improved little by little, and friends began to return from their summer travels. Janet and Dan got back from Italy, Ruth from Martha's Vineyard. People dropped by to eat burgers and drink beer. And late in the month, an invitation arrived, inviting them to a celebration of Trent's tenure.

Apparently, Vicki and Trent had not separated. But Harper hadn't seen or spoken to Vicki since the day she'd punched her in the nose. Harper had let Vicki's phone calls go unanswered, letting the questions of Vicki and Hank go unanswered, as well. Now, there was this invitation.

They couldn't go. Why would they? The friendship had

disintegrated. Trent and Vicki still hadn't come to see Hank. And, more important, Harper wasn't sure Hank was up to seeing his old colleagues yet. Or to having them see him. No, they couldn't go. She didn't even mention the possibility, set the invitation aside. But then one afternoon, she saw Hank reading it.

'Trent's party.'

'Yeah. No big deal.'

'Going.'

'We don't have to. Don't worry about it.' She had little trouble understanding him anymore.

Hank stared at the calligraphy. 'Neat ink.'

'Uh huh.' She didn't ask if he wanted to go. It would be painful for him to celebrate Trent's tenure, the position he should have gotten.

Hank picked up the invitation, turned it over, set it down. Scratched his head. 'A suit? Wear?'

A suit? 'Really?' He wanted to know what people would wear? 'No, it's not formal. I think just a sport shirt.'

'Go. We.' Hank was insistent. 'Let's.'

'Are you sure?' Harper knew even as she asked. She could tell by his voice; Hank was determined to be there.

A large white tent covered the yard beside Trent and Vicki's house. Professors and administrators lolled about, holding cups of punch, chatting, posturing, chuckling at bad puns. When Harper and Hank arrived, heads turned and conversation hushed. Not many had seen Hank since his accident. Now, suntanned and toned, almost steady on his feet, Hank strode across the lawn to the festivities.

Harper spotted Vicki near the tent, standing with Jim Hayden, head of the Geology Department.

'Hank.' A colleague – Harper couldn't remember his name – stretched out his hand, then hesitated, unsure if Hank would be able to shake it with his weakened right arm.

Hank did, though. 'Ellis.'

Amazing, Harper thought. Except that Hank hadn't smiled, the interaction had been completely normal; listening, nobody would have guessed that Hank had aphasia.

'How the hell are you doing?' The guy named Ellis slapped Hank on the shoulder, glad to see him. The head of the department left Vicki's side, rushing over.

'Hank. Great to see you.'

'Jim.' Hank glared at the man.

Other people were gathering around them, but Hank continued to glare at Jim. Why was Hank looking at him that way? It was embarrassing. Was he sore about Trent's tenure?

'Nice to see you again, Dr Hayden. I'm Harper. Hank's wife.' She intervened, shaking Jim's hand, not sure he remembered her.

'Of course, Harper. Glad to see you. Call me Jim. We're all just colleagues here.' His smile was permanent, his handshake indefinite.

Hank continued to eye Jim oddly, even as the crowd gathered, asking questions. Hank, how are you? When are you coming back to work? How the hell do you manage to look so good? 'How's he doing, really?' a stranger whispered to Harper. 'It's such a shame what happened.'

At first, Hank seemed uplifted by the swarm of attention, smiling at one colleague, embracing another. But the questions and comments came too fast for too long, and Harper saw his frustration rise. He simply couldn't say what he wanted to.

'I'm fine.' Hank frowned, concentrating, needing time. 'How been. You?'

'What's that, Hank?' People quieted, trying to hear him. Jim, the department head, turned his ear toward Hank, as if that would help.

'You. Good. Fine?'

'Sorry?'

'You want something, Hank? A drink?'

Whispers. People buzzed, well-intentioned, trying to be helpful.

'What did he say?'

'No clue.'

'I can.' Hank shook his head, emphatic. 'Talk. Now.'

'He has aphasia,' Harper explained. 'He's getting better, but it takes a while for Hank to get his words out.'

Nods and smiles. Platitudes. Empathy and embarrassment.

'Well, you sure look good, champ. Doesn't he? Doesn't he look great?'

'Maybe I should drop you on your head, George. Maybe then you'd get into shape like Hank.'

'Good to see you back, man.'

Harper's neck heated up, blotchy and mottled. 'Let's get some punch.' She forced a smile and led Hank toward the tent. The little crowd dispersed; the buzz of conversation rose again. And, suddenly, Vicki came at them from nowhere, like a descending hawk, wings spread, flapping, engulfing Hank. Pecking at his face.

'My God, Hank. Let me look at you.' She checked him out, hugging him. Her nose was markedly shorter, must have been fixed by a plastic surgeon. 'I was afraid you two wouldn't come.' She turned to Harper. 'I've been trying to reach you for—'

'Vicki. About my explosion.' Harper had prepared an explanation. 'I'm sorry—'

'No. I understand. Completely. In your shoes, I'd have been mad, too.'

Wait. She'd broken Vicki's nose, and Vicki wasn't even mad? Maybe Vicki felt guilty about what she'd done. Well, she should. At least Harper wouldn't have to explain about eating the drug-filled cake or the side effects of the drugs. At least not here at the party.

'Well, still. I shouldn't have hit you.'

Harper had half expected Vicki to have her arrested; instead, she wasn't even annoyed.

'I can imagine how you felt when you found out. But think about it. The way things turned out, what happened really didn't matter. Nothing's different than it would have been.'

Harper's face reddened. How could Vicki talk about her affair with Hank right in front of him? Negating its significance. Did she think he was deaf? The woman deserved that punch in the nose, maybe another.

Vicki kept babbling, playing the hostess, fawning over them until, from across the lawn, Trent sauntered toward them. Silently, Hank broke away to meet his friend.

'Excuse me—' Harper left Vicki mid-sentence and took off after Hank. He hadn't seen Trent since the accident, and she wasn't sure how the reunion would go. Hank might be bitter that his friend hadn't even once come to see him. Not to mention that Trent had received the tenured position that should have been Hank's. She doubted that Hank would cause trouble and knew the two men needed time together alone, but her instincts wouldn't let her. She stayed close, just in case.

'Hank. It is! It's really you.' Trent swayed slightly as he

approached, spilling punch on to the grass. 'Finally. We meet again, old friend. How you doing?'

Hank didn't even try to speak. He stood silent, facing Trent, eyeball to eyeball.

'Sorry about the tenure, Hank. Don't take it to heart,' Trent rambled. 'Under normal circumstances, this thing might easily have gone the other way.'

'Screw.'

Screw? Harper looked at Hank, startled. He was cursing at Trent. Oh Lord.

Trent raised an eyebrow. 'Sorry?'

'Vicki. Screwed. Win.'

Wait. Oh God! He wasn't cursing – Hank was referring to his affair with Vicki! Lord, for some bizarre reason, Hank and Vicki had both decided to air their secret right there at Trent's party. But why? Coming here had not been a good idea. Harper downed her glass of punch.

Trent smiled stupidly. Mutely.

'Hank.' Harper stepped over, taking his arm. 'I think we should—'

'Vicki screwed. Won. Not you. She.'

What was Hank's point? In a twisted way, was he telling Trent that he hadn't really won? That Trent might have tenure, but Hank had had sex with his wife? How could Hank announce that right in front of everyone? Harper pulled him away.

'Let's just go, Hank.'

Hank stood his ground.

'I'm – I'm not sure what he's trying to say,' Trent stammered, grinning. 'So good to see you, though. Both of you. Let's get together soon.' He started to walk away.

'Roof. Trent.' Hank declared, too loudly. 'You. Pushed.'

Trent stopped walking, stopped smiling. Harper froze. Pushed? Trent? Was Hank accusing Trent of pushing him off the roof?

Again, Harper saw Hank falling, sliding, arms askew. She squeezed her drink, counted faces. Fended off flashbacks.

Trent and Hank faced each other mutely.

'Look. No hard feelings,' Trent finally offered. 'It was an act of passion.'

What? He was OK with Hank and Vicki having sex?

Hank didn't move. 'Not OK. Pushed. You. Because fucked. Vicki.'

Harper translated: Trent had pushed Hank because of his affair with Vicki. She had trouble breathing. She couldn't believe what she was hearing. Why was Hank talking about his affair right in front of her, as if he didn't care if she heard? She wanted to leave. Pictured herself running for the gate. Speeding home, packing. Leaving.

But Trent was talking again. 'Hank. I don't really get what you're saying, but if it's what I think, just forget it. It's in the past. All of it. History. It was the heat of the moment. All is forgiven, pal. You didn't mean it.'

Wait. Trent was forgiving Hank? For having sex with Vicki?

'Frankly, if it was the other way around, if Harper had – if she'd done what Vicki did – I might have lost it—'

'No.'

'No,' Trent agreed. 'You're right. I wouldn't have done what you did—'

'No. Hoppa would. Not. Do. Like Vicki.'

'What's that, Hank? Harper's not like my Vicki?' Trent's smile was thin. 'Too bad; I suppose your Harper isn't as devoted as my Vicki.' He turned to Harper. 'Is that true?'

'Is what true?'

Trent stepped too close to Harper. He smelled like booze. 'Is it true that you wouldn't devote yourself entirely to Hank, doing everything in your power to further his career?'

Harper stepped back. What was he talking about?

Hank said nothing. He stood perfectly still, watching Trent, who shifted his weight and forced a grim smile.

'Hank, look, why don't we put all this behind us? I'm not proud of what went on behind the scenes, so to speak. But, on the other hand, you tried to push me off a roof.'

Wait. Harper must have heard wrong. What had Trent just said? That Hank had tried to push Trent? Not the other way around? What? Someone grabbed her arm. She spun around.

'Why did you walk away like that?' Vicki demanded. 'What have I done to make you so mad at me? We used to be friends, Harper. What I did – was it really so unforgivable?'

Harper strained to hear what Trent was saying. Something about 'screw him'. No. Screw Jim? Jim? Who was Jim? Unless . . . Did he mean Jim Hayden, the head of the department? Why was he cursing out Jim?

'Tell me, Harper,' Vicki asked again, drowning out Trent's voice.

OK. Why not, Harper thought. Go for it. 'Vicki, cut the crap. You really think it's no big deal that you had an affair with my husband?'

Vicki's jaw dropped. 'That I what?' She actually laughed. 'Oh my God. That's what you thought? Lord, no.'

She took Harper's arm and led her away from a cluster of guests. 'No wonder you got so pissed. Oh, man. That's why you punched me? You thought my affair was with Hank.' She shook her head.

'You all but admitted it, Vicki. You said you'd had an affair—'

'And I told you it wasn't with Hank.'

'But I read your emails. "I love you and always will." And "please don't tell Trent."'

'Oh God.' Vicki rolled her eyes. 'You read all that stuff and you thought it was about Hank?' Vicki looked over her shoulder, making sure no one could hear. 'You're so wrong.'

Harper folded her arms, unconvinced. She glanced at Hank, still arguing with Trent.

'I wrote those because Hank found out about my . . . relationship. He accused me of using sex to get Trent tenure and threatened to tell Trent about the affair. I wrote those emails begging him to keep quiet. I thought Trent wouldn't be able to handle it. But Hank went to Trent anyway.'

'Hank told Trent you were having an affair?' Harper was confused.

'Yes. Even though I begged him not to. As it turned out, though, Trent already knew. In fact, he'd known the whole time. And, worse, he didn't care. It actually amused him. He thought the affair would help him get tenure, too. I guess Trent's attitude made Hank even angrier.'

Harper still didn't get it.

Behind them, Trent voice boomed, gracious and magnanimous. 'Forget it, Hank. I forgive you. How about we call it even?'

'Maybe I'm slow, Vicki. But I don't see how your cheating on your husband could further his career.' People wandered by with plates of potato salad and grilled filet sandwiches.

Vicki closed her eyes. 'OK, I'll spell it out. My affair wasn't

with Hank.' She leaned over, whispering in Harper's ear. 'It was with him.' She nodded toward someone across the lawn.

Harper followed the nod, spotting a group of women surrounding the department head, Jim Hayden.

Finally, she understood.

'You had an affair with Dr Hayden.'

'Never with Hank. I would never. Neither would he.' She reached out and hugged Harper.

Slowly grasping the truth, Harper allowed, then returned the hug, elated.

Hank hadn't cheated. Her friend hadn't betrayed her.

Suddenly, Vicki let out a belly laugh. 'You broke my frickin' nose, Harper.'

Harper was giddy, silly, full of relief. 'Yes, I did. I got you good.' Her fist punched air, demonstrating. She was giggling.

'And—' Vicki bent over, cramping with laughter. 'And it was all—'

'All for nothing.'

'For nothing. A big fat mistake.' Vicki wiped her eyes, waved at a passing couple, waiting for them to move on. Finally, the laughter subsided. They stood catching their breath.

'Well, at least I got my nose done.'

'Looks good.' Another round of laughing.

'So,' Vicki panted, 'you're not mad?'

'Why would I be?'

'The tenure thing. I mean, Jim's head of their department. He has pull in deciding tenure. I told Trent I'd had the affair just to help him get it. I think he actually half believed me. He doesn't know how close I came to leaving him.' She met Harper's eyes. 'Truth is, I was head over heels.'

Yes, Vicki had been head over heels. But, thank God, she hadn't been head over heels with Hank. Harper kept jubilantly repeating that fact in her mind. Hank hadn't cheated. Hank hadn't cheated. She could sing an aria with those lyrics. She shouldn't have doubted him. And – God forgive her – she should never have been unfaithful either. She was appalled, mortified, ashamed, even though her behavior wasn't really her fault, had been drug-induced. Must have been. But Vicki was talking, wanting to make a date for coffee, like old times.

Harper looked across the lawn at Jim Hayden, his broad grin and dark tan, his easy confidence. His charm. And his best

quality of all: he wasn't Hank. Of course she'd have coffee with
Vicki. Like old times.

But behind them, Trent repeated his offer. 'Even Steven. You
don't tell anyone about my dear wife's indiscretions, and I don't
tell anyone how you came to fall.'

Harper finally understood. She pictured them, Hank and Trent
on the roof. Hank accusing Trent of orchestrating Vicki's affair
to get himself tenure. Trent denying it. Hank furious, coming
at Trent, maybe even trying to shove him. Trent dodging, Hank
slipping.

And falling.

A few feet from Harper, Hank smiled broadly and put a hand
on Trent's shoulder, declaring, 'Fuck.' He paused, forming
another word. 'You.'

Trent furrowed his eyebrows. 'Yeah? Well, fuck you, too.'

The two men faced each other, nose to nose, a staring contest.
Vicki and Harper stood by, silent. Tension mounted. Suddenly,
Hank swung, punching Trent's shoulder, bending him forward,
grabbing him with his strong arm, trapping him in a headlock.
Helpless, his drink spilling into the grass, Trent waited for Hank
to release him.

'Hank.' Harper tugged at his arm, trying to loosen his grip.
'Let him go.'

Vicki gaped. Didn't move.

'Hank!'

For a long moment, Hank held on to Trent, and Trent didn't
struggle. He simply endured it. People noticed, but assumed
two old friends were horsing around. 'Don't kill him, Hank,'
someone called. 'He owes me for lunch.'

'Go ahead and kill him,' a second voice disagreed. 'I want
his office space.'

Hank finally let him go. Trent was red in the face and sheepish,
seemed less tipsy. Maybe even sober. Hank put one bear-like
arm around him, the other around Harper, who put an arm
around Vicki. Connected at the shoulders, the four walked
abreast back to the tent where they sat together, eating, drinking,
laughing and talking. Almost like old times. It was a fine celebration, a feast, though Harper noticed that neither Trent nor Vicki
spent much time with Jim Hayden. As the evening wore on,
wine poured generously, and Hank's colleagues began to seek
him out, comfortable again, forgetting about his aphasia. Harper

was relieved to see him mixing, rebuilding his life, and, for the first time in months, she allowed herself to relax. Not worrying or planning. Not being afraid.

It wasn't until the end of the party, as she waited for Hank to say his goodbyes, that Harper noticed Sameh, quietly watching her from the shadowed corner of the tent. Harper took her time. She didn't flinch, didn't run for a lemon. Instead, slowly and deliberately, she met Sameh's eyes and stared at them steadily until Sameh turned and walked away.

When Hank was ready, he looked refreshed. Even happy. Harper took his hand and smiled, ready to go home.